CODDIWOMPLE

S.E. HARMON

This is a work of fiction. Names, characters, places, and incidents either are the product of the author's imagination or are used fictitiously. Any resemblance to actual persons, living or dead, events, or locales is entirely coincidental.

Coddiwomple © 2021 by S.E. Harmon. Cover Art © 2021 by S.E. Harmon. Cover content is for illustrative purposes only and any person depicted on the cover is a model.

All rights reserved. This book is licensed to the original purchaser only. Duplication or distribution via any means is illegal and a violation of international copyright law, subject to criminal prosecution and upon conviction, fines, and/or imprisonment. Any eBook format cannot be legally loaned or given to others. No part of this publication may be used or reproduced in any manner whatsoever, including but not limited to being stored in a retrieval system or transmitted in any form by any means, electronic, mechanical, photocopying, recording or otherwise, without the written permission of the author.

For my mother

FOREWORD

Coddiwomple—to travel in a purposeful manner towards a vague destination

This book started from that single word. I came across the word on one of those "odd words around the globe" lists many years ago, and it immediately became a favorite of mine. You can ask any writer, and they can immediately tell you two or three odd words that they just love to pieces. Gobsmacked, anyone? And querulous just sounds good on the tongue. The word wonder was so deep, it just made me stare out of the window for five minutes. I just knew that eventually —somehow, someway—coddiwomple would work its way into my writing. And so it has.

Yes, I like how it sounds, but I like what it represents even more. Life can sometimes seem like the most meandering journey, and we rarely end up exactly where we intended. But I suppose as long as we have purpose—to keep moving, trying, loving, laughing, living—we can deal with all the U-turns and pitstops along the way.

I thought it would be interesting to get into the mind of someone always trying to see "what's over there." Sometimes you need to see "what's over there" to realize what you have right here.

I hope you enjoy Cameron and Journey's...well, journey. Sorry, I couldn't resist.

Happy reading,

SEH

The world is big and I want to have a good look at it before it gets dark.

— JOHN MUIR

1

JOURNEY

The shipwrecks were terrible in their beauty.

I stood on the shoreline at Cape Cross, watching the fur seals in the early morning mist. The same fog that created amazing photography conditions for me had sent countless ships straight for the shrouded cliffs.

I'd been around the world, but I'd never seen such a desolate place as the Skeleton Coast. North of Mowe Bay was usually closed to the public, but I had special permission and a guide named Suva from a local tribe. Suva had told me the coast was known as the Land God Made in Anger. I could see why. There was no civilization as far as the eye could see, only miles of the desert meeting the frigid embrace of the Atlantic. Any creature that dared call the coast home was truly an example of survival of the fittest.

I picked my way along the rocky shore, taking pictures of the seals adeptly navigating the waves for food. The view was beautiful, but it damn sure wasn't peaceful. Between all the roaring, fighting, and barking in general, they were noisy as fuck. They didn't smell the best, either. Eventually my ears and nose acclimated, and I got lost in my work.

Critics never talked about the hard part of getting the perfect shot.

It certainly wasn't finding a worthy subject because that part was ridiculously easy. Hell, I almost felt *guilty* taking credit for my photos as a Journey James original. I shouldn't be tagging the photos *J.J. Sutton*; I should be tagging them *Mother Nature*. It wasn't like I'd created anything. I'd simply waited while Mother Nature did her thing, and then I captured the magnificence on film. So no, the hardest part wasn't finding something to take pictures of. Instead, it was exercising patience in weird positions while my extremities fell asleep.

No one talked about that. They spoke about getting amazing footage of wild animals, going to exotic locations most people never got a chance to visit, and seeing your images in print. If you were lucky, sometimes your work ended up in national magazines. They didn't talk about squatting and kneeling on the hard ground for hours at a time, with your eye practically glued to the end of a telephoto lens.

As the light started to change around eleven in the morning, becoming more perpendicular and creating less volume in my subjects, I took a quick break for lunch, berating myself for not getting more early shots. I was back at it by one o'clock, my belly full, ready to head down the coast. Suva and I took ATVs farther inland, down toward the riverbeds. I needed a picture of some springbok and wasn't calling it a day until I got it.

Hours later, I was reconsidering my dedication. Sweat coated me from my prickly scalp down to my scuffed, dusty boots, but I didn't move. As uncomfortable as it was, I needed the angle for the shot I wanted. Lying on the ground gave me a vantage point for a more dramatic impact, and the dimensions would make the target of my shot appear even more grandiose. Well, it would as soon as my target showed up.

My only company was Suva, who left me alone for the most part to do my thing. Oh, and a cheetah. Yeah, a cheetah. He sat on his ATV, leaning on the handlebars as he watched me with an air of mild amusement—Suva, not the cheetah. Suva had been a tour guide for most of his young life, so he was used to wildlife photographers and all of our quirks. He knew what lengths we'd go to in pursuit of the perfect shot, and he was used to corralling us when it was time to leave.

He cleared his throat, and I knew what was coming. Sure enough, he said, "You have less than twenty minutes before we need to get back to camp."

I didn't give him a response, and he didn't expect any. Even if my target never showed, I never left without a sunset shot. A photo of Cheetah with the darkening sky in the background would go a long way to salvaging the day.

The cheetah was a rescue, according to Suva. She was also the nosiest damn cheetah in the world, according to me. She'd spent most of her childhood with humans and it showed. I'd been on the reserve four days this week, and most of those days, I'd felt her tracking me. This was the first time she'd decided to let me see her. She sat close enough to monitor what I was doing, but never close enough to touch. I was *definitely* all right with that.

"If I can't get this shot in the next fifteen minutes, this whole day was a fucking waste," I muttered to Cheetah. "Stellar company aside, of course."

She groomed herself, clearly giving zero fucks that I'd been lying on my belly in the dirt for most of the afternoon with sweat trickling from my every pore. I didn't miss the irony that I was lying next to a cheetah waiting for pictures of glorified deer, but the heart wants what it wants. In this case, *National Geographic* wanted what it wanted, and I didn't intend to leave without a shot of some springbok.

Too bad *Nat Geo* wasn't interested in a picture of an extremely nosy cheetah.

"Apparently, you're passé," I informed her.

She yawned, exposing a mouthful of wicked-sharp teeth, clearly not concerned that the powers that be didn't want a picture of her beautiful mug. I'd taken several anyway, enough that she'd stalked off several times, tail flicking with irritation.

"I wish I could scratch you behind the ears," I told her. "I think you'd like it."

I widened my eyes in tandem with the narrowing of hers. "You're not going to claw my face off now, are you?" I asked, alarmed.

She flicked her tail and it thumped against my camera bag.

Suva chuckled. "Lahja, she is good listener, yes?" His Afrikaans accent was melodic and sibilant. "I've told her many things. If she ever starts talking, I may have to kill her."

"Well, now you've ruined any incentive she had to break the animal code of silence," I complained.

Suva laughed, his teeth flashing white against his umber skin.

The sun began its descent in the sky, molten gold surrounded by red and streaks of pink. I took a few pictures of Lahja, and she yawned in the middle of one, making it look like she was sticking out her tongue. I chuckled. "Well, I was looking for a new screen saver, and that's too perfect."

Just as I was ready to throw in the towel, there they were. A gathering of springbok made their way across the desert, leisurely, like I hadn't been waiting half a day for their asses. *And just where the hell have y'all been?* I was surprised they weren't carrying yoga mats and Starbucks cups.

I snapped photos, almost forgetting to breathe. The suspended dust that seemed to never go away only added to the atmosphere of mystery. When everything worked together—the lighting, the timing, the subject matter—it was pure magic. At least, it was until an approaching Land Rover ruined everything. After an obligatory pause for shock, the springbok scattered. Lahja loped off, glancing back at the vehicle once before she disappeared in the brush. I stood slowly, stiff down to my toes, hacking on a cloud of dust.

Irritation flickered through me as the tourist group passed. A woman in a panama hat waved from the back row, smiling widely, and even though she'd possibly cost me some shots, I couldn't help but smile in return. Her joy was fucking contagious. I didn't blame the sightseers. We were doing something that not a lot of people got the opportunity to do, and I'd be a fool not to take a moment to appreciate how special that was.

But for the moment, my love of nature was over. Now I wanted to appreciate how special a shower could be. I hobbled over to my ATV and climbed on, already dreading the bumpy ride back to camp.

"Are you in the mood for some dinner?" Suva's ATV roared to life beside mine. "Maybe some of that stew you like so much?"

My stomach rumbled, not even giving me the chance to decide. "Potjiekos," I tried, the word still strange on my lips.

He laughed in that way that foreign people do when you try to speak their language and wind up butchering the hell out of it. Like they were saying, *"Not quite, but I love that you tried. Bless your heart."*

"Close enough," he said. "I'll make a local of you yet."

I opened my mouth to say something when a shadow caught my eye. I turned to find a lion standing on the dunes, just a ghostly figure in the encroaching darkness. "Phantom," I murmured.

Christ, now my trip was complete. Those desert lions were the ultimate conservation story. They'd survived in a place where little else did. A rare sighting of the desert lion was photography gold. I cut the engine on my ATV, and Suva knew better than to argue.

The stew would have to wait.

BACK AT CAMP, I took the time to charge my camera batteries and downloaded the photographs. No matter how much I wanted to relax, those things went at the top of my list. Then I showered all the dust of the day off. The communal showers were clean and serviceable, which was more than I'd had access to at other campsites, so I couldn't complain—aloud. But my muscles and I wholeheartedly thought I deserved a few hours in my jetted tub right about now.

By the time I got out and dressed in some beat-up khakis and a black T-shirt, dinner was being served by the campfire. I hustled to join them. A woman in colorful tribe wear ladled out servings of the *Potjiekos*. My stomach growled ferociously as she handed me a wooden bowl, even as I opened my mouth to thank her. I grinned sheepishly as her brown eyes danced.

I sat in a camp chair next to Karl, a young photographer just starting out. I regretted my choice almost immediately. He spent a large portion of our dinner griping about losing a perfect shot because of a rogue shifting wind.

"It happens, kid." The guy on our left didn't hesitate to add to the one-sided discussion. He was tanned beyond tanned, well on his way from original recipe and approaching extra crispy—which was strange since I hadn't seen him without a hat the entire time we'd been here.

"I've been in the business over thirty years," he said, giving Karl a pitying look. "You're green now, but you'll learn. You're gonna miss more shots than you catch. And what does it matter anyway? You've been on one safari, you've been on them all."

Karl looked offended and angled his body toward me as he started going on about his plans for the next day. I listened with half an ear, eating my stew languidly. It was like sitting between two extremes—the kid wet behind his ears with too much fucking energy to even contemplate, and the old-timer to my left who couldn't be bothered to glance at the spectacle of Brandberg Mountain behind us. I guess my placement between them was perfect. Maybe I wasn't wet behind the ears anymore, but I planned to hang up my Canon 7D long before I was too jaded to appreciate a natural wonder.

I knew I had to get to bed soon because the days were long, but I wasn't quite ready to turn it yet, so I sat around the campfire a little longer. At one point, Nalani served us a local drinking brew that was dark and spicy. I wasn't sure of the ingredients, and to be honest, I wasn't too eager for the recipe. But it was cold and mellowed me even further as I sat around listening to stories, the hot air blowing my hair gently. Namibia was about as far from Coral Cove as I could get. My hometown was nice, with its seaside ambiance and tropical weather, but this… this was truly something special.

Someone tapped me on the shoulder, and I turned to find a young man dressed in all khaki. It took me a moment to recognize him as one of the employees of the campground. "Are you Jugahney?" he asked, his accent thick.

It took me a few seconds to realize he'd said my name. "Journey." I nodded. "Yes, that's me."

He smiled. "My apologies."

"No worries." Frankly, it was only fair because I'd been butchering their language for days. I may be a world-class traveler, but a linguist, I was not. My tongue saw letters placed in unfamiliar ways and started tying itself immediately. "Is there something wrong?"

"You have a call."

I widened my eyes. An international call made me nervous. It could only be from my family, and they wouldn't call if it wasn't mission critical. "Who is it?"

"A man named John. He said it was very important."

My brother. That only cemented the feeling in my gut. I was seven years older than John, and we'd been the closest growing up. There had been a lot of hero worship from his direction, and a lot of big-brother-protective mode from mine. Somewhere along the way, he'd grown distant. I knew he wasn't calling me in Namibia to chat.

"Is he still on the phone?" I half stood even as I asked the question.

"Yes, I told him I would try to find you. John said he would wait." He waved toward the small main office next to our sleeping quarters. "Please follow me."

Something is wrong, wrong, wrong. Years of being the family fixer made me anxious. Even though all three of the boys—men, now—were grown with wives and kids of their own, I couldn't shake that desire to fix everything for them.

I followed the poor man so closely that when he stopped to open the office door, I nearly plowed into his back. Unfailingly polite, he apologized to me even as I was apologizing to him. When I finally picked up the older model handset, I didn't bother with pleasantries. "What's going on?" I asked anxiously.

"Dad's in the hospital." John was matter-of-fact, as usual. No histrionics on his branch of the family tree. "He had a stroke. I thought you might want to know."

He what? My mind struggled to process what was very simple information. And then, John's little dig filtered in. "Of course I want to know," I snapped.

"I wasn't sure. If you're coming down, let me know, so we'll know to expect you."

If I was coming? My father and I might not agree on... well, anything, and he might not understand his artistic, gay son worth a damn. We might not be able to be in the same room for over ten freaking minutes without offending one another, and we may not have anything in common. He might not be over the fact that I didn't join the family business, and.... Wait, where was I going with all this again? Oh yeah, Dad was family, and that took priority over anything else. It always had.

"I'll catch the first flight out of here in the morning," I said, my mind already whirring with details to make that happen.

"Cam said if you did decide to come, he can pick you up from the airport."

"Cam?" It took everything in me not to stutter. I barely kept from saying, *my Cameron?* That was a silly thought in and of itself because it had been a long time since Cameron was my *anything*. Last I checked, he'd been engaged to a woman named Charlotte.

"Yeah, you remember Cam," John said dryly. "Your ex-fiancé?"

I could hardly forget. I pushed those thoughts aside for more pertinent matters. Travel arrangements would be a bit complicated, but I wasn't picky. All I needed was something with wings headed for the States. Since I always traveled light, packing was a simple matter as well. Years of globetrotting had made me an expert in categorizing what I truly needed, and what I thought I needed until my back had to carry it.

Cutting my assignment short was a little stickier. I felt guilty even thinking about it, but I wondered if I had enough material. I'd planned on at least a few more days, but none of that mattered now. Family was family. I'd make it work.

As if he could sense the direction my thoughts had taken, John snorted. "Glad you could make time for him to come back from Where the Fuck Ever Timbuktu."

"Well, we can't all be happy two feet away from where we dropped out of the womb," I said snidely. I immediately felt ashamed. For whatever reason, John and I brought out the worst in each other. "Sorry."

"Whatever."

It took me a few seconds to realize he'd hung up on me.

I ran my hands through my hair, processing my new reality. I guess it wasn't that much of a surprise that my father had a stroke. He was getting up there in age, and he didn't always take care of himself. Jack Sutton smoked, drank beer excessively, and ate whatever he wanted. And spoiler alert: what he usually wanted was deep-fried. But still. He'd always been larger-than-life and full of spit and vinegar.

I needed to see him with my own two eyes, to make sure he was okay.

I realized I was still standing in the office, looking at the phone stupidly. I gave myself a mental poke. *If you want to see him, you might wanna get a move on*, my brain was kind enough to remind me. *You're still in, well, Africa.*

I got moving.

A FEW HOURS LATER, I was on a plane out of Hosea Kutako. I sat across from a chatty woman named Molly. She'd gone on her first safari a few days before, which meant she was showing pictures to anyone with eyes and the inability to say no. I recognized her as the woman on the rig that had scattered my springbok. And no, I wasn't holding a grudge—much.

"Was this your first time on safari, dear?" she asked, scrolling through more pictures on her iPhone.

I half smiled. Despite my mood, her excitement was palpable. I gave up on wishing her phone would spontaneously combust. "No, I've been about five or six times."

She looked suitably impressed, even though that hadn't been my intention. "Oh my, that is just fascinating." She elbowed her companion, who was already half asleep. "Isn't it *fascinating*, Joe?"

From the looks of things, Joe was fascinated with the insides of his eyelids. He murmured something sleepily, his head lolling to the other side. Joe had good instincts. Might as well get rest because it made a fifteen-hour flight seem like... well, a fifteen-fucking-hour flight. Guess there was really no way to make that better.

"You must've seen some amazing things," Molly gushed.

I chatted with her for a good thirty minutes, trying to think of an excuse to extract myself from the conversation. Since stabbing myself in the thigh seemed like more of a lateral move, I laid the foundation for feigning illness by grimacing and rubbing my temples. By the time I finally pleaded a headache, it wasn't a lie.

Molly instructed me to get some rest in a loud whisper, and I agreed wearily, dropping my head back against the seat. She was quiet for a good five minutes, and I enjoyed the peaceful drone of the engine. Then she was back at it, waking Joe up with another well-placed elbow. I squeezed my eyes shut. *Better him than me.*

Safari was amazing. Namibia was amazing. The people, the culture, and the food were incredible, but now I needed to get home. I didn't miss the irony. A few short hours ago, I'd been thinking how glad I was to have this life, and how far it was away from Coral Cove. Now, I resented every single mile.

It was going to be a long flight.

2

JOURNEY

Fifteen hours and thirty minutes later, my flight touched down at Miami International. I was never gladder to not have to fuss with luggage as I hustled out of the terminal. I only had two things to carry—my battered duffel and my camera bag, which rarely left my sight even when I *wasn't* traveling.

I stepped out into the muggy night air, not at all surprised to find the hub still busy even at this late hour. After a few seconds of craning my neck, I spotted Cameron's black Jeep idling at the end of a long row of cars that hugged the curb. He hadn't seen me yet, but his head was clearly on a swivel, looking for authorities.

Even though nine cars were waiting in the same spot, idling at the curb was illegal. And Cameron *always* tried to do the right thing. It was one of his more endearing qualities. And most annoying. I huffed with soft laughter while I watched him look here and there as though he'd stolen the Hope Diamond. If I didn't hurry and get in the car, he'd probably wet himself.

He startled as I knocked on his passenger window, and a few seconds later, I heard the pop of the door locks. I opened the back door, tossed my duffel in, and got in the passenger side with a wave and a grin.

"Hey," I greeted him, putting my camera bag on my lap. I pulled on my seat belt before he could even open his Dudley-Do-Right mouth.

"Hey." He flashed me a tired smile and put the car in gear. As he pulled away from the curb, his relief was palpable, and I barely held in a chuckle. "Look what the cat dragged in."

And he wasn't very gentle about it, either. That proverbial cat had been dragging me by my face down a gravel driveway for the last five hours. Now that I was in a cozy seat with the AC on full blast, I could feel my body decompressing without my permission. I needed to hold sleep at bay until I made it home and could face-plant in the middle of my bed, which hopefully someone had bothered to put sheets on.

"Thanks for coming to pick me up," I said around a yawn.

"It's not a problem."

Cameron slammed on the brakes as another car cut him off, and suddenly I felt a little more awake. "So... how much is the Arrive Alive Fee in this Uber?"

The right corner of his mouth kicked up as we watched the car cut off another two lanes of airport traffic. "Shut up, JJ."

"I *did* ask you not to call me that, mostly because I'm not dy-no-mite."

He chuckled. "Well, I'll stop when everyone else does. And we both know that's never going to happen."

As he exited the airport terminal. All the friendly lights faded away and darkness and shadows took their place. Cameron navigated the busy traffic smoothly. I didn't try to back-seat drive. Drowsiness tugged at my subconscious again and I fought it back once more.

Cameron spoke into the quiet. "I wanted to let you know that I'm sorry about Jack. If I can help in any way, let me know."

His heartfelt words reminded me that I hadn't come home for an impromptu visit. My father wasn't going to meet me on the porch, fussing about me spending money on an Uber. One thing the Suttons never suffered from was a shortage of cars—that kind of came with the territory in a family of mechanics. The house wasn't going to smell of his special spaghetti, which was my favorite. He never admitted to making it just for me, but he did, and I pretended to believe that it just happened to be on the stove every time I came home.

He's not gone yet.

"Thank you," I said, a little subdued. "Do you know what happened?"

"Somewhat. Jack was in the grocery store when he fell to his knees and nearly passed out. He managed to call John, and thank God, John realized something was wrong. Your father was slurring his words and not making any sense. John called the paramedics, who took Jack to St. Mary's. Then he called me."

I tried not to feel disgruntled. It only made sense for my brother to call Cameron. My entire family still considered him part of ours, which was understandable. We'd made one hell of a team. After my mother's death, he'd been the first person in my life to help me shoulder the burden of taking care of my family.

Apparently, he still was. He was always right fucking here, doing the right fucking thing. As for me, I'd been lying on my belly in a national reserve, taking pictures of stupid springbok, while my father fought for his life.

"He's okay, JJ." Cameron's voice was soothing and sure, it immediately had a calming effect that I'd never cop to. "You know I wouldn't lie to you."

I blew out a breath. "I know."

Despite my desire to rush to the hospital, I knew it was far too late at night, at least, that's what my watch told me. My body was still in a different time zone. I usually had tricks to help me with the jet lag, but my rush to get home had made that impossible.

I glanced over at Cameron to ask if he could stop for food, and kind of lost my train of thought somewhere around those broad shoulders and strong corded forearms. I knew he'd probably come straight from work to pick me up because he was still in his dark blue scrubs. He owned a vet clinic in town named Happy Paws. Even though he'd probably put in a full day, he was still neat and tidy. Being neat and tidy from head to toe was kind of Cameron's thing.

Messing him up was mine.

He was still wearing his hair the same way as the last time I'd seen him, which was a little longer than usual but neatly tapered. God help the glossy chestnut strands if they tried for any type of rebellion. I couldn't really see his eyes in the dark, but they had always been the lightest of greens. Every time I came across sea glass I paused and thought about Cameron's eyes.

Fanciful nonsense.

I looked away. I guess I'd just put Cameron's hotness in the category of "Things That Hadn't Changed." What *had* changed was that I was no longer a glutton for punishment. We didn't fit together anymore, and we wanted different things. I knew that. I also knew that while he looked like a nice, sweet boy on the outside, he certainly didn't fuck like one.

But I digress.

I was glad to still have him in my life. No matter how difficult it was. We'd been best friends long before we'd ever become lovers, and I wasn't going to give that up. Besides, there was nothing romantic between us now. We'd both been in our twenties when we broke up, and we'd dated a lot of people since then. I didn't need to keep tabs on him because every time I came into town, nosy people made it their business to mention who Cameron was dating and for how long.

My last visit to Coral Cove had been three years ago, and Cameron had just gotten engaged to a lovely woman named Charlotte. She worked at a wildlife sanctuary for birds, which was where they'd met. I hadn't heard anything about a wedding yet, so I assumed they were still engaged. Hopefully, I would be somewhere far, far away when they finally decided to tie the knot. After they got married, they would probably proceed to have perfect babies with Cam's beautiful brown hair and Charlotte's gorgeous blue eyes. Cameron's sweet stepmother, Rosy, would enjoy her retirement bouncing so-said perfect babies on her knee. Then everyone would live together in a castle in an enchanted forest. And so went the book of *Fuck You, Happily Ever After Is Not Supposed To Be A Real Thing*.

Even though I knew we had to be getting close to my father's house, I felt myself starting to nod. It didn't help that years of travel had made me capable of sleeping pretty much anywhere. Or, that Cameron was such a safe, conscientious driver. I knew I was in capable hands.

I finally gave up and leaned my head against the door. To be more accurate, my neck gave up on holding up my head and it lolled against the window with a *thunk*. Cameron, that bastard, chuckled lowly. As I fell asleep, I imagined the brief touch of a finger on the back of my hand.

I WOKE in what felt like minutes, but as I blinked, taking in my surroundings, I knew it had to have been longer than that. Cameron's Jeep was parked in a darkened room of some kind and it was off, but probably hadn't been for long; I could hear the engine still ticking as it cooled. I was still buckled in and covered by a jacket that wasn't mine. The fabric smelled like Cameron and had a few strands of dog hair on it. I blew one away from my nose, a little amused. Everything he owned had a bit of pet hair on it. He should be the spokesperson for *Bissell* vacuums.

I rubbed my eyes blearily. Well, at least I'd woken up just in time for the good part of the carjacking. I checked my lap and found my camera bag. I sighed in relief. I might be about to die, but at least I had my Cannon.

The automatic lights suddenly winked on and Cameron came out of the side door of the house. He looked surprised to see me awake and sent me a rueful look as he came around to my side and opened the door. "I was hoping to let you get a little more sleep."

I knuckled my eyes some more, so hard that it left little sparklies in my vision. "I appreciate it. Really. Thanks."

"No problem." Without a word of warning, he reached in and

unbuckled my seat belt. I sat there like a toddler and let him, so maybe I was a little more tired than I thought.

I got out, shouldering my camera bag, and proceeded to stretch the longest stretch in history. It was a shirt-rising, spine-cracking ordeal to cap off what was now a seventeen-hour day of fucking travel. When I finished, Cameron was looking away, his face a little pink. I remembered then that he'd probably had a long day himself, which had been exacerbated by driving to the airport to pick me up. The trip was an hour each way.

I winced. "God, I'm sorry. I'm just taking my time here."

"That's all right. I don't have any place else to be."

"No, I've taken up enough of your time. Thank you for—"

"Will you stop thanking me?" For the first time since we'd left the airport, he sounded a touch irritated. "This is what you do for friends. We are friends, aren't we?"

"Of course we are." I wasn't sure why I felt flustered. "Let me get my bag and I can get out of your hair."

"I already took in your bag. And getting out of my hair is going to be a challenge." His mouth kicked up. "We're at my house."

And then he went inside... fucking went *inside* like he hadn't just dropped that little bombshell.

"Um. Why exactly would we be at your house?" Realizing I was talking to an empty garage, I threw up my hands. I had no other choice but to participate in my own kidnapping—albeit a friendly one. I marched over to the door he'd disappeared through and let myself in. It felt awkward just walking into his house, even though he obviously intended for me to follow.

I found myself in an airy, comfortable-looking living room. The décor was cozy and understated with oversized couches and a few patterned rugs. A few bookcases lined the far wall next to the entertainment center, which was unapologetically large to accommodate a big-ass TV.

I trailed my fingers over the light brown cashmere throw. It felt as soft as it looked and was clearly someone's favorite. There was a slight dusting of dog hair on the adjacent couch, which probably belonged to the big-ass dog standing in front of me.

Dog? Wolf? Who knew? The dog-wolf titled his head with unblinking blue eyes, assessing my very being with uncomfortable intensity. His coat was a beautiful brown, with a little gray and black mixed in. After a few moments, he gave me a wolfish smile. Technically, he was probably panting, but he looked like he'd made a fucking *decision*.

"Hey, Cam," I called out.

"Yeah?" His voice came from somewhere in the back, all casual-like, as if he hadn't just *literally* thrown me to the wolves.

"Could you maybe stop doing whatever the hell you're doing for a few seconds and come save my life?"

"What? I'm just making sure your room is ready." He emerged from a doorway in the back and came down the hallway. When he spotted us in our man versus *what-the-hell-are-you?* stare down, he chuckled. "I see you've met Kona."

"Yeah, we met. He asked me if I knew where you kept the all-purpose seasoning."

Cameron snorted. "*She* is very friendly. Intense, but friendly. She's a rescue that I'm fostering."

"Rescue from what?" I muttered. "I wasn't aware the hounds of hell had a catch and release program."

He laughed. "You'll get used to her. She really is a sweetheart."

As if to prove that she was at least part dog, she started scratching her ear. Our easy but careful banter ended, and awkward silence stepped in like a champ, only disturbed by Kona's tags jingling to the beat of her leg. At least the silence felt awkward to me. Cameron didn't seem to be bothered.

His eyes held fondness as he gave me a onceover. "You look good, JJ."

I fought off a blush and won, reminding myself that it didn't matter what he thought. About anything. We weren't together anymore, and he wasn't going to be my husband. The sun no longer rose and set in Cameron Foster's beautiful sea-glass eyes. I didn't respond.

He wasn't deterred. "So, what were you doing in Namibia?" He inclined his head at the camera bag on my shoulder. "Other than the obvious."

"Apparently someone at National Geographic was jonesing for a picture of some springbok. And I'm certainly not going to argue about traveling to Africa."

"Another entry for your dream book?" he asked lightly.

"Dream journal," I corrected, my tone matching his. "And yeah, it is."

That old binder was one of my prized possessions. I'd found it in my parents' attic after a particularly nasty hurricane. Part of the roof had given way and a corner of the glorified crawl space had gotten soaked. I'd gone up there to salvage what I could and had come across that journal. The sepia-colored binder had been imprinted with faint impressions of globes and world maps, the word *Coddiwomple* written in script across the cover.

I knew immediately that it belonged to my mother because my father would sooner give up fried food for life than journal his thoughts. I set the binder to the side, so I could take it home for myself. Secretly. We generally fought over any Mom Items we found. It was understandable—the building memories part of her life was over, so the ones we had would have to hold us for a lifetime. Normal items that she would've probably tossed were suddenly precious keepsakes. A crumpled hanky with a spot of lipstick had become more valuable than anything Indiana Jones found in the Temple of Doom.

Because no one was curious enough to wonder why I was carrying my sweater home rather than wearing it, I smuggled the binder home safely, right past my brothers' noses. When I finally got a chance to open it, I was surprised to find newspaper articles and pictures of classic tourist destinations. Machu Picchu, the Great Pyramid, Belize. It took me a few minutes of flipping through the journal to understand it was like an illustrated bucket list. A record of all the places she'd wanted to visit.

She'd never gotten the chance. Had never even been on a fucking plane. Her journal had been such a departure from what I'd known of my mother. She'd been a no-nonsense woman who acted like we needed a passport just to leave town. I'd never pictured her as someone with aspirations of travel... dreams of something beyond Coral Cove.

That journal had eventually become a bone of contention between Cameron and me. To hear him tell it, that tangible record of stifled dreams had been the catalyst for our breakup. I called bullshit on that.

Thankfully, Cameron didn't press. "Come on, I'll show you your room. You'll need some rest if you want to get to the hospital early."

We made a train of man, man, wolf as we headed down the hallway. Kona's breath was hot on the back of my thigh as she bumped into me a few times. Probably on purpose. I could see the open door of my room up ahead... which reminded me of something pretty fucking important.

"Er, Cam?" I followed him into a mint green guest room, which smelled slightly of PineSol. A small basket of toiletries and snacks was on the driftwood side table, probably Charlotte's touch.

"Yeah?" He looked around distractedly and snapped his fingers. "I forgot the towels, but there should be some extras in the linen closet."

"Yeah, about that. Why are we at your house again?"

"I thought it might be nice for you not to have to worry about getting your room ready. Just for tonight." He smiled. "I'm being neighborly."

"Neighborly...." I thought about that for a few seconds. Last time I checked, Cameron lived in a little cottage down by the water, not next door to my father. If I hadn't been so busy examining the inside of my eyelids when he pulled up, maybe I would've noticed. "You didn't."

He flushed. "I always wanted to buy property instead of renting. You know that."

Yeah, I did. But why this one? My father had been after us to buy that property during our engagement.

"*It's just close enough, JJ,*" he insisted. "*We won't be on top of each other, and it has good bones.*"

"*It's too big,*" I said, frowning as I looked over the two-story house. "*We don't need all that space.*"

"*When you decide to have a family, you will,*" he said sensibly.

And suddenly, I felt like my collar was a little too tight. Boy, all of this was happening pretty damned fast. Cam and I hadn't even walked down the aisle yet, and my father was ready for some grandkids.

"Sure," I managed as I dabbed my clammy brow.

He smiled. "*It's perfect for a young married couple starting out. Make sure you show Cam.*"

That was all such a long time ago, and I'd never planned to move back here or buy that house. So why did I feel like Cameron had encroached on my territory? I silently instructed myself to be reasonable.

Cameron winced as if he knew exactly what I was thinking. "I used to see the property every time I came over here to check on Jack, and I finally thought, wouldn't it be nice—"

"To get your nose *all* the way up my family's ass by moving in next door?"

Hmm. And just what part of that rejoinder was supposed to be reasonable? I reviewed my word choices and mentally marked them all with red Xs. *You get a D minus for diplomacy.*

"Nice. Real nice." His eyes were decidedly cool as he leveled me with a look, making me feel about two inches tall. Then he cut even *that* in half. "Don't take your anger out on me because you feel guilty that you haven't been here for them."

Even sweet, helpful kittens had teeth. I masochistically enjoyed being an inch tall for a few seconds before I nodded shortly. He wasn't wrong, and I wasn't mad. If you can dish it, you'd better be damned sure that you can take it. But frankly, I had no desire to stay in his perfect house perfectly decorated by his perfect fiancée while he judged me.

I leaned down and picked up my duffel, which he'd put at the end of the bed. "Thanks for the ride, Cam."

He blinked for a second before reaching for me. I evaded his grasp as I swept past him, and he cursed. "JJ, Will you just...." I was in the hallway before he grabbed my arm and jerked me to a stop. "Can you wait a fucking second?"

"Foster, I'm not in the mood. And will you call off your demon dog?" I looked down in irritation as Kona bumped her large head against my leg. "You're the one with your hands all over me. I'm no threat."

He let my arm go as if I was made of fire. "Sorry," he muttered, "she's not protecting me, she's trying to comfort you. She can tell something is wrong."

I looked down, and sure enough, she was rubbing against my leg and then glancing up at me in intervals. "Oh." I reached out hesitantly and gave her broad head a scratch, and she bumped me again. "That's... kind of sweet."

"Yeah, that's Kona for you. If owning a wolf hybrid wasn't such a commitment, we'd probably have people lining up to adopt her." He sighed, running a hand through his hair. "Look. I'm sorry. I shouldn't have said what I said."

No, it wasn't very nice to give people the truth right to the cranium.

"I shouldn't have said what I said, either." I frowned. "I think I'm just overtired and feeling a little sensitive."

"Stay," he said, removing my duffel from my shoulder. He seemed obsessed with that thing. I had a feeling if I wanted to leave his house, I was going to have to do it without my bag.

When he moved to take my camera bag, I pulled it back protectively. No one touched my equipment but me. He chuckled softly. "Fine, fine." He went back into the bedroom and dropped the duffel back at the end of the bed. I trailed behind. "You should get some sleep."

I glanced at the queen-sized bed, which looked all kinds of fluffy and comfortable. That sounded like a damned fine idea. "I think I will."

"I have to go in pretty early, but you're more than welcome to use my Jeep. You just have to drop me and Kona off first."

"You take her with you to work?" I couldn't help but smile. "That's kind of adorable."

He gave her a fond look. "She gets so excited and ready, like it's the first day of school. I almost expect to find her waiting at the door with a lunchbox between her teeth."

I chuckled at the mental image. "Thanks for the offer, but I think I'll just use Dad's car. He still has the Mustang, doesn't he?"

"His vintage refurbished Mustang?" Cameron raised an eyebrow. "Um, yeah, he does. And he still feels the same as he did when you were younger about letting his kids drive it."

I grinned. "Then he'd better hurry up and get well. May I presume he still keeps his keys in the bowl by the front door?"

He held up his hands. "I don't want any part of this."

"Coward." I waggled my eyebrows. "Maybe if you're nice to me, I'll give you a ride."

He laughed. "Get some rest, JJ." I watched him shamelessly as he headed for the door. Everything about Cameron Foster turned my crank—always had. He paused at the doorway and gave me a half smile. "I'm glad you're back home."

Before I could respond, he was gone, shutting the door quietly behind himself. I glanced down to find Kona standing there, looking at me expectantly. "You don't think you're staying in here, do you?"

She smiled a doggy smile. Apparently, she did.

"Fine," I huffed, as if I had a choice. "I guess I could use the company."

I had no delusions that she planned to sleep on the floor. Cameron treated animals like people. I wouldn't be surprised to see her on the couch with a beer and the remote control. After I stripped down to my boxers and flopped on the bed, she proved me right, jumping up next to me.

"You're lucky the bed is big," I informed her.

She didn't seem concerned with little things like bed size as she stretched out beside me, which was a pretty blasé attitude considering she took up quite a bit of it. I drew a line down the middle of the bed with the side of my palm, maintaining eye contact. "Your side." I pointed at my pillow. "My side."

Her tail beat an excited tattoo on the comforter. Thinking ahead, I got back up and opened my door a crack, just in case Her Highness, Queen of Bed Hogging, got sick of me during the night. Then I flopped back on the bed, which was exactly as soft as it looked. I fell asleep to the memory of Cam's little smile as he admitted he was glad I was back home.

Temporarily, I reminded myself as I drifted off. Kona migrated over to my side, and I curled my fingers in her fur. *This is all only temporary.*

3

CAMERON

It was going to be one of those days.

I knew that, even as I opened my eyes. Mostly because I'd made some questionable decisions regarding booze the night before. I didn't drink often, and when I did, it hit me hard. I had the alcohol tolerance of a kid skimming a bottle from his parents' liquor cabinet for the first time. My drink ad would look nothing like the suave *Dos Equis* commercial. *I don't always drink, but when I do, I wake up feeling like absolute shit.*

But fuck, being around Journey always messed with my head. A drink to take the edge off had turned into two and quickly segued into three. Then I'd decided that whoever created shot glasses had never had big boy problems and I got a better vessel from the kitchen cupboard. Things went south from there.

It was hard to believe it had been three years since I'd laid eyes on him. We still talked, of course, because we were dedicated to maintaining our friendship. A quick text here. A birthday post with a smiley face. The occasional photo of an elephant, which he knew was my favorite animal.

Once upon a time, even a few hours apart seemed like too many. Those days were long gone. Our current record was five months of no contact. And now, he was here, in my house, in the room right next to mine. Yes, I was the one who'd invited him, but I'd seriously underestimated the mindfuck factor.

God, had it really been over a decade since we'd been engaged? After all that time, it was hard to believe I could still want someone so much. Especially after the way he left. It didn't seem to matter that he saw me as an annoyance and perpetual interloper in his life. It didn't matter that we'd been apart longer than we'd even been together. It didn't seem to matter that we wanted different things out of life. I just looked at him and I *wanted*. The end.

It was probably perfectly natural. We were each other's firsts. For better or worse, you always remembered your first. I'd met Journey in high school, our freshman year. I'd gravitated toward him almost immediately, probably because our homelives were far from idyllic. My father had turned marriage into a spectator sport, and Journey's mother had passed the year before. We had more on our minds than what celebrity was wearing what and who had a crush on whom.

He was different from the others. More serious. Responsible. He always hurried home after school to take care of his brothers. He even worked at his father's auto shop on the weekends. I knew he understood what it was like to be the kid who never got to be a kid.

He'd made his interest clear even before he tried to kiss me. It was a clumsy attempt and I'd shied away—not because I didn't want to, but because I probably wasn't sticking around. I knew my father. Getting attached to one place and the people there was not a good idea. His marriages never lasted, and then he was ready to "start fresh."

But then there was Rosy, my stepmom. When I found out I was going to be able to stay in Coral Cove, I was ecstatic. That removed the final barrier between Journey and me. Even though it was late at night when I found out, I couldn't wait to tell him. I came over and knocked on his window until he stumbled out on the porch in pajamas, his sandy blond hair a mess. He barely had a chance to say my name before I pushed him up against the wall and pressed my mouth to his. It was my first kiss, and I had no idea what the fuck I was doing. It was artless and raw and the most amazing moment. It was my first taste of forever.

Or, so I thought.

Rebecca made noise from her area near the wall, and I glanced over at her kennel. All I could see was her plaid blanket, but it was moving up and down with her measured breathing. The clinic staff was all taking turns looking after her, and last night had been my shift. Luckily, no one cared if you were buzzed while babysitting, as long as your charge was a raccoon.

Someone had seen fit to raise her and then abandon her in a dumpster, where she'd been trapped for days. She'd needed fluids and food and a lot of care, and then I had to figure out what to do with a raccoon who was way too acclimated to people and not fit for the wild.

I rolled over on my back with a groan and stared up at the ceiling. The list of things you had to do as a fully functioning adult had never seemed less appealing. On that list was getting out of bed, putting on clothes, and trying to interact with people. I mentally checked the list again, but I couldn't find "rolling over and going back to sleep."

I convinced myself to get out of bed, keeping the whimpers to a minimum, and floated myself a few lies to get moving.

Lie #1: *You'll feel better after you shower.*

I did not. Less bleary-eyed and wet, certainly, but not better.

Lie #2: *You'll feel more with it after you get dressed.*

I did not, but at least I didn't have to worry about what to wear. I put on my blue scrubs and a comfortable pair of white sneakers. Then I tamed my hair and put in my contacts. A couple of blinks made me realize that my eyes were not in the mood, so I switched to glasses.

Lie #3: *You'll feel heaps better after you get something in your stomach.*

That helpful bit of advice sent me right to the garbage can, where my stomach and throat worked together to eject my muffin and juice with little ado. Afterward, I stood in front of the sink, brushing my teeth grimly. Like I'd said, it was gonna be one of those days.

Even after I finished getting ready, there was still no sign of Kona.

I glanced at my watch. I needed to get her started on her routine, so we could get going. And if she could appear magically in the hallway right about now, that would be great.

No such luck.

I scratched the back of my neck, looking at the partially cracked door to the guest room. I knew exactly where she was, and I felt strange about going in there when he was sleeping. Although, it *was* my house... even if, for the moment, that room was his domain.

I sighed and pushed on the door, widening the crack before sticking my face through the opening. Of course, because he *lived* to fucking torture me, Journey was not under the covers like a decent human being. Instead, he was sleeping on top, his face buried in the pillows, giving me an unfettered view of his body. Why wouldn't I want to start my morning with a visual of the body I no longer had the right to touch?

I knew every bit of him, from his mess of sandy blond hair to the freckles on his sun-kissed shoulders to the toes on his long, slender feet. Every fucking inch had seen my hands or my mouth or my dick... some important areas had seen a combination of all three.

He was a little more muscled than I remembered. Even though he was relaxed, I could still see the strength and definition in his back. The tattoo was new, too. It was of a small bird midflight on the right side of his back, just above his ass... that firm, round ass, which was barely covered in his navy-and-white striped underwear.

If you could call them underwear. He didn't even have the common decency to wear real fucking pajamas. I huffed. I mean, what the hell were those, anyway? Boy shorts? Why would someone wear such a thing? Probably to make some poor loser stare desperately at your ass.

I stared *desperately* at that ass.

I wanted to touch. I wanted to do more than touch. And since *none* of that would be happening, I put my googly eyes right back in my head. I was not a creepy pervert, and I would not linger in the doorway ogling Journey's ass. Nor would I think about it later when I was in the shower beating off to the memory. Okay, so I was a pervert and I certainly *was* going to do that other thing, but for now, I was going to do my utmost best to achieve normal.

A snort on the other side of the bed made me smile. Kona was stretched out on her side of the bed and his, her paws in his face, her nose under his arm. Journey was lucky she hadn't given him her business end to wake up to. I'd gotten the bad end of *that* particular deal on quite a few occasions. She had absolutely no boundaries, and when sleeping, tended to follow you in the bed like a heat-seeking missile.

I saw her eye move and knew she was playing possum. To be fair, she gave up the ghost rather quickly. When I snapped my fingers, she sprang to her feet and shook herself liberally. I winced as she bounded to the floor, shaking the bed quite a bit. Journey didn't move a muscle. I closed the door behind us quietly because he was going to be out cold for a little while.

I was already dreading the day she'd be adopted. She'd been dropped off at our clinic six months ago, probably because she'd either gotten bigger than they'd expected or maybe because of her rambunctious personality. I'd kept her at the clinic for a few weeks, but she'd gotten into so much trouble that I'd decided to bring her home. She was a sweet dog, but she was headstrong and wasn't used to being held accountable for her actions. She kind of reminded me of a teenager who'd been running wild and was suddenly placed with strict parents.

I let Kona outside, and she wasted no time reclaiming her backyard kingdom with a long howl. I chuckled. I wasn't worried about her howling which was, admittedly, one of her favorite activities. Even when he was there, Journey's dad certainly didn't have a problem with it. And neither did Marly, the town florist, on the other side. It helped that due to the lot size of the homes in the neighborhood, we weren't exactly on top of each other.

My house was an older structure, built in a time when building codes and permits were just a suggestion. That was probably why certain parts of the house were hotter and cooler for no damn reason at all, and why getting replacement parts for anything was an adventure. But the neighborhood was quiet—at least until Kona had arrived—and the backyard was huge, which made up for any number of architectural sins.

We were supposed to live here together.

I'd been dreading telling Journey that I bought the place, but I was glad I'd pulled off that particular Band-Aid. Hopefully he wouldn't think that I was still so hung up on him that I couldn't move on, which was absolutely not true, despite what my former fiancée Charlotte thought. Oh, and Beau, the guy I'd dated after her. We'd lasted a year before he claimed I was "holding myself back." Whatever the fuck that means.

Then there was Paola, the woman I'd dated after Beau. We got off on the wrong foot from the very beginning. I ended our first date early to help one of Journey's brothers. Mark was running late at the doctor's and needed someone to pick up his kids. I called Paola later to apologize and offered to take her out again to make up for it. She declined, but not before listing a whole host of reasons why I was undatable. A lot of those things involved Journey.

So yeah, that was one thing Charlotte, Beau, and Paola shared—they thought I was entirely too wrapped up in my ex's family. Another thing they shared? They were all delusional and wrong. I'd gone on a blind date recently with a nice man named Carter, and I managed not to mention Journey or his family once.

I smiled. I was so proud of myself.

After ten minutes, I whistled for Kona and we headed back in. She circled my legs, tripping me mercilessly until I brought out her vitamins. She gobbled them down with little ado. I was never quite so eager for *my* vitamins, but to each her own. I crunched down on my own fruity, chalky tablets and she looked up at me with pity. *Poor, ignorant bastard. He doesn't even know vitamins can be chicken flavored.*

I put Rebecca in a sling around my chest, like the baby she thought she was, and we all headed out the door five minutes later. When I got back, Journey would be gone, as it should be. I was just doing a nice thing for an ex because I still cared about him and his family. Just like when I brought over leftovers for his dad sometimes or made sure he remembered to put out his recycling bins on time. I was just being nice.

Kona ran in front of me joyously, circling back every few seconds to make sure I was coming. I was thankful I had a career that allowed me to bring her to work with me. As I buckled her in the back seat, she licked at my face impatiently, wrestling a smile out of me. When I finally found her forever home, she was going to make an excellent companion for someone. But right now, she was my best girl.

Becca glared up at me from her sling, her moist dark eyes accusing, as if she could read my mind. "I barely know you," I informed her. "I'm not going to add you to my best girl list."

She chattered angrily.

THE HAPPY PAWS vet clinic was only a ten-minute drive away from my house.

Since we were pretty much the only game in town, other than a small boutique vet place an hour away, we prided ourselves on being a comprehensive practice. The building consisted of three exam rooms, a surgical suite, an X-ray and ultrasonic suite, and my small office.

The staff included a vet tech, Lolly, and a vet nurse, Charles. Bailey, our always efficient and scarily organized office manager, rounded out the team. Bailey was as nosy as she was efficient. She loved to mother hen me to death even though she was younger than me. She was also probably the closest thing I had to a best friend.

I walked into a flurry of activity. Most of the team were preparing and stacking cages, which let me know that we had a callout of some sort. Kona only added to the chaos, barking for reasons only known to her.... Well, her, and apparently also Bailey's husky, Katya. She joined in the fuss as she greeted Kona with the song of her people, which involved a lot of howling. The two of them obviously had urgent dog/wolf business to get to, so I left them to it.

I handed off Rebecca to Bailey, announcing, "Your turn."

"Rough night?" she asked, her blue eyes curious behind dark-framed glasses as she got the raccoon settled. Her pink scrubs had cats wearing sunglasses all over them. Her wild, curly hair was pulled back in a clip that did absolutely nothing to contain it, and Rebecca immediately reached for a curl with adorable little black hands.

"You have no idea."

"Don't worry. I know how to handle a diva." She cooed down at the raccoon even as she freed her dark curls from those curious hands.

Rosy gave me a sheepish look as I jumped in to help prepare cages. Did I mention she was having a hard time with retirement? She was also in blue scrubs, her gray hair pulled back in its customary braid down her back. "I know what you're going to say."

"Then why do you keep making me say it?" I asked patiently.

"I was talking with Eric in the Sheriff's Department and he mentioned there is a hoarding situation going on at the Cooper place." She lifted a shoulder. "I figured you could use some help. Just for today."

"Uh-huh."

I loved working with her because she was easy to be around, and she was an amazing vet. But she'd been diagnosed with a heart problem five years prior, and the doctor told her to slow down. I worried about her. She was the only real mother I'd ever known.

My real mother died suddenly when I was six, and that was the last of stability as I knew it for a very long time. It wasn't that my father didn't love me; he'd been a fun-loving guy who was always quick with a joke and a smile. But he'd spent much of my life trying to find what he had with my mother, and five wives later, that was still very true.

Rosy and my father's marriage had only lasted a few years before he fell in love with a coworker, the lovely Gabriella, who would become wife number five. Gabriella hated the never-ending Florida heat and wanted to move up North, and I just remember being so damned *tired* when my father told me we were moving. I'd sat Rosy and my father down and asked if I could stay behind under the guise of finishing my schooling in one place. Truthfully, I just wanted to get off the merry-go-round once and for all. My father's expression had been a study in resignation as he'd ruffled my hair.

"I get it. If Rosy says it's okay, it's fine by me."

So yeah, it was a little hard to draw a hard line with her, which she absolutely took advantage of.

She sent me a cheeky grin. "You need my help. Looks like twenty-five to thirty dogs at last count."

For years, animal control had been dealing with the Coopers, an elderly husband and wife, who never allowed anyone on their property. The smell had prompted their closest neighbor to call the authorities, which started an investigation.

I knew from experience we were going to see a bunch of mistreated animals, malnourished, possibly feral depending on how much they'd had to fend for themselves. And worst of all, we were going to have to make some heartbreaking decisions about who could be saved, and who should be spared any further suffering. It infuriated and saddened me in equal measure.

I was determined to put my best foot forward for the animals who'd never had someone stand up for them a day in their lives, even if I was a touch hungover. I could be a hungover hero. It was an overlooked market, and the geniuses at Marvel comics should be ashamed of themselves.

"You can stay," I allowed. "But I do all the heavy lifting."

She all but clapped her hands in glee. "You're a good son."

She had me in the palm of her arthritic hand, and she knew it. "Yeah, yeah, yeah."

"I'm going to take this first batch of cages over in the van with Lolly," Rosy said, heading for the door. "Can you meet me up there with Charles?"

"Yep."

She paused. "You know, you don't look so hot. You're not sick, are you?"

"Nope."

"And you sure you're feeling good enough to—"

"Yep."

She left after one more searching look that I pretended not to notice. I was getting a lot of those looks lately because our town was nosy as fuck, and news of Charlotte's pregnancy had spread like wildfire. Just yesterday, someone had murmured "Poor Cameron" while I was in line at the coffee shop.

Some people had no sense of decency. If you're going to be a good busybody, you invest time in learning how to fucking *whisper* properly. Have the discipline to learn your damned craft. Even the smiley barista had sent me a sympathetic look and put an extra muffin in my bag. I half expected to find "Sorry Your Ex Found Someone Better" scripted in sugar crystals across the top.

It was all so unnecessary. Charlotte and I had thoroughly moved on from one another. She'd married a nice guy named Greg, and they were finally having the baby she'd always wanted. And I was happy, too. Well, happy-ish. Maybe I was a little lonely. I hated starting over. Some people loved the thrill of the chase, the nervousness and the butterflies that came with meeting someone new. To me, it just felt like I'd been working my way up Relationship Hill, and someone had dropkicked me back down to the bottom.

A throat clearing jolted me out of my thoughts, and I blinked to find Bailey looking at me with raised brows. God knows how long I'd been standing there, contemplating life. One of the office cats, Mr. Pickles, moseyed across her keyboard. Bailey shooed him off, but he came back for a second pass, clearly determined to put his thoughts in print.

Bailey pulled the cat in her lap and rubbed his head. "I have good news. I finally heard back from the observatory."

"The observatory." I looked at her blankly. "Do we have a pickup there or something?"

"The *observatory*." She clucked impatiently. "You know, the place with the beautiful trees and butterfly garden? The place I was trying to book for my wedding?"

Oh, riiiight. I combed my brain frantically, wishing I could do a keyword search for the words *observatory* and *wedding*. Maybe something had gone into my mental Spam Folder. It was usually pretty crowded in there.

I knew the important bits. I knew she was getting married to her long-term boyfriend, Garrick. I knew he was a great guy. And I knew I was getting them a toaster oven, the nice kind, with French doors and a rotisserie rack. Didn't I get credit for any of that?

Bailey narrowed her eyes. "You do remember, don't you?"

I nodded emphatically like I absolutely lived for her wedding musings and didn't immediately tune out the moment she started going on about anything wedding related. To be fair, if you weren't one of the people actually doing the marrying, it was a bit of a snooze. I was just a guest. All I needed to know was when and where, and what colors were on the no-fly list.

"We're on for the twenty-first of September," she continued. She'd stopped stroking Mr. Pickles, and he headbutted her a few times to get the petting factory up and running again. "So, don't make any plans."

That was almost four months away. I nodded again. "Got it."

"You're going to need a date."

"I don't *need* a date," I scoffed. "If I find someone between now and then that I'd like to bring, that's fine, but I'm not going to—"

"You *need* a date," she insisted. "Charlotte is going to be there, and she RSVP'd for two. I'm sure she's bringing Greg."

"So?"

"*So*, you're going to look pitiful and dumped! She's going to be all radiant and pregnant with her big, strong fireman husband at her side, and you're going to be all alone, drinking away your sorrows."

I perked up a bit. "It's going to be open bar?"

She snapped her fingers. "Focus!"

"It doesn't matter what people think," I informed Bailey. "I don't need to scrounge up a date to pretend I'm something I'm not."

"What, happy? And it wouldn't just be for show," she said. "You should get out there. A nice good fu—"

"Bailey!"

"I was going to say a nice fulfilling relationship might do you some good." Her eyes twinkled. She was a dirty little tart, and I loved her down to her bones.

"If you want me to find a fulfilling relationship, why did you make me create a profile on that trashy app?"

"Trashy?" She rolled her eyes. "It's a dating app. That's how people do things nowadays. You'd know that if you weren't so—"

"Young and hip and utterly fantastic?"

"I'll take not what the fuck I was going to say for one hundred, Alex. My point is that it wouldn't kill you to get out there."

"I've been out there, thanks. Three blind dates in three months, all of them more boring than the last."

"Well, you have been picking a certain type of person. I met a few of them, remember?" She rubbed Mr. Pickles as she searched her brain for delicate terms to describe my dating taste. Tactful wasn't exactly her comfort zone. "They were all of a particular age."

"Nothing wrong with someone age-appropriate."

And just that quickly, she gave up on trying to spare my feelings. "They were all boring as shit, Cam."

"Age does not equal boring. I'm forty years old and—"

"Thirty-nine," she corrected.

"*And* I'm not looking to date someone who thinks a good time is partying at a bar," I went on doggedly. "And just so you know, past thirty-five, it's all forty, Bee."

She paused for a moment, digesting that acrid-flavored nugget of truth. I didn't point out that she was also invited to the It's All Downhill from Here party. No RSVP required.

"What about my cousin Carter?" she finally asked. "You guys had a good time last month."

I'd say "good" was probably stretching it a tad. We'd had a pleasant dinner with nice conversation, and then we'd gone our separate ways. There had been no spark. No awareness of him as anything other than a good guy and a potential friend.

But I guess that's what I was looking for this time around. Not boring, but... safe. Safe was not your fiancé telling you that he was overwhelmed with responsibility and wanted to do something for himself. It wasn't your fiancé completely overhauling his life to trek to the rainforest and take pictures of wildlife. It certainly wasn't him telling you that he was going with or without you. I still remember my reply as I sat there blinking at him stupidly. *You wanna run that by me all over again? Take that shit from the top.*

"I'm not saying no," I said slowly.

"Good. I'll set it up myself. What day is good for you?"

"Err," I said eloquently. "I don't know off the top of my head. I'm an extremely busy man, Bee."

"Watching *Dateline* with your dog is not extremely busy."

"Kona is not my dog, but she always knows the killer before I do." I smiled fondly. "She's so gifted."

Bailey didn't find me amusing. From the look she gave me, it was clear that she thought I actually believed Kona loved Dateline, which was crazy. She preferred *20/20*.

"Feel free to leave that whip-smart humor home when you go out with Carter," she advised. "It might increase your chances of getting laid again before you die. Now when is good for you?"

"Can I have some time to think about it?"

She eyed me for a few moments, and I had a feeling my reading on the bullshit meter was quite odiferous. "Tonight," she said definitively.

Someone wearing cat scrubs shouldn't be so threatening. And yet....

"I don't think—"

"Just a quick bite and a drink at Riptide," she insisted. "You go there all the time anyway."

I grimaced, rubbing a hand over the back of my neck. "And it won't be a long, drawn-out thing?"

"I promise."

I agreed with a sigh. "Fine. Go ahead and set it up."

"Fantastic. And I'm glad you agreed because your love life is just sad." She gave the calico a scritch near his ears. "Isn't that right, Mr. Pickles?"

I thought it was only fair when he urinated on her a little bit.

Bailey squealed as she lifted him off her lap gingerly. "He has a bladder problem," I reminded her. After glancing around the floor, she decided to put him on her desk, mostly because he and Kona didn't get along all that well. "It's not his fault."

"I know that," she said, dabbing at her scrubs futilely. Mr. Pickles sauntered off, making sure to knock her pen and almost empty coffee cup off the desk first. Almost empty. Coffee splattered across her shoes and she groaned. "That damned cat."

My love life officially forgotten, she marched off toward the restroom. I wisely kept my yap buttoned, but I sent Mr. Pickles a wink. He might not have a great bladder, but there wasn't a thing wrong with his timing.

4

JOURNEY

The right side of room 402 was occupied by a sleeping patient who didn't stir as I entered. I walked past him quietly and ducked behind the curtain on the far side. The bed was empty, but there was still an untouched lunch tray on the bedside table. The TV was on mute, with a news show on the screen.

I checked my watch, only to find it was slightly after ten o'clock in the morning. Maybe they'd taken my father for X-rays or something. Well, it wasn't like I had anyplace pressing to be. I sat in the visitor's chair to wait.

I didn't particularly care for hospitals. The last time I was in this one, it was because my mother had died. The mind worked in mysterious ways sometimes. I couldn't remember what I'd had for breakfast, but I could recall every single detail of that night. The sights. The smells. The concerned face of the doctor and his smiley face tie.

My brain had recorded the event for posterity without even checking with me. *Look, kid, I know you're not going to want to remember any of this. You're gonna try to block this out, just so you'll be okay. But don't worry, I'll take good notes. I'm gonna make sure you're able to relive it every second... of every day... until the day you die. Cool? Cool.*

I'd been a teenager then, and I'd fallen asleep after a marathon gaming session that required a lot of Red Bull and Cheetos. I hadn't known it was my last day as a carefree kid, who spent six hours trying to beat some meaningless video game.

The ringing doorbell so late at night had woken us all up. With uncanny timing, my first thought upon waking was that I hadn't heard my mother come home. She and my aunt had gone out for drinks—their monthly girls' night. My second thought, as I glanced at the clock blearily, was that it was two in the morning. My third and final thought before I'd stumbled out of bed was, *Oh shit. This can't be good.*

I stood at the top of the stairs, my younger brothers practically glued to my back. John had been the next oldest behind me at eight, and he hushed the other two as we listened. The shock came first. Numbness followed shortly after. An impatient driver had gone around a tractor trailer in a curve and met her head-on. She never saw it coming.

Neither did we.

"You need to come to the hospital now."

"Now?" My father had questioned, a strange hitch in his voice. It wasn't a real question. He was already groping his pockets for his keys. It was just something you said while your brain hurried to process that the worst was actually happening.

The trooper's grim response had made me swallow hard. *"Right now."*

We Suttons weren't a very tactile bunch by nature, and the younger boys had made arguing a gladiator sport. But at that moment, it was hard to tell which of us was gripping the other's hand harder.

My father had been grim and strangely unhurried. It was only when I got older that I realized he'd already known she was gone. We'd arrived at the hospital, still a little disorientated and half dressed. I hadn't remembered to brush my hair and none of us had bothered to change out of our pajamas.

I hadn't known what it meant when they showed us to a sterile little room upon arrival, but my father certainly had. When the chaplain came in, even I started to get the picture. I realized later the little room was because they didn't want us to upset the other patrons in the emergency room with our reaction to the news. They shouldn't have worried because we were a stoic family by nature. I wasn't sure what the Latin was for "internalize your pain, and talk about it never," but it should go on our family crest.

As I rubbed sweaty palms on my wrinkled Spider-Man pajamas and stared at my father's ghostly pale face, the gravity of the situation hit me with the gentleness of a sledgehammer. We hadn't come to take her home.

We'd come to say goodbye.

The sound of a knock at the door and an overly cheerful voice on the other side of the curtain jolted me out of memories better left buried. "I'm here to take your blood pressure, Mr. Roberts. Do you mind if I turn on the light?"

Mr. Roberts seemed to feel like I did toward overly cheery people. He grunted and muttered, "Does it matter what I say?"

I listened with half an ear as she finished taking his vitals. The nurse had the patience of a saint. She kept up a steady flow of chatter that was truly remarkable, considering how little Mr. Roberts gave her to work with. After she finished, she flipped off his light. There wasn't much difference, what with the natural light streaming in through the window, but Mr. Roberts gave a sigh of satisfaction that made the nurse chuckle.

I expected her to leave, but a moment later, she popped her head around the curtain and nearly scared the pants off me. I grabbed my chest, because that's what you do when you aren't sure if your heart is going to fail or keep pumping.

"Oh, sorry hun," she said with a smile. "I'm glad you're here. He's in X-ray right now, but he's been asking for you."

"Yeah?" I barely held in a snort. I seriously doubted that.

"Yes, you must be John." She beamed.

"Nope."

Her smile lost a little shine. "Mark?"

"No."

"Um," she said hesitantly. "Matthew?"

I took pity on her. "Journey."

She looked nonplussed for a moment, clutching the pole of the blood-pressure machine like a lifeline. Then she reddened. "Journey. Journey, of course!" She began rewrapping the cord around the pole as if it had suddenly become mission fucking critical.

I was more than happy to let her off the hook. I'd bet a month's salary that my father hadn't mentioned me at all. It certainly wasn't the nurse's fault that Jack Sutton could be an asshole. Nor was it particularly newsworthy. He hadn't forgiven me for leaving, and I hadn't forgiven him for making it necessary. It was the suck-ass version of the *Circle of Life*.

"So, how's he doing?" I asked.

"Are you...." She hesitated. "Family?"

All right, that was starting to chap my ass a little. "His son," I said through gritted teeth.

"Oh, good. Right." She smiled widely. "We're just glad to see him close to getting back home. He's been impatient, to say the least. I keep reminding him that the stroke wasn't that long ago, but you know how it can be."

I frowned. John hadn't said a word about it. "I wasn't aware he was ready to be discharged."

"Of course. Either tomorrow or the next day, he'll be ready to go."

"Go? Go where?" I looked at the beaming nurse as though she'd said a dirty word. And in a way, hadn't she? Had that crazy woman implied that I might be taking my father someplace?

"With you, of course." She frowned. "He's going to need supervision and care while he recuperates. Where else would he do that?"

"I assumed here." I paused. "Isn't that what you all do?"

"Yes, we take care of sick people. Your father is well on his way to recovery."

She couldn't be suggesting I bring him home with me. And then it all clicked. *Ahh.* She must be helping herself to the good stuff. I shook my head, clucking my tongue. *High. In a hospital. Such a shame.*

"We have a lot of things to go over, but I brought you a packet to help you prepare your home," Nurse High as a Kite went on. "More information will be available for you in his discharge packet. We can go over his care instructions before he leaves."

"Care? As in me caring for...." For some reason, I had lost the will and ability to create full sentences. "No, you don't—"

"Is your house a one-story or two?" She pushed a packet of papers in my hand, and I glanced down at the manual dumbly. *Home Health Care and You*. "One would be preferable, of course, but as long as the patient has access to a bathroom, two stories shouldn't be a problem."

I had a loft. It was in a great neighborhood and had gorgeous brick walls and gleaming exposed copper pipes. And I had recently installed hardwood floors, and the shiny new planks were deathly allergic to being scratched up with any old-man furniture like a walker, which was yet another reason why I was so *not* doing this.

The nurse continued yammering on. "There are several safety features that you might want to consider installing tonight, of course. Nothing too crazy. Just a rail in the tub, nonslip stickers on the bottom of your tub...."

I almost choked. Nonslip stickers on my custom-built jetted tub? "Wait. I need you to hang on just a minute." I held up a hand to stop this shitty rollercoaster. It was too high, too fast, and I was *not* tall enough for this ride. "He isn't coming home with me."

Her eyes got all squinty at my tone. "You won't take him home?"

Now you're finally getting it. There was history there, a history she didn't need to know. The minutes to this little meeting were simple. I handed her back the home health care package, just to make sure she was smelling what I was cooking. "No."

"That's your decision, of course." Her voice was noticeably cooler, which was to be expected now that I was a deadbeat son and not an integral part of her patient's recovery team. "We can put him in nursing home care until he's well enough to be on his own."

Nursing home care? She held out the home health care packet with a raised eyebrow, and I took it back slowly. After delivering that killing blow—*Finish him!*—she turned and left, her vitals machine clattering behind loud enough to make Mr. Roberts grumble.

I sat there for a while, trying to wrap my mind around the idea of my larger-than-life father in a nursing home. He had such a lively presence, with a voice that was always a hair too loud and way too gruff. That guy. In a nursing home. The two images wouldn't gel. Neither would the idea of me taking care of him for any extended amount of time.

"I need to speak to my brother," I said to no one at all.

Speak, yell, throttle... it was all semantics at this point.

5

JOURNEY

I walked down Main Street with a purposeful step.
Coral Cove wasn't exactly a one-horse town, but it was small enough. When they'd built a Walmart on Third and Wiltshire, it had been an *event*. People took pride in helping their neighbors. And everyone knew someone, who knew someone else, who knew all your damned business.

As a teenager confused about life in general, I'd found small-town life stifling. With a wealth of experience under my belt, it was now strangely comforting. It was kind of nice to have a connection with your neighbors. In my building in Seattle, I wasn't even sure I knew my neighbor's name. I frowned. Evan, maybe? All I knew about him was that he enjoyed strong-smelling food and listened to a lot of Tori Amos.

Coral Cove was different. It was nice to know that Ms. Aldacott's cat, Rufus, wasn't lost. He "ran away" monthly to see her ex-husband, who lived on the other side of town, and then sauntered back a few days later. The big tabby had created his own fucking custody agreement and made sure his parents stuck to it, to the letter.

My brother Mark's wife, Laura, owned the bakery downtown called Sweet Times. She specialized in homespun Americana, but when she learned that Mrs. Crabtree's favorite dessert was a tarte tatin, Laura tried recipes for a couple of weeks until she perfected one made with plums.

My other sister-in-law, Mindy, made sure to include all the town gossip no one ever asked for in a newsletter. She emailed it to me monthly, along with photos of my nephews and nieces. I was addicted to her hometown missives.

Before long, I reached the garage. It was at the end of the street, which was a good location because it was easy to get to and close enough to the main highway to catch passing traffic. All three bay doors were open as I walked up. I could already hear the comforting sound of various tools going busily. Something low and country was playing on a Bluetooth speaker sitting on a crate in the corner.

Three years had passed, but not much had changed except the cars in the bays. I inhaled deeply, filling my lungs with the questionable bouquet of motor oil, grease, and dust. It smelled like home. I'd spent a lot of time here as a kid, sticking close to my father and learning everything he could teach me.

I hadn't really cared about working on cars. I'd just wanted to be close to him, and he'd been more than happy to oblige. As long as we were doing what he considered worthy work—man's work—he was happy as a clam. After I came out to him when I was fourteen, the garage became less of a place of refuge, and more of a place of tension. I was grateful that he hadn't thrown me out, but resentful because things between us felt... different.

I'd dug in, working harder than ever. Through action, I'd tried to prove that some things had changed, but I was still his son. I could still change a car's oil with my eyes closed, and I still had the touch when working with tricky foreign cars that none of the other mechanics wanted to bother with. It never felt like enough.

Mom's death had put our discord on the backburner. Soon, he had other things to worry about, other than the disappointment that was his oldest son. Jack Daniel's and Coke—yeah, he worried about them plenty.

I spotted a pair of legs in blue coveralls sticking out from under a little gray Civic and couldn't help but chuckle. We had a hydraulic lift now, but John thought old school was the best school. I kicked his legs gently, and he made a noise as he clunked his head on something.

"Goddammit, who the hell?" He rolled out from under the car, and I couldn't help the affection that suffused in me at just seeing his face... his grimy, sweaty face.

My brothers all took after my father—tall and broad, with brown hair and a dimpled chin, and the trademark Sutton blue eyes. I was a carbon copy of my mother, with sandy blond hair and light brown eyes, and I found it comforting to see her face every day in the mirror. The height, she could've kept to herself. I was five-eleven on a good day, which was galling in a family of men who were all six-feet-plus.

The day I realized all my younger brothers had surpassed me in height had been a dark one indeed. The youngest, Matt, had offered to grab a box of crackers off the top shelf that I couldn't reach. I stood there, long after he'd sauntered off, clutching a box of Ritz and wondering what deity I had offended to have such a fate befall me.

John grinned when he saw me. "Well, well, well, if it isn't Worldwide. So glad you could make time to mingle with the common folk."

I ignored the slightly caustic nickname. John was, of course, just being John. "Had nothing better to do," I said simply. "Where's Mark?"

"Test-driving a car. If I know him, he's gonna stretch it out."

I chuckled. Same old Mark. The nicer the car was, the longer the "test-drive." Our father got after him all the time about it. "Some things never change," I said fondly, tapping my fingers on my thigh. "How about Matt?"

"Home with the kids. Cal picked up a bug in daycare and brought it home to the rest of them. You know how crazy that can get."

"Ah." I nodded as if I understood. Truthfully, I didn't want to learn any more about kids than I already knew.

My brothers had seven kids between the three of them, each rowdier than the last. Those rascals had looked at our unspoken motto of working quietly and keeping your head down and said,

"Um, nah." The next generation of Suttons was loud for no bloody reason at all and firmly believed in having *fun*.

John and I made a little small talk about my flight. I'd stopped by the house earlier and found my room clean and orderly, and the bed was made with fresh linens. I asked him to thank his wife, and he said he would. I teased him about still being too tall, and he razzed me about still being too short. I informed him that I was perfectly average, and he reminded me that I only had two inches on his wife. I shot back that I probably had two inches on him in another place, and he pretended to take offense.

And that was about it. We stared at each other frankly, not bothering to fill the silence that settled between us. We hadn't seen each other in three years. We should really have more to say.

John sighed. "I know you didn't come all the way down to the garage to see how I'm doing. We've got all the pleasantries out of the way. Let's talk turkey."

We were a little beyond turkey. We were turducken at this point. Something was happening that shouldn't be happening, and I needed to know who'd thought this was a good idea.

I held up the caregiver folder the nurse had all but shoved in my hands. "Did you know about this?"

The way his gaze shifted away from mine answered my question, but he went ahead and added the words. "Maybe I did. JJ—"

I was already shaking my head. "You've got to take him."

His eyes widened. "Take him where?"

"Disneyland," I snapped. "Don't fuck with me, John."

At least he had the good grace to look guilty. "Look, I can't take him. I've got a family and the business to help take care of. With dad temporarily laid up, I finally got a look at the books. They're a mess."

"Are you guys in trouble?"

"I don't know." He shook his head. "Like I said, it's a mess."

"I can help with the books," I said impatiently. "You know I'm good at that kind of thing."

"That's a Band-Aid, JJ. What happens when you leave?"

"Well, I was going to snatch all the computers out of the office and stuff them in my suitcase," I said dryly. "But now, I'm thinking I'll probably just set up something easy to operate and show you how to use it."

"Oh." He looked a little nonplussed. "Well, that might work."

"I'm thinking it just might," I said with a grave nod. "Maybe Matt can take him."

"He's got school. Just went up from part-time to full-time, while he's working here."

"Mark?"

"He has his hands full with the kids. Since Laura opened the bakery, he's been helping out more at home."

I worked a hand behind my neck, massaging what suddenly felt like a huge knot of responsibility—albatross-sized. I didn't want to do this again. I didn't want to be the fixer anymore. "Maybe I can hire someone. In-home care, you know?"

"You mean throw your money at the problem and make it go away," John said flatly.

He made it sound like it was drug money instead of money I'd earned through my craft. Money that had provided the down payment for Laura's bakery and several family emergencies over the years. I'd left here with a camera and a dream, and I'd made it work.

Do not engage. Despite my sudden urge to introduce my knuckles to John's eye socket, I stayed calm. "And just what is the problem with hiring a qualified individual for round-the-clock care?"

John snorted. "You know dad isn't going to want a stranger in his house."

I knew he was right. So... Matty was out, John was busy, and Mark had his hands full with the kids. *Excellent.* The tension in my neck ratcheted up more. I ran a hand through my hair, already thinking logistics. "I guess I can bring him home with me for a couple of weeks."

"He doesn't like to fly. Hell, I don't think his doctors would even *want* him to fly so soon after a stroke. And he's going to need more than a few fucking weeks, JJ."

"Well, he's not going to be able to have everything his way," I shot back. "I'm trying to help, but he's going to have to work with me."

"Do you see him being comfortable in your place? In Seattle?" He lifted a mocking eyebrow. "His friends are here. His garage is here. *We* are here. You know that's not going to work."

He stabbed a finger at the Sutton & Sons sign hanging above the door. "And sons, Journey," he said through gritted teeth. "That includes you."

"I have a life someplace else, John. I can't just drop everything and come back here."

John made a sound in the back of his throat and rolled back under the Civic. A few seconds later, I heard the clunk of metal on metal as he got back to work. "I don't know why I expected anything different. That's what you do, right?"

"What the fuck is that supposed to mean?"

"It's supposed to mean that while we're here taking care of everything, you're off doing your Journey thing in your Journey world. You pop back here every so often, make sure everyone is alive, and then you're good for another couple of years."

I blew out a patient breath, wondering if it was all *that* despicable to whack someone in the head with a bottle of synthetic oil —probably.

"I don't expect you to understand," I finally said.

John ignored me like I was already gone. In a way, I guess I was.

I left without another word.

6

JOURNEY

I decided to do what I always did when I had a lot to chew on—be productive.

I headed to the hardware store and proceeded to buy supplies to fix things around the house. The top porch step was squeaky, and the weather stripping on the front door had come loose, letting the air-conditioned air out and God knew what in. One of the shower temperature knobs had been stripped, and the light fixture in the bathroom was broken.

And on and on the list went. My father had never been much for fancy décor, but he'd always kept the house shipshape. That probably meant he'd been feeling bad longer than he'd admitted. I added a couple doorknobs and a drywall repair kit to my haul and then hustled home.

I argued mentally with John throughout the day as I hammered and drilled, and I won all of our fights. *All* of them. Maybe he knew what it was like watching our father spiral after our mother's death, but he didn't know how it felt to be the oldest, and know that you had to *do* something about it. He didn't know what it was like to don the yolk of responsibility and take over.

To have everyone looking at you for answers.

I finished fixing the screen door and gave it a couple of test swings to make sure it closed properly. *Fix it, JJ. Mark needs to go to the dentist after school, and I need you to get him there. John needs new sneakers for basketball practice. Can you take him to the mall? Matt needs help with his homework. Would you mind pitching in? Fix it, fix it, fix it.*

Once I was sure they could stand on their own two feet, I'd put myself at the top of my priority list. I had no intention of getting sucked back in.

I heard a howl next door, and I knew Cam had probably let Kona out in the backyard. My fingers tightened around my screwdriver. Living next door to him was going to be just as hard as I thought.

I hadn't known putting my wishes first would cost me the love of my life.

"You quit your job," he said slowly, still processing. "And you're going to become a... a what now?"

"A wildlife photographer."

He stared at me some more. "And you've already booked a trip to the Amazon rainforest."

That was about the whole of it.

"I don't understand." He got up abruptly and began pacing a path across the living room. "This photography class was supposed to be something fun. Something just for you. You wanted to do something more exciting with a camera than taking portraits of families in their color-coordinated Sunday best. Isn't that what you said?"

"I did, yes."

"And now you're talking about turning your whole life upside down."

"Come with me," I said a little desperately.

"Go with you where?" Cameron all but snarled. "You don't even know where you're going."

"That's the fucking point, Cam. It's... it's coddiwomple."

He blinked at me as if I'd grown another head. "Dare I ask?"

"Traveling in a purposeful manner without a destination." When he continued to stare at me, mute, I made a sound of frustration. "I had to look it up, too. It was in my mother's dream journal—"

"Fuck, JJ!" He all but shouted, which gave me pause. Cam didn't yell, and he didn't lose his temper. He was so laid-back most of the time, weed thought he was too mellow. "I don't want to hear about that fucking thing again. You're lucky I don't burn it. We were happy before you found that fucking book."

I looked down, trying to tamp down my anger. We both knew if he so much as touched that book, my most prized possession, we were over. So I didn't bother to warn him about something so blatantly obvious.

"All I'm saying is that when I found... the thing, I realized that I was doing it, too. Granted, it was a bucket list I'd started on the back of a visa bill, but it was a record of all the things I was never going to do. Just like her."

"Your mom had a beautiful life, JJ. I don't think she would've changed a thing." He frowned at me. "Lori loved you. She loved all of her boys. Do you think she would've cast all that aside for a trip to some ancient ruins?"

"Well of course she wouldn't. That's hardly the point. She left a note, you know. In the back of the journal."

He stilled. "You never told me that."

I'd all but rubbed the ink off the note, I'd touched it so much. "It read, 'life can be the most amazing journey. Don't let it pass you by.' " I blew out a breath. "Don't you ever get tired of all this? Don't you ever want something exciting and different?"

When he finally answered me, his voice was icy. "No, I spent most of my childhood following my father from one new place to another. As soon as I got used to a school and a new neighborhood, boom, his marriage was over. I've finally found where I'm supposed to be. I'm sorry that's not enough for you."

"You've always been enough for me."

"Then why won't you stay?"

"Because I don't want a faded and forgotten binder of things I wanted to do."

My answer took him aback. He rubbed a hand down his face, and when that hand finally dropped, he looked tired... as if he'd aged several years in the weeks that we'd been arguing nonstop. "We're going around in circles."

"Then you'll come with me?" I asked hopefully.

He shook his head slowly, and my heart dropped to my toes. "No, my place is here. But I won't stop you."

I blinked. "You won't?"

"I never want to stand in your way. But if you go, you're going without me. Without us."

So, I went.

In my defense—and I needed one—I'd been young. Twenty-five and carrying more responsibility than someone twice my age. Still, sometimes I wondered if I'd done the right thing. Sometimes I *knew* that I hadn't. But life didn't give do-overs.

Cam's laughter floated over the fence as he told Kona she was a good girl, and she barked in response. Even though I had about a million things to do, I stood stock-still, hidden on the porch, just enjoying our proximity. The back door shut a few moments later, and I felt the loss acutely.

I sighed and tossed the screwdriver in my father's toolbox. Enough woolgathering about things that didn't matter anymore. I had a sink to fix.

Sometime around six, my stomach grumbled, clearly unbothered by my existential crisis. Since I couldn't be bothered with cooking, I decided to get some takeout. A quick google search led me to Riptide, an inexpensive pub by the beach with "oceanside vibes." I wasn't too interested in their "vibes" as much as I was the food pictures some kindly soul had posted. A beautiful, juicy burger in all its HD glory was all I needed to get me going.

I grabbed my keys, stuck my feet in some sandals, and headed out the door. I decided to walk because it was a nice night out. I glanced at Cameron's darkened house as I passed. His Jeep wasn't in the driveway, and I wondered where he'd gone. Too bad Cameron's whereabouts were none of my business anymore.

The waterfront bar was doing brisk business. It was just as beachy as their website portrayed, done in light colors with a thatched roof.

The walls were crowded as hell, with mounted surfboards, fishing nets, and shells. Tiki torches completed the look. But never mind all the kitschy beach stuff—the star of the show was the view. The half wall facing the water brought the ocean right into the bar and it was hard to look at anything else.

Eventually my stomach forced me away from the view and I approached the bar. The driftwood top was battered but clean. My butt had barely hit the stool before I spotted a familiar face behind the bar. A lazy smile appeared in his bushy red beard. "Well, if you aren't a sight for sore eyes."

I grinned at Hudson Smith, one of my good friends from high school. He was older and a little more rounded in the middle but still the same handsome devil he'd been back then. He wore a black shirt with the sleeves pushed up to the elbows and had an apron around his waist. "Hudson?"

"You were expecting someone else?"

I laughed delightedly. "God, I haven't seen you in...."

"A long damn time."

I opened my mouth to disagree, but yeah, he was probably right. "When did you get back?"

"Couple years ago." He shook his head. "Damn, JJ, you got old."

I laughed. "Shut up, Hud. What the hell are you doing here anyway?"

"I live here."

"*Here*?" I all but goggled.

"Yes, *here*," he teased, duplicating my tone exactly. "Anything wrong with *here*?"

"Not at all," I said hurriedly. It was just that Hudson had been more determined than *me* to get out of Coral Cove, and that was saying something. *"I've got a lot of plans and none of them include small-town life,"* he used to say.

"Maybe if you came back *here* a little more often, you'd know that it's not as small as it was when we were growing up," he went on.

I'd already seen that for myself. There were a lot of new shops and more people than I remembered. It was busy and bustling with small-town charm. I wondered if Hudson's about-face regarding small-town life had something to do with the death of his abusive father. Maybe he hadn't been so determined to get away from here, but away from *him*.

"You haven't been in any of Mindy's newsletters," I blurted.

He let out a great belly laugh. "Oh Lord, that woman. I love your sister-in-law, JJ, but she's a horrible gossip. I don't do anything even remotely interesting, so I don't think I'm on her radar."

I grinned. She might be a horrible gossip, but I loved her to bits. "I don't know, I think it's kind of interesting that you decided not to become an astronaut."

"Yeah, NASA said something about no beer bellies on the shuttle." He sighed sadly, rubbing his stomach. "Their loss, right?"

I chuckled. It was hardly a beer belly, but he wasn't the same beanpole I'd known. It fit him better, in my opinion. He looked like the kind of guy who cleaned up nice but wasn't afraid to have a chicken wing or six. Or in my case, twelve.

"I was bartending up in Orlando. My uncle had been after me for a while to take over for him. He was getting too old to handle this place, and I was tired of working for someone else." Hudson shrugged. "It seemed like a good time for a change."

"Wow," I shook my head, still smiling. "I thought you would've been the last candidate for small-town life."

"I grew up." He smiled back. "It suits me."

That it did. He looked... settled. Happy.

His phone dinged with a text and he checked it quickly. "Lord." He rolled his eyes. "Our dishwasher is still on break. My wife is handling the griddle back there, and everything has to be perfectly in order."

I goggled again. The Hudson I'd known had sworn off women and marriage because of his parents' volatile relationship. "That's... kind of amazing."

He arched a brow. "What, that my wife likes to take the whip to my hide if we're out of clean plates?"

"No, just...." I waved a hand. "Never mind."

He bustled off, and I surveyed the bar lazily in the mirrored back. I would readily admit to enjoying people watching, and this bar certainly had a lot of good candidates. Even though I hadn't been back to Coral Cove in a while, I knew most of the people in attendance.

Tim Cooper was sitting at the other end of the bar, nursing a drink and working on a crossword puzzle. I didn't know what he was up to nowadays—clearly, Mindy picked and chose who was newsletter worthy—but he used to man the gas station on the corner. And there was Amelia James and her husband, Anderson, playing some table game that required a lot of laughing and a pitcher of beer. If I remembered correctly, they had five kids. Somehow, someway, they'd suckered someone into watching their brood. They'd probably have fun watching grass grow, as long as it was outside of the house.

My gaze caught on another familiar face. Cameron was sitting at a table with another guy. Someone from work, maybe? They both had food and beer, and as the other guy took a bite of his sandwich, my stomach growled.

I looked away. After a few moments, my gaze slid back over to him without my permission. I was exasperated with myself but not surprised. Anytime Cameron Foster was in the room, nothing else could hold my attention.

He was working that classic, small-town good-guy vibe pretty hard, from the top of his shampoo-ad hair down to his neatly tied sneakers. The only thing rumpled about him was a slight stubble on his jaw, and I'd wager that was because he hadn't had time to shave. His wide-eyed expression made me want to laugh. It was clear he was trying not to fall asleep as his companion prattled on.

"So." I glanced up to see Hudson back, watching me with a tiny smile. "What's your poison?"

"Coke, no ice."

"Whoa, camper." He held up his hands. "Let's not get too risky."

Well... it's not like I was driving. "Add some Jack in it. And since you've got the grill nice and hot already, a burger and fries, if you please."

He cocked his finger at me in the shape of a gun. "Now we're talkin'."

As Hudson bustled off to put in my order and make my drink, my gaze automatically went back to the mirror behind the bar. Cameron flashed a smile at his companion, who was *still* chattering on, and I sat up a little straighter. *Seriously?*

I knew that fucking smile. That was his date smile. He had a crooked incisor that he didn't like, so he had a special way of smiling when he didn't want to show too many teeth. I found it ridiculous because his imperfect smile was just the cutest thing. What was *not* the cutest thing? The fact that he was on a fucking date.

Hudson slid a drink in front of me, and I blinked at him. "That was quick."

"Actually, it wasn't. You were just so occupied ogling your ex that you didn't notice." He clucked his tongue in mock dismay. "Still? Really?"

I didn't deny it. I pretty much eye-fucked Cameron every time I saw him. "No harm in looking, is there?"

"Nope." He popped the *p*. "Maybe you'd be interested to know that this is the second time he's gone out with Carter."

"I would not," I said primly. "I would, however, be interested to know what the hell happened to Charlotte. Last time I was here for a visit, they were engaged to be married."

"That had to be a while ago, then."

Three years, but who's counting? I flushed guiltily. "It was."

"Well, they broke up. She's with Greg now. The firefighter. One of the Branson boys," Hudson added, trying to jog my memory. "They're having a baby, and he's over the moon. He was in here yesterday buying rounds for everyone."

Hudson paused to watch me take a sip of my drink. He seemed to be waiting for something. A minute later, I gave it to him as I started coughing so hard, my eyes watered. *Shit.* Hud still had a heavy hand with the booze. I remembered that from days of raiding his father's liquor cabinet.

"You all right?" he asked somberly, eyes twinkling. "It would've been remiss of me not to give you the old buddy, old pal special."

Since I was busy hacking up a lung, I settled for flipping him the bird. Once I regained the power of speech, I went on. "I've been reminiscing about you too fondly. I think I glossed over all the memories in which you were annoying as fuck."

He chuckled. Someone at the other end of the bar called for a refill, and Hudson bustled off. He was back with my burger and fries a few moments later, and I tucked in before he could even bring me a napkin. The burger was juicy, and the fries were salty and crispy, so I forgave him almost immediately for being a giant pain in the ass.

I tried to keep my eyes off mirror Cam and his date, and for the most part, I was successful. For the most part. His date was handsome enough, with frameless glasses on a narrow, angular face and dark hair, graying slightly at the temples. He looked like just Cam's type. Stable. Distinguished.

Technically, I guess I couldn't know all that from a profile. But he was wearing a sweater vest, for God's sake. If there was a flag to represent stable and distinguished people, it would probably be in the shape of a sweater vest. He didn't look like the kind of guy who would quit a stable job taking portraits at a retail store to become a wildlife photographer.

I went back to my burger. My phone dinged just as I was finishing up, and my agent's name popped up with a text. The message was short and to the point. *They love the photos. Congrats.*

I texted back quickly, still working on the fries one-handed. *Thanks, Boz.*

How do you like Antarctica?

I snorted. It wasn't a question. That was sly agent speak for, "They need pictures of something in Antarctica. Before I slingshot your ass down there, do you need a thermal jacket, or you good?"

My fingers hovered over the *S* key. What normally would've been a shrug and a "sure" was suddenly a bit more complicated. True enough, I'd won all my mental arguing with that know-it-all John today, but somewhere around the time I was reminding him what an intolerable jackass he was, I realized he was kind of right.

Hudson walked by and reached for my plate. I just managed to grab the last fry before he snagged the dish and bustled off. I stuffed the fry in my mouth. *Maniac.* I hadn't even gotten to swipe it through the freaking ketchup. But then he brought me a fresh beer to go alongside the Jack and Coke I hadn't quite finished, and I forgave him anew.

Maybe I *had* let my familial duties slip a bit. Maybe. I got busy, and I lived so far away and.... Well, I guess I could insert any number of excuses after that. Truthfully, the longer I was gone, the easier it was to stay away. Maybe I was running a little bit. John was still an intolerable jackass, though.

I guess I could spare a few months to stick around. The summer, maybe. I could make sure my father healed the way he needed to, in the place where he was most comfortable. I resented the decision almost immediately, but I was going to stand by it.

Guess I was here for the summer, then. I sighed. *August, here I come.*

Someone slid on the stool next to me and cleared his throat as I texted Boz back. *On hiatus for the summer. Sry.*

The text bubbles appeared, reappeared, disappeared, and then reappeared again, all in the span of a few seconds. He finally just answered with an "ok" and a smiley face. That was one of the things I loved about Boz. He was always on my side and he didn't push... much. I knew if I stayed longer than the summer, I'd have some answering to do.

The guy next to me cleared his throat again. I rolled my eyes. Someone was either sick with a sore throat or trying to get my attention. I had the same answer for either of those scenarios—move several seats away and leave me the hell alone. I was about to make that suggestion when I heard a familiar voice. "You still take forever to answer a text."

I glanced over to see Cameron sitting on the barstool next to me, a half smile on his face. I looked up in the mirror instinctively, like I'd see him still sitting at the table. "Hey. You're here," I said stupidly.

"I am," he agreed.

I was starting to get annoyed. I'd only been in town for twenty-four hours, and I was on Cameron overload. Being around him took me back to a time I'd rather forget—not because it was so bad, but because it had been so damned *good*. And could he give the looking-good, smelling-even-better thing a rest?

"Did you talk to your brothers?" he asked bluntly.

That certainly got my thoughts off sex. "One of them." I eyed him. "I guess I shouldn't be surprised that you knew what they were going to ask me."

He hummed but didn't deny it. "So, what did you decide?"

"I figure it won't kill me to stay for the summer," I said a little begrudgingly. "At least that way, I can make sure my dad is back on his feet."

He only nodded. I watched him out of the corner of my eye as he fiddled with his drink, wondering how nosy was too nosy. Then I remembered I was in Coral Cove—nosy was a way of life. "How'd the date go?"

He gave me a look of slight surprise but answered gamely enough. "I'm sitting here with you. That should pretty much sum it up."

"Yikes."

"I'll just say that life can seem pretty short when you're listening to someone go on about life insurance."

I chuckled. "I don't know, I enjoy it when the Geico gecko does it. Maybe he just needs the accent to make it interesting."

Cameron paused as if that was a real fucking suggestion and then he shook his head. "Well, anyway, Carter is a nice guy. Just... not the right guy for me."

I checked my "nosy" meter once more and couldn't get a reliable reading. "Forgive me, but you don't seem all that torn up about it."

He shrugged. "We never had any real chemistry."

"Chemistry can be weird. Sometimes you can work side by side with someone for years and nothing, and then one day, bam, there it is."

And just why the hell are you trying to convince him to keep seeing someone else? I was as flummoxed as my brain was with my words. I shouldn't be trying to convince him to stay in the dating pool. I should be trying to convince him that there were piranhas in there. We may be done as a Sunday roast, but that didn't mean I wanted to watch him date someone else.

"I guess." He didn't seem all that convinced. "I was looking for something a little more instantaneous. More passionate. I haven't gotten any in the longest, so I don't think that's a big ask."

I could tell the moment he realized who he was talking to. I watched in fascination as he turned an alarming shade of pink rather quickly. "Oh God," he croaked, "I certainly didn't mean to confess that to you."

I laughed. "I'm kind of glad you did. I wouldn't want to be the only one who isn't getting any."

"Well, if you're interested, the rumor mill has all kinds of theories about who you should wind up with." He shrugged. "I heard some things at the coffee shop."

"Like what?"

"You sure you want to hear it all?"

I took a sip of my drink. "Hit me."

"Well, Mabel thinks you're *such* a good boy for coming home to take care of your father."

"Wait, *I* just decided that I was going to stay. How did she—"

"Call it a hunch. She also thinks you'd be a perfect match for her daughter."

"Is that so?"

"Yep. Gertie told her to hush, and that you'd be a better match for *her* daughter. But Gertie wasn't sure if she wanted to set you two up, because you never can stay in one place for too long, and you're not taking her daughter with you to Timbuktu." His mouth lifted. "That's when Anna informed them *both* that they needed to hush up because you were gay, and you didn't want either of their daughters. At that bit of news, Mrs. Edith one table over got very interested."

"And why's that?"

"Apparently, her grandson is a chef and very, very gay."

I laughed. "Oh, well, as long as he's very, *very* gay."

"Her words," he said with a chuckle. "And according to her, Mr. Hotshot Chef could do worse than settling down with a nice kid like JJ."

That made me laugh again. "Mr. Richards at the convenience store offered me a lollipop with my fill-up, you know." I smiled fondly. It didn't bother me, instead it was kind of sweet. "No matter how much I grow up, I'll always be a kid to everyone in this town."

He took a long pull on his drink. "Not everyone," was all he finally said.

There was a wealth of meaning in those two words. And it let me know he wasn't as unaffected by me as he let on. It was a heady feeling to know that no matter how much time had passed, no matter what the distance between us, *that* hadn't changed. He still wanted me, and I damn sure wanted him.

As nice as Hud's bar was, I was kind of done socializing and drinking if sex was on the table. I wanted to be someplace private, creating new dirty memories with what was, hands down, the best fuck I'd ever had. Cameron had a nice dick and knew how to use it. Tomorrow, I was being a good son and taking on a shitload of responsibility. Today, I deserved a nice, hard fuck.

"So, you and Carter aren't serious," I said casually.

Cameron snorted. "Hardly. We can't even get past small talk. I didn't think he was into me at all, but he asked to see me again next week."

"Then it wouldn't be wrong for you to go home with someone else."

"Someone else?" He stared at me blankly for a moment before his eyes went wide. He swallowed as his gaze dropped down to my mouth. I'd be lying if I said I didn't lick my lips slowly on purpose. "Oh."

"So," I prodded when he didn't say anything else.

"So." His cheeks were seriously pink now. And his ears.

God, he was so fucking cute. If he wanted the words, I'd give him the words. "You want to get out of here?"

"You and me?"

"It's not like we haven't done it before."

His mouth curved. "Nice pitch, JJ."

"I'm just sayin'."

"What are you just saying?" His brow furrowed. "You know this would be a bad idea."

Bad idea? He was the king of understatement right now. The two of us hooking up was *beyond* a bad idea. It was the heavy-weight champion of bad ideas. It was a bad idea meeting a shitty idea and having a horrible baby.

I wanted to do it anyway.

"I think we can handle it."

Those glass-green eyes pinned me in place as he skewered me with a searching look. "Can we?"

That wasn't a no.

"I don't see why not. As long as we both remember what it is and what it's not."

"Just that simple, huh?" He snorted. "Since when are you the glass-half-full type?"

"Optimism is the shit when sex is involved." I raised an eyebrow. "I guess the only question is... are you in?"

7

CAMERON

I was a little stunned. I couldn't believe Journey was serious about going home with me for a quick round, or two, of hot, sweaty, headboard-banging sex. I mean, he didn't *use* any of those adjectives, but I could connect the dots. Right now, those mental dots looked like tiny dicks, which was probably not normal.

Fuck if I didn't want to say yes. Tempted didn't even begin to describe it. It had been too long since I'd felt something more exciting than my own damned hand—since Charlotte, actually. And my hand, while always available, was kind of done with me. I hadn't regrown my virginity by choice, exactly. I'd always been that guy who needed a connection to take the final step.

It had been extremely frustrating in high school. While my friends were sleeping with anything that moved, there I was, activating turtle mode. And not the super-cool-ninja kind, either. Journey and I already had a connection, so that wasn't an obstacle. I wasn't stupid enough to think that time and distance had changed that.

His eyes glowed amber under the soft overhead lights. He looked calm and expectant. This was nothing for him, simply a quick fuck with an ex to scratch an itch, and then right back to normal the next day.

I wasn't wired like that. Sex and love were ridiculously, hopelessly, wonderfully entangled in my world, and I'd come to embrace that about myself. I was looking for someone ready to put down roots. Someone who didn't mind that everything I had was practically covered in pet hair, almost to the point that I hardly noticed anymore. Someone who didn't mind that my dedication to my job sometimes meant that my patients had to come first. Someone who wanted to take a relaxing walk after dinner with the dog we'd get together.

Journey and I had already been down that road, and at the end of it was a cul-de-sac of hurt. Only an idiot would contemplate making a U-turn.

"Cam?" I blinked to find Journey giving me a concerned look. "Are you okay?"

"No," I finally burst out. My dick nearly had a coronary and demanded answers immediately. *Forgive me because my hearing is a little blocked by your tighty-whities, but did you just turn down sex with your smoking hot ex?*

"I mean, yes, I'm okay. But no, I don't think the other thing is a good idea. Sorry," I added lamely.

"Ah." Journey looked a little disappointed but not angry. "Did I misread things?"

"No, it's just that...."

He waited patiently for a sentence I had no idea how to finish. "Your taste in guys has changed?" he guessed. "Maybe I don't do it for you anymore."

I barely held in a snort. Physically, I wasn't sure that was possible. He used to have guys hitting on him all the fucking time and that probably hadn't changed. I didn't normally think of the word beautiful when I thought about men. Handsome, yeah. Good-looking, sure. But I saw Journey and thought beautiful. All that messy, sandy hair and those golden eyes and sun-kissed skin—he was everything I needed to avoid in one beautifully wrapped package.

"I don't think it's smart for us to go down that road again," I finally said. I expected him to cop an attitude and get up and leave.

"I hear you." He smiled a little self-deprecatingly and he was even more charming. "Nothing for your ego like getting turned down flat."

"I don't think you need any help in that category."

"What I'm hearing is that you still think I'm hot. So hot, you can barely stand it."

I couldn't help but laugh. "Yes, like a brushfire in jeans and sandals."

"Okay, so let's forget the last five minutes happened." He blew out a breath. "Now that you've got me all wound up without any relief in sight, you should buy me a drink."

I shook my head, amused, even as I plucked out my debit card. I handed it over to one of the bartenders, who gave Journey a flirty wink. That made me even *more* certain turning him down had been the right thing to do. That young guy with the nose ring and painted-on jeans was more Journey's speed, not someone whose idea of a good time was a night in, a good show on TV, and a nice snack.

Wow, Cam, even zombies are urging you to liven things up.

Well, what the hell did zombies know? Their constant hunt for brains meant they didn't have any. I was youthful, I was fantastic, and anyone would be lucky to have me. I rewarded myself for being awesome with a mental pat on the back. A mini-yawn caught me unaware and morphed into a bigger one. No matter, being hip and young wasn't easy, so I probably needed to get home and check if the ass dent in my couch was okay.

"I can't stay long," I said. "I need to get back to Kona."

"Right. The dog that you won't admit is your dog."

"She's a foster," I insisted.

"Exactly. A Foster. As in Cameron Foster's fur daughter." He gave me a knowing look. "I bet you have pictures of her on your phone."

Pictures? Of Kona? Only about a thousand. I huffed. "I need photos to put on the adoption website, don't I?"

He chuckled. "Go ahead, Fossie. Trot out the kid photos. This is a one-time offer with an expiration date, and I'm only making it only because I'm starting to get a nice buzz."

I couldn't help but get excited. "Why not?" I kept my tone casual, as if he just hadn't given me the green light dog lovers lived for. He would rue the damn day. I pulled out my phone and started scrolling.

I expected him to make the appropriate noises and feign interest, but I should've known better. Journey always gave one-hundred-percent of himself and he was fully engaged, chuckling at the pictures of her acting goofy and awing at the pictures of her sleeping.

I suddenly realized how close we were sitting. Hell, I was leaning into his shoulder now that we were sharing the phone screen. And I was really enjoying the scent of his cologne or soap or lotion or whatever the fuck he was wearing that smelled faintly of coconut and lime. Being so distracted, I stumbled right into the pictures of Bear, which I generally avoided.

My throat tightened a little just looking at him. The German Shepherd's muzzle was flecked with gray, his eyes a little unfocused as he peered sweetly at the camera.

"Bear," Journey said with a soft smile. "He used to follow you everywhere. He never did warm to me."

"Bear was very much a one-man dog."

"When did he...."

He didn't need to finish the sentence. I knew what he meant, even without his suddenly awkward body English. I didn't gloss over the truth. "About a year after you left."

He grimaced. "Sorry."

Bear had been at my side since I was sixteen years old. A police officer had found the puppy in a dumpster and brought him into the clinic. I'd taken care of him until Rosy gave him to me, and we were fast friends from the very beginning. He'd been gone a long time now, but I still felt the loss. It was probably why I'd been hesitant to replace him. Every time poor Kona curled up at my feet, I wanted to tell her that she was barking up the wrong tree.

Journey bumped my shoulder. "Hey, you okay? You disappeared on me for a little bit."

I felt my ears warm, realizing I'd been staring at the picture on my phone far too long. If I got to the pictures I'd taken of his last day, sitting in front of his favorite snack that I rarely let him have—a plain hamburger—and smiling that doggy smile, but too exhausted to even try to eat, I couldn't guarantee what I'd do. Especially with Journey being so sweet and all. Rosy had helped him cross over the Rainbow Bridge later that same day, and he'd died peacefully, his big head resting trustingly in my lap.

I hit the Sleep button on my phone. "That's enough of that, I think."

"Hey," Journey protested.

"What, you were enjoying my dead-dog home movie?" I joked, even though I still felt a little raw. "For a double feature, I can show you the cat I fostered who ran away."

His knowing gaze called bullshit on my jovial tone. "You don't have to do that."

"Do what?"

"Make jokes about it. I think how you feel about animals is pretty amazing. They're the most wonderful, perfect, honest creatures, and they deserve the best."

Please stop, I wanted to say. *Please stop saying all the right things before I beg you to come home with me.*

"I do what I can," I croaked. "That's why I'm a vet, I guess."

"You've always had a way about you, Foss. There's just something about you that lets a person know he's in good hands." He propped his chin on his fist as he smiled at me lazily. "Huh."

I didn't like that *huh*; there was a wealth of meaning in that *huh*. "What?"

"I forgot what a nice fucking guy you are."

"I wasn't aware that was a bad thing."

"It's not." He certainly made it sound like one. I had a feeling any sort of offer of meaningless sex was now off the table. Sure enough, he went on, "I just don't do nice guys anymore."

I scowled. "I rejected you first."

He laughed. "Duly noted."

We talked, polished off a few more drinks, and time passed rather quickly. As the night wore on, it became harder and harder to remember why I'd thought us sleeping together was a bad idea. *You did the right thing*, I reminded myself. So what if I watched his mouth or his throat move? Who could blame me? And who knew a throat could be so damn sexy?

At one point, Journey went to the bathroom, and I wasn't even ashamed to admit I watched his ass the whole way. That perfectly fuckable, round ass. The only thing that brought me back to reality was a sudden wet spot on my shirt, which made me check to make sure I wasn't drooling like a dog. Luckily, I was still in control of my bodily functions. I'd just been mid-drink when I was temporarily paralyzed by the sight of Journey's ass in those jeans. I shook my head wryly, putting my drink down before I wound up wearing the rest. But really, his body should come with some type of warning.

Two glasses of water suddenly appeared on the bar in front of me, and I looked up into Hudson's grinning face. "I'm not drunk," I informed him. My statement probably would've carried more weight if I hadn't hiccupped at the end. "Maybe a little buzzed, but that's it."

He chuckled. "Just drink it."

Begrudgingly, I took a few sips while he stared at me like a bug on a microscope slide. "What?" I finally asked.

"You and Journey, huh? Don't think I saw that one coming."

I blinked at him stupidly. "Saw what one coming?"

He went on as if I hadn't spoken. "I mean, the way things ended between you guys? I didn't think you'd ever get back together."

"We're not getting back together."

"Mm-hmm."

"It's not a crime to have a drink and a chat with an ex, you know," I said exasperatedly. "And just what would you know about our breakup?"

"Mindy's newsletter." He gave me a no-duh look. "She had a feature story called "Ancient History," where she profiled lots of the town's favorite former couples." When I just arched an eyebrow, he added helpfully, "You guys were number two, right behind the Aldacotts."

God, this town really needed to let go of their hopes for a Journey/Cam reunion. And number two? What the hell was up with that?

"How did we score behind a couple that wound up in jail for tax fraud?" I demanded.

Hudson shrugged. "Mr. Aldacott used to make dynamite fudge, and he wasn't shy about sharing."

I squinted at him. "Don't you have work to do?"

"Yup. I was instructed by my wife to stay close and keep an eye on things, and that's what I'm doing." He grinned cheekily. "The window to the kitchen isn't quite big enough for her to do it herself."

"There's nothing to report," I growled.

"You two were gazing into each other's eyes," he singsonged. "There was quite a bit of unnecessary touching."

"I'm a toucher," I informed him. "Last I checked, it's not a crime to be a tactile person."

His mouth twitched like he was holding in a laugh and treated me to another judgy "mm-hmm."

"Nothing is going on between us," I said firmly. "The title of that article was perfect to describe what Journey and I are to each other. Nothing but ancient history."

"Is that so?"

"It is so."

A few bills landed on the bar next to my glass. It took me a couple of seconds to realize someone had put the cash there and the ceiling hadn't started raining money. *Hmm.* Maybe I *had* had a few too many.

I glanced over to see Journey standing there, his face impassive. I missed the slightly buzzed and flushed look he'd had before, those amber eyes warm on my face. I hadn't said anything wrong, but I certainly felt like I had.

"I'd better get going," he said. "Thanks for getting my mind off things, Foster. It was nice talking with you."

Things were moving a little fast for my buzzed brain. I tried to catch up, but my slightly throbbing head made me give up rather quickly. All I knew was that he was leaving and I didn't want that—not yet. "But—"

"Thanks for the drinks, Hud." He ignored me as he tapped the bar. "You know I'll be back. Best damned beer in town."

Hudson grinned. "You haven't had any other beer in town yet."

He winked and a little of that personality was back. "Then you know I'm telling the truth."

He touched my shoulder before he turned and left without a backward glance. I told myself it was for the best. At Hudson's arch look, I told him that, too. He snorted. "Sure. I've seen you in here on quite a few dates, Cameron."

"I don't know if one date a month can be categorized as 'quite a few.' "

"My point is that you had more fun tonight than you've had in a long time. He lights you up like nobody's business. Always has." That smug little smile of his was going to get him mugged one day. Maybe by me. "Tell me I'm wrong."

I wanted to, but I'd had enough of Hudson's judgy *mm-hmms* for the night.

8

JOURNEY

When I made it to the hospital the next day, my father was still in bed sleeping. He looked so... frail. I guess anyone could look like that in a hospital gown, but it just wasn't him. That still, pale figure was eons away from my blustery, ruddy-faced father, clad in his usual uniform of motor oil-stained jeans and an undershirt that had seen better days.

I knew how hard it was to get rest in a hospital, so I didn't want to wake him. I sat carefully in the visitor's chair, but I might as well have spared myself the effort.

"I'm fine," a scratchy voice said. I glanced up to find my father frowning at me, heavy brows slashing down over his eyes.

"I know you're fine."

"Then stop looking like at me like you're ready to throw flowers on my damn coffin."

"Like I'd waste good flowers on you, old man."

He chuckled and even that little bit of energy seemed too much for him as he sagged against the pillow. We stared at one another for a few moments, unabashedly cataloging the differences in our appearance since the last time I'd been in town. He finished first.

"You need a haircut," he said gruffly.

"You need a hairbrush," I said tartly.

I might've been teasing, but his hair was looking a little unkempt, and understandably, that was probably the last thing on his mind. It was a little thinner on top now and liberally streaked with gray, which was unusual. Dyeing it was his only real vanity, which he'd done since I was in high school. Nose hair trimming didn't make the cut. Neither did his ear hair, which probably accounted for his propensity to make people repeat themselves until they went insane.

"How was your flight?" he asked.

"Fine. Long."

"You get a lot of sleep?"

"Yep. Then I watched a few movies and read a little bit. The usual." For once, I was grateful for the small talk. "I also caught up on some emails and posted some pictures on my Instagram."

I might as well have said I did a little witchcraft for the puzzled look he gave me. "What?"

"You know. Email… Instagram.…" Confronted with another blank look, I shrugged. "Well, anyway, I got a lot done."

"You see your brothers yet?"

"I saw John, but not Matt or Mark." I tapped my fingers on my thigh. "Dad—"

"I'm not leaving my home, and I'm damn sure not going to Seattle."

He said Seattle like it was a curse word. I didn't ask what was wrong with Seattle because I didn't want to hear the list he probably had all cued up. He'd probably been working on it for years because he was just über prepared like that.

"You'll stay with me," he said.

"I already decided that, Boss Baby," I informed him, "but only for the summer. I'll give you until the end of August."

"I generally include September in the summer," he said craftily.

"That's crazy talk. September is fall."

"I go by the weather," he said confidently. "When the weather changes, the summer is over."

"The weather never changes. This is Florida."

"We have a winter," he said stubbornly.

"Yes, those two days a year when I have to wear a sweater are truly harrowing." I made a sound of exasperation. "If you tack on September, you have to add May as well. Where does it end?"

"Well, we're at the end of May now, so isn't that moot?"

I opened my mouth to argue some more, and then I realized we were both strapping on gear to spelunk in a rabbit hole. "The summer," I said firmly. "I'll help you get settled and then I need to get back."

"To what?" he demanded.

"I have to get back to my real life," I said slowly, as if talking to a very difficult child, which wasn't far from the truth. "Back to work. Back home."

"You *are* home. And work?" He snorted. "You call goin' round the country and takin' pictures work?"

"The world, actually. And yeah, I do." I tamped down my irritation. I wondered if there would ever be a time when he didn't try to talk down my profession.

"You would've done much better to join the family garage. What the hell is the point of naming the business Sutton and sons if—"

"My sons don't want to fucking join," I finished tiredly. "I know, I know. You need new material."

I swiped a hand through my hair. I'd thought we could maybe use this time together to foster a better relationship. Now, that goal seemed a little... lofty. We'd only been together for a few minutes, and I was contemplating watching a couple of episodes of *Forensic Files* with a pad and a pen to take notes. *How much planning makes a crime premeditated again? Asking for a friend.*

When the doctor and a nurse bustled in, my father did his best to hide his true personality behind a friendly veneer. Not that he wasn't a pleasant man, he simply had a lot of... tang. Like the human equivalent of ranch dressing that was slightly beyond its expiration date. Yes, that's it. He was expired ranch dressing forgotten in the car for a few days.

His doctor went over my father's conditions and plans for moving forward. He used a lot of hot-button terms like "wake up call" and "lifestyle change" in his speech. I didn't blame him—it was pretty obvious that my father had been letting his health slide for a long time. He had high blood pressure but hadn't filled his prescription in several months. He was diabetic, but hardly ever checked his sugar level. His cholesterol was off the charts, he was slightly anemic... and a partridge in a pear tree. Apparently, he'd adopted the "cross my fingers and hope I don't die" approach to health.

I listened with one ear while I gathered and packed his belongings, suppressing eye roll after eye roll as he promised them the moon and stars—anything to get discharged. The lies went as follows:

1. *Yes, I'll take it easy. I'm practically retired!* I had it on good authority he routinely worked ten-hour days. Retirement was a four-letter word.

2. *I won't miss one follow-up appointment.* He was the reason doctors' offices created cancellation fees. Enough said.

3. *Seasoning alternatives? How clever!* He managed a look of faux, wide-eyed amazement when the nurse told him about the wonders of Mrs. Dash.

4. *Of course, I won't use salt.* Oh, that one was a doozy. He'd managed to look offended when he swore that oath. I couldn't suppress a snort, and he sent me a quick glare. We both knew he'd eat a shoe if I put enough salt and butter on it.

I wavered between enjoying his antics and busting the little phony. In the end, they bought his dog and pony show and discharged him to my care. I glanced around the room for a few moments, making sure I'd gotten all his personal effects.

My father made a rude noise in his throat. "Are you going to stand there all day, or can we get out of here? Get my bag, boy."

How long was the summer again?

"Do you want to take your flowers?" I asked as I shouldered his bag.

"What do I look like, some kind of woman?"

No, seriously, how long is the fucking summer again? I bit my tongue to stop myself from lecturing him that you didn't have to be a woman to enjoy a get-well bouquet. Apparently, in his world, a man sniffing a bunch of lilies was a smite-worthy offense. "God forbid," I murmured.

"Don't know what your brother's wife was thinking, sending that crap," he grumbled. "Waste of good money, I say."

"Should he be talking so much?" I asked the nurse innocently. "That can't be good for his recovery, can it?"

Pilar hid a smile, but I couldn't tempt her to be unprofessional. "We enjoyed having you, Mr. Sutton, but I hope we don't see you again," she said. "We want you to stay nice and healthy and out of this ward."

He grunted.

"I'm good at interpreting his grunts," I informed her. "What I think he means is, thank you so much, Pilar. You've been such a big help. And you are more than welcome to take my beautiful flowers."

This time a little laugh broke free. "Oh, you," she said as she left. She took the lilies with her.

I wheeled him down the hall, his bag on my shoulder and a thick packet of discharge instructions under my arm—and that packet *was* thick. I could barely remember to take a multivitamin, and now I'd been drafted to keep my father alive. I felt a little overwhelmed, which meant I needed to make a list and just attack it from the top.

I stopped in front of the elevator, lost in thought. I needed to get a pill caddy. Maybe a walker with some wheels, too. The discount number they'd given him was all right in a pinch, but I should probably find something a little sturdier. I put a blood pressure monitor and a glucose meter on the list. Oh, and I needed to pick up test strips, needles, and insulin from the pharmacy.

Even my list was starting to get a little convoluted. I reminded myself to take a deep breath.

"Well?" I glanced down to find him looking at me questioningly. "Do I have to press the button myself? Or can you stop woolgathering long enough to make yourself useful?"

I stabbed the Down button so hard I almost jammed my finger. I could only hope the elevator didn't malfunction and open to an empty shaft. Right now, I couldn't be trusted to not push him in. They'd probably know I did it on purpose, which meant I'd have to go on the lam. But sometimes you had to be willing to don a disguise and escape to another country—that's if you're not a fucking slacker and you're dedicated to achieving your goals.

The elevator doors opened and, but for one doctor perusing something on a clipboard and sipping from a Starbucks cup, it was blessedly empty. I turned around and pulled my father's wheelchair in, so he would be in front. I had a feeling I wouldn't need to get too used to figuring out wheelchair logistics. My father was a stubborn son of a bitch and the moment he could walk, he would.

We were halfway down to the lobby before he spoke again. "I need to stop by the store and get something to wet my whistle," he said.

"I'm pretty certain we have water at home." I gave him a warning look. "We're not getting you any beer."

"What are you, my warden?"

"If necessary. Anything else?"

"Yeah, you can stop giving me that look."

"What look?"

"The look that says you don't know whether to help me or set me on fire."

"Don't tempt me," I said gravely. "And I wouldn't set *you* on fire. I'd torch your bed and let nature take care of the rest." The doctor looked up from his chart with a disapproving glance. "What? It's not like I asked you for a match," I said defensively.

He huffed and turned his back as well as he could, which was quite a feat since we were standing right next to each other. I sighed. *Jesus.* I thought I'd make it more than five minutes before being reported to adult protective services.

MY FATHER COMPLAINED the whole way home.

I wasn't even surprised. He complained about the way I helped him into the car. Apparently, the time it took me to get out of the parking garage was ridiculous. My driving speed was too inconsistent. Even the comfort level of his own fucking seat was unacceptable, as if I was responsible for every bump and pucker in the restored vintage Mustang.

"It's your bloody car," I informed him at some point, which took the wind out of his sails. He was silent for about two-point-five seconds before he declared that he was hungry and reminded me he needed to go to the drugstore for supplies.

"What kind of supplies?" I asked suspiciously. The drugstore was his place of choice to buy chewing tobacco, which was an all-star on the doctor's no-no list.

"A stick of deodorant and a new toothbrush," he snapped. "And *I'm* the parent, here."

That was entirely debatable.

"Well?" he prodded. "What about some lunch? Am I allowed to eat, warden?"

"You're allowed to eat, Prisoner 666. I'm just going over your list of approved foods in my mind. If I remember correctly, you need something low-fat, low-sodium, and low-sugar. Nothing spicy, either. And no citrus because of one of your new meds." I blew out a breath. "So...air. You like air?"

He snorted. "I put a steak in the fridge to defrost before I went in."

"Yeah, that goes on the no-fly list for now," I said, shooting him a sidelong look. "And please stop making it sound like you just checked yourself into the hospital for a quick tune-up."

"Might as well have."

"Really?" It was my turn to snort. "Because the way Cam tells it, you fell in the grocery store, right down the deodorant aisle."

"Which is why I still need sundries," he bellowed, "like I told you."

"Calm down, calm down," I huffed. "Jesus, you'll get your pressure up."

Whose bright idea was this anyway? I was many things, but

patient and nurturing didn't even crack the top hundred list of my best traits.

"Do you think you could drive a little faster?" He shifted in his seat, trying to get comfortable. "You'd think you were driving Miss Daisy."

Refresh my drink, in the movie, did they drive Miss Daisy off a cliff or no?

"I'm trying to keep the ride smooth for your sake," I said. And because irony was a thing, I hit a pothole that sent us both jumping in our seats.

"Great job," he managed to bark, even though clearly in pain as he clutched his side. He had a bruise there from when he'd fallen in the grocery store, and he was healing slowly.

"I didn't pave the freaking road," I snapped, before biting down on my tongue to keep from saying more.

Knockout drops. I added those to my mental list of essentials for when he got on my last fucking nerve, which was probably going to be often. Melatonin would work. In a gallon jug.

He made a sound of derision. "Good God, boy, are you seriously going to stop at a yellow?"

At his incredulous mutter, I pressed harder on the accelerator and the vintage Mustang roared like I was an extra in one of the *Fast & Furious* movies. I was hard-pressed not to smile. "You souped this up, didn't you?" I accused.

His lips twitched. "No other way to drive American muscle. Now hit it."

I did as I was told and *lookee* there, I felt a little better. "Are you that eager to get home?" I asked, navigating around a couple of slow cars that didn't get the memo that arriving safely was passé.

"I'm that eager to get a real damn bath. Sponge baths just don't cut it."

I grimaced. "Christ, I was hoping we could work up to me seeing you completely naked." I shook my head. "Not just, hi son, welcome home, check out my balls."

He looked as horrified as I felt. "What the hell are you talking about?"

"I'm assuming you don't want to ruin your welcome home party, for one, by cracking your dome on the side of the tub," I said dryly. "If you *did* want to go out that way, you shouldn't have told me. I think that makes me an accessory or something."

"I can give myself a bath," he said stubbornly.

"Day fucking one," I muttered. *Day fucking one* and he was already itching to be bounced back to the hospital.

I did a couple of minutes of deep breathing exercises that I'd been taught by an actual monk in a Tibetan village. I gave up on finding my center fairly quickly. No offense to the monk, but spiritual breathing was a lot easier on a quiet mountaintop than in a car with a grouchy old man. I decided to treat him like a three-year-old. I would give him an either/or situation and make him pick one.

"Look, you can either accept my help in the tub, or I can bring you a bucket and some soap, and I'll help wash you off bedside. And I'm not as cute as the nurse who was doing it at the hospital." I paused meaningfully. "Or as gentle."

"When do I get to take a shower?" he demanded.

"If you're making adequate progress, in a few days you can sit in the shower on a bath bench and use the handheld showerhead. That's *after* I install decals and… well, buy and install a handheld showerhead."

He looked aghast. "You're not going to be this way the entire time, are you?"

When I took on a job, I did it right, and he should know that by now. "Pretty much."

"What am I gonna eat?" he asked plaintively.

"I'll come up with something. Tomorrow I'll pick up some fresh ingredients." He made a face, and I rolled my eyes. "You'll like it. You'll see. One good thing about all my travels is that I've learned all kinds of regional cuisine."

"Regional cuisine." His mouth made a little *o* of horror before he snapped it shut. "Where's Mark?"

I sent him the gimlet eye. "At work. And the first person to bring you contraband is getting a demonstration on everything I learned from a Judo master in Japan."

It was mostly a lie—I *did* meet a Judo master in Japan, but I did a lot of watching and taking pictures, not learning. No one needed to know the specifics.

My dad slumped in his seat. "This summer is gonna be somethin' else."

"I heartily concur."

9

CAMERON

I pulled into my garage a little after eight.

I was tired as hell, and I wished I hadn't promised I'd meet Carter for dinner. But I had, so I would. I still had to get Kona fed and let her out before I headed down to the restaurant. Carter wasn't a stickler for punctuality, but I hated to be late. I glanced down at myself and grimaced. I certainly wasn't about to show up in dirty scrubs.

I got my but in gear, put out Kona's food, and then I showered while she ate. By the time she was finished, I was dressed in a casual button-down and nice dark-wash jeans. I grabbed some socks and shoes and tucked them under my arm, hustling Kona outside.

She wasted no time, thundering through the yard in a way that would make even Cujo stop and ask, "What the fuck?" I sat on the top step of my deck to put on my shoes and socks as she got down to serious business. She sniffed down the backyard thoroughly, making sure nothing had changed—grass-wise, of course—since we'd left for work. I watched with a little smile. She let out a joyful howl, which I took to mean everything had checked out and all systems were a go.

Across the fence, the atmosphere at Jack's house was more lively than usual. The glow of lights graced nearly every window and the driveway was filled with vehicles. I recognized most of them as belonging to Journey's brothers. From the sound of things, they'd brought reinforcements in kid form. Someone yelled something so loud that Kona paused, midstep, and a child started shrieking with laughter.

I chuckled, shaking my head. Bunch of hell-raisers. No wonder Jack didn't mind Kona and all her howling—raising that noisy brood had probably left him partially deaf. Journey knew how to wrangle them, though. Always had. Over the din, I could hear his voice as he threatened to knock some heads together if they didn't settle down.

Usually, Jack's house was the quietest on the block. He came home after work and sometimes had a beer on the porch. If I pulled up and he happened to still be outside, I went over to join him for a little while. I knew he'd never admit it, but now that his rambunctious bunch had lives and families of their own, he got lonely over there. They all lived within a twenty-minute radius, but things got busy. Relationships slipped through the cracks.

I wasn't surprised that Journey's arrival had brought them out of the woodwork. They'd always seen him as more of a father figure than a brother, probably because he'd been a surrogate for so long. His father had checked out after Lori died, just completely fell apart. It had been up to Journey to pick up the slack and without missing a beat, he had.

The wooden gate door between our houses suddenly rattled, and Kona went on high alert. A hand reached over to flip the latch on my side right before it swung open. I chuckled as Journey came through a moment later, closing the gate door behind him carefully. He looked completely relaxed in khaki shorts and a white tank top, with thong sandals on his feet. He had a pan in one hand and was eating something with the other—it looked like a pastry of some sort.

He gave me a jaunty wave as he crossed my yard. Kona skulked along behind him silently, keeping to the shadows. I wasn't worried. Sometimes she just liked to... stalk people. It was harmless. Probably.

By the time he reached me, the pastry was gone and he was

licking his fingers. From the looks of the half-empty pan, it wasn't his first. He inclined his head. "Foss."

I held back a grin. "Sutton. To what do I owe this visit?"

"I was hoping I could convince you not to call the police." He grinned cheekily. "Are we too loud over there?"

As if he planned it that way, some of the kids started shrieking and thundering footsteps sounded as they raced around the patio. There was a crash a moment later, and Mark boomed that "someone was gonna get it."

Too loud? I gave Journey a disbelieving look. "I'm assuming that question was rhetorical."

He laughed. "Sorry. Here's a peace offering, though."

I took the tray of half-eaten dessert bars. They looked like raspberry. I sighed wistfully as I visualized the evening I was passing up. There I was on the couch in pajamas with Kona at my side, and we were watching some junk television. These perfect raspberry bars were invited, too, and so was a glass of ice-cold milk. But no, *someone* had to try and be social and make a date.

There was another crash next door and Journey winced. "I'm not sure what those hellions are up to now, but I'm pretty sure some of them should be in bed. Why they all descended on the house *en masse* is a mystery."

You know why.

They loved him. Missed him. I had no doubts that he felt the same way because Journey would die for his brothers, no questions asked, and feel no regrets. But their family dynamic was complicated. Whenever he came into town, they fell into the same old patterns of looking to him for guidance and expecting him to do everything. That made him start feeling a certain kind of way—crushed with responsibility. Like his life wasn't his own. He started looking like a caged wild animal, and before long, he lit out of Coral Cove like his hair was on fire.

Sacrificing everything for a decade of his youth had left its scars. When I looked back on it, proposing to him and talking about starting a family probably hadn't helped. I'd started to see that caged-animal look in our final days together and I just hadn't known what it meant at the time.

Once when I had to stay late at work, I'd asked him to come home early to take out Bear. When I got there, the house was still dark, and Bear was a mess. He'd done his business on several of the rugs and himself besides.

After standing there in the odorous living room for a few moments, nonplussed, I'd figured I'd start with Bear. I'd assured him in the bath that it wasn't his fault, but he was morose. I could tell he'd felt like he'd done something wrong. There was nothing a good boy hated worse than feeling like he'd been a bad one. That had made me even more pissed at Journey.

I'd been on my knees with a bucket of soap and water, cleaning up the mess in the living room, when he'd finally made it home. He'd been apologetic and full of excuses that he'd had to help Mark at the garage.

"I'm so sorry," he finished awkwardly, realizing I hadn't responded to anything he'd said. He reached for the sponge. "Here, let me help you with that."

"I've got it," I said shortly.

"You're mad."

"I'm not mad," I said exasperatedly. "But when are you going to put us first? What happens when we have kids? You're not going to be able to just drop everything for Mark."

"Well, I'm not going to have to," he said with a little frown. "I don't want to have kids."

I couldn't have been more surprised if he shapeshifted into a wolf. I blinked at him for a few moments, dripping sponge forgotten in my hand. "Really?"

"Well, yes. Really."

He headed over to the bookcase, where we kept a glass treat jar, and pulled out a couple of Milk-Bones. He tossed them to Bear, who turned his back on the treats. After a second or two, Bear figured his point had been made, and he snatched them up. Journey leaned down to ruffle his ears, and

Bear leaned into his touch. He didn't know how to hold a grudge to save his life.

"I'm going to spoil you rotten tonight," Journey promised him, and Bear glanced up hopefully. "Just let me get into something more comfortable, and there will be a long walk around the neighborhood and belly rubs galore."

Journey rose and looked at me, surprised to find me still frozen. "Maybe I should've mentioned it earlier," he said hesitantly. "I just... I assumed we were on the same page."

"But you're such a natural at it." I was almost at a loss for words. "The boys...."

He grimaced. "Yes, the boys. I love them to pieces, but goddamn, they weren't the easiest."

"Our kids would be different." I felt like I was losing an argument I hadn't prepared for. "It's different when they're yours."

He snorted. "I think people have to say that. Otherwise, there would be a lot of parents rubbing their temples and murmuring, what the fuck have I done?"

I stared at him for a few moments, certain things falling into place. "Is this why you didn't want to buy the house?" When the realtor mentioned how great the backyard would be for kids, Journey had changed the topic so fast that we'd gotten whiplash.

"Cam. Honey...." He spread his hands, looking a little helpless. "I'm sorry. But I've already done my time."

Journey frowned at me as if he could read where my thoughts had gone. "Don't try to make me feel guilty, Cam."

"I didn't even say anything."

"I can read your body language. And why are you dressed up anyway?" Awareness dawned in his eyes as the obvious answer occurred to him before I could even open my mouth. "Ah," was all he said.

I scratched the back of my neck. Christ, this was awkward. "Just meeting a friend for dinner."

"That's what I figured." He paused. "Carter?"

I didn't answer, and he chuckled softly. He didn't bother to hide the appraisal in his gaze as he looked me up and down. He lingered an inordinately long time in certain... areas. "You clean up nice. Always have."

As usual, just a simple perusal from that knowing gaze took me someplace I had no business going. But no one ever talked about this part of breaking up. It was hard to forget how good we were together. He'd never hesitated to use those hands and that skilled mouth to *take me there*, and I always eagerly returned the favor. It was hard to forget how it felt to have him spread open under me, those amber eyes hazy with need. How it felt when he locked those legs around me and egged me on to take him apart.

People talked about the bad feelings and the regret, but no one ever talked about that other shit, like how being around your ex could take you back to a time when you could plow his ass all you wanted. I blew out a breath and raked a hand through my hair. So yeah, *Breaking Up for Dummies* could use a fucking update.

"Stop making it weird," I finally complained, "and stop looking at my dick."

"I wasn't," he said gravely. "But I'd like to point out that your dick *is* looking at me."

I huffed. At this rate, I was going to have to change my fucking jeans. "That's hardly my fault. He has a mind of his own."

"Clearly." His eyes twinkled. "You know what they say about all work and no play. It gives you the most horrific boner all day."

"They do not say that," I said with a chuckle.

And then, he cut right to the heart of the matter. "You know I'd take care of that for you. Right now, in fact."

Suddenly it was a little challenging to get air in my lungs. It was a moment before I could look away from his mouth. Another moment before I could dispel the image of him on his knees, my dick buried down his throat as far as I could get it. He was always amazing at that. As a bonus, it really got him going. It was hard for him *not* to come when he got to sucking my dick and stroking his own... and just where the hell was I going with that particular train of thought?

Oh yeah, I was looking for more than a quick fuck. I was looking for something real. And I certainly wasn't going to find that with a globetrotting photographer, who would probably shrivel up and die if he had to stay in one place for over six minutes. Been there, done that, got the engraved wedding band in the back of my closet.

This is how forever feels. Remembering that ridiculously short-sighted engraving made me wince. It also made my answer easy. "No thanks," I said abruptly. "I'd better get going. I don't want to keep Carter waiting."

"Right. Carter." He looked vaguely amused about something. "Hope you don't nod off in your soup."

"Cute, but I've had exciting," I said pointedly. "I'm looking for something a little different this time around."

Point for Cam. Your serve.

He stared at me for a second, and I wondered if he'd take me up on the dig. In the end, his mouth just quirked as he inclined his head in acknowledgment. "I hope you have a good time."

"Do you?"

"Not really, but that seemed nicer to say than, I hope you have a lousy time and decide you can't wait any longer to get laid."

I held in my amusement, but he wasn't quite finished. "I also hope you throw away all your principles about casual fucking and burst through my bedroom door like your name is Kool-Aid."

I couldn't hold back my laughter anymore. "You're an idiot."

"Oh yeah," he added helpfully.

His perfect imitation of the Kool-Aid man set me off again. "I hate you."

He smiled. "No, you don't."

No, I don't. I watched him cross the yard and disappear back through the gate. *But sometimes I wish I did.*

10

JOURNEY

My father and I had a little trouble settling into a routine, which was to be expected for two headstrong people. Most of my time seemed to be spent trying to stop him from doing things he shouldn't be doing, and there were a lot of things on that list. Some of his all-time favorites included: attempting the stairs unassisted, trying to lift heavy things, and eating foods on the doctor's incinerate-on-sight list.

He fussed; I ignored him. I badgered; he ignored me. I cooked; he bitched about what I cooked. I hid the salt and the sugar; he returned the favor by hiding the wheat germ and the oatmeal. At one point, he got one of the grandkids to help him install *DoorDash* on his phone. In the comments section, he put, *no doorbell, no knock, and leave it in the bushes by the road.* So yes, there was a little friction, but we were making it work. One week after I picked his ornery ass up from the hospital, he was still alive and so was I.

Other than running around behind a full-grown toddler, I found myself a little restless. Being tethered to one place too long usually did that to me. I continued to remind myself that this wasn't forever. My time in Coral Cove had a built-in expiration date, and soon, I'd get back to my real life.

It wasn't all bad. I was enjoying all the extra time with my nieces and nephews. I didn't get to see them often, other than on the phone screen. Kids changed so fast at their ages that missing six months seemed like three times that many. Usually by the time I rolled back into town, they had different likes and dislikes, and their previous best friend in the whole world had become chopped liver. So being so close was nice—different, but nice.

I perused the fridge with an eye toward dinner and realized I had enough ingredients left to assemble a stew. I'd made the stew earlier in the week and it disappeared fairly quickly. Once he got wind of what I was preparing, my father made sure to voice his complaints. Apparently, he now hated the stew, even though he'd had four bowls on Tuesday.

"Too bad, so sad," I called out as I continued to chop vegetables.

"How about some barbecue?" he asked hopefully.

"How about some tofu?" I threatened.

He sighed loudly and left me in peace.

My watch beeped as I was adding the beef stock. My überorganized sister-in-law, Laura, had suggested that I set some alarms on my phone for my caretaking duties, and I was grateful for the idea. In my line of work, I was known to lose entire blocks of time as I waited for the perfect shot. My schedule nowadays wasn't quite as free.

I checked my watch, and sure enough, the little note said OT. My father had occupational therapy twice a week, which he hated. Even though he knew what time OT was, he hadn't moved from his chair in the den to get ready.

"Dad," I called out. "It's time for OT."

Not a word in response. I might as well have been yelling into a canyon. Actually, no, at least the canyon would've had the good manners to throw me back an echo.

I sighed as I added spices to the broth and a thick cut of chuck roast. The back door opened with a creak, and I glanced over to see Mark come in carrying a foil-covered pan. "Hey," he said. "I brought the mower back and put it in the shed."

"I'll let Dad know. We were sick with worry," I said solemnly. "We were just about to put up missing flyers."

He rolled his eyes. "Laura told me to tell you hello."

"Did Laura also send some of her apple-cheesecake bars?" I put the lid on the Crock-Pot and rubbed my hands on a dish towel. I set the dial on Low and then thought better of it and kicked it up to Medium. "And just know, if you say no, it can and *will* affect our relationship."

"She doesn't make those anymore. Get with the times, JJ." He brought the pan forward with a flourish. "She makes dynamite PB and J bars with roasted chopped peanuts now."

I squinted at the pan suspiciously. "That wasn't in any of Mindy's newsletters."

He chuckled as he put the pan on the table and went over to the silverware drawer. He pulled out a couple of forks with a noisy clatter and held one out to me. "I'm surprised you even read those."

I took the proffered fork with a frown. He looked vaguely embarrassed. It wasn't the first time someone had insinuated that they thought I was looking down on small-town life. That couldn't be further from the truth. There was nothing wrong with homespun Americana—it just wasn't for me.

"I read them twice in case there's a quiz," I said lightly.

We dug into the PB and J bars, and I learned a hard lesson about doubting Laura's culinary prowess. They were so delicious that before I knew what was happening, we'd devoured half the pan. I glanced at the clock above the stove and cursed. "Dad," I bellowed.

"What?"

He knew damn well *what*. It hadn't even taken him a second to answer, probably because he'd been waiting for me to notice the time.

"At the risk of being repetitive, it's time for OT."

"I'm not in the mood."

I made a rude buzzer noise. "The answer we're looking for is, *I'm ready son, I just need to put on my shoes.*"

"I'm busy," he hollered.

"Watching *Bonanza* and eating pecans does not qualify as busy. Let's get a move on. Whatever you're wearing in"—I glanced at the time on my phone—"seven minutes is exactly what you're wearing. And if it's house shoes and that ratty robe, so be it."

"We all agreed you would sneak and throw out that damned robe," Mark said, his voice low.

"I *did*," I shot back, equally as quiet. "He dug it back out of the trash can."

"You gotta toss it on trash day," he said exasperatedly. "Don't give him the chance next time."

"There is no next time. He's on to me now." I had a feeling he was hiding it, mostly because if he wasn't wearing it, I couldn't find it. "We're lucky he doesn't lock that ratty old thing up in the safe."

The theme song to the old Western started playing as another episode cued up, and I yelled, "I mean it! Six minutes."

There was grumbling but definite signs of movement in the den, and Mark chuckled. "Gawd, I'm having PTSD flashbacks from my childhood. You're just as bad as you were back then."

"And don't you forget it," I said with a nod.

Trying to corral those hellions wasn't a job for the weak. I'd made it understood that if they wanted a ride to school, they had to have their butts up, ready, and fully dressed by seven. Anything they hadn't done by the time my boots hit the front porch had to be done in the car. That led to a lot of half-dressed mornings, swearing, and combing hair and brushing teeth in the rearview mirror.

I smiled. "I remember you beat the system by getting a buzz cut in high school. I think you could get ready quicker than a fireman after that."

"Still can," he said around a mouthful of food.

I took one more bite of PB and J bar before pulling the wrap back over the pan. There was no need to get fancy about storage. They weren't going to last the night. I stuck them in the bottom oven, where no one ever went.

When I glanced over at Mark, he was scratching the back of his neck, the way he did when he had something to say but wasn't sure if he should say it. His mouth opened and closed a few times.

"She's your wife," I said, plucking his fork from his fingers. "She can make you more. Stop eyeing my pan."

"No, it's not that."

Oh, good. I breathed a sigh of relief as I tossed his utensil in the sink. I'd been ready to stab his hand with a fork, but I'd hoped it wouldn't come to that. "What is it, then?"

"We still paddleboard, you know," he said awkwardly. "We try to get out there at least once a month. Since you're here, you should join us. Everyone would love to have you."

"Yeah?" I snorted. "Even John? I didn't get that impression when we last spoke."

"John... John is just being John."

"I have no idea what that means."

"Yeah, you do." His mouth quirked.

I absolutely did. And "John being John" encompassed quite a bit. John was a grouchy bastard, who'd never fully forgiven me for, well, anything. He hadn't forgiven me for leaving. And for not joining *Sutton & Sons*. I didn't know if he wanted me on their monthly paddleboard jaunt or not, but I was in either way.

"Sounds like fun," I finally said. "After all, I did promise Kelci I'd show her how to outswim her old man."

Mark didn't smile as I'd expected. Instead, his mouth opened and closed a few more times, and I sighed impatiently. "Could you stop doing that? Your gaping like a fish impression is fantastic. Just say it."

"I don't want this to come out the wrong way, but please don't promise my kids anything like that."

I blinked. That wasn't anywhere in the realm of what I'd thought he was going to say. "And why would that be, exactly?"

"Because we don't know if you're going to be here, JJ. And that's not fair to them."

In a perfect world, I could assure him I wasn't going anywhere. That I was done traveling and was ready to settle down in Coral Cove and do… what, exactly? I had no idea what life looked like without a pack on my back and a camera to my eye.

Of course, if it *was* a perfect world, I wouldn't have started my morning with an old man threatening to throw his bowl of oatmeal unless I brought him some 'real fucking sugar.'

I firmed my jaw. "Fine."

He sent me a guilty look. "Sorry, I just had to say something."

"It's fine," I said breezily. I grabbed the dish towel and wiped at the already spotless counters until he left.

It didn't feel fine.

If I hadn't taken a walk during my father's session, I would've never found her.

I spotted the stray dog on my way back to the building, lying under a park bench that was flanked by bushes on either side. I was fully prepared to coax her out of her hiding spot, but when I squatted down, she didn't even look my way. I was almost afraid to check, but I couldn't just leave her there.

I pulled her little body out as gently as possible. She still didn't move, even when I picked her up, but I could feel her little heartbeat thumping reassuringly beneath her prominent ribcage. "Thank God," I breathed.

She blinked, startled at the sound of my voice and probably surprised to find herself out from under the relative security of the park bench. She put up a token struggle that lasted less than ten seconds. She'd been roaming the streets too long and was out of fight. She went limp in my arms. It was like holding a teddy bear with sharp burrs in her fur. I stared at her, a little flummoxed as I wondered what the heck I should do next.

Water, I decided. It was a hot day out. I couldn't go wrong with water. Only I didn't have a bowl. Or water. I huffed. Two minutes in and I already sucked at this taking care of a dog thing.

I finally gave up on trying to figure out the best way and just did it the Journey way. I trotted across the street to the gas station and bought a water bottle and a pack of paper bowls. Then I went back over to the bench to show her my offering. She was still limp. I nudged the paper bowl closer, but she didn't move.

I put my finger in the bowl and then wet her mouth with the drippings, and for the first time, she perked up. She shoved her face in the bowl and went all psycho on the water, enough that I had to fill the bowl twice. Then she sat back on her haunches and looked at me. Her big brown eyes seemed to be absorbing my every feature. It was like she was saying, *"Thank you for seeing me."*

I scoffed at my fanciful thinking. "We need to find your owners. I guess I should put your cute little mug on a couple of fliers and post them around town."

She pressed against my leg and one of the burrs in her fur snagged on my jeans. "I probably should have you groomed first. Your own mother wouldn't recognize you like this."

She yawned at my perfect plan. Well, then. "Pet Smart, first. You need a leash and collar," I said crisply as I headed for the car. She followed me, albeit slowly, as if to show me those items were overkill. "I'm not naming you, either. For now, you're Thing One."

She didn't look bothered in the least.

My Pet Smart visit didn't go as I planned. A perky woman named Trish was thrilled at the thought of a stray finding a forever home. She assisted me with getting essential supplies, which in her world translated to everything but the kitchen sink. I kept reminding her that Thing One was *not* my dog, but that didn't deter Trish. Her cheeks glowed with joy as she showed me a super-cute leash and halter that were unbelievably tiny.

"Don't worry, you'll be able to adjust this for her after her grooming," she said, showing me how the buckle moved. "I have a feeling your dog is even smaller than she looks. You'll see once all that matted fur is removed."

"She's not mine," I reminded her for the fourth time.

"Of course," Trish said brightly. "Should we look at bowls for your little girl, here?"

I grumbled but wound up with even more stuff in my cart. The bed and toys I could justify, but the jacket and pajama onesies were just embarrassing—for both of us. I topped off the cart with a couple of bags of tiny treats, and Tanya gave me a knowing look.

"She's been through a lot," I said defensively.

"Mm-hmm."

My conversation with the groomer didn't go much better. A cute guy named Cesar informed me that Thing One couldn't get groomed until she had proper proof of her shots. I wanted to pull out my hair. I didn't know what was living in her fur, but I *did* know I didn't want it transferred to my carpet. And frankly, I thought Thing One would be a lot more comfortable in this heat without all the matted and muddied fur.

I checked my watch, realizing more time had passed than I'd thought. If I didn't leave soon, I'd be late to pick up my father. I put Thing One's new leash and halter on her, and then we left the grooming shop.

By the time I pulled up, my father was sitting in his wheelchair near the front entrance. I was one minute late, but God forbid he should wait in the air-conditioning like a reasonable human being. He'd rather risk heatstroke to prove a point.

I got out of the car, holding up a hand in warning. "I'm not in the mood for it," I informed him.

He closed his mouth and made a harrumph. I got him settled in the car and went back around to the driver's side. I slid in, only to find him looking in the back seat warily. He reached down slowly and pulled off his slipper.

"JJ, I think there's some sort of opossum in the car."

"Will you put your shoe back on?" I asked exasperatedly. "It's a dog." *I think.*

His face screwed up. "Well, whaddya get a damn dog for?"

"I couldn't afford a helper monkey for you."

"You're my helper monkey," he informed me. "A little chattier than I bargained for, but beggars can't be choosers, and all that."

"Hardy har har," I said dryly. "You're so hilarious."

"I know." He eyed the dog again, who smiled at him, her tongue hanging out as if to prove, *yes, I am a dog*. "Since you have time to rescue animals, you have time to take me to the store."

"Yes, master," I grumbled, putting the car in Drive. "Right away, master."

He didn't answer my sass, but his mouth twitched. I wasn't sure what tickled his funny bone more, my grousing or the fact that he got to ride me like a Grand Canyon pack mule. No matter. I drove him to the nearest Pick-n-Save and made the mistake of helping him find a riding cart. Once he got the hang of the controls, he couldn't shoo me and Thing One away quickly enough.

I huffed. "Good luck reaching anything on a high shelf," I called as he motored into the store.

"How's a short thing like you going to help me with that anyway?" He hit top speed, which I could still probably pass crawling on my hands and knees. He looked like a contestant in NASCAR for the Elderly.

Thing One and I got back in the car. After a few minutes of tapping my fingers on the wheel, I decided to make a quick stop at Wendy's. I picked up a plain hamburger and a cup of water for Thing One, and a combo meal for myself. Then I pulled back into the parking lot of the Pick-n-Save and rolled the windows down.

I set the dog up with a hamburger and occupied myself by trying to find her a groomer on my phone. There were only three in town, and I called them all as she sat in the passenger seat, looking perfectly at peace with life in general.

I hung up with the last groomer on the list. Like the rest, she needed a rabies certificate first. I sighed. It was stunning how a footloose and fancy-free life could be bogged down so quickly. Now, not only was I responsible for taking care of a grouchy old man, but I'd also acquired a dog-maybe-opossum.

"Well, I guess I need to take you to the vet," I informed her. "Fortunately, I have a good one on speed dial. I guess they can also check you for a microchip."

She didn't seem perturbed.

"You're not staying," I reminded her, "so don't unpack your Chewy box just yet."

She sniffed my hand for more hamburger. I opened my palm to show her that she'd cleaned me out, and she licked my palm once for good measure. I chuckled and scratched her ear.

"Is it strange that you're the most pleasant person in my life right now?" I asked. "Maybe I need to run with better company."

She gave me a happy doggy smile as if she agreed.

At least I got to see Cam. I wasn't going to hit on him again because I could take a hint, but seeing him was always a bright spot in my day. I had no intention of dissecting that feeling, though. Not even a little bit.

11

CAMERON

I was halfway through my third appointment of the morning before I realized something important: Kimble, a poodle mix, and his owner, Netta, were starting to look alike. They both had fluffy white hair, large dark eyes, and a little overbite. They seemed to realize it, too, because they'd started to dress alike. Today, they were both in white-and-pink striped shirts. All Kimble needed was a pair of small eyeglasses hanging from a pearl chain to complete the look.

"How're the seizures?" I asked, holding his muzzle still, so I could get a better look into his eyes. The left one was a little hazier than the right, but that was to be expected with his age.

"Only had two this month." She rubbed Kimble's ears to keep him calm, however, it wasn't necessary. He was always a good patient and the ultimate candidate for the Goodest Boy award.

I finished my exam quickly and let him down, so he could give the room a good sniffing. He'd already done it twice, but Kimble liked to be thorough. Now and again, he would pause and stumble. At one point, he got lost in the corner for a few moments, standing stock still and staring at the wall.

Netta wrung her hands. "I don't like the way the medicine makes him feel."

"It's perfectly normal," I said sympathetically. It could be hard to see a dog's personality that you knew inside and out change so rapidly, but he couldn't afford another series of seizures. "The side effects of the meds should wear off in a few weeks, and he'll be back to his normal self."

"And the staggering and falling?"

"His ataxia should resolve itself, but just in case, we can give him half the dose. Make sure you keep him in a place where he can't hurt himself." I paused. "He could also stand to lose a few pounds."

Kimble chose that moment to back out of the corner. He turned and stared at me with his better eye, as if he knew exactly what I'd said. "Just a few." I rubbed his ear fondly. "It'll be better for his joints. And with his seizures, we don't need to compound things with another health issue."

Kimble yanked his face away from my touch. It was probably because I'd surprised him. Or, because he was calling me a *jerk* in doggy language.

She sighed. "He doesn't like diet food."

"Who does?" I asked with a grin, making her chuckle.

I finished up with them and headed out to the front. Bailey gave me an expectant look. "Everything all right with Kimble?"

"Right as rain. Make sure you give Netta some of those samples of the diet food."

"Again?"

I hid a smile. "She can't forget when she brought him home all those years ago and he was nothing but skin and bones. Her heart is in the right place."

"Now her head just has to join it. An extra pound on that dog is like ten on my body," Rosy said from behind me. She had no tolerance for people who overfed their pets. Something bumped into her from behind, and only her quick reflexes kept her from falling as she grabbed the desk.

She turned and gave Kona an exasperated but fond sigh. "And have you found a home for this dog yet?"

"I'm working on it," I said.

"She's a menace, and you're falling in love with her," she accused.

I didn't bother to deny what we both knew was the truth. I didn't fall in love easily, but when I did, I fell hard. "Aren't you supposed to be retired?" I asked pointedly.

Bailey handed Rosy a patient folder and pointed at room two. "Ms. Wallace brought in Phoebe for excessive itchiness." She handed me a clipboard with a patient intake form as Rosy disappeared down the hall.

"Hey," I protested even as I took the form. "I always get to see Phoebe." She was a sweet, pregnant dalmatian, and I loved dalmatians.

"You have the Oslo kittens, Rex's guinea pig, and if Rosy's not done, a new patient," she informed me.

I sighed. Well, maybe I could at least stick my head in the door and say hello. I glanced over at the lobby and nearly dropped my clipboard to find Journey sitting in the waiting room. He had a small dog with snarled fur on his lap, and he was frowning down at something on his phone. He glanced up and met my gaze. He smiled, those gorgeous amber eyes lighting up, the slightest impression of a dimple creasing his cheek. I was momentarily captivated. He should be on a goddamned magazine, not behind the camera.

I tried to pretend my heart rate hadn't kicked up a few notches. He was just a new patient, he wasn't ridiculously attractive, and I wasn't happy to see him at all. Or something like that. I squinted at him. "This is pitiful, even for you," I teased.

"What?" His eyes twinkled. "You think I scrounged up a dog just so I could see you?"

"Like I said. Pitiful."

"If you would agree to all my wicked demands, I wouldn't have to resort to such tactics."

I opened my mouth to respond in kind, when I remembered Bailey sitting there. I glanced back to find her watching us in fascination, her gaze ping-ponging between us. *Jesus, Cam, you're at work. Think you could keep it professional?*

"Come with me," I said crisply.

He looked a little startled at my change of tone, but he got up gamely enough. Bailey gave me a thumbs-up as we passed that was fucking impossible for Journey to miss. Sure enough, I heard him cover a laugh with a cough. I let him precede me into the examination room, doing my best not to stare at his ass. I was a professional at my place of business and… and oh, wow, he smelled so good it was ridiculous. I was tempted to hold my breath as he passed close enough to brush up against me.

I closed the door behind us, aware I was blushing. Damn Bee and that thumbs-up. "Sorry about that."

Journey smiled. "Well-meaning friends, right?"

I chuckled, feeling my tension ratchet down a bit. "Exactly. She's the one always trying to set me up on horrible blind dates."

"Horrible?" He raised an eyebrow. "I only know about the boring ones."

"Then I guess you don't know about the one who set his menu on fire," I said. "He leaned a little too close to the candle in the middle of the table."

"That could happen to anyone."

"He dropped the flaming menu on the table and the table linens caught on fire."

His amber eyes widened. "Well… that's still within the range of it could happen to *you*."

"Then he decided to put it out with his gazpacho."

Journey let out a charming little laugh before slapping a hand over his mouth.

I chuckled, too. "It's funny *now*. It wasn't funny when I was sitting there blinking glorified tomato soup out of my eyes."

He laughed again. "To me, that just means you weren't with the right person. If you were with the right person, something like that would've just made a funny story, not a horrible date."

"So, you're saying I should hold auditions where my dates throw soup in my face and see if I find it hilarious."

"Cold soup," he specified, "and I would pay good money to see that."

When I realized we were just standing there smiling at each other, I internally rolled my eyes. For God's sake, I could and *would* be professional, and that was all there was to it. I took his well-behaved charge off his lap and put her on the exam table.

I began going through a basic examination, something I'd probably done a thousand times. She looked to be a large percentage Shih Tzu. "What's her name?" I asked.

"I don't know. I just found her."

"I know. I saw that on your intake form. I meant, what do you call her?"

"Thing One for now."

"*Thing?*" I gave him a horrified look, clapping my hands gently over her ears. She tried to lick me for my efforts. "You have to give her a real name, Sutton."

The small smile that spread across those full, plump lips flustered me. God, why did he have to be so damned attractive? If I had a checklist for a type, he'd check off every fucking box. But back to the dog.

I put my stethoscope in my ears and placed it against her chest. "I'm just going to have a little listen," I told her. She looked up at me trustingly.

I listened to her heart for a few seconds, hearing the strong, reassuring beat in my ears. No murmur. I checked the lungs too and gave them the all-clear. I moved cautiously and deliberately during the exam, so as not to startle her, but she was friendly as could be. And ridiculously attached to Journey already, judging from the way she kept trying to keep a part of her body in contact with his. *Join the club, little lady.*

I put my stethoscope back around my neck and felt her belly. "She's a little undernourished. That's to be expected if she's been on the streets for a while. Other than that, she seems to be pretty healthy." She wiggled her butt a little, and I smiled down at her. "Little thing like you probably had it hard out there, all alone in the big bad world, huh sweetheart?"

I looked up from her big brown eyes into Journey's lighter ones.

He looked softly amused but didn't comment. I flushed anyway. As usual, I forgot myself when I was with an animal. They were the kindest, most understanding beings on Earth, and I'd always thought so, even as a little boy. That hadn't changed one whit after being around humans for almost forty years.

I was cautious examining her mouth, but other than trying to lick me to death, she didn't show any aggression. "Her front teeth are broken, but I'm not sure what from. That's why I originally thought she was a little older."

"How old is that, exactly?" He got even closer, and I tried my hardest not to breathe in his pleasant, crisp scent.

"About three years old." I checked her teeth again. "Looks like she needs to have a few pulled. That happens with smaller dogs."

He looked concerned. "How is she going to eat?"

"It'll be better for her overall health to get those bad teeth out of there," I said. "She'll still have enough chompers to work with."

"How much are we talking?"

I quoted him a price that didn't even make him flinch. He just nodded. Of course. I'd followed his career in the years since he'd left, and he did pretty well financially. I'd fallen in love with his work from the beginning, even when he was just taking pictures at the retail store, so I wasn't surprised the world had as well. His work had been featured everywhere—from magazines to galleries and everything in between. I was happy that he'd found what he was looking for. I was just sorry he left me to do it.

But enough of that maudlin shit.

I stepped back. "If you're ready, you should make an appointment, so we can handle her teeth. And I'm assuming you don't have any flea and tick prevention, so we can set you up with some Frontline Plus. We'll need to do a heartworm screening, too, so we can put her on a preventative."

"Check, check, and check." He looked eager as a schoolboy. "Anything else?"

"One other thing. For God's sake, Sutton, you've got to get her groomed. And named."

"That's two things," he said cheekily. "Any recommendations?"

"For a name?" I blinked. "That's kind of a personal choice."

"Grooming," he said with a soft smile.

"Oh. Right." I liked when he found me a little ridiculous because it came with more of that special smile. "Dapper Dogs on Main Street. If you mention me, Sally will probably get you in today."

"Done." He lifted Thing One off the table and clipped her leash back on. "I think I'll try out the name Biscuit for a bit. See if that fits her personality."

"And just how the hell do you act like a biscuit?"

"Dry and flaky," he said, as if it was obvious. He looked at me expectantly. "So, I'll see you later, then?"

I blinked. "For what?"

"All the sex," he said, a little twinkle in his eye.

I huffed out a laugh. "Get out."

12

CAMERON

Kona officially took the award for the worst at fetch. Bear had been a champion at the game, and it was guaran-damn-teed that I got tired of playing before he did. Kona seemed to enjoy human fetch better, which involved me throwing the stick and then getting off my rump to retrieve it. The way she was panting, tongue lolling out, it almost felt like she was laughing at me. I threw the stick again, and she yawned.

I chuckled. "I give. You win."

She sent me a *finally* kind of look and exposed her belly. I took the hint and gave her a good scratch. Her leg started to twitch like a rabbit. I pulled back after a few minutes, and she gave me a narrow-eyed look. I got back to scratching.

May had turned into June and the Florida weather had turned with it. We were now in the "Dear God, I don't think people are supposed to actually live here!" stage of the year. I'd dressed accordingly in cargo shorts, a lightweight T-shirt, and some sandals. I checked my watch. Journey and his father were due home any moment. He usually got Jack settled inside and then we took our dogs for their afternoon walk.

I could hear a truck pulling into the yard next door, but I didn't need to get up and look—Mark's pickup had a very distinctive sound. Jack's house had become a hub, and one or more of his boys came by every night. A couple of doors slammed and the sound of arguing children floated across the fence. Kona gave a short howl of greeting.

"Hey, Foster." Mark appeared at the fence suddenly, making me jump a little. "I heard Kona and thought you might be out here."

"Hey, Mark. How's it going?"

"Hot as hell, but I'm still living."

He braced his arms over the fence. It was a pretty tall fence, but he was a pretty tall guy. Journey was the only short stack in a family of tall folk. Mark was about my height and broader just about everywhere. He was a carbon copy of Jack—brown hair, blue eyes, and a square chin. He looked like that guy on the football team that dated the head cheerleader, married her after high school, and had a few kids. *Oh, wait*—I smiled a little, thinking about their cute brood of three—*that's exactly what he did.*

He held up several bags of KFC. "You hungry? We've got plenty."

"No, I'm good, thanks."

"Well, more for me. I told Pop I was coming over for dinner, but I'm not eating Journey's latest creation, straight from the streets of Bumfuck Wherever." He shuddered. "You know he made something called a beepin' bop last night?"

I hid a smile. "A bibimbap?"

"Whatever. He keeps saying that my palate needs to be educated, and I keep telling him my palate already has a degree in *What Normal Folks Eatology*." He shook his head. "I figure I'll get all the food dished up before he brings Pop home from therapy, and then he'll have no opportunity to even touch the stove."

I tried not to laugh. "I'm sure he knows how to cook something...." I struggled for the nicest way to put it. "Less adventurous."

"And I'm sure he does not. I don't even know how to pronounce some of the stuff he put on the grocery list on the fridge."

This time I couldn't hold in a laugh.

Mark shook the bags at me again. "You sure that's a no on the chicken? Because once John and Matt get here, this food is history."

"I'm sure."

"All right. Oh, and I texted JJ earlier, and he should be here in about twenty. Enjoy your walk." His expression got sly. "If that's what you two are really up to."

I widened my eyes. "Of course that's what we're doing."

"Your 'walks' have been getting longer and longer. Last night, it took an hour and a half."

"So?"

"So, the dog park is ten minutes away."

"It's not what you think," I said hotly. And sure, maybe both dogs got to whining as we sat on a park bench, chatting way too long, but still. Exercise was good for them. "We let the dogs play for a while."

"You sound like JJ," Mark said gleefully.

"That's because it's the truth. It's not like that." My ears burned. It was exactly like that. "Don't you have some chicken to eat?"

At least he waited until the front door banged shut behind him to laugh—loudly. I harrumphed and took Kona inside for water. Yes, Journey and I were walking our dogs together almost every day, but it's not like we'd planned it that way. One night, I'd been walking to the dog park and he'd been coming back from the park. It only made sense to sync up.

I winced. Because that's what you do with the ex who you haven't got over. And yes, I finally admitted that shit. Two weeks in, and I also realized something else—I hated living next door to him. That was probably something I should've considered before buying the house next door. But in my defense, he hadn't been *here* at the time. When your ex is usually a continent away, the world is a wonderful place. You're well-adjusted and happy, completely over him, and the way that he looks at you does *not* make you weak. I'm just paraphrasing here.

It was another twenty minutes before I saw the Mustang come by, and Kona and I wasted no time in moseying on over. Journey gave me a little wave before he went to the trunk of the car. He pulled a wheelchair out and went around to the passenger side. Before he could reach the passenger door, someone threw it open.

"Dad, will you hang on just a second?" Journey asked, his voice exasperated. I could tell it probably wasn't the first time they'd butted heads today. Hell, judging from the irritation on his face, it probably wasn't the second or third time, either.

"I may not be able to drive my car, but I can still get *out* of it on my own," came the grouchy reply. Jack nodded at me. "Foster."

I nodded back. "Sir."

Journey started to say something three different times before he finally snapped his mouth shut. He began getting out bags, and when I offered to help, he shook his head. That left me standing there awkwardly to watch Jack struggle out of the car to make the short steps to his wheelchair. My fingers curled into my palm painfully as he nearly lost his balance.

He staggered one last time before he plopped into the wheelchair. "See?" He sounded triumphant, his color high.

Journey shut the trunk and came around to the side, several bags looped around his wrist. "Yes, you're a real-life Iron Man," he said dryly.

After a few seconds, his father's triumphant expression melted into something cross. "Well?"

"Well, what?" Journey asked.

"You'd better get me inside before I expire in this heat," his father snapped. "Where's your mind, boy?"

I took the bags hastily off Journey's wrist before his father caught a Walgreens bag of prescriptions right to the face. Journey gave me a nod of thanks before he took the handles of the wheelchair and began pushing Jack up the walk. I pitched in to help get the chair up the porch steps. Jack didn't argue, which let us know how much his earlier display of independence had tired him out.

Once we had him on the porch safely, Journey sent me a grateful smile. "Thanks for your help."

The fading sunlight caught his eyes, turning them into molten gold like some big cat in the Sahara. I looked at that little sprinkling of freckles on his nose. I'd kissed those freckles so many times. And that wide, generous mouth, which now had my full attention. Just a single step forward and I could have his lips against mine.

I wanted to take that step.

A little dumbstruck at how much I wanted him, I blinked and took a step backward instead. "Um, yeah, of course."

Jack hid a guffaw behind a cough. "Good God, you two."

Journey sent him a glare as I turned red. "You know, someone killed Grumpy Care Bear. They don't talk about it, but everyone knows that's what happened."

I laughed as Jack shrugged a *what're you gonna do* kind of shrug. I put the Walgreens bags on his lap, and he nodded in thanks. "Do I smell chicken?" he asked hopefully.

"You always smell chicken. You're like a hound dog for fried foods." Journey turned to me. "You should stay for dinner. I'm making tom kha gai."

"What the hell is that?" Jack demanded.

"It's soup, Dad."

"Jesus, JJ," Jack complained. "Have you ever heard of chicken noodle? What have I done to deserve this?"

"Plenty." Journey's mouth twitched with amusement. "Hang on, Cam. Let me get him inside. It's probably a prosecutable offense to inflict him on innocent bystanders for this long."

As the door closed behind them, I heard Jack demand, "And just what does *that* mean? Paul at the barbershop said I was a *delight*."

"He's ninety-two years old. He also said that to a chair," Journey informed him.

I chuckled as Jack gasped in outrage.

The next time the door opened, Journey came out with Biscuit, who was wearing a pink leash and halter. She'd been to the groomer recently and looked all kinds of adorable. She'd been shaved down low, probably because she had been too tangled for a puppy cut. The top had been left long and it was currently pulled back in a little bow, like a little blond ponytail.

Despite Journey's initial apprehension that Kona might eat his dog, we found that they got along like two peas in a pod. Two suspicious peas in a pod. They eyed each other quite a bit, but there was no hostility. Now, they mostly ignored each other.

I didn't know what I'd expected from Mr. Commitmentphobe, but this love affair with Biscuit wasn't it. He'd already brought her into my office twice for "illnesses"—both of which had been gas-related. Biscuit certainly knew how to clear a room, but Journey didn't seem to mind. He was so gone over that dog it was unreal.

I guess it was only people he had a problem committing to.

"Aren't you the sweetest little Biscuit," I said to her with a smile.

"I've changed my mind about that name. She hasn't been presenting like a Biscuit."

"Presenting... like a biscuit?"

"Exactly. She's not the least bit flaky." He shook his head. "She's quite focused and smart. And vibrant, which is why we're going with Skittles for now."

I chuckled. "I'll make sure to change the name tag on her file."

He peered up at me. "Are you ready?"

There just wasn't a chance I was going to say no. I nodded, and we set off a few moments later, Skittles walking slightly ahead and Kona walking to the other side, so they could ignore each other thoroughly. Journey's arm slightly bumped against mine.

This was stupidly, dangerously close to the vision I'd always had of our future, once his brothers hadn't needed him so much and things were settled down. I hadn't known all the particulars of what I wanted things to look like, but he and I had certainly done a lot of walking our dogs together after work.

"How were the Hendersons? Did they check out to adopt Rebecca?" At my negative headshake, he snorted. "Why am I not surprised?"

"I felt like they were in it for the novelty," I said with a frown. "They just weren't the right family for her."

"She's a raccoon, honey, not a newborn."

I glanced his way, but he was busy reining in Skittles as she tried to take off after a lizard. I wasn't sure he was even aware he'd used the endearment, and it wasn't the first time. Maybe I wasn't the only one having a hard time drawing a line between friends and... more. I decided not to address it, but only because I didn't want to make things awkward and *not* because I didn't want him to stop.

"She's a living creature," I said, "and she's been through so much. She deserves a good forever home."

He chuckled softly. "You're something else."

"What?"

"Why don't you just admit that you're keeping her? And Kona? And those two chinchillas you brought home last week?"

"They're all just temporary guests," I informed him starchily.

"Hotel Foster seems more like Hotel California. You can check-in, but you never leave."

He was not the least bit funny, and I poked him in the side. "Whatever."

"All right, then. If you're so determined to get them adopted, then you should know that I finished touching up the photos I took of the chinchillas last week. They came out wonderfully." He smiled. "Should I send them to Bailey to list on the website?"

"Send them to me," I said quickly. "I'll handle it."

His mouth twitched. "Sure you will."

At least he didn't laugh in my face. I'd count that as a win. "Did you really finish their pictures, or were you just baiting me?"

"A little of both." He reached over to pat my cheek. "Bailey liked them so much that she wants me to take some pictures of the foster dogs."

"Oh, you don't have to do that."

"I want to. We were spitballing some ideas last night, and she wants to do a spotlight on senior dogs that I think would be pretty cool."

I smiled. His enthusiasm was pretty cool, too. "You get just as excited taking pictures of shelter dogs as you do of taking pictures of a cheetah."

"Taking pictures of incredible things is easy. Making people see how incredible normal things can be is where the real challenge begins."

And with that, he launched into a more thorough explanation of what he meant. Very thorough. He lost me somewhere around Art Wolfe and Brian Skerry, but I wasn't bored in the least. I could probably watch him read the entire US Tax Code Guide and ask for more. He got really animated, his cheeks pink and eyes sparkling with excitement about f-stops and defining angles and... whatever-the-fuck else he was talking about.

We'd walked several blocks and reached the park before he wound down. I saw the moment realization hit him that he'd talked the entire way. He flushed adorably. "Sorry. Here I am just going on and on."

"I like hearing you talk."

"Still, I don't want to talk your ear off like that guy on your date."

"What guy?"

"Carter," he said with a frown as he gave Skittles the full length of her leash to run. Instead, she sat on her little butt and looked up at him. With a sigh, he started walking and she followed. "I just remember looking at you and wondering if you'd actually fallen asleep with your eyes open."

"Oh. *Oh*, right," I said as I winced. Talk about no fireworks. I shouldn't have to jog my memory about a man I'd been out with three times. "Carter."

"Yeah, him." He seemed unconcerned that I had the memory of a goldfish as he sent me a casual glance. "You ever go out with him again?"

"Yep. One more time." I tried to school my expression, so as not to be rude to the absent Carter, but it was hard holding back the grimace.

I might as well not have bothered. Journey's eyebrows shot up. "He had to be better than gazpacho soup guy."

I paused. "You know, you certainly have a way of putting things into perspective."

"I'm just saying." I expected him to drop it, but he pressed on. "What was so wrong with him?"

"Nothing I can put my finger on specifically. He just wasn't what I was looking for."

"That's vague."

"Well, sometimes you just know. I mean, he's always on the phone a lot, checking this or that, or posting something on social media."

"What else?"

"He seemed to have a lot on his plate with work and his kid. If you can't make time during the early stages of the relationship, that's a bad sign. It only goes downhill from there."

Journey's mouth twitched like he wanted to laugh. "And?"

"And he was really into astrology and kept nodding to himself when I did something that matched certain aspects of my sign. Like I'd say I didn't enjoy doing something, and he'd nod and murmur, *well, of course you don't. You're a Leo.*"

This time he did laugh. "You remind me of John."

I frowned. I liked John, of course. In fact, of all the brothers, I probably saw him the most. His daughter had a couple of hamsters—Cheddar and Monterrey—that were regulars of the Happy Paws clinic. Monterrey liked to eat things he shouldn't, and Cheddar was such a freaking follower. So yeah, John was good people, but he wore a lot of plaid and communicated mostly in grunt form. I didn't know if I was digging the whole *you remind me of John* thing.

"Care to explain that?" I asked.

"John always had a very clear idea of the woman he wanted to end up with. Not so much what she looked like, but what she would do and how she would act. He had a vision of this Gisele Bündchen lookalike who acted like June Cleaver and fucked like a Dannica Downs."

I furrowed my brow. "Who?"

"Some porn star he was obsessed with when he was younger."

Talk about something I didn't need to know about John. "Yikes."

"Yikes indeed," he said, his eyes twinkling. "John taught me the lifelong lesson about knocking on doors before you open them. No matter what. Knock hard and long, and if someone says, *I need a minute,* you fucking give him that minute."

"My dad taught me that lesson with one of his ex-wives. I was hoping with time the trauma would fade, but clearly it hasn't." I shivered in memory. "We should start a support group for people who've seen too much. Our mascot will just be a pair of googly eyes."

He laughed, reining Skittles back in as she started barking at another dog. "We should probably head back."

I checked my watch and realized he was right. It was getting late. As we turned and started walking in the direction we'd come, Journey picked up his thoroughly forgotten train of thought. "My point was that John's wife, Mindy, isn't anything like the person he thought he wanted. She's pretty and sweet, but not even close to the Stepford-wife blow-up doll he seemed to be looking for."

"And?"

"*And* that's because he was looking for an idea. Not a person. He thought he knew exactly what he wanted. Then he met Mindy and all those ideas went out the window."

It was so close to what Bailey had been saying that it was a bit unnerving. Searching for love without parameters was rather frightening. "I don't see what's so wrong with looking for someone who wants the same things."

"It's not wrong, but sometimes you can find happiness in unexpected places." I stared at him for so long that he started to look a little unsure. "Not that I'm anyone to give life advice."

I glanced at a familiar Jeep as we passed and blinked when I realized I was passing my driveway. Fuck, our walks always seemed too short. I wasn't a fiend for exercise, I just... liked his company. I didn't realize I'd walked him clear to the door until we were standing on the porch again, like a goddamned date. I blushed.

He seemed to realize it, too. "What the hell are we doing?" he asked quietly.

"I'm not sure what you mean," I hedged.

"Cameron."

My name on his lips made me feel weak. "I don't know. I just know that every time I'm around you, I want more."

"I offered you 'more.'" The look he gave me could've melted plastic. "Did you change your mind?"

His *more* was not my *more*.

I blew out a breath. Getting involved with him would be stupid. We were just looking for different things, and we didn't even live in the same state. Most of the time, we weren't even in the same damn country. It was already hard enough to make relationships work without all that added pressure. Good Lord, look at me already. *Relationship*. My ex offered me a quick, fun, dirty fuck, and here I was writing *Journey + Cameron* in my notebook.

I shook my head slowly. "I don't think it's a good idea."

"No 'think' about it." He gave me a wry smile. "It's not."

I chuckled. "Look, we've already been there, done that. I'm looking for something real. You're looking for Mr. Right Now."

"Yep." He didn't look the least bit sorry about that. "Mr. Fuck Me Right Now."

"Please." I groaned. "If you care about me at all, don't make me picture it."

I needed little encouragement to go down that road. I had a very clear memory of the last time we'd fucked. If I'd known it was going to *be* the last time, I would've made it last longer. It wouldn't have been just a perfunctory fuck before going to work. I would've made sure to rim him first. Sink to my knees behind him and bury my tongue in that perfect little bubble ass. Getting rimmed was one of his favorite activities, and he usually wound up begging me for it, bent over with his cheeks spread so I could get to him better. Sometimes I could make him come like that, too, with just my tongue buried in that tight hole. He would fuck my fist desperately as I worked him over—

"You're picturing it right now, aren't you?"

"What?" I croaked. I glanced over to find Journey looking at me, a slight smile on his lips. There was no hiding that I was stiff as a pole. "Well, you made me."

"I'm guessing your hand is going to be very busy tonight," he teased.

Busy? My hand was going to take out a restraining order on me. I sighed. "I'd better get going."

"Would you like me to bring you some soup tomorrow?"

I chuckled at his innocent look. "Advancing your campaign to get in my pants?"

"I'm offended." His eyes sparkled. "I also want in your shirt. If memory serves, you have nice abs. But I need a refresher just to be sure."

Cameron in his twenties had nice abs. Cameron nearing forty had okay abs, but I was still willing to help him with his research. "I want you." I sighed a little wistfully. "Stop telling me that I can have you."

He made a sound of amusement. "I'm not going to be around all that long," he said. "You'd better make up your mind quickly."

Yeah, that was part of the problem.

13

JOURNEY

After my walk with Cameron, I was more than happy about the distraction that was my family. I started with plucking a fried drumstick right out of my father's hand. The cursing had practically turned the air blue, and no, he didn't give a fuck that there were kids at the table. We finally compromised—at least, that's what I called peeling all the skin off and putting the meat on his plate. He blistered the air again.

Kids today. I shook my head at the missed opportunity. If they'd had the foresight to create a swear jar, they'd be set up for college by now. Too bad, so sad. My agent called, which gave me an excellent excuse to hide in the kitchen. Frankly, there's only so many times you can listen to someone use the word *motherfucker*.

I put in my AirPods to take the call while preparing my soup. Now that I knew Cameron was going to eat some of it, I had to bring my *A+* game and that involved chopping the veggies properly and not rushing each stage, so that the flavors could develop. I wasn't too concerned with my sudden desire to impress him. It was perfectly normal to want to impress someone you wanted to fuck clean through a wall with your cooking prowess. I think.

Boz sighed. "Are you even listening to me?"

"Of course I'm listening. I have my AirPods in." I tossed in some chopped ginger and gave the pot a little stir. "If I could hear you any better, you'd be inside my freaking skull."

"There's hearing me and then there's listening," he said patiently. "What do you think about my show idea?"

"I don't want to do an adventure show." I felt smug as I was able to prove that I was listening and burst his bubble all in one breath. I didn't like a lot of attention—that's why being behind a camera was perfect for me. "Why on earth would I want to be on TV? It's like you don't know me at all."

"You like to travel, you take pictures, and your name is Journey, for God's sake," Boz huffed. "An adventure show is pretty much your destiny."

"If I say I'll think about it, will you leave me alone?"

I could hear his shrug. "Possibly."

"Possibly, he says," I grumbled. "Not getting harassed is supposed to be one of the benefits of having you so very far away."

"Yeah, about that," he said pointedly. "Just when are you coming back to Seattle?"

"I'm staying for the entire summer," I said as I stirred. "I told you that."

"Okay," he said slowly. "Forgive me for having questions. This was all kind of out of the blue."

"Well, strokes aren't big on giving notice," I said dryly. "It's hard to update your calendar properly."

"Don't be such a sarcastic asshole," he said, "even though I'm pretty sure that's your default state. I'm just making sure you're not thinking of staying."

"Of course I'm not moving back here," I insisted, a little surprised at how strange those words sounded on my lips. "Don't talk crazy."

"Good."

The silence that fell between us was a little awkward, which was unusual. Boz and I were normally on the same page regarding my career. But I just... I didn't want to talk about the future right now. I wanted to cook my damn soup and enjoy time with my family. I didn't want to talk about work or going back to Seattle. I still had things I wanted to do here.

I wanted more paddleboarding with my brothers. More chatting with Laura while I "helped" her bake, which was code for eating batter and dough when she wasn't looking. I wanted more nights with my dad in his recliner watching TV, and me on the couch working on my travel book. More of me fixing things with him watching over my shoulder, telling me how to do what I already knew how to do, and irritating me to death. Oh wait, that's a different list—the Let's Have Fucking Less of That list.

And then there was Cam. Seeing how he'd been very clear that nothing was going to happen between us, he probably shouldn't be on my *more* list. But I wanted more flirty walks in the park with him. More of those intense green eyes staring at me when he thought I wasn't looking. More of his shy smiles and kind nature. More of the way he got flustered when he was around me. I wanted more of everything. *More, more, more.*

I grimaced. I had to be careful. I was starting to sound like that blue girl in *Charlie and the Chocolate Factory*. And we all knew what happened to that poor bastard.

I finally broke the silence, since Boz had clearly been struck mute. "Look, I need to get back to making dinner."

I tossed out the excuse like I needed both hands to churn butter. It wasn't my best dodge, but he sighed and let me off the hook. "I'm sending you a sample itinerary of what your first season on the show would look like."

"Boz...."

"First stop, Thailand."

"Boz!"

"Just *think* about it."

"I will."

He was satisfied with my begrudging agreement, and we got off the phone a moment later. I removed my AirPods and carefully put them back in their case—they were pretty much the most losable thing I owned.

When I turned around, Mark was standing in the doorway, an inscrutable look on his face, his daughter Olivia on his hip. She was in a yellow sundress that was oh-so-cute. She was trouble in chestnut pigtails, yes, but cute.

"That Boz?"

It was clear Mark already knew, so I didn't bother to answer. I wiped my hands on a dish towel and walked over to him, so I could take Olivia. He frowned but let me have her. I settled her against my hip, all heavy and warm. I tugged one of her pigtails, and she frowned at me. "That's not nice, Uncle JJ."

"Sorry, Livy." I wasn't sorry in the least and to prove it, I tugged at the other pigtail. She giggled.

"I guess I shouldn't be surprised that you're already itching to get gone," he said, clearly spoiling for an argument.

"I'm not in the mood," I said, not looking his way.

Olivia didn't seem to notice the tension as she gave me a gap-toothed smile. "Uncle JJ?"

"Yes, sweetheart?"

"Will you come to see my art at the center?"

"Of course I will," I said, chucking her on the chin.

Her eyes lit up. "Maybe you could even teach my class!"

I realized then that I had no idea of several things: how old she was now, what kind of art she was doing, and what kind of center she was talking about. But in my defense, kids *did* grow fast. And there were a *lot* of them in the Sutton brood. Between Mark and John and Matt, they had like, eight kids. I remembered faces, nicknames, and for the most part, ages. I couldn't be counted on to remember hobbies, too, could I?

"Um...." I glanced at Mark for help, but he was too busy dipping a spoon in my soup. "Mark? A little help here, please?"

"They cut the art program at her school a year ago. So now, people volunteer once a week to teach a class at the center," he said distractedly, blowing on the spoon. "It's not a strict medium. You just arrange for an activity for the kids and make sure they don't kill each other for a couple of hours."

"That sounds more like a parent thing." I was more than willing to tool around her classroom and make the appropriate "oohs" and "aahs", but this was something else entirely. Since Mark was too busy burning his tongue on my soup, I directed my attention at Olivia. "Maybe we could do something just the two of us."

My father came hobbling in and made a beeline for the fridge. I watched him with a gimlet eye to make sure he didn't get anything that he wasn't supposed to have. When I was sure he was only getting sparkling water, I looked back down at Olivia.

Her delicate brow furrowed. "I want you to meet my friends."

"Maybe some other—"

"I love you," she said winningly, and I narrowed my eyes at her winsome expression. She had the trademark Sutton blue eyes and she knew how to work 'em. Not to mention, anyone who didn't melt when a kid said 'I love you' was a monster. It was like the Grinch litmus test.

"I don't know, Livy," I said doubtfully.

"I *love* you," she repeated with more emphasis, clearly puzzled why her kid magic wasn't working.

"I love you, too, sweetheart." I lowered her to the floor because I might not remember how old she was, but I damn sure knew how heavy she was. My back had started to voice complaints, and I was too old not to listen.

"You should do it," my father advised. "Anything is better than having you underfoot all the damned time."

I decided not to address him categorizing my cooking of his meals, cleaning of his clothes, and making sure he didn't accidentally off himself with medication as 'being underfoot.' If I did respond, he would probably have something smart to say in kind, and then I'd have to finally choke him to death. There's a place they have for people who do things like that. He shuffled back into the living room, oblivious to my internal debate about strangulation and legal strategies to get away with it.

Olivia tugged at my shirt, and I looked down right into a glare. "I said I love you."

"I'm not deaf, kid," I said dryly, plucking my shirt out of her chubby little fingers. "I'll give you and your band of ragamuffins two hours of finger painting, and that's it."

"We want to take photos like you do," she said slyly, proving that you could never be too young to have a plan and execute that plan with an assassin's accuracy.

"So you've run this past your merry band? I should've known." I squinted down at her, working the logistics in my head. A few disposable cameras and traipsing around the park for an hour, I could do. "One hour and we'll do the pictures."

"You've got a deal." She smiled and skipped off toward the living room.

Outmaneuvered by a... how old was she again? "You're like four, right?" I called out.

"Six," Mark informed me, busy dipping his spoon back in the pot. "But nice try."

"Your daughter is a charlatan. And could you stop double-dipping? It's gross." I suddenly understood the desire to rap someone's knuckles with a wooden spoon. "I promised I'd bring some to Cam, and I don't want him getting your cooties."

"Well, this is unexpectedly tasty for something I can't pronounce." He paused. "Since when does Foss get top billing around here?"

I would've loved to wipe that smug little smile off his face. "Unlike you Neanderthals, he's interested in something that isn't a hamburger," I said with a sniff.

"Well, well, well." He eyed me with interest. "I didn't know it was like *that*."

"It's not like that"—I paused—"whatever that means."

"You're *cooking* for him," he said gleefully. "That's so adorable."

"I am not," I said hotly. "You're lucky I can't find a wooden spoon."

"Hey, Laura, come in here," he called out. "Journey's got a crush, and it's so adorable it freakin' hurts to watch."

Laura hustled into the kitchen and she wasn't alone. Mindy practically hip-checked her out of the way like a championship hockey player, trying to get to me first. *Oh God, I'm gonna be in the newsletter,* was my last thought before they mobbed me with questions. I did my best to fend them off, insisting that Cam and I were *not* getting back together again.

Cameron had made his position on that issue clear, so despite what they seemed to think, I wasn't lying. And so what if I was starting to wish that we were getting back together? I stirred my soup vigorously. No one asked me about all that.

14

CAMERON

I generally prided myself on doing the right thing, but lately, I'd been trouncing all over that policy. I couldn't seem to stay away from Journey. Our nightly walks had continued. We'd also taken to meeting in the mornings for coffee. He'd started bringing me some of his culinary creations for lunch, which, despite what his family seemed to think, were pretty amazing.

I lingered near the front desk in the clinic, pretending to look over the chart of the patient who'd just left. Bailey glanced up at me with a puzzled smile. I mentally projected the idea of her being very, very thirsty. *Coffee*, I tried beaming her way. *You need coffee now.* She scratched her ear and went back to typing.

I huffed. There was no avoiding it—Journey was coming by in a few minutes to deliver me lunch, and she was going to witness it. I had no chance of playing it cool. Every time I had a conversation with him, I turned into a teenager trying to talk to a crush. My version of EL James' book would be *Fifty Shades of What the Hell is Wrong With Him?*

As if I'd conjured Journey up, the door opened and he came in, his little dog under his arm. He was wearing some distressed jeans and a gray T-shirt, his hair a little messy as usual and falling in his face. My fingers itched to touch, and I gripped the clipboard reflexively.

He greeted Bailey and me, and at the sound of his voice, Kona came bounding out of the back like her best friend had come calling. He laughed as she barreled into his legs. His smile was pretty much the thing I'd been waiting for all day and I hadn't even known it. He leaned down to pet Kona, who soaked up the attention.

"He's not here for you," I informed her as he rubbed her ears.

He laughed and held out a Tupperware container. "As promised. Let me know if you like it. The family won't touch it, so I have plenty."

"They don't know what they're missing." My stomach rumbled as I took the container eagerly. It smelled strongly of garlic and spices. "This is great, thank you."

"What is it?" Bailey asked curiously.

"An Ecuadorian stew. Seco de chivo." At her blank look, he clarified, "It's not quite the same because I didn't have any goat, but I made do."

I was willing to try pretty much anything he put in front of me, but I had to admit, I was *exceedingly* glad he couldn't get his hands on any goat. "I can't wait to try it," I said as I checked the clock on the wall. *Damn.* I was disappointed to find I was still a few hours away from lunch.

"It's nice of you to stop by," Bailey said. "Again."

"I was in the area," he said, stumbling a little as Kona tried to wind through his legs. She often forgot that she was closer to wolf than cat on the species scale. "The place my father goes to for OT is right down the street."

I could feel Bailey's eyes on me, and I wished her into the cornfield. Not forever. Just for the next hour or so, or until she forgot about whatever vibes Journey and I were putting out. I bulged my eyes at her and hoped she understood that to mean, *don't embarrass me.* After a little huff, she inclined her head. Luckily, Journey didn't seem to notice our wordless exchange.

I pointed at his tiny dog, who was wearing a black shirt that read *Security.* She'd been Pumpkin, Scooter, and Peanut in the past two weeks, and I was almost afraid to ask what name he'd landed on now. "So?"

"Fifi," he said promptly. "That's Fifi LaRue to you peasants."

I chuckled. "For God's sake, will you settle on a name already?"

His phone rang and he glanced at the screen before letting out a groan. "I gotta go. If His Majesty has to wait over one minute, he has a complete meltdown." He put his phone on the counter to let Fifi down and then spent a few seconds adjusting her harness. "I'm stopping by Laura's bakery on the way home. Want me to get you something sweet?"

My ears burned. We both knew what kind of "something sweet" I'd like, and it wasn't baked goods. "Yeah."

He grinned cheekily because that's what you do when you're a walking temptation. "See ya tonight."

I knew better than to think Bailey would let any of that go. Sure enough, the door had barely swung shut when she cleared her throat. I pretended to be busy looking at my next patient's chart. She cleared her throat again.

I was about to offer her some Robitussin when she finally gave up on being subtle. "That was certainly interesting."

"Was it?"

"Indeed. Of course, I've heard talk about your little nightly walks in the park, but I just assumed that was the town rumor mill working overtime. Now that I've seen you two together, I guess Gertie from the dry cleaner was right, and Madge owes her ten bucks."

I sighed. "You people need a hobby."

"I don't see you denying it."

"What would be the point? Clearly, the *National Enquirer* already has the story and the pictures."

"So give me the details," she said eagerly as Kona bumped her head against my leg and tried to jump up on me.

"There are no details," I said exasperatedly, pushing Kona back down on the floor with a firm reprimand. She gave me the saddest face she could muster, which worked to make me feel monster-like. I reminded myself it was for her own good. "We're just friends."

"Just friends," she repeated.

"That's right." A bit of tan caught my eye, and I watched Mr. Pickles pick his way down the counter on quiet paws. I hoped he was in one of his *I'm About to Knock All This Shit Off This Desk* moods.

"Just friends who walk their dogs together every night."

"That's correct."

"And just friends who bring one another lunch and desserts."

I eyeballed her smug face. "Is there a point to you reiterating everything we already know?"

"No, I just wanted to talk about your Victorian dates of chaste walks through the park." She smiled innocently. "Four more years, and you might be ready to hold his hand."

I gritted my teeth. "Nothing is going to happen with him. *That* I can promise you."

Her face fell as she dropped her teasing tone. "Cam, I know there's a history there that makes things difficult. But pretending something isn't happening between you isn't doing you any good."

"We already tried it once," I finally said. "It didn't work out."

"Yeah, and you were both in your early twenties. I tried a lot of things in my early twenties that didn't work."

Yeah, I'd seen the photographic evidence. "Bangs," I muttered.

"What?"

"Nothing," I said quickly.

She narrowed her eyes. "My point is that you're not the same person you were back then, and neither is he." When I didn't respond, she went on. "You think ignoring how you feel about him is going to make it go away?"

"I'm not pining over Journey, for crying out loud." I took the intake form of the next patient, a cockatoo named Gary. "But I'm looking for something different this time around, if that's all right with you. Someone older. Someone more—"

"Boring."

"Settled," I continued doggedly. "Someone ready for—"

"Death," she volunteered cheerily.

"Commitment." I glared. "Remind me why I don't fire you again?"

"Because I'm efficient as hell, and I work for peanuts. You're still in love with him," she said. "Admit it."

"I am not. He's the absolute last thing I need in my life."

Her eyes widened, presumably from the vehemence of my words. Granted, I was harsher than I should've been, maybe because I didn't want to admit just how appealing I found him. "Cam," she began.

"I'm serious." I was a little done with everyone in my life trying to push Journey and me together. Especially since I wanted him so damn badly. It was like not being able to have sugar and everyone making it their business to shove homemade cheesecake in your face. "He's not someone you can trust your heart with, and I don't plan to go down that road again."

I checked her face to make sure she got what I was saying. Other than the fact that her eyes suddenly seemed a lot larger than usual, I couldn't get a read on her expression. "Cam," she said urgently.

"No, I mean it. Stop suggesting it. I'm not going there again, especially with him. Let it go, okay?" My back suddenly felt quite prickly, and I understood why Bailey suddenly seemed to be having an eye problem. The sound of a tiny dog sneeze confirmed my suspicions. I turned around to see Journey standing there, one eyebrow raised.

"I left my phone," he said, picking it up off the counter. There was a certain quiet dignity there. He scratched Kona's ears while I stood there awkwardly, embarrassed down to my toes. He was the king of graciousness right now, and I was an ass.

I winced. "I didn't mean—"

He waved a hand. "It's all good. I'll see you around."

Good to know I could still pick out a lie when I heard one. He would not be seeing me around, and anything we'd had going on between us was done and dusted. *Just like you wanted,* my subconscious gloated. I watched as he walked out, his tiny dog trailing behind.

"Fuck," I groaned.

Bailey shook her head. "I told you he was standing there."

I ran a hand through my hair, resisting the urge to pull hard.

"How is saying my name with varying degrees of intensity telling me he was standing there?"

"What do you care anyway?" Her voice was deceptively casual. "You said you're over him."

"I am, but I didn't want to hurt his feelings."

Bailey's phone rang just as she opened her mouth, which was damned good timing. She held up a finger warningly in my direction as if telling me not to move, but then she glanced at the screen and let out a gasp. "The florist!"

She got up so fast, Mr. Pickles let out a startled meow. He gave her a dirty look and sauntered off. Bailey didn't seem to notice as she hustled down the hallway. I only caught, "I would never ask you for peonies. I don't even know what they are!"

The back door slammed.

I looked down at the Tupperware container in my hand. He'd written *eat up, buttercup* on a piece of tape on the top. There wouldn't be any more casual flirting. No more... possibilities. I didn't know why that made me feel so bereft. I took a few more moments to reflect on the state of my idiocy in general before I got on with my day. Work to be done, patients to be seen.

Just like always.

15

CAMERON

My week was unusually busy and capped off with a difficult surgery for Rory, a favorite patient of mine. He'd been attacked by another dog in the dog park and had gotten the worst of it. I wasn't surprised because he was a gentle giant and didn't have an aggressive bone in his body. According to his devastated owners, he'd spent most of the attack cowering and whimpering.

I was supposed to get out of here and leave his care to Charles, who would stay overnight, but it was hard to leave him. The bandage across his abdomen covering his incision still looked clean, so that was good. I squatted down in front of his cage in the kennel room, rubbing a hand over the drowsy goldendoodle's head. Usually I couldn't get a hand near Rory without being licked to death, but now he just stared at the wall of his cage blearily.

"You did great, buddy," I told him softly.

His eyes closed and then popped open again as he tried to fight off the lingering anesthesia, but he didn't have a chance against the drugs and drifted off.

"Why are you trying to take my job?" Charles asked from behind me.

I turned to see him shaking his silver head. "You know I trust you.

It's just hard to leave him like this. Rory's been a patient of mine since he was a puppy."

"I know, but he's going to be okay." He gave me a fond smile. "I hear he has a great vet."

I chuckled. "Well, when you put it that way."

I stood, my joints creaking. I always felt that way after surgery. Being stooped over for hours on end took its toll. I needed a hot shower, and I had to get home to Kona. Bailey had dropped her off at my house and given her food and water, but Kona hated changes in her routine. She expected my ass to be on the couch by a certain time, and I didn't plan to disappoint.

Rory whimpered in his sleep, and I hesitated at the door. Charles gave me a little push. "Out," he said, "and get something to eat, too. Real food, not take out."

"Who's the boss here again?" I grumbled, but I knew better than to disagree.

I stopped at the market on the way home. As I coasted into a parking spot, I noticed a familiar Mustang a few spots over. I briefly debated not going into the store at all. By unspoken agreement, Journey and I had been avoiding each other. Ignoring each other? I wasn't sure. Being neighbors made that tedious and, not to mention, ridiculous. We'd gotten through a broken engagement—we could get over a few careless words. Granted, they were *my* careless words, but still. I owed him an apology, and hopefully, we could get back on track as friends. Just friends.

I got a basket and started to shop, keeping an eye out for him the entire time. Much as a hunter who finally set his sights on his prey, I finally got my chance. We came face-to-face as I rounded the corner of the dry goods aisle. Startled, I went to one side and knocked a display with my hip.

"Oh shit," I blurted, putting one hand on the frantically quivering rack. I could only hope I wasn't about to end a long day by chasing Pringles cans as they rolled down the aisles. Luckily, the display gave one last shiver and the tower of cans settled down.

I turned to Journey, who thankfully hadn't used my distraction to disappear again. The look he gave me was decidedly cool. I searched for something to say and came up with something brilliant.

I gestured at his basket. "Cooking?"

Nice one, Cam. You've only had a week to come up with that amazing icebreaker.

He clearly wasn't in the mood to toss me a bone as he started walking. "Yep."

I nodded and followed... because that's what you do when someone doesn't want to talk to you. I looked in his basket, which was overfilled with fresh ingredients. "Looks good." I winced. More inane chatter. *You don't even know what he's making. How can it look good?*

"Hopefully, it will be," he said. "I only need to find the sesame oil."

"There aren't many products like that here. Brannigan's on Third is more of a specialty store. They'd probably have it."

"Thanks."

He headed for the checkout counter. I became aware that I was still following him around with my sad little basket of three items because I hadn't even finished my shopping. But I couldn't seem to stop. And since there was only one other person in line, I probably needed to stop stalling and apologize. "Look, about the other day—"

"Forget about it," he said absently, perusing the candy bars next to the register. "I already have."

Molly, our cashier, gave us a friendly smile as she finished with her other customer. "Hey, Cam. And Journey, it's good to see you again. How's Jack?"

"Doing better every day," he said, putting his items on the belt. "Thanks for asking."

He put a divider at the end of his groceries, right behind a rolling cabbage that understood the end was near and was trying to make a break for it. I sat my basket after the divider without unloading it.

"I was just telling my mama the other day how thrilled he must be to have you around after you being gone so long." Molly squinted at him. "You stickin' around awhile, hun?"

If I hadn't been staring at him like a crazed stalker, I would have missed the slight tightening of his jaw before he evened out his expression. "We'll see," he said noncommittally.

She turned her attention to my basket with a dismayed expression. "Cam, is that all you're getting?"

I glanced down at my pineapple, box of crackers, and half pound of deli ham. I nodded, and with a shrug, she resumed swiping Journey's items. I could hardly tell her I'd stopped in the middle of shopping because the object of my stalking affections had wandered by, which fucking reminded me of something important. He was nearly halfway finished with his checkout, and I hadn't apologized yet.

I lowered my voice a bit. "So, we're okay, right?"

"Cameron." His voice was exasperated. "Yes. It's okay. I've been turned down before. Although, maybe not as many times with the same person. You should start punching my loyalty card. One more and I get a free frozen yogurt."

I snorted. "I haven't been that bad."

"You have. But I get it. Message received, loud and clear." Done with our conversation, he tossed two KitKats on the conveyer belt.

All right, I'd done what I'd come to do. No need to keep talking. I shifted from one foot to the other. "I've missed you on our walks."

And just like that, his hold on his blank expression slipped. Irritation wreathed his brow as he stared at me—hard. "Cameron."

I winced. "I know, I know."

"I'm trying to figure out what your damage is," he said quietly, but no less intense for the lack of volume. "You said you didn't want me to pursue you, and I'm not. You were extremely vocal that you don't want to go there again, *especially with him*. I accept that."

I started to get a little annoyed. He was acting like this was easy for me, and it wasn't. "I remember what I said."

"Now you've hunted me down to apologize, and I said we're good," he steamrolled on. "What else do you want?"

"I don't know."

"Don't you?"

I want you. That answer was pretty easy. I just didn't know if I could *have* him that way without taking us back to a place better left forgotten.

Molly was doing a poor job of pretending not to listen. She was so into our conversation that she rung up the cabbage twice. Blushing, she called for the manager. We waited in silence as the manager sauntered over, in no particular hurry, and keyed in his code. When he finished, Journey paid and left without speaking to me again, his arms laden with bags. I didn't blame him. What else was there to say? Either I was in or I was out.

Molly widened blue mascara-rimmed eyes at me. "Are you just going to let him go?"

I blinked at her. "What do you expect me to do? Physically restrain him?"

"Good Lord, Cameron." She looked appalled at my cluelessness. "Go after him."

Just like that? Was she mad? She hadn't even rung up my items. Judging from the look on her face, she wasn't going to, either. "I can't—"

"Go."

"It's not that simple—"

She waved me off. "Don't make me repeat myself, sugar. Get on, now."

When someone starts talking to you like a mutt digging in the trash, you'd better not argue. Even I knew that. By the time I rushed out in the parking lot, I was relieved to see Journey still loading up the back of his dad's Mustang.

"Need any help?" I offered.

He looked askance at me, brow furrowed as he put the last bag in the tiny trunk. "I think I can handle a couple of bags, Foster."

"Right-o." *Right-o?* I shouldn't be allowed to speak to people—ever. "I guess I'll be seeing you, then."

"We live next door to one another, therefore the likelihood of that is pretty high, yes."

"I don't do hookups," I blurted. "I never have. Especially not with an ex. It just gets messy."

"Good of you to rush over here and tell me that. Again. I'm starting to take it personally." He shut the trunk and not gently either. "And now you owe me a fucking frozen yogurt."

I grabbed his arm before he could turn away and promptly forgot what the hell I was going to say. His skin was warm and soft. I couldn't see the hairs there all that well, probably because he was so fair, but I could feel them under my fingertips. His pulse thrummed at hummingbird speed under my touch. "I wasn't finished."

"Then finish." His voice wasn't that steady, letting me know he was just as affected as I was.

"I can't stop thinking about you. I can't stop remembering how we were... together. I'm making an exception to my own rules."

"An exception for what?"

"An exception for us," I said, frustrated that I wasn't being clear. "Having a little fun."

"Like Poker? I do love Poker."

"You *know* what I mean."

His eyes were amused as he blinked at me innocently. "Do I?"

That rat bastard was going to make me say it. I sighed. "Fun like sex," I said loudly, and someone gasped nearby.

I glanced over to see Mrs. Wallace clutching her purse as she hustled past. I cast my eyes heavenward. I wanted the last five seconds of my life back—immediately.

"She's in my stepmother's gardening club," I said conversationally. "That's not going to bite me in the ass at all."

He bit his lip, clearly trying to keep from laughing. "I want to hear more about this fun sex. Do you have any candidates in mind?"

"I did. But he's kind of a dick." I released his arm reluctantly. "So. How do we do this?"

He smiled, tilting his head, those golden eyes lit by the sun. They looked like warm honey. I'd always loved those damn eyes. A man could get lost in those eyes and never find himself again.

"Well, I was hoping to have you in the parking lot," he said.

I huffed. Too bad those eyes came with that smart mouth.

"Are you busy tonight?" he asked.

"Yeah. Unfortunately. I have to go check on a dog I operated on, and then I have to get home to check on Kona."

"Tomorrow, then," he said easily. "I'll be over around eight o'clock."

I was transfixed by his mouth. It had been a long time since I'd had those lips under mine, and I wanted to rectify that desperately. So, I hit the pause button on overthinking and did what I'd been wanting to do since he got in my Jeep at the airport.

I crushed my mouth to his with zero finesse. He made a startled little noise, his hands flying up to my arms, but he didn't push me away. Instead, we used grizzly bear rules: when someone mauls you, you maul 'em back. He gripped the back of my neck with both hands, his mouth slanting over mine impatiently. I nipped at his bottom lip and that grip tightened painfully.

He slowed things down and softened the kiss. I followed his lead without even thinking as his mouth explored mine, tasting me. Teasing me. Reminding me of what he liked and how fucking good we were together. I felt like I couldn't quite catch my breath, but it wasn't enough to make me stop or pull away.

Fuck breathing. Breathing is for losers.

The sound of a nearby car horn startled us apart. I almost stepped toward him again before I remembered we were in public. "I want you," I said, just in case I hadn't made that perfectly fucking clear.

His eyes sparkled warmly. "Yeah, I think everyone in the Pick-n-Save pretty much got the memo."

I glanced around to find that yeah, we had attracted a *bit* of notice. Pamela, who ran a yoga studio in the plaza, nearly pushed her grocery cart into a garbage can. I had no idea who was manning the register since Molly was peeking out of the automatic doors.

"Sorry," I said. I wasn't sorry in the least.

"I want to get fucked," Journey murmured, "but maybe not on the hood of my father's car." And now it was an uncomfortable situation in my pants again. I barely held in a whimper. He titled his head to the side, considering me for a moment. "You're picturing it, aren't you?"

"You made me," I said defensively, trying to get my dick under control.

He chuckled before getting in the car. "See you at eight, Foster. That's if you don't change your mind."

As if there was a chance of that.

16

CAMERON

I woke up the next morning with a stomach full of nerves.

When I checked the forecast, the weatherman predicted a ninety percent chance of me backing out. I spent much of the day in that strange place between anxiety and anticipation. I thought about canceling no less than five times, but my dick kept hanging up the phone. My nervousness bled over into my job, distracting me and making me an absolute butterfingers for most of the day. Around four in the afternoon, Bailey got sick of me and shooed me out the door.

No matter. I had plenty to do before eight o'clock. Logically, I knew there were only a few things I *needed* to do—shower and make sure I changed the bedsheets—but in Cameron-world, that list got a little bit longer.

I started with feeding Kona and Becca and the chinchillas. Then I let Kona out in the backyard to run while I buzzed around in the kitchen and threw together a quick sheet-pan dinner. The pork chops and root veggies could do their things while I got the house—and myself—ready.

A little "sprucing up" of my already tidy house turned into spring cleaning. At one point, I went full-on crazy and dragged out the steam mop. I didn't know much about having casual sex, but I knew a steam mop wasn't supposed to be involved. By the time I was done, everything was sparkly fresh and the house smelled overwhelmingly of PineSol. I opened a few windows and turned on some fans while Kona gave me dirty looks.

That dog truly needed to learn how to let bygones be bygones.

"What's done is done," I informed her as I headed for the bedroom. She trailed behind me, nails clicking on the hardwood floor.

My sudden desire to clean like royalty's arrival was imminent had cut into my time, so I made my shower quick. With a towel tucked around my waist and my hair still dripping, I headed for the closet. Kona tracked my every move, lying on the rug beside the bed. I pulled out the first thing I saw that wasn't workwear—black trousers and a charcoal button-down shirt. I held it out for a minute, wondering if it was a little too dressy. She gave me a skeptical look.

"What?" I asked. "Too much?"

I didn't know what wolf-hybrid speak was for "you're doing the most," but she managed to convey it with just a look. I put the outfit back and tried again with some khakis and another button-down.

Kona panted.

"What's wrong with this?" I demanded. "It's the button-down part, isn't it?"

I finally shut my closet door and went over to my dresser. "We like to call this the *I like you, but I'm not that into you* zone," I informed Kona as I pulled out a pair of jeans and a gray Henley. "So, if he's offended, this is your fault."

After I was dressed, I glanced around the bedroom to make sure everything was in order. I'd changed my sheets and made the bed with so many throw pillows, it could've doubled as Genie's vacation bottle. I took off half the throw pillows, like a sane person, and stashed them in the closet.

I'd put condoms and lube in the top drawer of the nightstand—after opening the brand spanking new box of condoms and taking out a few, just so I wouldn't look too pathetic. All that did was remind me I hadn't had sex in three years, and even then, it hadn't been all that great. People still swiped right for sexless monks, didn't they?

There was a knock at the back door, which brought an abrupt end to my madness. That was unfortunate. Quite frankly, I'd been interested to see what I'd get up to next. Given another thirty minutes alone with my thoughts, I might've started power washing the house.

I opened the door to find Journey standing there, a small bag in his hands. The smile on his face immediately put me at ease. "Sorry I'm late. It was harder than I thought to give the old man the slip. He thinks I'm checking the mailbox."

I barked out a laugh. "Seriously?"

"I didn't say it was a good excuse. I just needed something to get me past Deputy Dog's nose."

"Speaking of dog noses...." I looked at his feet, but apparently he'd left his little companion at home. "Where's Fifi?"

"Sascha," he corrected. "Her name is Sascha now. Last I saw, she was perched on my father's lap, and they were watching TV. Even though he's still pretending he doesn't care for her."

"God forbid Jack should admit to liking a purse-sized dog."

He chuckled. "He's completely gone over her. If you see him around town with Sascha in a satchel, just pretend you don't notice."

He looked good in well-worn, soft-looking Levis and a button-down shirt. He smelled even better. I gave Kona a sideways look as she pushed her way in front of me. *I told you button-down shirts were okay.* That would teach me to take advice from someone whose beauty routine consisted of shaking out her luxurious fur.

"Can I come in?" he finally asked.

I flushed as I realized I was only standing there staring at him. He looked amused as I stepped back to let him in. I closed the door behind us and stood there feeling all kinds of awkward.

I gestured at the bag in his hands. "You didn't have to bring me a gift."

He reached in the bag, plucking out a bone. Kona went on high alert, sitting on her haunches with her ears pricked. "I didn't."

I chuckled at his sly grin. "Bribery? Really?"

"I know how to get on a girl's good side. I was at the boutique shop across town getting some treats for Sascha, and I couldn't resist."

I gave him a look of betrayal. "You've been patronizing the business of my competition?"

"You don't sell fancy-ass dog treats." He didn't look the least bit sorry. "Is she allowed to have this? It's in bone shape, but it's made of oats and honey and carrots."

"Yeah, go right ahead." As he leaned down to give it to her, I hurriedly added, "Just drop it on the floor, though. We're still working on her manners, and I'm sure you need all those fingers."

He dropped the bone like it was on fire, and Kona snapped it up. She trotted off to find a good hiding place to enjoy it, just in case Journey changed his mind. The chomping of teeth followed as she massacred her treat.

The oven timer went off, and I hustled off to check the food, Journey trailing behind. My kitchen was homey and elegant with rustic accents and scalloped crown molding. French country kitchen at its best. It wasn't exactly my style, but I didn't cook enough to bother with remodeling.

I checked the pork chops, only to find them just about done. "Another five minutes or so, and I think we'll be ready. I hope you're hungry."

I turned to find Journey looking at me curiously. "You made dinner?"

"Yeah, I hope you still like pork chops."

"Love 'em."

He leaned down to peer in the oven window. I did my best not to ogle his ass. Oh wait, I was *allowed* to do that, wasn't I? Was I also allowed to close the distance between us and grind my dick against it? *Asking for a friend.*

Oblivious to my pervy thoughts, he straightened. "Everything looks delicious."

"I hope it doesn't disappoint." I wiped my palms down my jeans nervously. "I thought maybe we can watch a movie after. And I bought a cheesecake from Laura's bakery."

"Um, okay."

Journey looked surprised at all the effort I'd put into everything. He hadn't even seen that I'd set the table yet. I was suddenly embarrassed. "And after dessert, I thought we could get married and adopt a couple of kids."

He chuckled. "Will you fucking relax?"

"I'm just no good at this. As you can see. I was barely able to restrain myself from lighting candles." I let out a breath. "Tell me something, have we completely lost our minds?"

"Probably."

And then, he pulled my face down and kissed me, just like that. Much like the last time his lips were on mine, I melted against him like a pat of butter dropped on a steaming hot baked potato. He deepened the kiss, licking against the seam of my lips until I opened, and then invaded my mouth with his tongue, making my cock jerk. Suddenly dinner seemed like a bad idea. That was a lot of time wasted on eating when we should be spending that time fucking. When he pulled back, I chased his mouth a little. I didn't want to let him go—not yet.

"Any rules you want to put on the table?" he asked.

It was hard to look away from that soft mouth, still damp from our kiss, but I managed. There were some things I had to say before anyone lost their pants. We hadn't been together that way since we were twenty-five. We were just kids, really. A lot of things had changed since then.

It was a kick to the teeth to realize the person I'd once shared everything with didn't know me anymore. And I didn't know him, either. Maybe that was for the best. Tonight wasn't about our past, and quite frankly, it wasn't about our future. It wasn't about failed relationships either, who'd left whom and who wasn't understanding enough. Tonight was about doing something I wanted to do, and not thinking about the consequences. Defining it further would ruin it completely.

"I don't have any rules, per se. I just have a few things we need to get clear."

"Like what?"

I tugged on my ear. Nothing I was about to say would probably go over well. "I don't think you should stay over at any point. Not because I don't want you to," I added hurriedly at his raised eyebrows. "But because it would blur the lines."

He didn't look all that pleased with that rule, but he nodded slowly. "Fair. Anything else?"

"Cuddling afterward should probably be off the table, too."

"No cuddling?" His eyes widened. "Jesus, Cam, why don't we just fuck in an alley like a couple of feral cats?"

"You saw them, too?" I made a face. "I don't think they're spayed, either."

"Cam."

"Sorry. I just want us both to remember what this is, and what it isn't."

"Duly noted," he said shortly.

There. I mentally dusted my hands. It wasn't my intention, but I'd definitely killed the romance in the air. "I've got to turn the oven off. And then we can get started."

"Should I clock in first, or is this a freebie?" he said sarcastically to my back.

I shrugged. I'd laid out terms for a reason and it wasn't to be a dick. I had to protect myself from being sucked in by Journey again. I was happy before he'd blown into town, and I'd be happy after he left —as long as I kept my distance.

He still looked a little sulky when I got back to the living room. This time when he kissed me, it was different than before, less sweet and more aggressive, his tongue demanding entry and not asking. I gripped his hair and went along for the rough ride. I didn't realize we were moving until my back hit the wall.

Oh, someone really didn't like those rules. I smiled against his mouth. No surprise there. Journey still hated people telling him what he could and could not do. I slid my hands down to his ass and gripped. He was firm and round in my hands, and my dick jerked against his, and…. Oh yeah, our dicks were against one another, which was *glorious*.

I knew we were being stupid, and I knew this was probably going to blow up in my face. My fears disappeared like smoke. "How's that?" I gasped against his lips.

"Not bad." He gave an experimental roll with his hips, and I groaned. "Not bad at all."

A little rolling turned into a lot of grinding. I gripped his hips and set the rhythm—not so fast that it would be over in seconds and not so slow that it was frustrating. Need rolled through me like a tidal wave as I fit my mouth to his again. I kissed and nibbled and licked at his lips, but he kept pulling out of reach. I wasn't even sure he realized he was doing it, since his eyes were closed. He was focused as could be on maintaining that urgent rocking of his hips.

I wished I could stop long enough to do things properly. Naked would be a good start. But the couch was too far, and my bed might as well have been on Mars. I took us both down to the floor. The results of my efforts put him flat on his back, and me between his spread legs. He lifted them a bit, so I could get better access, and I took advantage. I ground against him, finding that perfect rhythm again and making us both groan.

His hands flew around my neck as I gave him more of my weight, leaning down on my forearms. I finally had the perfect angle to kiss him as deeply as I wanted, so I did, plunging my tongue inside his mouth and mimicking the thrusts of my hips.

My smooth thrusting turned into mindless rutting, and I took a moment to note that nothing—*nothing*—should ever feel this fucking good. Blood pounded in my ears as I realized things were going about to end with or without my permission. My mouth slid off his. I tried to slow down, but he dug his fingers in my hips and sped me right back up.

"No," was all he said, stretching up to take my mouth again.

I let him have his wicked way with me for a few more moments until I felt that impending orgasm again, teasing at the base of my spine. "I'm about to come," I gasped against his mouth.

"That's kind of the point."

"Not in my fucking pants, it isn't."

He chuckled. "I don't think there were any rules in your Sexamation Proclamation regarding orgasms. Go ahead."

Music to my ears. There was no right or wrong, or insert A into slot B. Just doing whatever the hell felt good. I stopped holding back. The friction between us was just right, and our perfect rhythm broke, becoming choppy and frenetic. His fingers digging bruises in my hips only made me wish that he was touching my actual skin. *Next time, next time, next time,* I internally chanted. This train had officially left the station—all aboard the *Shit, I Finally Got Some* Express.

Only a few seconds later, I felt that rush.

Oh fuck, there was nothing like that fucking rush. I buried my face in his neck and rode the wave. Journey went rigid and still beneath me, and I distantly heard him moan. My heartbeat was loud in my ears as I struggled to catch my breath. I fully expected the embarrassment to set in, and I waited... and waited. But it never did. I only felt satisfied and sleepy. I also felt very warm feelings for the man who'd made me feel that way.

When I looked down at him, he still had his eyes closed. I pressed a kiss on his mouth, but he didn't respond, too busy lying there like a dead fish. Probably too satisfied to move, which was gratifying. Or dead, I thought uneasily, which was awkward.

I poked him in the side. "You're still alive, right? Because if you're not, I need time to come up with an alibi. I can't have people around town thinking I fuck people to death."

He chuckled, opening his eyes, and they were a little unfocused, his pupils blown. His cheeks were still a little flushed. "We should've done that sooner."

I kissed his nose before I answered. "Agreed."

Journey yawned widely, and I suddenly regretted all my big talk about rules and keeping things impersonal. I wanted him in my bed, all warm and soft and sleepy. I grimaced. Thank God I'd set some parameters for myself.

"I should get going," he said, sitting up. His hair was even messier than usual and that was saying something. He ran a hand through the unruly mass of sandy waves, grimacing as he looked down at his pants. "I don't suppose you have something I could borrow to wear home?"

I eyed him critically. I was a little bigger and taller, but I had some sweats with a drawstring that might work. "Yeah, I'll rustle up something. If you want to shower first, the bathroom is right down the hall."

His mouth quirked as we got off the floor. "Glad your little rules don't include throwing me out to do the walk of shame past my father."

I flushed. "Shut up," I said without heat.

Journey headed for the bathroom, and I went to my bedroom to rifle through my drawers. By the time the shower started, I'd found everything I needed. I put the folded sweats and a fluffy towel on the floor in front of the bathroom door. I gave the door a little tap with my knuckles.

"Yeah?" he called out over the water.

"I'm leaving you some clothes and a towel right outside the door."

I thought I heard him chuckle before he said, "Thank you."

"No problem."

As I started to walk away, I heard him call out again. "Oh, and Cam?"

"Yeah?"

"Will you get your ass in here, please?"

Well, since you asked so nicely. I opened the door a crack, letting out some lemon-scented steam, only to find him standing there with the shower door open. He was getting water everywhere, but I couldn't care less.

I took a few moments just to take him in because that's what you do when you come face-to-face with a naked sex nymph in the wild. I eye-fucked him to my heart's content, head to toe. His skin was smooth and a creamy peach all over, the fine blond hair getting darker and thicker the lower I looked. The hairs were almost a light brown when it got to the thatch around his dick... which got me to look at his dick. He was a little smaller than me, and a little less thick, slightly curved to the left.

God, he was so fucking sexy. And he knew that shit. Owned that shit. He didn't try to cover up an inch, letting me look my fill without moving. Well, the parts he could control, anyway. His dick continued to jerk under my frank perusal, which was sexy as fuck.

When I finally got back up to his face, his mouth was quirked with amusement. "Seriously? Leaving the clothes outside the door like a sweet old nun? You weren't even tempted to get a peek?" He tsked. "You've changed, sweetheart, and not for the better."

I blushed even as I laughed. "It seemed like the polite thing to do."

His eyes sparkled. "You're such a fucking prude, and I love it. Now get your ass in here."

He'd barely finished speaking before I was pulling my shirt over my head. Even though I'd just been completely satisfied less than ten minutes prior, I was more than ready to go. Hey, I hadn't had sex in three years. I had a lot of catching up to do. Besides, he'd called me a sweet old nun.

"On your knees, Sutton," I told him as I chucked my pants. "As much as I enjoyed coming in our pants like teenagers, I have a more exciting orifice in mind this time around."

He raised an eyebrow even as he sank to his knees on the wet tile. "Is that fancy Cam-speak for a blow job? Because good grief, Foss."

I huffed in amusement as I sank my fingers into his wet hair and angled his head perfectly. I was doing the world a favor by putting something in that mouth of his. "Open," I instructed softly.

He worked me over like a pro, taking his slow, sweet time to turn me inside out. My legs shook so bad that I braced myself against the wall, not trusting I could hold myself up. At one point, I slammed my hand against the shower control, turning it off. I didn't want to hear water against tile—I wanted to hear all those filthy sounds his mouth made in all its acoustic glory as he slurped and licked and sucked me into oblivion. He only backed off and started over twice before he let me come. I cursed as I shot down his throat, two of his fingers in my ass, his other hand working the base of my dick.

He kept his eyes on mine the entire time, which made it hard to maintain my emotional distance. Well, now I knew.

My list of rules already needed a fucking update.

17
CAMERON

I got roped into Bailey's wedding madness on Saturday. She texted me at a godawful hour in the morning, reminding me to get my butt down to the tailor by nine thirty—sharp. I was starting to feel less and less enamored of her love story. I was close to floating the idea of elopement and Vegas, but then I remembered that she knew where I lived. *I choose life.*

When I walked into the little shop, it was already full of people from the wedding party. Garrick, the groom, immediately became my favorite because he shoved a cup of coffee in my hand before he even said hello. I thought about informing him that his wife to be was a harridan with no respect for sleep, but he had to already *know* that. Besides, telling someone that his future wife was annoying as hell seemed like more of a best man thing.

Garrick's younger brothers Blake and Clark were also there getting measured. They were both redheaded, brown-eyed, and about the same height. They even had some of the same mannerisms. When I asked if they were twins, they scoffed at me, which probably meant that neither one of them had ever walked past a mirror. I couldn't tell them apart to save my life, so I just mashed their names together and referred to them both as Blark.

Garrick's college roommate, Beau, I knew a little more intimately. I'd dated him for six months before he'd pushed for us to move in together. When I'd said I didn't think it was a good idea, he'd accused me of still being in love with Journey. *And don't you dare deny it,* he'd snapped.

So... yeah. Good times.

Also in the room was a shy guy named Ben, who happened to be the tailor, and his assistant. The guys kept up a running chatter that I listened to with one ear, my thoughts drifting to Journey. No surprise there. I wanted to meet with him again, but I didn't want to seem too desperate. I mean, we were supposed to be having fun and keeping things easy breezy. None of that included texting someone less than six hours after he blew you in the shower and you returned the favor for him on the sink. Right?

I was too old for games and keeping score about who liked whom the most and who texted first. Journey wasn't going to be in Coral Cove much longer. I didn't want to waste any of that time trying to play it cool. With that decided, I pulled out my phone and unleashed a literary masterpiece.

Hi.

Luckily for me, he didn't seem to care about the night after rules, either. He texted right back, no cooling period required. *You're cute.*

Not that I'm about to argue the obvious, but that's a bit random.

I just thought you should know. In case no one told you that today.

The tailor did, I teased back.

Tell that homewrecker mitts off.

I chuckled.

"Surely Cam wouldn't mind," Garrick said to my left. "Isn't that right, Cam?"

"Right," I said distractedly.

"That's fantastic."

"Wait." The relief in his voice made me look up from my phone. That relief was normally reserved for *will you bail me out of jail,* or *can I crash on your couch...* the answer to both of which was "no." "What's fantastic? And just what did I agree to?"

"You said you'd go with Bailey to the cake tasting. I'm allergic to just about everything, so I won't be able to give her much of an opinion."

"Why don't you guys get a cake that you can eat?" I asked with a frown.

He shrugged. "If you can find a cake with no peanut butter, chocolate, nuts, or strawberries, be my guest."

"That list really cut me off at the knees," I said after a moment. "Why aren't you in a bubble?"

He chuckled. "You already said you'd do it. You can't take it back now."

"I only said yes because I wasn't paying attention," I grumbled.

"And just what could be more important than listening to every word that comes out of my precious mouth?"

"He was texting," Beau tattled for reasons only known to him.

"Texting who?" Garrick demanded. "This is my day, Foster."

"Getting fitted at the tailors is not *your day*, Groomzilla," I said exasperatedly. "And it's none of your concern who I was texting."

"It was probably Journey," Ben said absently. I gave him a look of surprise, and he blushed furiously, realizing what he'd said. "Turn, please."

"Did Mindy send out a newsletter?" I demanded.

"Yes," he said promptly as the entire room said "no." There were numerous groans as Ben blushed some more. Poor thing wouldn't last six seconds under interrogation. "Sorry, it was a secret lovers edition," he admitted without further prompting.

Hell, forget interrogation, the detectives would only have to ask nicely.

"There was a picture of the two of you in front of the supermarket, and it was...." Ben looked in danger of expiring on the spot. I almost offered to fan him so he could cool off. "It was intense."

"They were only talking in that picture," Blark said.

"Not the one on the back," Blark #2 interjected helpfully. "They were kissing in that one."

"There was a back?" Garrick sent his brothers an irritated look. "Mindy needs to go digital."

For Pete's sake. I huffed. "Journey and I are just friends. Whatever happens between us stays between us."

"And Mindy," Garrick added.

And unfortunately, Mindy. "One day, I'm going to break that woman's computer over my knee," I grumbled.

The one good thing about being busted was that when my phone binged again, I didn't have to bother being sly. *U busy right now?*

I sighed regretfully. *Yep.*

He wasn't deterred. *I want to see you tonight. I need my Cam fix.*

I barely held in a smile. I loved the way he approached things without artifice. I followed his lead. *I want to see you, too.*

We should do dinner, he suggested. *Plus something dirty.*

I hesitated, mostly because that sounded like a fucking date. *Dinner?*

Dinner. I don't think sharing a meal was banned on your little list.

I chuckled. I should've known he'd still be bitter about that. *Dinner, then.*

And a movie, he prompted. *Then all the dirty things.*

And just like that, my day took an upswing.

I pressed sleep on my phone and stuck it in my pocket. When I looked up, I found myself the target of many sets of very interested eyes. "Not a peep to Mindy," I warned.

Garrick grinned. "Yeah, we'll see."

18

JOURNEY

Cameron was getting better at this fling business.

There was a different kind of energy about him from the moment he opened the door to let me in. For one thing, he hadn't bothered to get all spiffy. Not in an *I can't be bothered to look nice for you* way, but more of a *what's the point of getting dressed when I'm just going to get naked* kind of way.

I took a few seconds to enjoy the sight of him in some gray sweatpants and a plain black shirt, his chestnut hair rumpled, his feet bare. The look in those intense green eyes let me know we weren't going to make it through dinner—or a movie. He confirmed my suspicions a few seconds later when he pushed me against the wall. The door slammed behind us.

"Blargh," was all I managed before he took my mouth.

He kissed me, his hands dropping to my ass as his tongue danced with mine. I struggled to catch up as he kissed the daylights out of me. It took me a moment to realize I wasn't on my feet anymore as he lifted me. My back thudded against the wall and my legs came up around his hips automatically.

"Too much?" He was a little breathless as he rutted against me.

Yeah, no. "You should show me your bedroom." I nipped at his full lower lip. "I want to do things that require a flat surface."

"Putting you down is pretty much the last thing I want to do right now."

Before I could protest, he was striding across the living room. I blinked in surprise even as I tightened my hold around his neck. I may not be a towering tree like most of the men in my family, but I wasn't exactly a *small* man.

"I can walk," I said automatically.

"Yep, I've seen you do it," he agreed, even as he made a beeline for the bedroom.

Hmph. I resigned myself to enjoying some primo He-Man tactics, but if he threw his back out before he threw *my* back out, I was gonna be pissed. I had a quick impression of a neat room with comfortable furniture and a beachy vibe, all done in gray and white. He deposited me on the bed, where I landed with a bounce. I didn't know what had gotten into him, but I was going to find out. And bottle it for retail use.

I opened my mouth to say as much, only to find him whipping his shirt up and off over his head. His sweatpants were next, and he shucked them off with little ado. Then he was quite naked at the end of the bed, and I didn't know where to look first. He was solidly built all-around with broad shoulders and well-defined legs. I'd felt that strength firsthand when he carted me to the room like a sack of potatoes.

My gaze got caught somewhere around his dick, which was already hard and thick, pointing in my direction. A bead of precum pearled at the top and started to slide off. His hand was there before it could get far, and he used it to slick his erection. I watched, a little slack-jawed, my dick doing its level best to join the party by punching a hole in my pants.

"Journey."

"Huh?" I finally stopped watching long enough to travel my attention up that body to his face, only to find his eyes amused.

"I think you're a little overdressed," he said.

"Oh, right." I made no moves to do anything about that, far too engrossed in watching him stroke his dick some more.

He chuckled. "Seriously?"

Yes, seriously. *He doesn't even know how hot he is. Poor bastard.*

I huffed as I sat up on the bed, pulling my shirt over my head. When I stopped there, he gestured at my well-worn ripped jeans, and I lost those, too, tossing them unceremoniously onto the floor.

"I did your evil bidding," I said, shifting to the end of the bed so that my feet were on the floor. "Now bring it over here, Foster. I want a taste."

I didn't have to ask twice. I watched his cock bob against his stomach as he walked over to me, not stopping until he was between my knees. And then I started my torture, stroking and pumping my hand down his length. I included his balls in my play, rubbing them and cupping them alternatively. I put my other hand against his stomach, and I could feel the muscles contracting beneath my palm.

"I thought you said you wanted a taste," he said huskily. "Don't tell me you're all talk and no—"

Whatever smartass thing he was going to say was lost in a moan as I leaned forward and took his balls in my mouth. His hand sank into my hair, not directing my actions, but just cupping my skull. It was more intimate than I'd expected, but I didn't call him on it. Instead, I teased him mercilessly, sucking his balls in my mouth and letting them slide out slowly. He growled and I looked up at him from beneath my lashes.

He let out a painful laugh. "I hate you so much right now."

"No, you don't." I gave him a wicked smile right before I took him in my mouth. I took every inch, not stopping until my nose was buried in his pubes.

"Jesus," he breathed as he widened his stance even farther.

It wasn't long before I realized that teasing him had a horrible side effect—I was teasing myself as well. I was dangerously close to coming and we'd barely gotten started. I took myself in hand and started to stroke as I sucked harder. Cam seemed to realize my intent as he started rocking his hips to meet my mouth.

"Question," he said breathlessly, and I hummed in response. "Do you still hate getting fucked after you come?"

I nodded... that's pretty much all the response you can manage when your mouth is full of dick. Things were just too sensitive after an orgasm. I'd let him know early on that if he wanted to have me that way, it needed to happen before I came. Figures he'd remember that.

"That's all I need to hear," he said, even though I hadn't said anything. He pulled out of my mouth, and I made a sound of protest. He leaned down, his fingers tightening in my hair painfully as he pulled my mouth up to his. I felt completely possessed by him and I fucking loved it.

He kissed me thoroughly. "I *am* getting inside of you tonight. That's a fucking promise."

Like I was going to argue with that. He got on the bed, and I wasted no time straddling him, my knees on either side of his hips. Those big hands secured on my ass, lifting and gripping me, and my hands flew to his shoulders. I leaned down to suck his full bottom lip into my mouth and worried it between my teeth.

The new angle was just perfect. His dick settled against the crease of my ass like it was meant to be there. I shifted a little until he slid between my cheeks and across my hole, and we both sighed with pleasure. At least, mine was pleasure. I think Cameron's sigh was laced with pain.

"Well, there goes any chance I had of dragging this out," he said exasperatedly. "Why can't I fucking take it slow with you?"

I laughed. "Look at it this way. We made it to the bedroom, and we're both naked. That's progress."

"I guess," he said crossly. "But I didn't even get to finger you yet, and I'm about to blow."

My mouth made a little *o* as I thought about that for a few seconds. I stopped him from fucking my crease abruptly, much to his dismay, and issued some sage advice. "Get the lube."

I busied myself kissing the sensitive spot behind his ear as he rifled through the bedside table. He arched up against me, trying to give me more access even as he cursed my name. Granted, my actions probably made it a little harder for him to find what we needed, but teasing Cam had always been a favorite activity of mine. It was a few moments before I realized he'd given up on anything productive, and his hand was just resting in the drawer.

I laughed and reached across him to get the supplies myself, only to find that they were *right fucking there.* "If it was a snake, it would've bitten you," I informed him as I tossed the bottle of lube on the bed. The box of condoms was next. The half-empty box.

I raised an eyebrow at him, and he flushed, which was fucking adorable. He didn't answer my wordless question, taking his time to prep me instead. He took his excruciatingly slow-ass, sweet time. He kept going long past the time I told him that I was good to go. Fingering my hole and sucking on my tongue was his new favorite activity.

Eventually, I had to call it, grabbing his wrist before I came. "I think that's enough, don't you?"

Those green eyes were a little dazed and unfocused. "A few more minutes."

"No more minutes."

Despite my ban on teasing, I put the condom on him as slowly as possible... because payback was a bitch. And when I added a little lube, I slicked it up and down a few more times than necessary, causing him to glare at me. But eventually, all the teasing was done. The blunt tip of his dick nudged between my cheeks, settling at my entrance. I braced my hands on his shoulders, waiting, more than ready for my reward.

And then...nothing.

I looked down into Cams eyes. I wasn't even sure that he realized his brow was furrowed. "Everything all right down there?"

"Yeah, of course." He blew out a breath. "I'm just... I'm just more out of practice than I thought."

"Is that all?" I laughed softly and rubbed his shoulder. "I don't want practiced. I hate those guys who think they're God's gift. You know the type."

"Sure," he said easily.

Too easily. I stared at him, even though he suddenly had trouble meeting my gaze. "You do know the type, don't you?"

"I said I did." His tone was defensive. "It's just that... it's been a long while."

"How long?"

"Three years."

I goggled. "Three years?"

"Three years."

"Three years," I repeated slowly, as though trying out the words for the first time.

"Three years," he confirmed.

"Wow." I scratched the back of my neck. "Three. Years."

"Maybe we can ask Alexa what those words mean," he suggested.

"How... how does that even happen?"

"What can I say? I'm a one-partner kind of guy," he teased. Whatever those words did to my expression made him hurriedly add, "Usually."

"Uh-huh." I tapped my fingers on his shoulder as I thought. "May I ask why?"

He sent me an incredulous look. "Now?"

I didn't blame him. All systems were a go. But I had questions. My dick had questions. My ass *definitely* had some questions that needed answering before liftoff.

"Well, it wasn't because I have anything against casual sex. It just worked out that way." He shrugged. "I've dated a lot, of course. But I have to care about a person to get physical."

"So, how many people are we talking?"

"Other than you?" He looked a little flustered. "Two."

"Two?"

"Two."

"Two," I repeated, just to be sure.

"Once again, I can help you define some of these words if you need help." After a pause, he quirked an eyebrow. "Now that I've put my cards on the table, what's your number?"

I tried not to look guilty, but I wasn't quite sure I pulled it off. "Not two."

He laughed. "You do realize you're blushing, yes?"

I did. I shifted uncomfortably, and he gave a little hiss when his dick slid up my channel, which reminded me that I had a hard dick at my disposal. Enough with all this jibber-jabber. "So, you're okay with everything we're doing?"

"Well, it's not like I'm a virgin."

"I'm just making sure!"

"All right, all right, calm down." His hand moved up and down my thigh in a soothing manner. "You'd think I told you I was a confirmed monk."

"If you were so gung ho about this, then why'd you hesitate earlier?" I squinted down at him suspiciously. "It was like all systems were a go and then... they went."

He didn't deny it. He frowned. "Like I said, it's been a while. I don't want to hurt you."

Oh, was that all? I felt my mouth pull into a half smile without my permission. He was sweet in the very best of ways. "You won't," I assured him, reaching back to guide him into position. "I can promise you that you won't."

He groaned as he slid inside me, one solid inch at a time. And yeah, there was a little pinch of pain as my body worked to accommodate him, but I certainly wasn't going to tell him that now. It was a good burn, the kind that woke me up and made me feel him everywhere. I finally took the entire length of him and let out a shaky sigh. It was good. So fucking good.

"I want to be good for you." His voice was a whisper near my ear.

My words were a little choppy because I couldn't seem to catch my fucking breath. "You already are."

I rolled my hips experimentally, and Cam let out a little whimper. He wasn't the only one who wanted to be good. I was one of three lucky folks who'd planted a flag on Mount Cameron, and I intended to make it memorable. I started a slow, steady rhythm, lifting and coming back down as his hands locked on my upper thighs. His eyes slammed shut, and I immediately felt the loss.

"Open," I demanded, and there was movement behind his lids for a few moments before they finally lifted. His gaze was heavy-lidded and unfocused, and I couldn't look away.

I wanted to relish every moment. Take my time. Take Cam to the brink and then stop before starting all over again. But we'd been teasing each other too long. Almost by mutual agreement, we became frantic.

He dug his heels into the bed to get traction and gripped my hips, digging in the flesh there. I held my own, slamming my hips downward until we had an almost violent rhythm. Cam's mouth was slightly open, his face twisted in a painful grimace, and I had a feeling I was looking at a mirror of my expression.

"Fuck, I'm about to come." His voice was almost unrecognizable, tight with tension and hoarse with strain. He gripped my ass, ramping up our rhythm to an even higher cadence.

I finally broke our locked gaze, closing my eyes. I stopped trying to brace myself and lay across him flat, my forehead against his. His mouth was open against mine, not really kissing, just breathing each other's air as we hurtled toward the finish.

And there it was.

As my orgasm gripped the base of my spine, and there was nothing I could do to slow the tide. My mouth slid off his and across his cheek, ending up somewhere in the crook of his neck. My voice was muffled as I shouted his name, my release warm between us. He groaned a few seconds later, chasing me over that cliff and freefalling after me, and I felt him pulsing in my ass, which made my dick jerk as I spurted a little more.

I collapsed onto him, feeling a little wrecked. My palm had landed on Cam's chest, and I could feel his heart going *pitter-pat*. His hands finally released their death grip on my ass and traversed my damp back a few times.

"Was that just me, or was that really, really good?" he finally murmured near my ear.

"It's just you." I couldn't resist teasing him. It wasn't like he didn't have the evidence of how much I enjoyed it on his stomach, threatening to bond us together permanently.

He pretended to take offense. Or, maybe not so pretend, because he proceeded to tackle me. After a startled squeal, I got myself together and went on the offense. He had the size advantage, but I was no slouch. If you grow up with rowdy brothers who are bigger than you, either you learn a thing or two about dirty tricks, or you wind up in the laundry hamper.

We finally decided to cry uncle mutually and lay there panting on our backs. My hand was still secured in his, and I wasn't sure if he realized it. Then he squeezed it, so I guess he did. I wondered where handholding went on his little no-no list.

I didn't pull away.

19

JOURNEY

I was pretty sure my father was on to me.

He didn't have to be a great detective. I was getting some on the regular from a great guy. Of course my mood had lifted. I found myself humming while I did household chores and smiling goofily for no reason at all. A sad song came on the radio and I changed the channel since I wasn't in a place to even relate to that shit.

I was disgusted with myself. This was only after three weeks with Cameron. What was I going to look like by the end of summer? Dear God, we were going to start wearing *I'm With Him* T-shirts in public, and then people would stone us to death for being corny as fuck.

I tried to apply myself to being normal.

After an appointment with my father's cardiologist, we decided to have lunch. He lobbied hard for Gloria's, a little hole-in-the-wall that prided itself on being cheap and serving big portions. Their main ingredient was not "love" as their sign proclaimed, but grease.

I agreed we could eat there as long as I got the final say-so on the dish. I thought it prudent to compromise because he was starting to remind me of a caged animal. Any moment, he was going to go feral, and I'd come home to find him passed out in the middle of a fast-food feast, a half-eaten bucket of chicken on his chest.

We sat across from each other in a booth, and when he tried to pick up a menu, I gave him a look. He put it down with a sigh. I picked up the one on my side and perused it, taking an extra-long time just to make him squirm.

I landed on a turkey sandwich with a side salad for him before ordering a chicken sandwich and fries for myself. If he was extra nice, I'd give him some of my fries. I handed back the menu to our waitress, Glenna. "Could you also add a burger meal to my order?"

My dad raised an eyebrow. "I'm stuck with a turkey sandwich special and you get a crunchy chicken sandwich and a burger?"

Glenna gave me a smile and a wink, answering before I could. "We're a few doors down from the vet clinic. He's probably going to bring his hunny a little something."

"Cameron is not my hunny," I said with an arch look. "He's just a friend."

"Mmm." She eyed me skeptically over her pad, pencil still poised. "Then it probably wouldn't interest you that he likes his burgers medium rare with extra pickles and no onions."

I paused, thinking of a way to thwart her nosiness, but the woman had me dead to rights. My dad made a sound of amusement and impatience. "Stop teasing the boy before I expire. I'd like my turkey club sometime this century, Glenna."

She winked at me again. "I'll bring your meals first and the to-go order about ten minutes later, so it'll be hot."

"Thank you," I said begrudgingly. *Not so much for the nosy convo but everything else.*

After she bustled off, a silence descended on our table. I felt a little awkward about what Glenna had revealed, but it wasn't like my father hadn't already suspected. When you break out into "Your Song" by Elton John while you're doing dishes, people notice that shit. They also notice when you go to the mailbox for the mail and come back two hours later with no fucking mail.

I fiddled with the saltshaker. Didn't mean I had to talk about it, though.

Apparently, my dad didn't get the memo. "So. You and Dr. Foster."

"Me and Dr. Foster what?"

"Well... you know. You boys getting back together?"

"Don't you people have Netflix?" I demanded.

"I'm just saying that it's been a long time coming. You could do a lot worse than Foster, you know."

"We're not getting back together, Dad."

"Why the hell not?"

Well, I could hardly clear it up for him, could I? *Well you see, Dad, Cameron and I decided we're not right for one another because we still want different things out of life. But the chemistry is out of this world, so we decided to fuck each other into oblivion before I leave town again.*

"We're just looking for different things," I said vaguely.

"Oh." He seemed dissatisfied with my nonanswer. "So you *are* open to a relationship, then? Because you haven't brought anyone around."

"Err—"

"You want my advice?"

"Not even a little bit."

"Put yourself out there," he said sagely. "You'll never find love if you don't take chances."

"I'm not in the market for—"

"My friend from church has a son you might hit it off with. You know Suzette?" He peered at me until I shook my head. He clucked his tongue impatiently. "You *know* Suzette."

I hadn't the foggiest. His level of distress increased, all because I couldn't remember some rando from a church I only set foot in at Christmas... if that.

"You have to remember Suzette," he said stubbornly. "She's the one with all the crazy hats."

"Oh," I said, before he started shaking me. I still wouldn't be able to pick her out of a lineup, but whatever. "*That* Suzette."

"And her son George," he prompted.

Now *him* I remembered. George took great pride in being an usher. He equated shuffling parishioners into the right pew at the same importance as being a Navy SEAL.

I cleared my throat. "Um, so George is... er, gay?"

"Well, I didn't interrogate the man." Just like that, he was irritated all over again. "He likes Cher and knows the lyrics to most Broadway show tunes."

Close enough. Guess that made my grandmother a little gay, too, and anyone who had ever shaken a glitter stick and fist-pumped the lyrics to "Song for the Lonely." Hmm, maybe he had a point. Now I had that song in my head, too.

I cleared my throat, trying to come up with some claptrap to get him off my back. "I'm in more of a single place right now. Trying to get to know me a little better before I jump into a relationship."

My dad snorted as he picked up a newspaper someone else had left in our booth. "That sounds like a bunch of malarkey."

Well, *of course* it fucking was, but he was supposed to be too polite to say so. I let out a huff of breath. "You could make this easy on me, you know."

"I'm an old man, JJ. I get my entertainment when and where I can."

"I bought you a Roku."

"It was too complicated." He unfolded the newspaper leisurely. "Watching you turn red and scramble to explain away your relationship with Foster is on the highlight reel of my day."

I glared. Before I could respond, Glenna dropped off our food. My father wasn't one for a lot of chitchat while he was eating, so he promptly occupied himself with his sandwich and newspaper. For my part, I pulled out my phone and picked up where I'd left off working on Cameron's YouTube channel. I hemmed and hawed over the name for a bit, before finally deciding on *VetLife*.

Bailey had been so pleased with our spotlight on senior dogs that she asked me to compile some of their videos on YouTube for easy access. I'd thought it was a fantastic idea, especially since it made Cameron squirm. He hated the thought of random people being able to watch him work. I loved the idea of being able to secretly get my Cameron fix anytime I wanted, even if I was like a creepy stalker behind a computer screen.

I finished my sandwich in record time and glanced up to find that my father was chewing slowly and only halfway done. He was determined to savor his few moments of food freedom. I decided not to rush him. I even pretended not to notice when he salted the tomatoes on his sandwich—twice.

Instead, I kept working. I nicked a couple of photos off Cameron's Instagram page, one of the few he'd graced with his actual face, and then a few from his stepmother's facebook page. I didn't know why the two of them were pretending she'd retired because she was in the office practically every time I stopped by. Then I used the photos to make a catchy little intro that I still had to find the right music for.

"Oh, that's cute."

I glanced up to see Ms. Aldridge, leaning over my side of the booth. She was the town librarian, and seventy if she was a day. She held monthly puppet shows at the library with milk and cookies afterward that made her a big hit with the kids... and an even bigger hit with parents, who needed a freaking break. After spending some unadulterated time with my hyperactive nieces and nephews, I could relate.

I smiled as I pressed play on the intro again. "Yeah, I think I like it."

"I wasn't aware that you and Dr. Foster were...."

I peered up at her, but she didn't finish. We blinked at one another, letting that fragment dangle for an inordinately long time before I prodded, "Were...."

"Were," she confirmed.

"Oh, were!" I shook my head. "We're just friends."

She looked crushed. "That's too bad. You two were so good together back in the day. You could do a lot worse than Dr. Foster," she added loyally.

"That's what I told 'im." My father wet down his thumb liberally before turning the page on the newspaper, and I shuddered to see one of my pet peeves being played out in HD. "But you know kids today. They think they know everything."

Small-town life. I hid my amusement. "If you two hens are quite finished clucking...."

"Well, actually I do have a favor to ask," she said hurriedly. "If you have a little spare time, I could use your help."

"What's up?"

"I'd like you to come to my son's surprise birthday party. I'd be tickled pink to have a professional take pictures of him and all his little friends."

Little friends? I raised an eyebrow. Her son was older than I was, and last I'd heard, Thomas was in his fifties and worked at the bank. "Err... Tom?"

"No, Peter."

"I'm sorry," I apologized. "I wasn't aware you had another—"

She flipped her phone around, and I found myself nose to screen with a corgi in a striped sweater vest. "That's... Peter?" I questioned.

"Of course." She swiped to show me another picture, and this time Peter was in a shearling jean jacket. He looked up at the camera smugly. He was cute, and he wasn't about to let you forget it. Two pictures in, and I was fairly certain other dogs constantly wanted to punch him in the schnoz.

I looked up from the screen. "That's the Peter who's having a birthday party?"

"That's the one."

"The... surprise birthday party," I said delicately, just to make sure we were on the same crazy page.

"Yes, he's always wanted one."

My father snorted and pretended it was a sneeze. I kicked his foot under the table, and he grunted, snapping his newspaper up straight.

Oblivious to our byplay, Mrs. Aldridge nattered on. "I invited all his friends, and there's going to be a specially made cake, with dog-friendly ingredients. It'll be shaped like a bone, of course."

"Of course," I agreed. "Any other shape would be a slap in the face."

"Exactly. You should bring Sascha!"

I wasn't about to deprive my little girl of the chance to socialize.

And wear one of her new sweaters. *Take that, Peter. You're not the only one who can rock a jean jacket.*

"So, will you?" Mrs. Aldridge prodded.

Attend your dog's surprise birthday party and take photos of him and all his equally confused dog friends? I sighed. "Sure." Why not? It made as much sense as anything else I'd done since I got into town, up to and including jumping into bed with my ex-fiancé.

"Marvelous! And if you see Peter, not a word." She put a finger against her lips, and my dad snort-laughed again. I took great pleasure in kicking his shin again, too. He grunted and sent me a glare over his newspaper.

"Not even if I wanted to," I assured her. "Mum's the word."

She didn't turn around and go back to her meal. Instead, she moved into our booth next to my father, who sighed loudly enough to rattle his newspaper. She proceeded to fill us in on all the details regarding Peter's party, reveling in her new role of hostage-taker. When Glenna swung by our table and dropped off my to-go order for Cam in a brightly colored bag, I breathed a sigh of relief.

I slid out of the booth and picked up the bag. My father made a show of folding his newspaper carefully, and I waved him back down. "You should stay and chat," I said. "I'll be right back."

He sent me a horrified look. "But—"

"I won't be long."

Mrs. Aldridge smiled as she pulled out her phone. "Now, what do you think of these balloons? Silver or gold?"

THE CLINIC WAS DOING brisk business as usual. Three people and their loyal companions waited in the front—a woman with a hairless cat, a guy with two napping schnauzers in scarves, and a kid with a big terrarium perched on his knobby knees. The terrarium appeared to be empty, and the nameplate at the bottom read *Dwayne*. My gaze traveled up the kid's shirt to the giant lizard-looking thing draped across his shoulders.

I stared at Dwayne for a few minutes, hoping he was as placid as he looked. He stared back, unblinking. After a few moments, he licked his eye. *Christ.* Guess being a vet wasn't all cute puppies and kittens. Sometimes you had to check in on the Dwaynes of the world and see what's shaking in the Lizard Kingdom.

Dwayne licked his eye again, and I suppressed a shudder. I was starting to think he was doing it for shock value.

"Hey, hun." I turned to the front desk to find Bailey giving me a tired smile. "I don't have you on the schedule. How's Sascha doing?"

"Her name is Honey now, and she's doing fine."

"I'm glad to hear it. You here to see Cameron?"

"Yes, but don't worry, I won't take up too much of his time." I paused, giving her a critical once-over. Bailey's personality was usually as big as her smile, but she seemed a little subdued today. "Everything okay?"

She sighed a little. "It's just been one of those days. You can go on back, hun."

When I got back to Cameron's small, tidy office, he was leaning over his desk and writing busily. He managed to look hot even in wrinkled blue scrubs flecked with dog hair, which really wasn't fair. He was clean-shaven today, his hair neat and tamed. I flashed back to the night before when his jaw was covered in stubble and his hair was a mess from my fingers. I wasn't sure which look I preferred—wholesome, trustworthy guy, or guy I just fucked until the bedframe gave out.

It was a cheap frame, okay? And that's exactly what I told Cameron as he looked up at me in disbelief from our position on the floor. I didn't know how much he'd paid for it, but it had to be the frame, not exuberant fucking. I was no nympho.

He turned in his chair when I tapped on his door. "Hey," he said, a tired smile crossing his face.

Just the sound of his voice sent a little shiver down my back, which was ridiculous. But I could practically *hear* his words from last night, as he'd hoarsely said my name. He'd followed that up with, *"Fuck, I can't hold back. You're so fucking tight."* I shifted, trying to think clean thoughts. Pure thoughts. Like him putting his forehead against mine as he fucked me relentlessly, saying, *"Nothing feels better than this. Nothing."* And, *"If you keep that up, honey, I'm not gonna last."*

Needless to say, I kept it up. And he sure as hell didn't last.

Okay, maybe I was some type of nympho. Or, maybe I'd just been sex starved for a long time. Good grief. No need to trundle someone off to sex therapy yet.

I held up the bag of food and set it on his desk. "Delivery. I take tips and I don't have change for any big bills."

He chuckled. "I didn't expect to see you today."

I bet. He was methodically spacing out our time together, and I was trying to play by his rules. Some days it took everything in me not to just show up at his front door. My ideas for excuses ran the gamut from unoriginal to criminal—borrowing a cup of sugar to pilfering his mail—so I could pretend they delivered it to the wrong house. In the end, I did nothing. I had no choice but to let him set the pace. This was his show, and he wasn't afraid to let me know it.

"Where's Kona?" I asked.

"She's been temporarily banned." He made a face. "She tried to play with Bailey's foster squirrels. It wasn't like she was trying to *eat* them or anything. But to hear Bailey tell it, Kona was all but sprinkling them with lemon pepper."

I laughed. "Not my Kona."

"Exactly."

Had his eyes gotten greener since the last time I saw him? Was that even possible? They were a little red-rimmed, though, and I had a feeling it wasn't from lack of sleep. The tip of his nose was a little pink as well.

"What's wrong?" I asked quietly.

He didn't look surprised because he knew me as well as I knew him. If there was something wrong with me, he'd know it with just a look, too. "It's just been—"

"One of those days," I said dryly. "I heard. Don't bullshit me, Cam." Then it hit me. "It was a black-coat day, wasn't it?"

He gave me a short nod, and I felt his pain in my heart. He called them that because euthanasia was always the hardest thing for him to handle.

"I had to put down a long-time patient of mine. Socks, the cat. His owner, Tessa, was devastated. She's had him since she was a kid." He sighed, running both hands down his face. "All these years in practice, and it's still the hardest thing."

His stepmother, with a wealth of experience under her belt, had told him that it was the kindest thing they could do as veterinarians, and they'd fallen out for a week. Eventually, he came around to her way of thinking, but I knew he still struggled with it. Someone with a heart as big as Cam's always would.

I hesitated before coming closer because I wasn't sure where physical comfort fell on his taboo list. Then I decided I didn't give a fuck. I *had* to touch him right then. I took both of his hands in mine.

"You remember what you told me about euthanasia. Sometimes doing the best thing is the hardest thing." I rubbed the back of his hands with my thumbs. "It allows you to focus on the quality of life. They don't have to suffer like we do."

"You remember that?"

I remember everything.

I sidestepped the question. "How old was Socks?"

"Fifteen. And Tessa didn't name him Socks because he had white paws or anything like that. He got his name because he kept stealing her socks."

I chuckled. "What the hell was he doing with all those socks?"

"Hell if I know. He would hide them in the couch cushions and shit. He was the funniest little cat." Cameron looked vaguely embarrassed. "Look at me carrying on. I have a roomful of patients waiting."

I didn't bother to address that nonsense. "It brings you back to Bear, doesn't it?"

He smiled faintly. "A little bit."

"I should've been there for you when that happened." I should've been there for a lot of things. "I'm sorry."

"This isn't about that."

"Cam—"

"I don't want to go there, Journey." His voice was serious as he pulled his hands out of my grasp. I felt the loss immediately. "I mean it."

Of course he didn't want to go there. Because *there* included talking about our feelings, and the past, and we'd said we wouldn't do that. *There* meant going beyond the boundaries of just having sex into the realm of talking about something that mattered. *There* meant talking about a future between us, not just the right now.

To go *there,* I'd have to break past this wall he'd erected. The Cameron I used to know didn't have any walls. The way I'd left had done that. I'm sure he'd met others along the way who'd added a few bricks, but the foundation of that wall was mine. I had no right to try and demolition my way back through.

I wanted to, though. Our relationship had never been smooth sailing, but we'd always had the counterweight part down. Neither of us had to be constantly strong. Sometimes one of us would have to provide more stability and balance, so the other side could be weak... even if it was just for a few minutes. My muscle memory itched with the need to do that again.

I wanted to press a kiss in his hair and wrap my arms around him. I wanted to whisper "I've got you" in his ear. I wanted to feel his vulnerability in a tangible way when we were fully clothed, not just when it was dark and quiet and we were skin to skin.

I didn't have the right to do any of that. Not with the way I'd left. But I could touch him sexually, though. He'd given me permission for that. I moved into his space, backing him up until his butt hit the desk. His eyes flared wide even as he zeroed in on my mouth. "Oh. This is that kind of visit." His voice was a little husky. "I thought this was just a lunch drop-off."

"This is *DoorDash Gone Wild*. It starts as food delivery, and then...." I sank my fingers into his hair and pulling him down to my level. "Things get a little wild."

I kissed him then, long and deep and lingering. He pulled back first, breathing a little unsteadily. "We can't," he insisted, "not here."

I rolled my hips against his, and he gasped a little. "You're right," I agreed amiably. "This is a place of business."

I looped my wrists around his neck loosely as his hands went down to my ass automatically. He was obsessed with it, and I didn't mind in the least. It wasn't a good day unless my ass had Cameron's mark on it—fingerprints and/or handprints. I wasn't all that picky. I raised an eyebrow, and he blushed. He let go immediately, sliding his hands back up to the small of my back.

I chuckled since the move just brought us even closer together. "That's not much better, Foster."

He groaned. "Fuck, I know."

He looked down at me, clearly waiting for me to make the first move. I was waiting for the same damn thing. I was very clear about what I wanted, and Cam would never admit it, but his natural sweet nature brought him dangerously close to people pleaser territory. It was important that I knew, *for sure*, that I wasn't pushing him too far out of his comfort zone.

Awareness flared in those glass-green eyes as he huffed out a soft laugh. "Really?"

"Yep." I forced myself to be still, even though I wanted to climb him like a tree. "Green light?"

It was his turn to attack my mouth. We stumbled back against his desk. I was so caught up in trying to eat him alive, it took me a few seconds to realize that he was working down my zipper. He wasted no time pushing my jeans down to my knees, which really wasn't necessary unless we were fucking.

I bit my lip to hold in my laughter. He was such an ass man, but he would never admit it. Sure enough, his hands stole back to my behind, and he squeezed, lifting and separating my cheeks. *What did we say about fucking in the office again?* I wondered hazily. *Was it just yes or fuck yes?*

"You. Want to feel you, too," I managed.

His pants were a little easier since he was wearing those scrubs. I pushed them down impatiently, enough so I could pull him out of his boxers. He was already thick and hard in my hand. He returned the favor, letting go of my rear to take me in hand.

His thumb skated over the head of my dick, and I bucked involuntarily, barely managing to hold in a whimper. "You used to be shy," I accused.

"You corrupted me," he insisted.

He nudged my hand off his dick and took us both in one of those big, calloused hands. He started jerking us off slowly, and my eyes nearly crossed from pleasure. It was rough going at first, even with the precum leaking from us both, but I couldn't be bothered to look for a lube substitute. He let me slide out of the warm haven of his fist, and I made a noise of protest.

I needn't have worried. He wasn't done with me yet. He held up his palm to my mouth. "Lick," was all he said.

Well, fuck, when you put it like that. Right before I made contact with his palm, I paused. "Wait, you haven't been fondling a dog's balls or anything today, have you?"

He gaped at me. "Why would I fondle a dog's balls?"

"Well, I don't know what you vets do." I continued to eye him suspiciously. "Whatever it is you do with dog balls, you haven't been doing that, have you?"

"Can we stop talking about dog balls?" His tone was exasperation and amusement all rolled up into one.

"Gladly," I said with dignity.

"And I wash my hands quite a bit," he informed me.

"Good to know, Ball Fondler."

"JJ, I swear to God—"

I licked his palm thoroughly, maintaining eye contact the entire time. His tongue slid out to trace his lips as he watched, transfixed. I wanted to keep teasing him, but I wanted him to touch me more. A few seconds later, I had my wish as he took us in hand again. It felt good enough that this time I couldn't help but let out the whimper.

"Shh," he said softly by my ear.

I buried my face in his neck, his skin warm against my lips. I felt the orgasm tingling at the base of my spine and knew it was going to be a doozy. He stopped just as I was ready to let go.

I pulled back far enough to see his face. "Please tell me you don't have carpal tunnel."

He laughed painfully. "I don't want to make a mess."

Oh. That. I guess it wasn't the best idea for us to come all over our clothing. Extremely satisfying, but not the easiest to explain to the people who seemed to make a hobby of playing *Clue: The Journey and Cam Edition*. I pictured Bailey with a magnifying glass to her eye. *My guess is he was fucking Professor Plum in the office with a lead pipe.*

"I think I have the solution," I said, right before I sank to my knees.

He watched, a little slack-jawed, as I took him in my mouth. It didn't even qualify as a blow job. Three seconds after he was in my mouth, he went off like a rocket. I made it my business to swallow every drop.

"Fuck," he whispered, his hand tangled in my hair like he wanted to keep me in place. It was unnecessary. I wasn't going to let him go until I had to. He was lucky we were in a place of business. I would love to push him back in that rolling chair and ride him until I was spurting all over my stomach.

Just the thought sent me over the edge, and I let him slide out of my mouth as I rested my head on his thigh. I came on the floor, biting on the inside of my cheek so all I let out was a couple of gusty breaths. We stayed there for a couple of minutes, too satiated to move until reality intruded.

Cameron seemed to realize where we were at the same time I did. He pulled me to my feet, giving me a sheepish look as he took over righting our clothing. He zipped me up before pulling up his scrubs and knotting the tie again. I grabbed some tissues from his desk and wiped my mess off the floor, and then I tossed them in the trash. We both washed our hands in the sink in his office, which was wonderfully convenient.

That should've been enough. I had no explanation for why I pressed my lips to his again. It wasn't sexual. Just a few moments when I could enjoy being close to him... or at least it started that way. He slipped his tongue against my mouth, and I opened readily, deepening the kiss. He fisted his hand in my hair and tugged gently, and I pushed him away before we went at it again.

A dog barking startled us apart. Cameron looked mussed and ridiculously kissable, his mouth still a little wet. I ruffled his hair, not even bothering to try to achieve the perfectly groomed look he'd had before I'd gotten ahold of him.

"Bailey is going to be able to tell what we were doing in here," I said with a wince. She was going to give him the business. "Sorry."

"Completely worth the hassle."

I was glad to know he felt that way, too.

"Come over tonight," he said. "Just for an hour or so. We can have a quick dinner and then... whatever."

Goddamn, his blush was just the cutest thing. "I like whatever," I said gravely, and he swatted me. I headed for the door before I started kissing him again.

"JJ," he said when I was almost to the door.

"Yeah?"

"I'm no expert in flings, but are you sure we're doing this right?"

I chuckled, gesturing at what would now be known as the scene of the crime. Someone should just draw a chalk outline of our dicks. "Doesn't it feel right?"

He didn't laugh as I expected. "Yeah. It does."

My smile faded as I sobered quickly. I knew he wasn't just talking about the sex. Somewhere along the line, I'd started thinking about us as potentially... *more*. I didn't know how that would work, especially if it hadn't worked the first time, but Cameron made me wish things could be different.

If I thought there was a chance he'd take me back, I'd go for it, logistics be damned. But he'd made it clear that he wasn't willing to go there again. If he thought we were in too deep, he'd call even this "fling" quits. I couldn't have that. Not yet.

"Don't forget to eat your lunch," I said lightly before I left his office.

I HOOFED it back across the street to find my father doing the crossword puzzle. He smirked when he saw me. I tried not to flush as I slid into the booth. I folded my arms when he didn't say anything. There was no *possible*, earthly way he could know what I'd been up to.

"Your zipper is down," he said casually.

I looked down so quickly, my eyeballs almost caught whiplash… only to find my zipper perfectly zipped. I huffed as his mouth curved. "We're just friends."

He nodded knowingly. "That's what I do for all my friends. I hang out near their jobs, hoping to catch a glimpse of them. And when that fails, I buy them lunch and hand deliver it. And by deliver it, I mean—"

"If you've ever loved me at all, you won't finish that sentence," I pleaded.

He chuckled. "You should invite him to your brother's shindig."

"Once I figure out what a shindig is, I certainly might."

"Every year he has a barbecue to celebrate his and Charlie's birthday. You know that. It's next weekend. The boys invite Foster every year, but he never accepts. Probably thinks it's a pity invite. I think it would mean something if you were the one doing the inviting." He sent me a stern look with his pen poised over the crossword. "You didn't forget your brother's birthday, did you?"

"Of course not," I said automatically.

It wasn't a lie, exactly. I just hadn't been around to attend one of his beach barbecues in many years. John and his firstborn son, Charles, were born on the same day, and they always celebrated together. I had a feeling that would get old one day, but as a five-year-old, Charlie seemed to love it. He also loved Paw Patrol and chicken nugget pizza, so his taste was pretty questionable.

"Every damn year." He clucked his tongue. "You've missed three of 'em, so this year has to be special."

"I already got Charlie a camera, and John a new grill, old man. Top that."

"I will," he vowed.

"Maybe I'll make them something special as well." I perked up. "You know, when I went to Egypt—"

"If I can't pronounce it, I'm not eating it."

"How delightfully closed-minded of you," I said sourly. "I don't know why I bothered to learn regional dishes for you heathens."

"Neither do I. You should've learned how to make some damned fried chicken. And some macaroni and cheese."

I rolled my eyes. "Mom already taught me how to make those things."

We both froze a little. Even all these years later, we didn't usually bring her up. It wasn't because we didn't remember, rather it was because we remembered all too well. It was like avoiding a tooth in your mouth when you're eating because it's sensitive and sore. If you never addressed it, eventually you just learn to chew a different way. We'd learned to live a different way, tiptoeing around the subject of Lori Sutton.

My father looked at me wistfully. "I never knew she taught you that."

"Sure did. I also know how to make her special sage-and-sausage stuffing, braised short ribs, jalapeno-cheddar cornbread, and her pecan pie." I eyed him. "What the heck did you think she had me in the kitchen for?"

He shrugged. "I don't know. I thought you were just in there helping."

"With Mom, helping very easily turned into learning."

I smiled. She'd been the most patient teacher. She'd had the most engaging laugh, and she'd never let me get away with shortcuts.

"You want to chop like this, honey." She watched as I copied her motions, julienning the basil. *"Curl the fingers of this hand inward and let your knife do all the work."*

Sometimes the grief would hit me in the weirdest of ways. Maybe that was because back then, I hadn't dealt with the pain. I'd tucked it all away wherever it would fit. Over the years, the memories just became little pockets of sadness, waiting for me to discover them at unexpected times. After her death, there was no time to grieve. I'd been too busy trying to hold us all together, even if half the time I hadn't known what the hell I was doing. I wasn't the best Captain, but I saw the freaking icebergs. And I never let us hit them.

John is doing poorly in school, there's no time to cry. Mark just got caught joyriding without a license—nope, no time for a breakdown. Dad didn't make it to work today because he's still in bed hungover, and customers are starting to call about their cars.... Seriously, are you still trying to fucking cry?

"Maybe you could make some of her favorite dishes for the party," Dad ventured.

He was lucky I was a sentimental old fool. "Maybe I will."

"And for dinner," he pressed.

"We'll see." I narrowed my eyes. "If I do, you're only getting a taste. That stuff isn't exactly for the health-conscious."

"We'll see," he parroted my words back without shame. "Now, go and invite your fella."

"He's not my fella," I said automatically. "What Cam and I have is a little casual for the whole hanging out with the family bit."

He snorted. "Cam is family. Always has been. You two might've removed some rings from your fingers, but precious metals don't break a family." He gave me a meaningful look. "They don't make them, either."

"Tell me this is it," he said, rubbing my plain band with a featherlight touch. *"Tell me this is forever."*

I sat there for a few moments, determined not to get lost in that particular memory. Because thinking about Cam putting that band on my finger was painfully linked with me taking it off. I'd left it on his dresser, sure in all my infinite wisdom at twenty-five that I was doing the right thing. Over the years, I wished I hadn't been quite so quick to return the ring. Wallowing in your misery wasn't the same without a proper talisman.

I watched my dad figure out the crossword, tapping my fingers on the table. I wasn't going to move on principle. Not one inch. Cam and I knew what we were doing, and we didn't need any interfering busybodies. Family barbecues were not in the cards.

Dad finally sighed. "For God's sake, JJ. I was hoping to get home before Judge Judy starts."

I huffed as I pushed away from the table. Yes, he'd worn me down quicker than tissue paper. At least I got to see Cam again, even if it was for a few seconds. Dad hid his amusement poorly.

I growled. "He's still not my fella."

"Whatever. I'll be right here." He scratched his chin. "Maybe I'll have some pie while I wait."

"You will do no such thing."

"Mm-hmm."

Oh, I knew what the hell that meant. So, I stopped by Glenna's station to give her some marching orders. "Don't serve him so much as one spoonful of pie," I told her. "He gets fresh fruit and nothing else."

She stood up straighter, looking smart as any soldier. "You got it, hun."

I headed for the door. As I stepped into the sunshine, I heard an upraised voice. "What do you mean you're not going to serve me any pie? I'm a paying customer, dammit." That was followed by an even louder, "Cantaloupe!"

I chuckled to myself.

20

CAMERON

Saturday, I threw on some board shorts, a T-shirt, and some sandals and then headed down to the beach. The strip was as busy as I expected, and it took me several minutes of stalking scantily-clad beachgoers before I found someone leaving. My prey took an inordinately long time mounting his surfboard on top of his SUV, but I persisted, even when the cars started to line up behind me. Even when someone honked repeatedly. Even when the cop on a Segway motored over to see what the hubbub was all about. Surfer dude finally peeled off with a cheerful wave, and I gave him a wave in return before I took his spot.

I got out and had a good, long stretch. John and Charlie couldn't have asked for better weather for their birthday party. It was sunny, but the heat was tempered by a little ocean-scented breeze, which was just enough wind to lift my hair, but not enough to blow sand in my face... or my burger, because I *was* having a burger. Unfortunately, this wasn't a dog-friendly beach. I'd gotten more than one mournful look from Kona as I left the house. She could always tell when fun was afoot and she was missing out.

It took me a few minutes to grab everything I needed from the car —my shades, a beach bag, and a couple of colorfully wrapped gifts.

The shades went on my face, the beach bag strap over my shoulder, and the gifts under my arm. Then I headed down the strip, following the occasional sign that read *Sutton Party!*

I chuckled at the last Sutton Party sign because it read *Really? You should see us by now.* I topped a dune and squinted down at the bottom to find the party area, decorated with colorful balloons. They'd picked a secluded spot, and I could hear music coming up from the beach. Jack was already set up in a beach chair, a drink in one hand and Honey on his lap. Clearly, he hadn't gotten the no-dogs-allowed notice. Journey was setting up beach chairs and tables by himself.

I sighed as I picked my way down the sandy dune. I wasn't surprised in the least. His brothers were fully capable of handling setup on their own. They'd done it the three years he hadn't been here. But the moment he came back home, they just fell into the same old patterns of leaning on him—hard. It was like they couldn't help themselves, and he didn't know how to tell them no.

I came up behind Journey as he was cursing the bum leg of one of the tables. He was only wearing a pair of navy-blue swim trunks, putting all that peachy skin on display, and the bird tattoo was only half visible on his lower back. I wanted to brush a kiss on that tattoo, which had become one of my favorite spots to touch. It always made him shiver. But quite frankly, the less I touched a nearly naked Journey in public, the better.

I settled for pressing my lips to his sun-warmed shoulder, just for a second, and he jumped a little. "You'd better be wearing sunscreen."

"Hey! You made it." He sent me a big smile before delivering a kick to the table leg. It snapped in place, and I chuckled. "And yes, I am."

"Mm-hmm." He was a notorious sunscreen shirker. I was tempted to put some more on him, just to be sure, but I resisted. He *did* smell a little coconuty, but then again, he always smelled like that. I thought it might be from his shampoo.

Judging from the number of personal belongings—beach bags, towels, a couple of discarded bottles of sunscreen, and plenty of flip-flops—I was probably the last to arrive. "Where are the birthday boys?"

"They're in the water already with Mindy and some of the kids. I think Laura took her crew on a seashell hunt."

"And everyone else?"

"Right over the next dune. Mark struck up a game of volleyball with some of the younger folk—"

"The *younger* folk? What are we, ready for the retirement home?"

The wind blew his sandy hair in his eyes, and he shook it back. "Do *you* want to go play beach volleyball?"

I shuddered. "Hell no."

"All I'm sayin'." He shrugged. "The only thing I'm interested in spiking is my drink."

I snorted. "What about Matt? Did he make it yet?"

"Yup. He's manning the grill, so we should have burgers and dogs and corn on the cob in about ten minutes."

Well, Matt was certainly excused, but I had no idea why the rest of them weren't helping. I bit down on the inside of my cheek to keep from asking. "Where do you need me?"

"Well, I'm almost done here. I've got the beach chairs all set up and the snack table. This table is for the presents and that one over there is for the drinks and ice." He glanced around, and I could almost see him ticking things off his mental list. "Shit, I forgot to get the ice."

"The Circle K is right up the road," I said. "Someone can make a quick run."

He shook his head. "They're all having fun, I don't want—"

"JJ, it won't kill them to get some ice," I said exasperatedly. "Stop treating them like kids."

He was a little surprised at my vehemence but gave me a little nod. "Habit, I guess." He looked at the gifts still tucked under my arm. "I see you're my first contribution to the gift table."

"Yep. I hope John still fans out over Star Wars because I got him a lamp in the shape of the Death Star. And for Charlie, a robot dinosaur."

He laughed. "Well, that's just perfect. His dinosaur phase is still going strong. As for John, I don't think his Star Wars phase will ever end. He's gonna love it."

I pretended to wipe sweat from my brow with relief. "Where are the other gifts?"

"Still loaded up in the back of Laura's SUV." He snapped his fingers. "I should probably go get those."

"JJ."

"I'll get someone to help," he said, rolling his eyes.

He absolutely wouldn't. "You've got someone to help. All I need is Laura's keys." I put the gifts on the designated table and held out my hand. "I'm going to marshal the troops, and we're going to get busy."

He looked like he wanted to argue, but Jack's voice interrupted whatever he was going to say. "Listen to him, boy," he said mildly. "We were just talking about this, weren't we? When they jumped out of the car and ran down here like kids, whooping and hollering? And you had to get me down here by yourself?"

I gave Jack a nod of approval. "I'm glad someone else is trying to talk some sense into you."

Journey grunted as he lifted a couple of cases of beer to take to the drinks table. "Yes, you're both taking turns riding my back like a pair of monkeys, one heavier than the last."

Jack and I looked at each other appraisingly, trying to determine who was Regular Monkey and who was Heavy Monkey. "He's talking about you," we said simultaneously.

THE DAY PASSED all too quickly in a haze of good food, family, and relaxation. At some point, I was dragged into the volleyball game by Mark, and then into the water by some of the kids. I made the mistake of playing sea monster and dunking Livy, and she came up demanding, "Again, again!"

It quickly became a hostage situation. I was forced to dunk the rest of the crew as the sound of giggling and squealing split the air.

Laura finally paid my ransom in the form of kid kryptonite—sugar. She clapped her hands at the edge of the water and called out a single word. "Cake!"

I gave her a grateful look as I made my way back to a beach chair next to John. He offered me a beer from a cooler near his feet, and I waved him off. I didn't need a drink. I needed aspirin and some sleep. Also maybe some therapy for my kid-related PTSD.

As the sun made its descent in the sky, Journey pulled out his camera. I smiled faintly as he tried to get organic photos of the kids, and they all delighted in thwarting him. "Stop looking at the bloody camera and act freaking natural," could be heard more than once. I chuckled as Charlie did a headstand and crossed his eyes.

"I wonder if he'd be interested in taking some pictures at Bailey's wedding," I mused. "Not the whole thing, of course, but I think she'd get a kick out of having a JJ Sutton wedding photo."

John snorted. "Like he'll still be here by then."

Right. I felt like he'd sucker punched me, which was ridiculous. I'd known Journey was leaving from the beginning. I'd been so determined to push his looming departure out of my mind that I'd actually managed to do so. "It was just a thought," I murmured.

"Anything regarding the future and my brother is a stupid thought."

I frowned. "I think you're being a little hard on him."

"Not that I agree with you, but he's my brother, so I get to do that."

"Well, he's my...." At John's arched brow, I faltered.

"He's your...," he prodded.

"Friend," I finished lamely, ignoring his resulting snort. "He's my friend, so I have the right to be concerned about him. And you. I still think of you like family."

"Don't be stupid," he said, "you *are* family."

"Thank you," I said dryly. "I love my Welcome to the Family, You're a Fucking Moron gift basket."

He sighed. "Sorry, I just get a little riled up when I talk about Journey and his ways."

"So I heard. He told me you said he was off in his Journey world doing Journey things and throwing his dirty money around." I eyed him narrowly. "Even though you certainly didn't seem to mind the college funds he set up for the kids. Or when he floated you that loan last year."

"I appreciate everything he's done," he shot back.

"He didn't do it for kudos. And he's done a lot more for you all than pay the occasional bill." As his jaw tightened, I pressed my point. "Tell me I'm wrong."

"I know all that."

"Do you? I don't think you know all the sacrifices he made for you guys," I said mildly, trying not to come on too strong. But fuck, he wasn't a kid anymore. He should be able to apply an adult lens to his childhood.

John let out a sigh. "I really don't want to talk about this right now."

Too bad. "Did you know he wanted to go to college in Rhode Island? One of his photography idols was alumni there and created a program for photojournalism. He got accepted, too. Partial scholarship." I eyed John, who was fiddling with the label on his beer. "He decided it would be selfish to leave you boys and he put all that aside. Then he decided to go to community college, but even that became too much. Your dad... wasn't taking care of the business as he should, and JJ had to step in."

"That's a nice euphemism for dad getting fall-down drunk and sleeping the day away," he murmured.

Maybe he used the adult lens now and again after all. It was time he used it for his brother. "Did you know he used to run track? He was pretty good at it, too."

"I remember," he said, a small smile playing on his face. "Why do you think I ran the 440 when I was in high school? The coach thought I was better suited for the 200, but if JJ did it, I wanted to do it, too."

"Well, if you remember that, then you also remember he had to quit. There was no more time for frivolous things like track practice.

Or French club. Or jazz band." I winced. "Not that he was good at that last one, but still. It was something he liked to do."

"The trombone." John shivered. "Why the trombone?"

I concurred, but Journey's lack of talent regarding musical instruments was beside the point. "More sacrifice. Do you know what that was like? One day he was a kid, free to join random clubs and hang out with his friends. The next, he was in charge, trying to hold everything together. His childhood ended the day your mother died, John. And he spent the next fifteen years making sure yours didn't."

I held up a hand when he opened his mouth. "I *know* he didn't always succeed. And I know it sucked for you guys. No one is saying you had a cakewalk. But maybe it's time for you to give credit where credit is due."

"Why are you telling me all this now?" he asked quietly.

"Because someone should've said it a long time ago. It should've been him, in a perfect world. But he loves you boys so much I don't think he ever would."

Just when I thought my words might be sinking in, John's face hardened. "I did my time." A muscle in his jaw ticked. "I did my time."

"Excuse me?"

"That's what he said to you."

I thought about that for a few moments, my brow furrowed. Not because I didn't remember the words—those, I remembered perfectly. But as far as I knew, we'd been alone.

"Where were you?" I finally asked.

"In the kitchen. I came through the back door. I heard you guys arguing, and I didn't want to interrupt."

"That doesn't excuse you for being a dirty little eavesdropper."

"That's not the point. Apparently taking care of us was so miserable having kids with you was akin to being thrown into Shawshank." His jaw worked as he stared at the ocean. "I did my fucking time."

"He was young and felt trapped," I said quietly. "He said a lot of things he didn't mean. So have I. And so have you, quite frankly. You're forgetting that I was there when you were a bratty, smart-mouthed kid, John. You said some things that your mother would've tanned your hide for."

He didn't deny it. *"You're not my real fucking father,"* was on the list—a lot—but it wasn't the worst. That honor belonged to what he'd spat at Journey after one of their last blowups. John had blown off curfew to go to a party, and it wasn't the first time. He should've known that Mark would spill the beans about his whereabouts. He *definitely* should've known that Journey would show up and drag him out by his collar.

They'd gotten in the car, each slamming their door harder than the last. They'd argued the entire way home as I drove. I occupied myself by concentrating on the rain-slick roads and giving John warning looks in the mirror when he got too mouthy. He hit all the hall-of-fame greats—*you're not my father, you're ruining my life*, and *it was just one fucking party*. There was nothing to say when he loaded the final barbed arrow in his quiver, though.

"I wish you would've been the one who died instead of mom."

The resulting silence in the car had been awful. I'd never seen Journey look quite so defeated or withdrawn. And I'd never forgotten his response as he stared out the window at the passing road.

"So do I."

From the look on John's face, he was lost in the same memory. Hopefully, he'd gloss over the part where I threatened to throw him out of the moving car if he ever spoke to his brother like that again. I'd never been so furious. Journey had seemed checked out, his head against the seat, his eyes locked on the passing scenery.

When John spoke, his voice was hoarse. "If I could have one back, that would be it. I've apologized many times since, but that would be it."

"I know. Eventually, we all have to grow up, John." I blew out a breath. Hard conversations weren't my specialty, but this one was long overdue. "If anyone deserves your understanding, it's him. Whatever he chooses to do, wherever he chooses to go... you need to be supportive. He's earned that."

John swallowed. "He'd be happier here," he finally said.

"That's not up to you."

Or me. He didn't deny anything I said, which I took as a positive sign.

"If you're so understanding, then why haven't you forgiven him yet?" John asked.

"I have."

"Then why are you still punishing him?"

"A, what do you mean? And B, how did this become about me?" I asked defensively.

"He wants to get back together with you, but you keep slamming that door in his face. And everyone knows about this supposedly casual fling you guys are having." He snorted. "Since when have you felt anything casual for JJ?"

I flushed. I wasn't surprised everyone knew because we weren't exactly being covert about it. I also suspected Mindy had sent out another newsletter with an update. And pictures. Netta was reading something in the waiting room when I brought out Kimble, and she nearly broke a finger jamming it in her purse.

"I can't be the reason he stays." My voice was subdued. "He's living his dream."

John hummed. "You can have more than one dream, Foss."

It was hard to tamp down my irritation, but I managed. I'd certainly given him a lot of unsolicited advice this afternoon, and he had the right to do the same. But John didn't understand. How could he? His wife wasn't going anywhere. She loved John, this town, and their kids, so just what the fuck did he know? He didn't know what it was like to lose the love of his life to a backpack and a dream. I had to keep a safe distance from Journey, so I could remember what this was.

And everything that it wasn't.

"I'm not falling in love with him again," I finally said. "Not when he has one foot out the door."

"Oh, Foss." He looked at me with a mix of fondness and sadness. "You say that like you have a choice."

"John." We both glanced up at the sound of Mindy's voice as she marched by, a kid dangling from her grip. His hair was smeared liberally with frosting and tears streaked his chubby cheeks. "I need you to talk with Mandy while I get this one cleaned off."

We watched them proceed to the shower area with wide eyes. I wasn't sure the slow trickle of the courtesy beach shower was going to handle all that.

John shook his head as he levered himself up from his beach chair. "Duty calls. I appreciate the talk." He grimaced. "And no offense, but I think I'm set on sharing feelings with you for a little bit."

I sent him an earnest look. "I promise, nothing but football, hockey, and boobs until Christmas."

He chuckled. "I'm not sure I want to hear your thoughts on boobs," he said as he walked away, presumably to find the mischievous Mandy.

"My thoughts on boobs are a delight," I called after him.

"Should I even ask?"

I glanced to my right to see Journey standing there, a slight smile on his face. He looked exhausted but pleased with himself. That was probably due to the camera hanging around his neck. He was tanned and probably a little sunburned, judging from his slightly rosy shoulders.

"I told you to put on more sunscreen," I fretted, like any good mother hen.

"Don't mother me, Fossie." He grinned as he leaned down and braced his hands on either side of my beach chair. And suddenly we were face-to-face, those warm amber eyes so close I could see the gold sunburst pattern in his irises. "Hi," he said.

"Hi," was all I managed before he gave me a smacking kiss. He tasted like Funfetti cake. I was hard-pressed not to suck on his tongue. The knowledge that my swim trunks might be loose, but hid very little, kept me on the path of righteousness. That and the fact that I could probably talk my way into his bed tonight. No sane man could watch JJ's ass in swim trunks all day and not pencil in some time to fuck it. And I was an *extremely* sane man.

"I'm glad you could make it," he said.

"So am I."

I knew we were smiling goofily at each other, but I couldn't seem to stop. Not even with the attention we were attracting.

"Kiss, kiss, kiss," Charlie chanted, and we laughed.

A few others took up the hue and cry. I was just thankful that Mindy was otherwise occupied. She would've probably pulled out a pad and pen—I was pretty sure she was writing Journey and Cam fanfiction.

"What do you think?" he asked, his amber eyes sparkling. "Should we give 'em a show?"

What the hell? There was plenty of time tomorrow to think about how stupid we were being. "Let's give 'em somethin' to talk about, Sutton."

"Oh God," he groaned, "don't do that."

"Do what?" I asked innocently.

"Get all Southern. You put on an accent so thick, Paula Dean would ask for a goddamned translator."

"Well, butter my butt and call me a biscuit."

"You're not even *from* here." His eyes danced. "Weren't you born in Pennsylvania?"

"Kiss," Charlie reminded us.

Journey chuckled right before his mouth met mine. We kept it perfectly chaste, like two nuns who had to buss cheeks to get their rosary beads back. That didn't stop everyone from making exaggerated "oohs" and "ahhs." Matt even gave us a wolf whistle that made me pray for my tympanic membrane. When Journey pulled back, his cheeks were flushed and he was laughing.

I'd never seen a more beautiful sight in my life.

"All right ya'll." He clapped his hands. "It's getting late, and I need to get all these tables and chairs back to the rental store." His statement was met with groans and boos. "You can still sit on towels! I'm not paying a late fee because you think you're too good for sand."

Journey met some vigorous booing with a cheeky middle finger, and people started vacating their chairs. Surprisingly, John immediately started breaking down tables. After a moment, Mark got up and joined him. Matt maintained his position, drinking a beer, until his brothers dumped him out of his beach chair and onto the sand. After a few moments of hushed conversation, he got up and started helping, too.

I turned to find Journey looking at me, a brow raised. "Should I even ask what you said to him?"

"Something you should've said a long time ago."

He huffed. "Nosy bastard."

"He's not a little kid anymore, JJ. None of them are."

"I still want to protect them. How is this your business anyway?" he demanded without heat.

Everything about your happiness is my business. Since he'd shown me what it was like to have a real friend in high school, I'd been willing to walk over coals for him. Decades and struggles of life hadn't changed that. I didn't bother to answer his rhetorical question. Instead, I kissed him on the tip of the nose and started helping break down the chairs.

It took us about a half hour to get everything loaded up in the cars. We had to make the back-breaking trip up the dune and walk the block to Mark's truck several times. I didn't mind. Manual labor kept me from pondering how very screwed I was.

I frowned as I put the last chair on the back of the pickup. Journey had been pretty quiet as well as we made trek after trek. He knew what I knew—that we were fooling ourselves with this stupid fling shit. We were as into each other as we always were. All that was left was to never talk about that shit ever.

Journey closed the truck bed with a clang. "One last step. I have to get Dad and then it's back to the rental store."

"I'll go to the rental store. You take care of your dad."

He started shaking his head before I could even finish speaking. "I couldn't ask you to—"

"You didn't ask me to do anything."

He gave me a doubtful look as he hesitantly put the key fob in my palm. "You're sure?"

"Yeah."

"You're a lifesaver." He kissed me on the cheek. "I'll see you in a little bit."

"Yep."

I got in the truck and adjusted the settings to my liking. As I tilted the rearview mirror, I used it to watch him walk away until he disappeared back over the dune. He looked exhausted but happy. I wanted to shoulder some of his burdens. Now that I wasn't a selfish twenty-year-old kid, I knew how.

A couple of chattering DJs shook me out of my thoughts, which I desperately needed. I needed to do normal stuff. Journey-free stuff. I started the truck. Normal was good. Normal was healthy. Normal was not falling in love again with someone who had itchy feet and a well-stamped passport.

"Now," I told myself firmly as I pulled into traffic. "Stop thinking about Journey."

And because Murphy's Law is always determined to prove itself, the first strains of "Don't Stop Believin' " suddenly filled the car. I sighed and cast a look at the radio. "Seriously?"

21

CAMERON

Bailey's cake tasting wasn't going well. She and Laura's assistant, Moira, had different ideas about flavors. Bailey was all about traditional. Moira, who I had a feeling didn't get to make cakes for weddings often, was determined to flex her pastry school muscles. There had been no less than four skirmishes, and we were only three samples in.

Currently, Moira was in the back, looking for a special sample of fig and guava cake that we just *had* to try. It didn't sound all that tasty, but my tongue told my brain he was taking point on this. My tongue's platform—cake was fucking cake. My taste buds thought that slogan was a real keeper, so I kept my fork ready.

"What did you think about the Italian buttercream?" Bailey asked as she flipped through the laminated sample book. "I think I liked it more than the American. What do you think?"

I wasn't even sure which had been which.

"I don't know," I said helpfully.

I had bigger fish to fry. Early on, I'd suspected Journey didn't know what he was doing with this fling business, but now I knew for sure. He didn't even know how to text properly. He was supposed to send me skeevy messages at ungodly hours of the night, like the innocuous, *You up?* We weren't supposed to be texting each other throughout the day. Or call each other most nights. Or having dinner with each other and *talking about our day*.

When we were kids, I'd known him better than anyone on earth. Then we'd broken up and time marched on. The core of who we were as individuals was the same, but there was a whole period of his life I hadn't been a part of. And while I was curious about the experiences that had shaped him as a person, it was safer not to fill in those gaps. So, what did I decide to do?

I sighed, propping my chin in my hand. I filled in the fucking gaps.

Now I knew that one of his favorite places to visit was Meteora, Greece, and his favorite subjects to photograph were birds because it was challenging—they were small, fast, and rarely kept still. I knew that he got that scar on his knee when he fell off a rock trying to get the perfect shot of an owl. And that his scariest moment in the field was when he was bluff-charged by a black bear.

I also knew what he sounded like when he came, so undone and uninhibited that if I wasn't already *there*, watching him orgasm usually did the trick. Older Journey was a lot freakier than younger Journey had been, which scandalized and fascinated me in equal measure. When he'd asked me to call him my slut and smack his ass while I was fucking him, I didn't think my cheeks could've gotten any pinker. Or, my dick any harder. I still wasn't sure if he made the request because it turned his crank or because he enjoyed hearing me stumble over the words. *Fucker.*

We hadn't switched things up yet with bottoming. I kept meaning to, but I was entirely too busy enjoying myself. Although, we'd gotten close a few nights ago. In preparation, he'd rimmed me thoroughly while I jacked off and did my best not to come. Before I knew it, he was putting a condom on me and getting on top.

"You said you'd fuck *me* this time," I'd informed him crossly as I gripped his ass. It was all hot air because there was no way I wasn't getting inside him.

"I know what I said," he'd informed me cheekily, adding a little bit of lube.

And then he'd taken me inside with one smooth thrust, and I had nothing else cogent to say. "So glad you're a top," he'd said a little dreamily.

I'd smacked his leg, trying not to laugh. "Stop saying that."

I guess it was win-win either way. I certainly wasn't going to complain about getting to fuck those perfectly round, firm cheeks, which I'd proceeded to do—vigorously. He'd urged me on the entire way, goaded me, really. I couldn't go fast enough or get deep enough for his liking. I'd finally had to flip him on the bed facedown, just so I could drill him like we both needed. And to get a break from his back seat driving. Back seat fucking. Whatever.

I scowled. It was like he realized our time together was almost up and he was trying to get as much action as he could before then. He was storing me up, like a sexual camel.

"How long is a fling?" I asked Bailey suddenly. She paused, making me realize that I'd cut her off midsentence. I flushed. "Sorry."

She raised an eyebrow, flipping another page in the sample book. "Were you even listening to me?"

"Of course," I said confidently. Well, I heard most of it. She'd said something about buttercream and meringue and... well, who the fuck knew. I was in a potential crisis here. "If you answer my question, I can give you my undivided attention."

"Good, because you're supposed to be helping me pick out a cake."

I was the wrong person for this outing. Cake and I had a very simple relationship and it was real and true. I needed it on a plate with a heap of frosting. The only garnish I needed was a utensil, preferably a fork that understood it was about to work like it had just joined CrossFit.

I shrugged. "I already tried to give you my input."

"Telling me I'd better go with chocolate is not input."

"Chocolate is always a crowd-pleaser." I made a face at one of her decadent finalists. "Almond amaretto sounds like a cake that wants to be alone."

She huffed. "Just what do you know about complex flavors?"

"That's what I've been telling you," I said exasperatedly. "Now. How long is a fling?"

"A fling is a fling until you both decide it's flung."

I briefly wondered if that would make more sense if I wrote it down. In the end, there was only one real response to that. "Wut?"

She shrugged. "I told you from the beginning that this was a stupid idea."

"You absolutely did not. You told me to go for it. Then you got on my case about inviting him as my plus one to the wedding."

"Yes. I said go for it. Not have a stupid fling. You're not a fling type of guy." She contemplated a picture of a glorious, vanilla tower of cake with gold-leaf accents. "This whole thing had heartache written all over it from the start."

"Well, why didn't you tell *me* that?"

"I did. Or maybe that was Irene from the deli." She frowned. "Or the florist?"

"Bee."

She flapped a hand. "Well, the point is that I told *someone*."

I slouched in my chair. It squeaked dangerously under me. Everything in this shop was clearly created by forest nymphs, but I was done being gentle. A chair that couldn't handle my rump roast didn't deserve to live.

"Okay, let's say I'd told you from the very beginning that having casual sex with an ex was a stupid idea and things wouldn't end well." Bailey put a sticker on a yellow buttercream cake as a possibility. "Would you have listened?"

Well, of course not. I'd wanted him and to hell with the consequences. I didn't answer because I had no intention of wasting my time stating the obvious. Bailey made a sound of satisfaction and went back to her cake book.

It would help if he was kind of a dick or had some horrible traits I could hang my hat on. I'd thought I might've had something a few days ago when he took Kona and the newly named Scribbles for a walk. I'd volunteered to stay behind and start dinner. It started to rain only a few minutes after they left.

They were back ten minutes later, soaking wet, and proceeded to track mud all through the house. To top it off, Kona did her best water sprinkler impression in the living room and the usually well-behaved Scribbles followed suit. Journey got the worst of it, but he didn't even get mad. He just laughed at their antics—*Laughed!*—like a maniac.

By the time dinner was ready, he'd cleaned up everything. He'd even bathed the dogs. And Kona hated baths, but she was laid out on the side of the couch she'd claimed, dry and fluffy, looking content with the world in general.

Journey came down the hall, wearing a pair of my sweats and a T-shirt, toweling off his sandy blond hair. My clothes on him were a bit baggy and loose, but he'd cinched the drawstring tight. I could hear the soft hum of the dryer. And it was so perfectly, ridiculously something I could see us doing every day for the rest of our lives that it had stopped me in my tracks.

I wanted this.

I stood there, clutching the platter of chicken and roasted potatoes like they were the last food items on earth. When I'd put that ring on his finger all those years ago, *this* is what I'd wanted.

"*Tell me this is it,*" *I said, rubbing the plain band with a featherlight touch.* "*Tell me this is forever.*"

When he saw me staring at him without saying anything, he blushed a little and apologized for wearing my clothes again. I assured him that it was fine, and we sat down to eat. Well, we both sat down, but he did most of the eating. I did a lot of reflecting on stupid people who did stupid things that ended stupidly.

Moira bustled back through the kitchen doors, a little display box in her hands. It contained round frosted circles on sticks decorated like bumblebees. "You know, I had an out-of-the-box idea," she suggested, her hazel eyes dancing with excitement. "Cake pops!"

Bailey's eyes widened with burgeoning outrage, and I whispered, "Back in the box. Get back in the box."

Moira squeaked, clutching her bumblebees. "Lemon with Italian buttercream?"

"Go get it," I advised. "Hurry."

It took me a few minutes to calm Mount Bailey down. When she could finally speak, the little monkey didn't hesitate to jump right on my back. "So, about this plus one situation—"

"No."

"I'm just trying to figure out my seating chart—"

"Nope."

"Cam." She sighed, clearly debating on whether she should say what was becoming glaringly obvious. "Why don't you tell him how you feel?"

The bell tinkled as someone entered the shop, but I was too irritated to notice. It wasn't that simple. And I was the worst flinger in the history of the world. I thought about him too often, and every time we hung up the phone, I wanted to call him right back. That shit had to stop.

"I have no affinity for Journey other than sex." Her doubtful look only ramped up my irritation. "That's it, I swear."

"And nothing more?"

"We're just fucking, Bee," I said, purposefully harsh with myself. I needed to remember that. "No feelings involved."

"Wow." I looked up at the sound of a familiar voice and saw Journey standing there, frozen behind Bailey. His eyes were a little wide. "Just... wow."

I wanted to pull out my hair. Because why *wouldn't* he walk up just as I was spouting such callousness? Again. "How the fuck do you keep doing that?" I practically shouted.

"I'm picking up a box of assorted goods for the kids in my photography class," he said mildly. "We're going to take pictures of them and eat them, then take pictures of the remnants. It's all very Brillat-Savarin."

"Who?"

"Tell me what you eat, and I'll tell you what you are?" When I continued to look at him blankly, he shrugged. "Well, it's going to be fun anyway."

"Right." I sighed. *Cleanup of my big mouth on aisle two.*

"I just had another thought," Moira said from the backroom. "Who needs cake at all? Brookies are all the rage nowadays. What about a monogrammed brookie for each guest?"

Bailey's wrought iron chair made a screech against the floor as she pushed back from the table. I shook my head sadly as she stormed off toward the back, eager to confront a rogue baker who had no sense of self-preservation. I stood as well, turning to face Journey full-on.

"I tried to tell her," I said.

His smile was a little tight. "Moira does like to push the envelope."

Just looking at him, I could tell he'd been out taking pictures. His hair was a little wind-blown and he was wearing what I'd come to know as his field clothes—well-worn, faded jeans and an equally faded T-shirt with some battered Converse. He liked to wear something comfortable that he didn't mind getting dirty.

I cleared my throat. "I'm sorry."

Those amber eyes were cautious on mine. "It's okay."

"It's actually not." I owed him more than an apology, but that was a good place to start. "Are you mad?"

He shook his head slowly. "I'm not mad, but I'd also like to think that we're friends."

"We are."

"I can get 'just fucking' with anyone. I wanted to have sex with you."

"So did I." I felt a little flustered. "So *do* I."

"Then why do you keep trying to make it seem like it's tawdry and less?"

If he could be honest, so could I, even if it felt all too vulnerable for my comfort. Even if I might ruin everything. "Because I have to remind myself."

His brow furrowed. "Remind yourself of what? How disposable I am?"

I drew back as if he'd struck me. Is that what it sounded like? "Of course not."

"Then what?"

"I have to remind myself of what this is, or I'm going to be in real trouble when you leave, all right? So just... please forgive me."

He seemed to be chewing on that because he didn't speak for a few moments. "You're not the only one who's having trouble with this, Cam."

More charged silence filled the room but neither of did anything about it. Actually, it wasn't completely silent. I could hear Bailey and Moira arguing in the back, but the world was all white noise when Journey was looking at me like that. Like maybe... maybe we could be something else.

I blew out a breath. "Should we just stop this now? Go cold turkey?"

He snorted. "Do you think we could pull that off?"

"Not really, no." I gave him a little half smile. "Do you hear us carrying on? I think one of us has to scratch JJ and Cam on a tree now."

"Not it," he said with a sniff. "I'm a wilderness aficionado. I'm not defacing a damn tree."

I walked the few steps to close the distance between us. Then I kissed him, because I had to. I liked the way he smelled, all coconut and lime. I liked the way he stretched up to meet me halfway. I liked the way his mouth was soft and familiar. I liked the little humming sound he made when I pulled away.

"Come with me." I held out my hand, and he took it gamely, his palm sliding roughly across mine. "Bailey is going to be a while, and she doesn't need my help anyway. She might not know what she wants, but she knows *exactly* what she doesn't want."

He glanced at the back doubtfully. "Are you sure?"

"Well... no. But I *am* sure I don't want to be witness to a bride-on-baker crime."

He chuckled, letting me tow him out the door. "Where are we going?"

"I want to spend the rest of the day with you, and I'm tired of pretending otherwise."

He didn't say anything as we walked down the street. I wasn't towing him along anymore, but I didn't see the need to let go of his hand. We'd reached my car before he finally spoke. "This is everything we said we wouldn't do, you know."

"I know."

The sun caught his eyes as he looked up at me, making them gleam like molten gold. "Maybe we should just ditch the rules and let things run their course."

I frowned. "We know where that leads."

"Would that be such a bad thing?"

God, John was right, about one thing at least. Journey was thinking about us getting back together. It's not like I was any better. I was falling in love with him all over again, and I didn't know how to stop. But he wasn't ever going to be happy in our little cove. When he left—and he *would* leave—he wouldn't just be taking that well-worn duffel. No, he'd be taking my heart, too—again.

Then why the fuck do you keep giving it to him?

A frown pulled at the corners of his mouth as the silence lengthened. "We're not the same people we were back then. Things are different now. *We're* different now."

I reached down to brush a flyaway hair out of his eyes. I wasn't even sure if he was aware of how he leaned into my touch, light and fleeting as it was. "Not different enough."

He stared at me for a few moments before accepting my decision with a nod. "Okay. I have to accept that. But you're not getting rid of me just yet, Foss."

"I wasn't trying to."

"We still have a couple of weeks left before the end of summer. I want to go to your house and do all those things we said we wouldn't do."

"Even though we know we're being stupid."

He lifted a shoulder. "Pretty much. You in?"

"Of course." I smiled. "Let's go be coupley and stupid."

WE SPENT THE DAY TOGETHER, exactly as planned. We didn't do anything particularly newsworthy—in fact, it should've been too boring to even think about. It wasn't. We stopped by the market and bought ingredients for dinner and then went home and cooked together. We ate, took the dogs for a walk in the park, and then settled down on the couch to watch TV. Then we fucked like rabbits for a while because we're not *actually* eighty years old.

I took him on the kitchen island because it's my house and I can be freaky if I want to. Then again in my bed because I was old and fucking on marble wasn't all that comfortable. The angle was all wrong and kneeling on a barstool wasn't safe. Well, anyway, we wound up in bed and checked a few more things off a very X-rated list. Rimming and getting rimmed was at the top. So was coming so hard I saw stars.

I fucked him through my orgasm, my hips moving almost without my permission. He groaned, tightening around me in every way possible. "God, that's just so fucking good," he managed. "You just have no idea."

"I'd like to," I said pointedly.

"Yeah, yeah, yeah. You'll get your chance to get dicked down later, Fossie." He reached back and gripped my hip. "Now harder."

I did what I was told because that's what you do when someone is strangling your dick with his slick, tight hole.

Neither one of us moved afterward. Twilight turned into darkness, shadows lengthening in the room, and still, I made no effort to get up. Not for cleanup. Not to turn off the TV still playing in the living room. Not to pick up the mess we'd made when *someone* swept everything off my kitchen island to provide room for fucking. I won't say who it was, but I will say that *I* would never do something so impulsive—and hot.

"I should get back."

Journey's words were the first either of us had spoken in over half an hour, and leave it to him to ruin the bliss of cuddling. I didn't acknowledge his statement, but I did let go of his hand where our fingers were interlaced. I rolled off him and onto my stomach, my face in the pillow. I felt a gentle kiss on my shoulder a moment later.

He groaned as he got out of bed. "You mind if I use your shower?"

"Yes, I mind. Kissing, yes. Fucking, hell yes, but don't you set one damn foot in my shower," I said, dry as toast.

He swatted my behind. "I swear to God, you used to be so damned nice. I think your pleasant nature is draining out of your pores or something."

I shrugged. That's what happened when you were on a constant diet of wanting the thing you shouldn't want. The thing in question padded to the shower. A few moments later, I heard the water turn on.

He didn't take long. He was back before I could drift off. The bed depressed on either side of me as he kneeled on the mattress. I could smell his coconut-scented shampoo. I *may* have bought a bottle to use when I beat off in the shower. I'm weak, all right?

He leaned down and kissed my nape. "Are you busy tomorrow? I thought we could go to Fork."

I squinted at him over my shoulder. "What is that, some sort of position? Is that the one where you—"

"No," he said quickly. "And please don't pull up an X-rated Power-Point presentation."

I shrugged and dropped my face back into the pillow. "Fork you."

He chuckled. "*Fork*. It's that new restaurant in downtown Miami. It's a bit of a drive, but it's supposed to be nice with views of the city. They have a lot of fusion cuisine, which I knew you like."

"Oh."

"Oh?" He poked me in the side, and I flinched, even though it didn't hurt. "Is that a good oh? Or an, *oh crap, I need an escape hatch* oh?"

"I never need an escape hatch when I'm with you." I gave him a moment to enjoy the sweetness of it all before I added a squirt of lemon. "But that sounds suspiciously like a date."

"It's just a meal, Fossie." He thrust against me lazily a few times, and I found myself arching up to meet him. "And then, I think we should come back here so I can fuck this ass."

Another few thrusts, and I let out a soft moan. He chuckled wickedly. "You good with that?"

"Apparently."

He kissed me one last time before levering himself off the bed. I heard him gathering his clothes and starting to dress. "I'll be here at seven, and you'll be ready in your nice black slacks and that green sweater that makes your eyes pop."

"I'm not wearing a fucking sweater in this heat," I said crossly. "And how did you know I never know what the hell to wear?"

"Kona told me." Journey chuckled as Kona the traitor rolled over with a long sigh. "It's a lightweight sweater. Practically a shirt with long sleeves. We're also going to be inside ninety percent of the time."

"It's that other ten percent I'm worried about," I complained. "I might pass out, right there in the entrance of Spoon."

"Fork," he corrected with a chuckle. "If you pass out, I'll roll you to the table and you'll have a nice meal waiting when you come to."

Hmph. I rolled out of bed as he started putting on his sneakers. "You don't have to get up," he said. "I know how to let myself out."

"I know." I yawned as I pulled on my boxers. "Kona needs a bathroom break, or she'll never give me any peace."

I didn't even remember how normal people woke up anymore. I woke up to Kona an inch away from my nose, treating me to a hot breath facial. When she was certain I was awake, she barked in my face. Just once. It was a particular joy of hers, and one more thing I would keep from the owners of her future forever home. Some things had to be discovered.

She padded behind us as we headed for the front door. I let her out but stayed on the porch since I was barefoot. It wasn't all bad because I got another chance to kiss Journey one more time before he left. Okay, maybe more than once. All right, we wound up kissing on the porch for a bit, long enough for Kona to have done her business ten times over. Journey's hands looped around my neck lightly, but I decided to make better use of mine and grip his ass possessively. From the way he hummed against my mouth when I squeezed, he didn't seem to mind.

Our kisses were unusual, though. They weren't our usual combustible, dirty, openmouthed affair. They were softer and hesitant, almost like we didn't want to spoil the magic of kissing under the soft glow of the porch light, with nothing but the vague sound of cicadas around us.

It was an unfortunate repeat of our kissing session in the kitchen earlier, after we'd finished doing the dishes. He'd backed me up against the sink and we'd spent a good ten minutes doing our Hallmark best to audition for a cheesy Christmas movie. He was the city chef who wanted my restaurant, and I was the hometown cook of few words who was *never* going to let that happen.

He pulled back to stare at me for a few moments, his face solemn. I searched his expression, but I couldn't tell what he was thinking. I only knew that he was in a strange mood, just like me.

He finally broke the oddly charged silence between us. "So, that happened."

I didn't even need to ask what he was talking about. "It did," I agreed.

He let out a breath and dropped his hands from my neck. Reluctantly, I let him go as well. Alright, maybe I copped one last tiny feel of that world-class ass, but then I let him go. "I should get going," he said unnecessarily.

I, too, enjoyed stating the obvious. "It's after midnight. We should probably get inside, too." I glanced around for Kona. "I'm surprised she hasn't voiced her displeasure. She usually gets water and a small treat when she gets inside after her last call, and God forbid if either of those things takes too long."

Journey chuckled as he looked around. "I don't see her."

Neither did I, now that he mentioned it. Usually, I only had to say something that *sounded* like the syllables of her name and she came running. I whistled a couple of times, and Journey called her name a few times as well. I frowned when she still didn't appear. I didn't even hear any rustling in the bushes. I called her name again, my pulse kicking up a few notches.

"Hey." Journey bumped my arm, clearly picking up on my rising worry. "Your yard is fenced."

"I'm not worried," I said automatically.

"The pulse in your neck says differently, but okay," he murmured.

I ignored him. I'd been soft kissing on the porch while my dog—I mean, my foster dog—was unsupervised. My yard was fenced, but she was clever. And big. It probably wouldn't take too much for her to leap the fence and disappear. There was a wooded, dense area nearby, and a highway behind that.

You should've thought of that and raised the fucking fence, I told myself sternly. *Good God, Cam, how could you be so fucking irresponsible?*

"Kona," I called, trying to sound as calm as possible.

There was nothing but the slight rustle of the trees from the wind. I was about to step off the porch when Journey chuckled. I scowled at him, wondering what the hell could be so funny about this situation. He pointed at my Jeep. "Cancel the amber alert."

I squinted at the windshield to find Kona sitting in the passenger seat, panting, ready for her ride. My relief came out in a whoosh of air. At Journey's upraised eyebrow, I flushed. "I knew she was all right."

"Mm-hmm. Good thing she's not your dog, huh?"

I scowled. "I'm glad to know you aren't perfect. I was waiting for the other shoe to drop and it's a doozy."

He laughed. "I'll get her. You stay here since you couldn't be bothered with shoes. Don't worry, I'll be careful with your baby."

I wasn't worried. Kona was generally suspicious of strangers, but she and Journey had clicked immediately. He chalked it up to the bone he'd given her, but I knew differently. Kona was more than capable of turning down bribery. She'd been known to take a treat from a hopeful stranger and give him her rump to kiss.

I watched as he opened the passenger door and ruffled her ears. I whistled, and she came running, clearly unbothered that she hadn't gotten to go anywhere as my copilot. She panted happily as she mounted the porch and bumped my legs repeatedly. Even though I wanted to give her a stern lecture about scaring the daylights out of me, I couldn't help but smile back. Adventure was what you made of it, and dogs *always* made the most of it.

I waved at Journey as he headed down the sidewalk. I stood there long after the lights came on in the living room next door, long enough to see them flicker off as he headed upstairs.

Kona yawned widely and then licked her chops.

"I suck at casual," I told her, and she gave me a *no-duh* stare. "You were supposed to be a foster situation and let's be real, I'm not giving you up."

The *no-duh* stare down continued. I sighed as I opened the front door and gestured for her to go back into the house. She paused, one paw inside and one paw still out, debating on whether to cooperate.

"Life would be so much simpler if you were human, or I was a dog. We could just get married and live happily ever after." I eyed her in case she didn't get the full picture. "Strictly platonic, of course."

She barked quickly in agreement, which was… rather insulting.

"I'm a good lay," I informed her, "despite whatever you've heard."

I was also trying to convince a dog of my prowess, which meant I probably needed some fucking sleep. "In," I said firmly, pointing at the front door. She looked at me with a hurt expression, and I sighed. "No, I wouldn't treat you that way if we were married, but we're not. So *in*."

She sashayed past, tail in the air.

22

JOURNEY

My photography class was going swimmingly. With six classes under my belt, I was back by popular demand. I'd gotten lucky. I'd expected a roomful of bored kids, but they were eager and ready to learn. According to the director of the community center, I ranked right behind McDonald's and Vampirina with their age group. That was pretty damned high, considering I didn't come with a McToy and I wasn't purple.

I had no lesson plan. Mostly I just shot from the hip and tried to expose them to different kinds of photography. I gave them a topic to start with and let their creativity do the talking. That was what art was all about. If nothing else, I could teach them that.

They turned in their cameras at the end of class, and I went through each kid's pictures, then printed out the best ones to hang on the wall at the community center. My current favorite was a picture of an ant crawling across a leaf. It made me smile. They were taking my words to heart and trying to find the unusual in the usual.

I decided to end the week by taking my art-turned-photography class on a little field trip. Field trip was probably a little ritzy of a term, since it was just the eight of us walking two blocks to the nearest park, holding hands to form a chain the entire way. My niece,

Livy, made sure to secure her hand in one of mine before anyone else could. My unofficial teacher's pet, Camila, snagged the other.

Acting as our unofficial mascot, my dog led the way, her little tail waving in the air like a plumed feather. Her name was Snickers this week, and it was starting to seem like a pretty good fit. Despite not knowing where the hell she was going, she was determined to be in front. She kept looking back at me to make sure she wasn't off course.

My charges were ridiculously excited and talking a mile a minute. I didn't care what they did, so long as no one let go of anyone's hand. I got them across the street safely which was, from my perspective at least, the scariest part of the trip. The way I acted, you would've thought we were crossing a six-lane highway, blind, and Snickers was our reluctant guide dog. In reality, it was a little access road that hardly anyone ever used.

I closed the park gate behind us with a sigh of relief. All students were accounted for and no one had broken so much as a nail. Looked like I wasn't going to be tarred and feathered by an angry parent mob just yet.

I passed out the cameras I'd stashed in my backpack as they chattered excitedly. I'd given up on being thrifty with disposables. Instead, I'd bought some inexpensive cameras on Amazon that were kid-friendly.

"Remember, these are not toys," I said. They'd heard the speech at least three times before, but I doggedly went down the list of dos and don'ts. "Don't remove the SD card. In fact, don't even look at the SD card. Don't put the camera in any water you may come across. Don't put *yourself* in any water you may come across. Try not to—"

"Drop it," they shouted in unison before looking at me expectantly.

"Exactly. And please don't open the—"

"Battery compartment," they filled in.

"Okay, yes. But other than that, have fun."

"What should we take pictures of?" George asked, bouncing on the heels of his feet.

"Good question. I want you guys to focus on sky art today." I cast a look upwards and got caught on the beauty overhead for a few moments. It was one of the best subjects in the world, slightly different every day but always beautiful. "Clouds, birds, airplanes—"

"The sun?" Trixie asked.

I tugged on her braid in fond exasperation. I swear to God, kids could take the safest activity and turn it into a nail-biter. It was like they had a divining rod for danger implanted in their little bodies. "Don't look at the sun, kid."

The always curious Otto lifted his hand. "Power lines?"

"Knock yourself out." I handed him a camera. "If it's in the air, it meets the criteria."

"Unicorns!" Livy shouted.

I chuckled. "If he's airborne, then yeah, he qualifies, too."

I watched them scurry off with a small smile. All right, fine, so maybe I was enjoying myself a teeny-tiny bit. That was a surprise, since I'd been soured on teaching at a young age. Coaxed into service in middle school by my aunt, my first customer had been my cousin Tyler. Tyler hadn't been the best student on a good day, and being taught by your younger, know-it-all cousin was not a good day. Several of our sessions ended with us locked in combat, rolling on the floor.

Once, he'd even ended our lessons abruptly by stuffing me into a garbage can. I remember being grateful that it had been freshly dumped, right before he slammed on the lid. He sat on top of it for a while, drumming his heels against the sides. That led to another lesson on how to project your apology outside of a garbage can, so your cousin will have mercy and let you out. Apparently the words "it's not my fault you're a dumbass" should not be incorporated into that apology.

Anyhoo, being crammed in a garbage can like Oscar the Grouch did not improve my impression of teaching. Molding young minds required a certain level of patience I didn't possess, and a certain level of enthusiasm I found hard to maintain. But I was working for free and doing the parents of Coral Cove a fucking favor, so they would just have to deal.

I let the kids do their thing, milling about and making sure no one got lost. Head counting was my newest favorite activity. At the forty-five-minute mark, I whistled to bring them back in. They came back in ones and twos, sweaty and excited and loud as fuck. I started collecting the cameras, some of which were dirty for no reason at all.

"It's my turn to hold Snickers," Julia screamed, also for no reason at all.

I rubbed my ear with a wince. That kid had a primo set of pipes. "Holy sh—sugar, Jules. Go ahead." She clapped her hands excitedly and kneeled like I'd shown them before to pick up a wide-eyed Snickers. "Be gentle, though."

"This was lame," Gregory said as he held out his camera.

There was one in every crowd. "Duly noted." I put his camara in my bag and moved on to the next.

Camila, otherwise known as the teacher's pet, shot him a sizzling glare. "It was not lame. I had fun."

"See, Gregory? Camila has the right idea," I said mildly. "Life is what you make of it."

"It's not Africa," he groused. "Or Japan. Or any of the other cool places you've been."

I remembered how impressed he'd been our first class, looking through a portfolio of some of my favorite shots. "Everything doesn't have to be an exotic location," I reminded him. "Every picture can't be of the Big Five."

He looked at me suspiciously. "The big what?"

I clucked my tongue in impatience. "Haven't you ever seen the squirrel series? Or the rats fighting in the subway?" I collected the last camera and zipped up my backpack. "Photography is about finding beauty in unusual places."

I did a quick headcount, already expecting seven. Six. I frowned as I did it again to the same results. I waited a moment, my heart thumping an uncomfortable tattoo in my ears. I sent up a quick prayer that I'd forgotten how to count to seven and did it again. *Still six.*

"Uncle JJ!"

I whipped around to see Olivia running across the field, a piece of paper flapping in her hand. "Oh, thank fu—dge," I said, aborting my well-earned curse as I remembered all the little ears listening. I rubbed my chest, my heart rate still a bit fast. Yeah, this was *so* the last field trip we were ever going on.

By the time she reached me, I was able to speak calmly. "Livy, you've got to stay with the group."

"But Uncle JJ, you gotta see this!" Her big blue eyes were distressed as she shoved a flyer up at me. "Just look!"

I frowned as I took the flyer and found myself face-to-face with a picture of Snickers. *My* Snickers. She was wearing a plaid harness and sitting on some kid's lap, but yes, that was my Snickers. Or Raisin, apparently, I corrected as I read the flyer.

Lost. Five-hundred-dollar reward. Three years old. Goes by the name Raisin. Please contact Jillian Carver if you have information.

I swallowed thickly. "We don't *know* this is her. Lots of dogs look like this."

The kids didn't seem to share my trepidation because they were excited to be part of solving a mystery. Gregory was the first one to do the logical thing and shout, "Raisin!"

She wiggled madly with excitement in Julia's arms, and my heart made its final descent to my shoes.

"Raisin! Raisin!" The kids started yelling her name with varying degrees of enthusiasm and she yipped excitedly, her tail going a million miles an hour. I guess I'd be excited, too, if I couldn't talk, and someone finally landed on my real name.

I folded the flier in quarters and tucked it away in my pocket. "Come on, you guys," I said, trying to restore order around the lump in my throat. "It's time to get back. Your parents will be there soon."

What had started as a pretty good day had just taken a turn for the worse. How was I supposed to give her up when she'd come to mean so much to me? How was that fucking fair? But did my attachment to her trump that of her real family? They'd had her—potentially—for three years. I'd had her for three months.

It seemed much longer.

Well, I knew one thing—I wasn't about to turn Snickers over to someone who'd lost her in the first fucking place. Not without seeing who they were and what they were about. For all I knew, it could've been a hoarding situation. Or an abusive one, where Snickers had managed to get herself free. Cam had told me stories about homes like that.

And of course, if all else failed and the Carvers were wonderful, I could just run away to Mexico with Snickers. Raisin. *Whatever.* I glanced around at the kids walking along beside me, chattering and whining about being too hot.

Fuck, that was a lot of witnesses to bribe. I had to save my money for me and Raisin now because life on the lam wasn't cheap. She'd become accustomed to a certain type of living and that included specialty treats and a monthly spa day. Although, weren't kids cheap to bribe?

I decided to test my theory and clapped my hands together. "Who wants an ice cream cone on the way back?"

The roar of approval was deafening. I nodded in satisfaction and gave Raisin an appraising look. Now we just had to brush up on our Spanish, just in case.

23

JOURNEY

The Carvers were disgustingly perfect.

Well, I didn't know that for sure, but on the surface, they certainly seemed to fit the bill. I stalked them online as soon as I got home. There were more ads for Raisin on various Lost Pet websites and one on Craigslist as well.

Jillian and Brian Carver had been married for twenty years. He was a tax attorney, and she was a stay-at-home mom with their three kids, all under the age of ten. They had a large two-story house with a pool that was properly gated, which I only knew because I was in my car outside of their house. And no, I didn't think I was being weird at all. That's what you *do* when you're vetting someone who wants to take away a teeny, tiny dog that was already lost once.

A little girl with her long brown hair in a messy braid played on the front lawn. She looked a lot like the kid in the photo on that flyer. I checked again just to be sure. Yep, that was definitely her.

"I put together my favorites for the gallery and sent them to your email," Boz said, startling me. I'd forgotten he was even on the phone. "I need you to take a look tonight and tell me what you think."

"What gallery?" I asked absently. The little girl was playing a game with her dolls that seemed to require putting a lot of them in time out.

"What gallery?" Boz practically shouted.

"*Ouch*," I winced. "Thank you for that. Also, where can I find a good cochlear implant?"

"Sorry, sorry. But jeez, you've been so distracted lately. Have you given any thought to our show idea?"

"Our show?" I chuckled. "If I recall correctly, you had an idea, and I said I'd think about it."

"Journey Forth," he blurted. "That's the working title. You get it?"

"Got it," I said before he wet himself with joy at his cleverness. "I appreciate everything you're doing for me, Boz, but I still need more time to think."

"To think," he repeated as if the words were foreign.

"Yes, it would be a big commitment."

"Doing what you love," he said slowly. "Exploring legends and lore from around the world. Traveling. Adventure. It practically has your name written all over it."

I rolled my shoulders uncomfortably. "I read the pitch, Boz. I just don't think it's right for me."

He waited a couple of beats before he shook his disappointment off. "You still haven't answered my email about the trip back to the Amazon."

"Wait, what?" That certainly got my attention. "When did I say I'd go to the Amazon?"

"A couple of days ago," he said exasperatedly. "You said you were just getting out of the shower? I told you about the trip then, and you said yes."

Oh, right. My face burned. Actually, I'd said "yes, yes, yes" because Cam had gotten out of the shower and started plying his evil trade on my body. "Right." I cleared my throat. "Refresh my memory. What is this trip about?"

"Well, since you won't do the trip to Chiang Mai—"

"I told you, I won't do any elephant camps."

"I heard you the first six times. I'm just saying that it turned out to be a good thing."

That wasn't what he'd said when he'd blistered my ear for a half hour, but his memory loss was not my problem. "I'm glad we're on the same page." I paused. "Wait, why are we on the same page, again?"

"You know Logan Adderly?"

I'd worked with Logan five years ago. He was a self-proclaimed adventurer who'd found success on an expedition show. His specialty was treasure hunting, and even though he'd never found jack shit, he was fun to work with.

"Of course," I said promptly. "What about him?"

"He's in the middle of a project chronicling a trip through the Amazon. He's mostly completed the writing part of the project, and Graham, his photographer, dropped out suddenly. Logan asked for you specifically."

"Why did Graham drop out?"

"Well, he died."

Yeah, that'll do it. "Oh."

"Anyway, Adderly immediately thought of you, since you've been to the Amazon already, and you've worked together before. I thought it would be perfect since you've always talked about going back."

The Amazon certainly wasn't for everyone, but even perpetually sweaty and covered in bug bites, I'd fallen in love. The flora and fauna had been beautiful beyond measure, and the Matsès people were kind and generous with what little they had. As a bonus, I'd even gotten an award out of the deal. My photo of the veiled stinkhorn was the kind of gold photographers lived for. It only bloomed at night and lived for a few hours, so getting a picture of it had been something special.

"It's a fourteen-day trip," Boz went on. "He needs an experienced photographer, Journey. You know that."

"I do," I agreed. Going off into the Amazon half-cocked was a good way to get killed. Just about everything had the potential to be deadly, and for every creature you spotted, there was another one camouflaged already watching you.

It should've been an easy yes.

Before I'd arrived in Coral Cove, I felt itchy and tense at the thought of sticking around. Now the thought of leaving was doing the same damn thing. Maybe I was just destined to feel out of place, no matter what I did. Except with Cam, I thought wistfully. When I was with Cam, I felt like I was right where I belonged. I needed more time to make him feel the same way.

Saying goodbye had always been the plan, but that was a stupid plan. I didn't know how we'd make it work, but I wanted to try. We could fucking *try* at least, couldn't we? That was probably something we should talk about. I guess it was a good thing I'd asked him out to dinner. When we were at his house, we couldn't seem to get any farther than the damn couch before somebody got naked.

The trip was only two weeks, but I didn't want to remind him of my job, which was ridiculous. If there was ever going to be anything between us, it needed to happen in real-world circumstances. Not this summer bubble we'd created. And yes, maybe I *was* leaving again, but this time, I had some things to say. He might not agree to my terms, but he was going to hear me out.

I cleared my throat. "Like I said. Let me think about it some more."

He was silent for a moment, so long that I checked the screen of the phone to make sure the call hadn't failed. The timer was still ticking away, so I guess he was just processing.

"I thought you said your dad was getting better," he finally said.

"He is."

He was silent some more and then he gasped. "You don't want to leave."

"That's not true," I denied automatically.

"What're they doing to you in that town?" he demanded. "Is this a Stepford situation?"

"I gotta go, Boz. And don't worry, I'll be back before you know it."

I hit the End button to the sound of his spluttering and went back to my spying. Some of the dolls earned their way out of time out, and the little girl started rearranging her toy army.

I gave Raisin a skeptical look where she sat grooming herself in the passenger seat. She didn't seem to care that her person was right fucking *there*. Didn't that speak volumes? She didn't have an affinity for this place of perfection. Of course, I hadn't let her out of the car. I grumbled as I stuck my binoculars back to my eyes.

Yes, I brought binoculars. I was a fucking professional.

I hadn't realized how much room I was making in my life and heart for this little ball of fluff that barely weighed ten pounds. But it wasn't like I could take her with me everywhere I went anyway. Some people traveled with their dogs, sure, but in foreign countries it was all red tape and complications.

I lowered my binoculars before someone called the cops. I was stalling. She had to go back to her family, and I had to find a way to let her go. "Tomorrow," I said hoarsely into Raisin's unblinking gaze. "I'll bring you back tomorrow, okay?"

I sank my fingers into her fur, and she stretched out on her side, exposing her belly. Not tomorrow. Today. Tomorrow wasn't going to make a damned bit of difference—it was just another shitty day with a different name. And I'd never put off doing what needed to be done, even if it was hard.

I lifted Raisin and brought her to my chest, where I kissed her about a dozen times. She looked at me with wise old brown eyes as I told her I loved her and kissed her nose some more. She usually hated that, but she allowed it because dogs were as intuitive as they were sweet. She knew something was going on.

I got out of the car. The little girl playing on the lawn glanced at me once with curiosity and then dropped her toy when she saw what I carried in my arms. She came running pell-mell in my direction as Raisin squirmed against me madly, trying to get free. I had no choice but to let her down before she hurt herself.

"Hold on, hold on," I muttered as I unhooked her leash. The moment she heard the clip release, she took off.

She and the little girl met somewhere in the middle of the yard as

I stood there with my hands in my pockets. In a second, I'd go to the door and talk to her mom to let her know she was back and give her a good report. But for right now, I watched the girl crying and petting Raisin while the dog licked her face madly.

I reminded myself that I wasn't giving anything up.

She'd never been mine in the first place.

24

JOURNEY

I took my time getting home. Truthfully, I wasn't all that eager to go back without Raisin because it just made it all too real that she was gone. Instead, I busied myself doing all manner of useless things. I stopped by the drugstore and bought things that I already had. I went by the gas station and topped off my tank, even though it was already over three-quarters of the way full. I enjoyed a nice carwash as well. Then I stopped for a vanilla ice cream cone. I indulged my masochistic tendencies by eating it on a bench at the dog park while the sun went down.

It was after ten by the time I decided to head home.

I heard the water running as soon as I walked in the door and let out a groan. After my father had gotten stuck in the tub twice, we agreed that he should hold off on baths. Showers sitting on the bath bench only. He *knew* that. It was like he woke up in the morning, yawned, stretched, opened his irritable little eyes, and pondered, *what can I do to make Journey's life more miserable today?*

I marched upstairs and caught him red-handed, sitting on the side of the tub and struggling to get his shirt over his head. Because there was a God, his boxers were still on. "What're you doing?" I demanded.

He startled but then gave me a defiant look over his lily-white shoulders. I was almost tempted to get some shades. "What's it look like?"

"It looks like you need a damn tan. It also looks like you're trying to bust your head open on the side of a slippery tub, but that just can't be the case."

He harrumphed. "I can take a bath by myself, goddammit."

I tried to be understanding and empathetic. That wasn't normally such a tall ask, but my meter ran kind of low at night. It had to be a tough blow to realize there were some things he just wasn't able to do, but I was leaving soon, and he needed to make smart choices.

I sighed. What the hell? I could haul his ornery rump out of the tub once more for old time's sake.

"What if I sit over here by the toilet?" I offered. "We'll draw the curtain. That way I'll still be close by if you need me, but you'll have privacy."

He didn't fight me on it, which I took to mean, *Yes, Journey. Thank you for being so kind and understanding and coming up with a wonderful solution.*

He grunted no less than five thousand times getting settled in the tub. "And maybe we could talk about something," I said after a few moments. "Hearing you squishing and squashing things around in there is giving me nightmares."

"The Dolphins sure are putting together a good team for next season—"

"And not sports, either."

He was silent for a moment. "I guess we could talk about why you haven't been back here in three years."

I blinked. "So... the Dolphins, you say?"

"I'm serious."

"So am I." I was genuinely confused. "Since when do you want to take a dip in the feelings pool?"

"You have a lot of time to reflect when you think you're going to die, JJ." His voice was quiet. "I haven't always done things the way I should with you, and I know that."

I was silent while I chewed on what exactly to say. It was easier not to talk about it. Hell, it was easier not to even think about it, but forgetting wasn't quite as simple.

It took me an hour at my mother's wake to approach her casket. I touched her hands gently where they rested, folded, over her stomach. They were encased in lace gloves. I stared at those gloves. It didn't hit me until then that this was not a nightmare I could wake up from. It was all too real. I couldn't believe lacy fucking gloves did the trick.

Seeing her hands—busy, work-rough hands—encased in those lace gloves made me sick to my stomach. My mother didn't wear gloves, and she certainly didn't wear anything as fancy as lace. It made me wonder what the hell they were trying to cover up. Discoloration? Something worse?

I swallowed as I stepped back. My father was still slumped in one of the fold-up chairs, his eyes glassy and unfocused. Family milled about, talking quietly, but he took no notice of any of them. He'd taken off earlier that morning without telling anyone where he was going or what he was doing. Getting thoroughly smashed had been more important than helping the boys pick out their Sunday best for the funeral. Luckily, the boys were with my aunt, who'd flown in to town for a few days. I was relieved. This... this was not the way they should remember our mother. Or our father.

At some point, my Uncle Theo pulled me aside. "He's been here long enough, I think," he murmured. "Take him home and maybe get some water in him."

I didn't know Uncle Theo and Aunt Tina all that well because they were a lot older and didn't visit all that often, but I appreciated him being there. In the four days since my mother had passed, I'd made a lot of grown-up decisions that were above my paygrade. It was a relief to have an adult telling me what to do.

I hauled my father up by his elbows and guided him outside. He lurched alongside me, stumbling and muttering. I helped him into the passenger seat of the car and went to get some bottled water from the helpful funeral director. By the time I got back, he was half asleep.

"Than' you," he slurred, trying to take the water and immediately spilling some of it all over himself.

I steadied the bottle long enough for him to take a few long swigs. "You're welcome."

He blinked at me over the rim like he'd just seen me for the first time. "Look just like your mama."

I was the only Sutton boy who did. They all looked like my father, each stockier, taller, and more blue-eyed than the last. "I know," I said softly.

"Not gonna leave me, are you?"

"No."

"Can't lose you, too. You and the boys, that's all I got," he said with surprising alacrity before he slumped in the seat again. "Look just like Lori."

He started to snore. How had my life turned so quickly? I stared at him for a few moments, disquiet rumbling through my body like a summer storm. Because this was only just the beginning. I knew that like I knew my name.

THE SOUND of a loud squeak made me wince—I knew the sound of butt cheeks against porcelain when I heard it. But I preferred anything over getting lost in memories better left buried.

"What do you want me to say?" I asked quietly.

"Whatever you're thinkin'. You know my rule. You boys can say anything to me, as long—"

"As we say it respectfully. I know."

He'd drummed that into us when we were growing up and it had been strangely freeing. Nothing was off the table, as long as we kept a civil tongue in our heads when we brought it up.

Respectfully, I thought he dropped the ball. He'd put a lot of burden on me, and I'd just been a kid. *Respectfully*, I thought he'd fucking checked out when he could least afford to. I was glad he'd finally decided to straighten up and get the help he needed, but *respectfully*, it had been a case of too little, too fucking late. A litany of things I could say ran through my head. I didn't care for any of them. In the end, there was only one thing that really needed to be said.

"I needed you... the boys needed you. And you were nowhere to be found." I swallowed. "I don't want to stir up the past, but I don't know how to pretty that up, Dad."

The sound of water had completely ceased on the other side of that curtain. "I know. I can only say I'm sorry."

"I know that." I was a little exasperated with myself. "This is all in the past. I don't even know why we're even talking about this."

"Because it can't truly become the past until we do," he said gruffly. After a few moments, he asked, "Did you know I used to play basketball back in the day?"

"Yeah, I did." I nodded even though he couldn't see me. "I saw some of your team pictures. Mom used to say you were cute in your basketball shorts."

"All the time," he said fondly.

"They were far too short, Dad."

"That was the style back then."

"Your knees were very knobby."

"And I passed them along to you," he said, sounding a tad smug.

He wasn't wrong. "Was there a point to this story?" I asked crossly.

He chuckled. "Well, my father used to work a lot and rarely had time to come to any of my school events. I understood, of course, because we might not have been dirt poor, but things were always tight. Still, he'd always made time to come to my games... until he didn't."

"What happened?"

"He needed the extra hours at work, so he'd be able to support us. He was doing what he had to do, and that was much more important than a silly basketball game."

I wasn't sure where he was going with his story, but I knew it wasn't good. "He wasn't working," I guessed.

"Nope. I found out he was spending time with a woman from church. He let me borrow his car sometimes, and I came across some of her things under the seat. A lipstick and a roll of lifesavers." He made a noise of derision. "Mom didn't eat candy, and she damn sure didn't wear lipstick."

"Did you confront him?"

"I did. And he convinced me to keep it a secret for years. It ate me alive. I was relieved when someone from the church found out and told my mother."

My grandmother had been very vocal about my grandfather's philandering ways before she died. As a kid, it had seemed like something that happened so very long ago, but hearing it from my dad's teenaged perspective was strange. It made the events feel fresh. Visceral. I could imagine his devastation at finding out, then having the horrible choice of betraying his father or hurting his mother.

"Why are you telling me this?" I asked.

"Because I had to move past it somehow. You know, when you're a kid, your parents seem like these omniscient, all-powerful beings who aren't supposed to make mistakes. They're always supposed to be there when you fall. They're always supposed to make you feel better when you're hurt. As I got older, I realized that parents were people, too. Flawed. He fucked up, but I still loved him."

Well, there you go. I didn't need a map to find that correlation. "I hear you," I murmured.

"Do you?" His voice was hoarse. "I fucked up, JJ, and I'm so very sorry."

My knee-jerk reaction was to say that it was okay and that he didn't need to apologize, but that would be minimizing the courage it took for him to broach the topic at all. Maybe I needed to hear it. And maybe he needed to say it.

"Thank you." My eyes were starting to burn a little, and I dared those suckers to fill with tears. Not on my watch. "You're more than forgiven."

"Good." He sighed. "That's good."

He didn't stay in the tub much longer. I helped him out and started tidying up the bathroom while he dried off and dressed in some pajamas. After a few minutes, he called, "Would you mind making me a snack?"

"No. What're you in the mood for?"

"Some of that tomcat soup?" he asked hopefully.

I chuckled as I picked up the damp towels and tossed them in the laundry bin. "It's tom kha, Dad, and yes, I will."

I spent a few more minutes toweling off the wet floor before I flicked off the light and headed through his bedroom. He was in bed, up against the headboard, dressed in striped pajamas. His face was a little flushed from exertion, but he looked pretty pleased that he'd accomplished it by himself.

"I'll be back up in about five minutes," I told him as I headed out his bedroom door.

"Journey?"

I paused but didn't come back to the room. "Yeah?"

"Thank you."

"It's just soup."

"Not for the soup," he said carefully.

"You're welcome." I smiled faintly. "Not just for the soup."

25

CAMERON

My Saturday started normally enough, but by noon, the back of my Jeep was filled with cats. Daisy, Quentin, Ollie, Storm, Frost, and Pumpkin. I glanced in the rearview mirror as I headed over to the clinic. I had six small kennels back there, each one holding a disgruntled cat, and at least as many scratches on my arms.

Their elderly owner, the lovely Ms. Price, had passed away early in the morning. She had no family, and even though she had a few friends, none of them were willing to take on her brood of six. We only had room for three, and frankly, even that was pushing it. The rest of them would have to be fostered out, which meant Bailey would have to do her magic. She had a gift for wheedling some of our reliable fosters to make room for *just one more*. The cats were well-behaved, so at least we had that going for us.

Well-behaved for now, that is. I glanced up in the rearview again and found myself the target of several pairs of unblinking eyes. I had a feeling Ms. Price's absence hadn't quite sunk in yet. They were used to having a lot of undivided attention from a woman who treated them like her children.

I pulled up to the backdoors of the clinic to deliver the cats into the waiting hands of Rosy and Lolly. They would check them out while I handled our regular schedule. It was going to be a ridiculously busy day, which kind of sucked for all of us. To be fair, Ms. Price's day had probably sucked a little more.

When I came in, Bailey was feeding her foster squirrels, a phone receiver tucked between her ear and shoulder. "Hey," I mouthed. "Schedule?"

"In the printer," she answered in a regular tone. "And I'm on hold. Our X-ray machine is on the fritz, and they need to get out here and fix it."

"Again?" I sighed. This day was just getting better and better, and that was *before* I spotted the giant cardboard box on the counter. I didn't see any air holes in it, which was hopefully a good sign.

"Those better not be kittens," I warned. "Or puppies or ferrets or any sort of live animal that people seem to love transporting in boxes. The inn is full. And the manger."

"Wrong on all counts," she said, placing one of her squirrels carefully in its lined basket. She picked up another and started the feeding process all over again. "You just missed Journey."

I held in a curse. It wasn't a big deal—we lived next door to each other, for crying out loud—but a smile and a kiss from him would've gone a long way to restoring my mood. Then I thought about what she'd said. "Wait, he brought the box?"

Even as I posed the question, I was lifting the flap. I peered inside to find the box chock-full of high-end dog supplies. There was unopened dog food, some collars, harnesses, and one of those fancy fountain water bowls, still sealed in the original packaging. I picked up one of the Kong toys—it still had the tags on it. As relieved as I was not to find a furry face in the box, I was still confused. Why would he get rid of all of Snickers' things?

I looked at the contents for a few moments before my heart kicked into overdrive. Maybe something happened to her. "Is Snickers okay? What happened? Why didn't he call me—"

"Will you calm down?" Bailey tsked. "And I think her name is Raisin now. I don't know exactly what happened because he was in a rush. My best guess is that he gave her away, so he doesn't need all this stuff anymore."

"Gave her away." I looked at her blankly, trying to process words that weren't making a whole lot of sense. I looked down at the unused princess pillow. I remembered that he'd bought two because they were on sale. "Gave her away?"

"Well, I'm just hypothesizing here. He didn't stay long, and I didn't want to press."

"Why... why didn't he bring her *here*? I would've rehomed her."

"Yeah, right into your home," she teased. "What's the count now, a wolf, a raccoon, and a couple of chinchillas?"

And a rat named Barney, but who was counting? Like I said, the inn was full.

When Bailey noticed I wasn't amused, she sobered. "Look. I know it drives us crazy when people do that, but it's none of our business."

It felt like my business. Right now, it felt a lot like I was still in love with a guy who was addicted to throwing people away like yesterday's newspaper. "I guess," I finally said. My jaw was so tight it was starting to ache, so I worked on unclenching.

Bailey sighed. "JJ is a good guy. He probably found a great home for her. You know he wouldn't do anything less."

"I know that." He was a good guy all right, but Jesus Christ, what was it about commitment? I was surprised he even had a cell phone contract.

"Besides, where was he supposed to keep her anyway?" Bailey went on. "He was only supposed to be here for the summer. Is he supposed to take her with him to the Amazon?"

"The Amazon?"

"Yeah, he was on the phone at the coffee shop with some guy named Logan." She leaned forward as she gave me the scoop. "Greta seems to think he was talking about heading to the rainforest in a couple of weeks. He seemed jazzed about it, too."

She continued chattering about whatever else Greta managed to hear, but I turned her out, too busy catching up on all this new info.

So this was it, then. Damn, I'd known it was coming the whole summer, but the reality was a bit of a slap in the face. He was cleaning house, getting rid of things he didn't need, and jettisoning entanglements... like his dog. The next thing he was going to chuck to the curb was me. The first time, I hadn't seen it coming. At least this time around, I'd known what I was getting into from the beginning. I did a quick mental check to see if that made things easier.

Nope, not even a little bit.

Realizing I hadn't said anything in some time, Bailey's chatter died down to nothing. She bit her lip. "I'm sorry, Cam, I wasn't thinking. Greta probably heard wrong anyway."

"No, it's fine," I said calmly. The truth of that settled in my bones. *I just got caught up in something that wasn't even real.*

I had no one to blame but myself. When we were together, it was so easy to forget how different we were. Journey wanted more adventure. More traveling. More of the world. After a lifetime of moving here and there with my father's every whim, I wanted stability. I'd etched out a life here in Coral Cove, and I had no desire to change any of that.

I'd been caught up in a fantasy where Journey moved here permanently and stayed with me. A future where we built something together. But that wasn't reality. Reality was his life in an easy carry-on and seeing the world from behind a camera lens, chasing that next cover and that next perfect shot. Hell, he didn't even really have a home. He had an impersonal loft in Seattle that he used to rest his head in between jaunts around the world.

I shook my head. That's probably what this whole dinner thing on Friday was about. You were supposed to dump someone in a public place... you know, so that person couldn't make a scene. At least, that's what I'd heard. I hadn't been the dumper all that much. I'd been the dumpee plenty, though. Under "Cause of Dumpation," most of them had listed that I was hopelessly in love with my ex.

Wonderful.

I could still hear my father's voice after he found out about my breakup with Journey the first time. *We're built for heartbreak,*

Cameron. He'd been drinking and reflecting on the demise of his most recent marriage—his last, to hear him tell it. Newsflash—it wasn't. His arm had been heavy around my shoulders as he slurred, *There's nothing quite so painful, or pleasurable, as love and the heartbreak that follows.*

I hated it when the old man was right.

I blew out a breath as I plucked my schedule off the printer tray. I had a bull terrier named Norman up first, and seeing regulars always lifted my spirits. I headed to exam room two, more than ready to dispel the pall Journey had cast over everything.

As if he had a sixth sense for when I was thinking about him, my phone pinged with a text from Journey. *We on for tonight?*

I paused in the hallway, knowing I should say no. A clean break was best for both of us. It was the smart, healthy thing to do.

Yes, I texted back. *See you at 8.*

Sometimes the smart, healthy thing to do was overrated. Obviously, having sex one more time and some sparkling dinner conversation would help me move on.

I headed in to see Norman, whose owner was picking him up later. I looked down at Norman as he looked up at me, his cute overbite on full display. I took the opportunity to let him in on a few facts of life.

"If you see a cute guy or girl dog that sparks your fancy, just keep on walking," I told him. "They're not even worth your time."

He licked his chops.

"I'm serious. Relationships are a suck."

He looked up at me, head tilted as if to say, *"Hey, you remember what you did to my balls, don't you?"*

"Oh yeah, sorry about that." I scratched my head. "But your mommy told me to. Now yes, I told her it would make you happier, calmer, and more comfortable in general, but she's the one who made the final decision. Just thought you should know."

He licked his chops again as if that was brand-new information. I wasn't above passing the buck, and Norman should know me well enough to know that by now. I started the examination, satisfied that we were once again friends.

In other words, life went on.

26

CAMERON

Journey and I were probably going to be late for our reservation.

That was mostly because when Cameron Foster had a plan, he stuck to it. I was on him the moment he showed up at my door, looking hot as fuck in slim-fit gray slacks and a black button-down. I felt bad for how wrinkled he was about to be, but those pants needed to be on my floor. I backed him up against the wall, tunneling my hands in his hair.

"I thought we were going out," he said against my mouth.

"We have time."

He let out a helpless whimper as our bodies notched together in a perfect fucking fit. I ground against him as he gripped my forearms. I thought I might have him until he glanced at his watch. "Yeah, we really don't."

"Then let's make time."

I strove for a playful tone, but it didn't quite land. He pulled back, looking at me with his brow furrowed. "Everything okay?"

"Of course. Why wouldn't it be?"

"Because you look like you don't know whether you want to fuck me or fight me, Foss."

That was... pretty fucking accurate. "It's nothing you need to worry about."

"Look, if you had a bad day, or you're not in the mood for this date, we can—"

"It's not a date," I said, working his zipper down. "Dating would imply that we're something serious, and this was just supposed to be a summer thing, right?"

He frowned but didn't stop me from pushing his pants and boxers down around his knees. "It certainly started that way, but—"

I cut him off with a kiss, my mouth demanding and aggressive on his. From the way he nipped at my bottom lip, I could tell he was irritated. Luckily I knew how to get him going in no time at all. I broke the kiss and dropped to my knees. Neither one of us spoke. He looked down at me, those golden lion eyes half-mast and glittering with annoyance. I raised an eyebrow and gestured for him to turn around with a spin of my finger. He huffed, not moving a muscle, and I did the motion again.

He didn't stand a chance.

When he finally complied, like I knew he would, I wasted no time spreading his cheeks. His breath hitched and that was *before* I licked my way down the length of his crease. He quivered but didn't make a sound. I chuckled because that was the most hilarious thing I'd seen all damn day. Did he think he was going to be able to stay silent through one of his favorite activities? Hope truly does spring eternal.

I slowed things down, licking at his rim and then dipping my tongue inside—just the tip. He widened his stance, his breathing a little choppy. He started to stroke his dick, and I batted his hand away. He made a sound of protest. And then, I was burying my tongue in his ass as far as I could.

"Oh fuck," he breathed, bracing his hands against the wall. His forehead joined them a few moments later as he muttered curses. "What the hell are you doing to me?"

"Gotta get you ready," I said, my voice low. "Wouldn't want to hurt you."

I tunneled my tongue inside him again and again, taking the time to turn him into a writhing, sweaty mess right here in my foyer. Then I took him against the wall, hard and fast, like I could fuck away my fears. I didn't let up until I came, so hard that I nearly saw stars. I stayed inside him for a few moments, trying to catch my breath, kissing his neck and behind his ear—any part of him I could reach, really. After I finally slipped out, I turned him around so I could take his mouth fully.

I pushed him against the wall and kissed him, only to find he was still hard... which was fucking perfect. I reached out and stroked him a couple times a little roughly, root to tip, just like he liked. He groaned, his hips jutting forward to meet my movements.

"Now," I said simply, knowing he'd know exactly what I was talking about. "I don't care if you've never topped before. No more stalling."

His mouth quirked. "How did you know?"

"Just had a feeling."

I turned, pressing my hands and upper chest against the wall. There were a few moments of breathless silence, and then his hands were on my shoulders. His hands mapped my back slowly, down to my waist and then skirting over my ass before he gripped it reverently. He fitted his front against my back, pressing me further against the wall.

"I didn't want to share this with anyone else," he said, his words a whisper across my skin. "I know it's stupid, but I just—"

"It's far from stupid, JJ."

He prepared me almost reverently, taking his time even after I told him I was ready. Repeatedly. And then he entered me on a curse, breathing heavily against my back. Even as I struggled to adjust to his girth, I regretted making him fuck me at all. Not because of the burn, which was just about the best feeling in the world, but because of the emotion that came with it. The feelings were too big; the love I had for him was too fucking much.

"You okay?" He asked quietly, one hand gripping my hip, the other braced on the wall beside my face.

Far from it. I nodded, unable to even speak. He started moving, and I could only hang on for the ride. I didn't know how to stop giving him pieces of myself. I wasn't even sure I wanted to try.

So yeah, we were a little bit late for dinner.

The maître d' at Fork was about as impressed with our timeliness as the valet had been with my dusty Jeep. I turned to Journey to share the joke as we followed our starchy host, but he seemed distracted. He'd been quiet the entire ride like his mind was elsewhere. I left it alone.

Our two-person table wound up being right against the window, giving us an unobstructed view of downtown Miami nightlife. The Yelpers had been dead on about the ambiance at Fork. It was perfect for a date—romantic but not cheesy. The food was accessible and not pretentious, which was great because the three dollars signs next to their rating meant we'd be ponying up some dough. The atmosphere of the restaurant was great, but the one at our table, not so much.

"How's your osso bucco?" I asked inanely.

Journey glanced up at me from where he'd been mashing most of it up with his fork. "Huh?"

"The osso bucco?"

"Oh." He looked down at his plate as if seeing it for the first time, as though he hadn't been picking off of it for the better part of a half-hour. "It's good. Quite tasty."

"Do you want some of mine?" I gestured at my miso-glazed salmon.

"No, I love osso bucco. That's why I ordered it."

Then the silence was back. I drummed my fingers on my thigh under the table. He looked like he was thinking heavy thoughts over there. I'd be thinking heavy thoughts, too, if I'd given away a helpless little dog. I reminded myself not to jump to conclusions.

Just be a fucking adult and ask him about it already.

"I got the supplies you left," I said casually.

"Oh, did you? That's good." When he looked up from his plate, his eyes were a little wistful. "I remember you told me that some of the dogs waiting for adoption have nothing, so I knew it would go to good use. I also had a couple of months left on a Farmer's Dog subscription that I forwarded to the clinic."

It was then that I knew I was completely wrong. He'd loved that dog to bits. Whatever had happened, he hadn't dumped Snickers because he was cleaning house and getting ready to be footloose and fancy-free again. "JJ, what the hell happened with Snickers?"

"My niece found a lost flyer, and things went to hell," he said with a faint smile. "I'm being dramatic, of course, but that's what it felt like."

"A lost flyer... you gave her back to her owners?"

"Yeah. They were moving into a new house, and one of the movers left the door open. Apparently, Raisin has always been too curious for her own good. The gate wasn't finished, and Raisin didn't know the area." He shook his head. "Jillian said it was the perfect storm for Raisin to get lost."

"Jillian?" I asked faintly.

"The mother. I had my doubts about giving her back, but you should've seen how happy their little girl was. Raisin was pretty stoked, too. She barely looked at me when I left." He sighed. "I was going to give them all the stuff I'd bought for her, but they already had a ton of supplies. It seemed like overkill. And you know how I overbuy."

"Oh, wow." I rubbed my temples. I was such an idiot. That would certainly teach me to assume the worst. "I'm so sorry. When I got the box, I thought.... It doesn't matter what I thought."

He furrowed his brow as he thought about that for a beat. Then his eyes widened as the implications of that set in. "Wait. You thought I just *dumped* her somewhere?"

I flushed. "Um," I said eloquently.

He sat back in his chair and stared at me for a few moments. "I'm going to need more than that 'um,' Foster."

"I know, I know. I'd just had a callout from a client of ours who passed. She had no one to take her treasured cats...." I winced. "I'm sorry. It was a bad time for me to think you'd dumped Raisin, that's all."

His expression was grim as he looked at me without speaking, so long that I was tempted to squirm. "Cam," he finally said. "We need to talk. There are some things I need to say, and clearly, there are some things you need to hear."

And here it was. I watched him pull out his phone, feeling a little numb. Had he written some sort of kiss-off speech? Was there a checklist he needed to reference? *Ten Easy Steps To Being A Heartbreaker*?

The first time, he'd said all kinds of pretty words to make it seem like it was him, not me. With distance and perspective, I now believed that he'd been truthful about that. But back then, my ears had played that kids' game Telephone with the information. His "it's not you, it's me" had reached my brain as "it's so fucking you. How *could* it be me?"

I decided to beat him to the punch. Maybe it was petty of me, but goddamn it, I couldn't hear him cast me aside again.

"This isn't working," I blurted. It was almost a relief to hear the words out there in the open. I no longer had to deal with the potential pain of losing Journey. I'd finally just rip the fucking bandage off so the bleeding could just *start* already.

He went still, his finger poised over the screen of his phone. "What?"

"This. Us. You and me." I gestured between us so wildly, a little miso flew off my fork and onto the table. I put my fork down a tad sheepishly before I wound up accidentally impaling a fellow diner. Enough people were already getting hurt tonight.

"So, I'm guessing that would be a no to my question," he said dryly. He turned his phone around, and I looked down at the screen to see a ticket of some kind. An airline ticket?

"I already know you're going to Brazil," I said with a frown.

He enlarged the screen and brought it so close to my face that I reared back a touch. I took the phone from him before he poked me in the fucking eye. When I looked down at the ticket again, I read the entry under the name of the traveler. *Cameron A. Foster.* I blinked at it in confusion for a few seconds before I looked up at him again.

"What?" I asked brilliantly.

"I was kind of hoping you'd come along. And don't just say no before you hear me out," he said quickly. "I'm not talking about forever, I'm just talking about two weeks, here. It's not an easy trip, but I think you'd love it. I can't think of anyone who would appreciate the native animals more, Foss."

His eyes practically glowed with excitement, and my heart sank. God, he came *alive* talking about travel. It just solidified everything I'd already known.

"It once took me twelve hours to capture a photo of a lettered aracari. You know, the one for that cover shot of *Nat Geo*?" He shook his head wryly. "Twelve hours for two quick camera snaps, and then he was back inside that tree."

"The lettered aracari."

"Yes, it's a bird—"

"I know what it is," I said impatiently. "I can't just pick up and go to Brazil."

"Why not?"

The man talked about going to another continent like it was a trip to McDonald's. I shook my head. "My God, I really can't believe we did this shit *again*."

"What are you—"

"We have to be the most masochistic sons of a bitches that I've ever met." I made a sound of frustration. "We're in the same place we were before, only now I love you more. How stupid is that?"

His breath hitched at my words and his eyes softened. I wanted to smack him. He didn't fucking *get it*. "I love—"

"Don't," I said sharply.

"Okay," he said carefully, as though I was a wild animal that needed calming. "But not saying it doesn't make it any less true."

"It doesn't matter," I said with exasperation. "Nothing has changed, and we still want different things. Don't you see that?"

"No, I don't," he said promptly.

"No? Okay, then, Mr. Commitment. How do you feel about marriage?"

"Marriage?" He looked a little taken aback, those beautiful amber eyes widening a bit. He cleared his throat a few times. "It's certainly skipping a few steps, but it's not like we haven't considered it before."

"No one's asking anyone anything," I reminded him. "I've seen your version of 'consideration.' I have your version of consideration in my underwear drawer."

His gaze sharpened. "You kept our rings?"

"Well, I'm not that crazy broad in *Titanic,* so yeah, I kept them." I scowled. He didn't need to know that I'd put them together on a chain and worn them around my neck for five years, either. Rosy had finally made me take them off when she said I was torturing myself. "That's not the fucking point. What about kids?"

"I like kids. Kids like me." He shrugged. "What else you got?"

"So, you'd be open to having a few?" I gave him a mocking look because I was all about calling bullshit tonight. "How does that fit in with your impromptu trips halfway around the globe?"

"Okay, maybe not *now,*" he allowed, "but in a few years, who knows?"

"I'm forty. I don't want to have to use the nursing home shuttle to pick them up from daycare."

"You're thirty-eight. And fine, that's something we should talk about." It was his turn to be exasperated. "I want this to work, but obviously you don't. You're just throwing up obstacles and that's not productive at all."

I was already shaking my head. "You know, back then I didn't get it. When you told me you felt trapped and that your life was passing you by? I didn't get it then, but I do now." I thought about that for a few seconds and made a derisive noise. "Hell, maybe I got it then, too, but I just couldn't see past what I wanted."

"Which was?"

You. I've never wanted anything else. I gazed at him for a few moments. "It doesn't matter what I want. You're still looking for something, JJ. I don't know what it is, or what it looks like… I just know it isn't here."

"You're so fucking stubborn," he said.

I shrugged. If it helped him to get angry at me, then so be it.

"I guess you're just perfect then," he said heatedly. "You've never had a question about where you belong or what you wanted to do. You've never doubted that you were doing the right thing and living your best life."

"I never said that."

I wasn't sure he even heard me as he steamrolled on. "Maybe I'm not as perfect as you. But at least I can recognize when I've found something special."

"Don't," I warned him again.

"I'm not," he shot back. "I'm certainly not saying that I've enjoyed our time together. And I'm not saying that every time I think about leaving, I feel queasy. And I'm certainly not saying that walking away from us would be stupid."

"You're saying it," I growled.

"No, I'm not. I'm also not saying that I don't feel like this was ever a fling. I'm not saying that this was our second fucking chance."

"That's not what we agreed upon," I snapped. "You're breaking all the rules—"

"Fuck the rules, Cam," he said so loudly that a diner nearby gasped.

I glanced over to find an older woman and her companion staring at us. When I looked at the other side, another table of patrons was sitting so still and quiet, they could've doubled as cardboard cutouts. I checked twice to make sure they weren't. They'd probably been listening for God knows how long. Hell, I'd been so caught up in our shit that I'd forgotten we were in public at all.

"Could you lower your voice?" I hissed.

"I will not fucking lower my voice," he shot back in an absolutely lower voice.

"Well, I'd kind of like to not get kicked out of here."

"Who cares about that? This place is overrated anyway." He raked a hand through his hair. "I love you. I love the way you make me feel, and how thoughtful you are... how much you care about animals who have no voice. You protect them, and as long as I've known you, it's made me want to protect you. When we're together, I don't care about all the obstacles. I just want us to be together. And I want you to want that, too."

"JJ," I said hoarsely. *Please stop saying all the right things.*

"I want you to take a chance on us." His gaze was intense on mine. "But I can't do all the heavy lifting by myself."

I didn't know how to respond to that. I struggled to come up with words until I realized that I didn't *have* to respond. I'd already said my peace. He just wasn't ready to hear it.

After what seemed like an interminable period of silence, he seemed to realize that, too. He sat back in his chair. "Are we done?" He asked unsteadily. "Because I really don't want to be done."

"I think we should be. For both our sakes." The words stuck in my mouth like peanut butter, but I managed to get them out. I licked my suddenly dry lips and forged on. "For God's sake, JJ, I can't have you and lose you over and over again. That's not healthy for either one of us."

"Cam—"

"No. Whatever this is…. Whatever this *was*, we shouldn't do it again."

"Wow," he said softly, almost to himself. "Just…wow."

I couldn't agree more. There was nothing else to say—*wow* really did a fantastic job of encapsulating it all.

27

JOURNEY

I woke in the middle of the night and couldn't go back to sleep. I tried though because I had to be at the airport at seven in the morning. That meant getting up at five, which was only a few hours away. I tossed and turned for a little bit before deciding to do something more productive. I got up, flicked on some mindless TV, and put the volume on low. Then I hauled out my duffel from under the bed and started to pack. I wasn't all that pressed about it, since after all these years of travel, I could pack in a snap.

I left out one outfit of jeans and a short-sleeved shirt, my camera bag, and a small zippered pouch of sundries. Then I brought my duffel downstairs and put it on the couch. I wasn't even sure the whole process took me over fifteen minutes. Packing done, I sat next to my bag and pulled out my laptop to prepare for my trip.

I took a moment to enjoy the irony of ordering from Amazon *for* the Amazon before I started putting things in my cart. I ordered some camping supplies I'd found helpful in the past and then some camera equipment to be delivered to my Seattle loft. The conditions of the Amazon were hell on my gear. The humidity fogged up my lenses inside and out, and the canopy of trees made lighting a challenge. I needed to be ready for any eventuality.

When I finished that, I clicked on the email from Boz regarding the gallery. I downloaded some of the photos they'd chosen, chuckling when I saw one of Lahja midyawn with her sharp teeth on full display. Figures. It didn't feel like it had only been four months since I'd been face-to-face with a cheetah, taking these pictures. It seemed like someone else's life. The longer I was in this town, the farther away it felt.

I wasn't sure if that was a bad thing.

"Where did you get this?"

I startled, looking over my shoulder to see my dad. He was frowning at something in my unzipped duffel. "You're going to have to be a little more specific, Pops."

He pulled out my mother's journal, handling it carefully. "I didn't know where this had gone."

"Well, I'm not giving it back, if that's what you're after," I said tartly. "I've had it as my constant companion now for over a decade. You might think it's fanciful nonsense, but Mom's journal made a huge impact in my life."

"That's all well and good. But that wasn't her journal," he said gruffly. "It was mine."

I stared at him, more than a little nonplussed. "Why didn't you ever say anything?"

He shrugged as he rubbed his thumb over the cover. "I didn't know you had it."

"So you... you wanted to go to all those places?"

He smiled. "Surprised? You're not the only one who had dreams, JJ. Why do you think I named you Journey?"

I never asked. "I always wondered what you guys were thinking naming us John, Mark, Matthew, and Journey. Apostle, apostle, apostle, and what the fuck?"

"You were first. We hadn't hammered out our system yet." He chuckled. "Besides, it fits your personality."

"I have a what the fuck personality?"

"There's no good answer to that."

I watched as he came over and sat on the couch with a sigh. He was moving a lot better, albeit slowly, and had ditched the walker and cane.

"Why didn't you ever try to go to some of these places?" I asked. "What happened?"

"Life happened. Lori and I had jobs and responsibilities and things got busy. There was always something that had to take priority over daydreams." He shrugged. "The pipes needed fixing. The roof sprung a leak. The AC went on the fritz. There were bills to pay and things to be done."

"But surely, at some point, you could've made time to do something just for you."

He waved a hand. "Eh, Lori got pregnant with you, and then John.... I needed more hours at the garage because kids are fucking expensive. Eventually, it all became just a pipe dream. It was more important to put food on the table than waste time thinking about places I was never going to see."

"Wow," I said quietly. It was the second time I'd said as much tonight, and I was just as bowled over. My father had never expressed any interest in traveling. He'd never expressed any interest in much of *anything* outside of Coral Cove.

"Yeah, well." He looked over at my open computer with interest. The picture of Lahja was still up on the screen. "You take that picture? Can I see?"

"Sure." I passed him my computer and showed him the arrow. "Press this to go forward and this one to go back."

I watched him going through my pictures, still a little flummoxed at his revelation. I huffed out a laugh at the irony. Here I was thinking we were as different as could be, and we shared more than I could've imagined.

"You know... you don't have as many responsibilities as you used to," I ventured. "John, Mark, and Matt are good with handling the business when they put their minds to it. And you don't have any pets to take care of."

He kept scrolling through pictures. "What's your point?"

"Maybe you should come with me on a trip sometime. It's never too late to check off some things on those travel lists."

He stilled, his finger frozen on the arrow key. "I don't know about all that."

"Think about it," I urged. "You don't have to give me an answer now."

"I wouldn't be able to get my special muffins for my breakfast," he blurted.

"For God's sake, Dad, they have muffins in different countries."

"Not Laura's special wakeup blend," he said stubbornly. "And what about my bills?"

"Autopay."

"My yard!"

"The boys can take care of it." I raised an eyebrow. "You gonna keep coming up with excuses, or are we gonna get you a passport?"

He grunted. I translated his Dad-speak again. *Thank you, Journey, for caring about my well-being. I'll take your thoughtful offer under careful consideration.*

I heard a howl outside and I smiled wistfully—Kona. If I went out there now, I could probably catch a glimpse of Cam in his backyard. I stayed right where I was. I glanced over to find my dad giving me a look. The *I'm about to get all up in your business* look. I sighed.

Sure enough, he asked, "Did you tell him how you feel?"

"Tell him how I feel?" I snorted. "I practically flayed myself open for the general amusement of our fellow diners at Fork tonight. I think Cam is done with me."

He scoffed. "That boy loves you. Always has. He's just scared."

"Yeah, well he's not the only one," I shot back.

He hummed as he continued flipping through my photos. "Good."

I frowned. "Good? Why's that? Is that some solution to a riddle I've never heard of? One fraidy-cat plus one fraidy-cat equals happiness?"

"No," he said pointedly. "And you should feel free to stop being a wiseass."

I huffed. "All right. Then why?"

"Because love is supposed to be scary. You're supposed to be scared of finding it. Keeping it. Losing it." His fingers tightened on my laptop at the last one. I didn't blame him. That one was the worst. "If you're not scared, you're not invested enough. Not with your future or your happiness. And definitely not your heart."

"Since when do you get so deep?"

"Still waters, JJ. Still waters." He closed my laptop and put it on the coffee table. "Love is why you came back to help get me on my feet. Love is you scheduling a walk-in bathtub installation next week that you think I don't know about."

"That was fear, Dad," I said helpfully. "I'm still scarred from seeing your ghostly white hide when I had to help you out of the tub."

He ignored me. "Love is why we ate that shackazulu you prepared yesterday."

"Shakshuka."

"Whatever." He paused. "Did I ever tell you how your mother and I started dating?"

I shook my head. "No."

"We were set up on a blind date with other people. I wound up sitting down at the wrong table." He went on as I chuckled. "We were talking for a good fifteen minutes before we realized the mix-up. By then, I knew I didn't want to let her go, but her date arrived and mine spotted me from over by the bar."

"Did you get her number at least?"

"Not yet. We spent the next twenty minutes making moon eyes at each other across the restaurant... at least, that's what my date said before she threw a drink in my face and stormed off."

I laughed. "She sounds like a real peach."

"Yeah, I dodged a bullet there. I guess what I'm saying is that sometimes you just know. So." He leveled me with a look. "Do you know?"

I knew that I woke up thinking about him. I loved his smile, especially the shy one that had no business charming the pants off me like it did. I loved that he could be quiet and reserved but still funny in his own way. I loved falling asleep with him next to me. I knew that I loved him with everything I had, and I knew that he loved me back.

"Yeah, I know." My voice was husky when I finally answered. "And lately, I've been thinking that Seattle might be a little far for home base."

"Foster?"

I thought about that for a few moments before I shook my head. "Not just Cam. I also want to be closer to John and Mark and Matt. Mindy and Laura. My nieces and nephews. You."

"I'm fucking last?" He raised an eyebrow. "After all the good advice I gave you? I bared my goddamned soul, JJ. I'm going to probably need therapy."

I chuckled. "Now, I just need to figure out what a life here looks like."

"You will," he said confidently.

"How do you know?"

"Because you never shy away from a challenge. You're a Sutton through and through. Do you remember that shoot you did in Tanzania? How you fought off that Caiman who got ahold of your camera bag?"

A startled laugh burst out of me. Crafty reptile. The irony hadn't escaped me—I'd traveled halfway around the world to get eaten by the uglier cousin of something in my own backyard.

"Wait." My brow furrowed. "How do you know about that?"

"I follow it all," he said promptly. "I have it all in a binder."

I blinked at him in surprise. "You started another journal?"

He nodded. "You know, I didn't know how well the name Journey would fit you until you grew up. You're happiest with the dust of the world on your feet."

"I think I'd give it all up for Cam."

"You shouldn't have to. Settling down doesn't mean boring, JJ. It just means you know where home is when you're done seeing the world." He raised a meaningful eyebrow. "You don't have to change everything about your life. Just show him that you know how to come back."

I planned to do exactly that. "Thanks."

"Don't mention it." He smiled. "You know, you remind me so much of myself at that age. Just better. I loved you since the first time I saw you." Before I could get too misty, he admitted, "Second time, actually. You weren't the most attractive baby in the world."

"Thank you. You're warming the corners of my cold little heart."

"I think they used some sort of suction on your head," he said with a frown. "It was all oddly shaped and red—"

"Thank you," I said loudly. "I get the point, but this sentimental trip has taken a wrong turn."

"Well, we'd better get some rest if I'm going to take you to the airport." He yawned and levered himself up from the couch. "Five o'clock, right?"

"Yep."

Now that he was driving again, he'd taken back control of the Mustang. Due to a minuscule ding in the door that happened on my watch, he informed me that the next time I'd be behind the wheel, he would be in a casket.

"Dad," I said hesitantly. He paused at the stairs, giving me an expectant look. "I'm sorry you didn't get to go on your journey."

It took him a few seconds to gather himself enough to answer. "Oh, I did." He blinked rapidly. I knew better than to mention his slightly watery eyes. "And it was better than I ever imagined it could be."

Now *my* eyes weren't exactly dry.

"Fuck," he exclaimed. "Didn't I tell you that was enough emotion? I ought to take you out by the woodshed."

"You've been threatening us with that for years and I haven't seen it happen."

"How do you know?" he demanded. "You're not even my oldest child. You used to have a brother named Phil. I took him out by the woodshed and well...."

I chuckled, feeling bad for poor, dead, imaginary Phil. "Goodnight, Dad."

28

CAMERON

Our monthly pet adoption event wasn't easy to pull off. It required a lot of legwork—advertising and permits to secure our space in the grocery store parking lot. There were enclosures to be transported and set up, and a refreshment table to stock. Even when the event began, the work wasn't done. Dogs needed to be walked and fed during and afterward. Potential adopters needed to be supervised socializing with the animals. Needless to say, there were a lot of moving parts involved in making the day a success.

Luckily, one of Bailey's superpowers was guilting people into helping out. She usually brought Mr. Pickles with her when she was drumming up volunteers. He wasn't much of a people person, but he could meow pitifully on command, which made him an invaluable member of Team Beg.

The entire staff was all-hands-on-deck and I'd given everyone instructions to make sure the senior dogs took top billing. We were all clad in khakis and blue T-shirts with Happy Paws scripted on the front in white writing, so it was easy to spot all the volunteers. I took no responsibility for the fact that a third of them had already signed up to adopt a pet. Why should I be the only soft-hearted fool living in a menagerie?

I was even happier to be working than usual. Anything to keep my mind off things was aces in my book. Anything to keep from remembering the day he left. I'd gotten up early and watched his yard like a hawk through my living room window. I'd seen Journey and his father in the semidarkness of the dawn, loading up the car with his bags. They were chatting as they disappeared in the house one last time and came out a little while later with travel mugs. Then I watched the taillights of his father's Mustang as they drove off. A couple of hours later, Jack was back alone. He made his way into the house, a contraband bag of McDonald's clutched in his hand.

And that was that.

Kona had bumped my leg anxiously, and I'd rubbed her ears. Eventually, I'd let her get up on the seat with me, and she'd climbed her big, furry butt into my lap. That's about how long it took me to process that Journey had left. I mean, yes, I'd told him to go. But who does the hurtful shit you goad him into doing? What happened to all those sweet things he'd said about loving me? *You mean those things that you practically threw back in his face?*

I winced. Well... yeah. Those things.

The town gossips had been hard at work since his departure. People were using their *poor Cameron* voices again. No one mentioned his name, as though it was an incantation. Mrs. Grimes had brought me a casserole to take home as if someone had *died* for Chrissake.

Well, if they were waiting for a show, they weren't going to get one. I could be perfectly dead inside and pleasant on the outside. I was an excellent multitasker.

I leaned down and ruffled Daisy's ears. The beagle had a sign on top of her enclosure that read Adopted! with a smiley face. "Susan lets her other dogs sleep on the bed," I told her, as she looked up at me with doubtful eyes. "You're going to love her pack, I promise."

"I'm not sure you even know they're not human at this point."

I turned to see Rosy standing behind me, a little half smile on her face. I straightened as I turned to face her. "And you're so much better? You bought your dog a monogrammed jacket."

"Bella is a retired police officer, Cam. She has a fucking job." Her blue eyes twinkled. "A dog with a pension is allowed to buy a damned jacket."

I chuckled. "Speaking of which, where is she?" There was very little Bella liked more than a car ride and a trip into town, except maybe taking a bite out of a fleeing suspect's ass.

"I left her at home. I got her a new Kong toy and couldn't pry her away." She shaded her eyes as she looked up at me with a frown. "How long have you been out here? You look a little flushed."

"It's hot," I said, sidestepping her original question and the hand she tried to press against my forehead. It's not as though I had a real answer anyway. I came early and stayed late until all the animals were adopted. "Of course I'm flushed."

"Mm-hmm." She gave me a knowing look, one that had broken me down many times over the years. "Why don't I take over from here? You can go do… whatever it is you do on a Saturday."

"I'm good, but thanks. Aren't you retired?"

"I can be retired and useful. Now get on with you." She waved her hands. "Why don't you go see your boyfriend? Take him out for a movie or ice cream."

"I can't do that," I said sourly.

"Well, why the hell not?"

"One, because we're not in junior high. And two, because Journey left. Over two weeks ago."

Bailey skirted by us, busy as the cartoon bees on her sneakers, with Kona following close at her heels. Bailey slapped another Adopted! sign on one of the enclosures, looking extremely satisfied with herself. I wasn't sure how she'd gotten someone to sign up for Pookie—a pug mix that'd once eaten a roll of change and pooped quarters for a week—but I wasn't about to ask any questions.

When I glanced back at Rosy, her face was a thundercloud of anger. She was not a woman who lost her temper easily. She was easy-going and as laid-back as could be, and I could count the times on one hand I'd ever heard her yell. From the looks of things, this might be one of those times.

"What?" I resisted the urge to step back. "You look like you're ready to hurt somebody."

"If he shows his face in this town again, I certainly will." Her cheeks were pink with anger. "How *dare* he? Does he not know how much you love him?"

"Um... I didn't tell *you* that I loved him."

"It's obvious," she snapped. "I look at the two of you together and I just know. Or at least, I thought I did."

I sighed. "This is exactly why I didn't want to tell you. Frankly, I'm surprised you hadn't heard."

"I don't pay the town gossips any mind." She huffed. "If you listen to those old biddies, I'm bored and struggling with retirement, and won't get out of your hair down at the clinic."

Even a broken clock was right twice a day. "Err."

"Hush. I can't believe that boy would do this to you again."

"I know. Can you believe he wanted me to go with him?" I asked indignantly.

She blinked at me for a few seconds. "He did?"

"Yes, unbelievable, right?" I shook my head. "As if I could just pick up and go to the Amazon."

"The Amazon?"

"That's what *I* said. He's chronicling some explorer's adventures through the rainforest through photos. He's hoping to see some pink dolphins or some such."

She fiddled with one of the bracelets on her wrist. "You love dolphins" was all she said.

"That's it?" I peered at her. "I've heard more about your preference in oranges."

"Cara Cara oranges," she said definitively. "They're just so damned good."

"That's fantastic. Do you have anything to say about the topic at hand? Something helpful?"

"Well, it's going to take me a minute to come down from my anger," she said apologetically. "I thought that you'd finally opened your heart to give him a second chance and he'd decided to leave you again."

"That's exactly what happened."

"No, it isn't."

"What part of him going to the Amazon is not leaving me?" I demanded.

"He wanted you to come with him."

"I can't just pick up and leave. You know that." I gave her a look of frustration. "And aren't you supposed to be on my side?"

"I was. I am," she said patiently. "I never thought he was right to leave the way he did the first time because he was running away. But now, he's just living his dream, honey. And it sounds like he wants you to be part of that."

"It's not that simple."

She lifted a shoulder. "It never is. Look, I'm not trying to get in your business."

"Good, because there seems to be a rash of that going around."

"*But* I wouldn't feel right if I didn't speak my peace. I love you, Cam. Always have." She smiled ruefully. "I didn't even want to meet you at first, but your father insisted. He brought in this little boy with big green eyes, looking shy and a little lost. Then you asked hesitantly if it'd be okay if you had a snack."

"You gave me apples and peanut butter," I said with a chuckle. "I remember."

"I was a goner right then." She shook her head. "I partially blame you for my divorce from your father, you know."

"*What?*" I asked incredulously.

"Just own it, dear." Humor lurked in her eyes. "You silenced all the doubts I had about marrying him. I wasn't sure I wanted to be his wife, but I wanted to be your mama almost immediately. Still do."

God, this woman. My father didn't have the greatest judgment when it came to women, but in this one instance, he'd certainly gotten it right. "You already are."

She immediately pressed her advantage, as any mother would. "Then listen to me. Your happiness is my happiness. And he makes you happy." She spread her hands in an *I'm sorry, but I've gotta say it* kind of gesture. "I remember thinking that when you guys left my house that night."

Digging up fond memories of Journey was not exactly on my list of top ten slammin' things to do. "Thinking what?" I asked begrudgingly.

"That you'd found something special. I've seen you date other people over the years, Cam. You didn't look at them that way. Not once. Not even in the beginning, when the relationship was fresh and new, and no one had gotten on anyone's nerves just yet."

I wanted to deny it on principle, of course, but in the end, I let it be. Rosy had always known me better than anyone else, and I wasn't in the mood to lie. She had me dead to rights. I loved Journey more than anyone or anything, but that wasn't enough. And now that we were all caught up on the *Life Sucks Big, Hairy Balls, And Not The Good Kind* files, we could all move on.

"What's your point?"

"I thought I already made it. Several times. But perhaps I need to hire some sort of skywriter to make it clear for you." She had the same expression that she used to get when she tried to help me with homework—like she knew she had to be patient, but she wanted to wallop me one. "Are you really going to let him go?"

"My whole world is here. *Here.* Not across the globe." Why was it so hard for everyone to understand that?

She shook her head as she pulled her phone out of her pocket. I watched impatiently as she tapped on the screen for a few moments. "Your whole world," she finally said, turning the screen around to face me. "Is right here."

I stared at the picture she'd taken of the two of us at her kitchen table. They'd gotten to talking about those specialty dog treats he kept buying at that boutique, and how great they'd be for the Happy Paws clientele. One thing led to another, and before I knew it, they were whipping up an oatmeal batch right at the table.

He was pressing the mix into a silicone mold and the only one my mother had was shaped like roses. *Now picture these in the shape of a bone,* he'd said earnestly. *I've already ordered some on Amazon. There's one that looks like a paw that's just the cutest thing....*

The memory made my chest ache. It certainly didn't help to look at pictures of that moment, either. I didn't need to see how adorable it was when he bit his lip in concentration as he worked. And I certainly didn't need to see how I looked at him. I mean, *really*. You should only look at people like that in a cheesy jewelry commercial.

"This is what matters, honey," she said as the phone went dark. She put it back in her pocket. "Everything else is just longitude and latitude."

"You really wouldn't care if I left Coral Cove?"

She smiled. "No, as long as you come back... and you *will. Come. Back.* You're mine in every way that counts, Cameron. I know you know the way home." She paused. "And I'll dog-sit Kona, just to make sure."

"What about the clinic?"

"Let's be real. I'm not *really* retired. I'd love to get back in there again, maybe on a part-time basis. That way, if you wanted to take off for a couple of weeks, we could work that out."

"I think he'd be a fool to let JJ go," a voice came from behind us. We both turned to find Glenna from the diner standing there, listening unabashedly.

"Are you serious right now?" I demanded.

This entire town was just shameless. I wasn't about to tell them that I had no intention of letting the best thing that had ever walked through my life go. I just had to figure out what I was going to do about it, and how I was going to get him back. The fact that he was currently knee-deep in a tropical rainforest was really tying my hands.

"He should go and surprise JJ. Just hop on a plane tonight and go." Glenna sighed, her little dachshund sitting at her feet. The equally nosy Wiggles looked on board with his mother's plan. "It would be so romantic, just like a movie."

"Maybe it will start raining when he gets off the plane," Norma said, her eyes a little dreamy. Apparently, we had another Journey/Cam fanfic writer in our midst. "They can stare at each other for a moment, completely shocked, and then run into each other's arms."

"You debark in a terminal," Rosy said, in her all-too-practical manner. She seemed pleased to ruin Norma's movie moment with a good dose of reality. "And Journey wouldn't know he was coming, so why would he just be standing in the airport?"

"Cameron should bring flowers," Tanya suggested from behind us. I turned to find her filling out an adoption form while Bailey held the clipboard steady for her. Bailey gave me an apologetic shrug. "Roses. Everyone loves roses."

"No, no, no. That's not right." It was Tim from the gas station's turn to be a big buttinsky. He marched over to us, shaking his head.

His cat Tina was in his arms, looking at peace with the world. Tim was the only person she liked. I always told potential adopters that all cats were not standoffish and that they were loveable creatures. Tina constantly did her level best to prove me wrong.

"Get him some bamboo," Tim advised. "It'll last longer than the roses and send a better message. I love you, and here's some peace and harmony for your living room."

His suggestion started an argument between them all that I could only listen to with an expression of bewilderment. What the hell was happening to my life right now?

Mrs. Wallace plopped a hand on her bony hip and demanded, "What kind of damned fool makes a romantic gesture with bamboo?"

I cut them all off with a shrill whistle and all heads swiveled in my direction. Even Tina stopped kneading Tim's arm with her tiny paws. "Okay, everyone, listen up, because I'm only going to say this once. I am not buying roses. I am not getting on a plane. I am not buying bamboo. We will not be kissing in the rain."

I winced at Glenna's crestfallen expression. I felt like I was writing the world's meanest Dr. Seuss book entitled *Miss Me With That Bullshit*. "When, and if, I see Journey again, it will be because that's what *we* want to do. Not as general amusement for the town."

"When and if?" Norma asked, clearly distressed.

"When and if," I confirmed. "Besides, why should I be the one to go find him? He left me. *He.* Left me." I paused for a few moments, finally acknowledging the hurt of that. Too bad I was acknowledging it in front of quite a few people. *Too fucking bad.* They wanted to know what was going on with me? Well, buckle the fuck up.

"I love him, more than anyone and anything I've ever loved in my whole life, and apparently that wasn't enough to keep him here. You'd have to be a fucking idiot to throw that away."

"Cam," Bailey said urgently.

"No, I'm serious, Bee. Fuck that. *Fuck. That.* Why should I put myself out there again? Why should I lay it all on the line for someone who doesn't seem to know that he's mine? He is mine. *Mine.*" At the thought of him moving on to someone else in Seattle, I huffed out a breath and they were lucky it wasn't accompanied by fire. "Mine, mine, *mine.* And I'm his. Why is that so hard to fucking understand?"

She widened her eyes, probably because I was turning the air blue in front of all these decent people, and I couldn't seem to stop. "Cam—"

"I mean, really, what does the rainforest have that we don't have? Sure there's the plants and beautiful rivers. And the animals." Thinking about it, I frowned. "So, maybe the Amazon has a lot. But *I'm* here."

"Cam—"

"Love like ours doesn't come around every freaking day. When it does, you don't throw it away. So yeah. *Fuck that.* Fuck it sideways." I nodded once. "And that's all I have to say about that."

"Wow." A voice came from behind me, freezing me in place. That voice was familiar—very familiar. "That's... a lot to unpack."

I didn't turn around. Instead, I did the only reasonable thing. I gave Rosy a beseeching look. "Just tell me he's not standing there. If God loves me—and I mean *really* loves me—JJ won't be standing there."

Her eyes glinted with amusement. "God just wants to be friends."

I sighed, even as I sent Bailey a glare. "For God's sake, Bee. The words are *Journey is right behind you.* It's very simple."

"Sorry," she said with a cheeky grin. She didn't look very sorry at all. "You were on a roll."

When I turned around, yes, he was standing there, and yes, seeing him was like taking a long drink of lemonade after a thirsty day's work. He didn't look all that mad that I was airing our business before all these people like freshly washed laundry. He didn't seem to notice them at all because his eyes locked on mine.

"I'm not even going to ask how the hell you keep popping up when I'm saying something I shouldn't," I finally said.

"Shouldn't." His voice was a whisper. "But did you mean it?"

"Err." I tried to think back to everything I'd said during my frustrated rant. There had been a lot of 'fuck this' and 'fuck that' in there. At one point during my rant, I was pretty sure I'd told someone to fuck something sideways.

I scratched my head. "Which part?"

"The part where you said you loved me. More than anything or anyone in your entire life." His mouth quirked. "I believe you said it right before you called me a fucking idiot."

"Oh, did I?" I asked faintly. "Yes, I meant it. The love part. Not the idiot part."

"Did you also mean it when you said that I was yours and you were mine?"

"Actually, he said *'mine, mine, mine'*," Tim stage whispered helpfully. When we both looked at him, he held up a hand. "In the interest of accuracy."

I cleared my throat. "Yes. I said those things. And... yeah, I meant them. I know I should've been telling *you* that, and not everyone else in town, but—"

He strode over to me and grabbed me so hard and fast that I squeaked. And then, he kissed me soundly. It took me a few seconds to unclench and get with the program, but then I was kissing him back so hard that it was difficult to tell who was in control of the kiss at all.

Realizing we were putting on a show for everyone—both four-legged and two—I finally pulled back. No one looked particularly disturbed. Quite a few faces were wreathed with smiles. Glenna and Norma gave a happy sigh as Rosy circumspectly wiped her eyes. Tim started a slow-clap, and Bailey hushed him quickly.

It was hard to look at them long because that meant looking away from Journey. Those amber eyes smiled up at me. "You didn't answer when I texted that I was coming," he said huskily. "I thought that was a bad sign."

"You texted me?"

"Yes," he repeated with more emphasis. When I continued to look at him cluelessly, he furrowed his brow. "This morning. And yesterday."

"Kona ate my phone, and I haven't had a chance to replace it." Considering, I amended that statement. "Well, she didn't eat all of it. Just parts... the good parts. The parts that make it a phone. It's uncanny really."

He gave Kona a look of betrayal. "Bad girl."

She smiled happily. In her world, bad was good, good was good, she was the goodest girl, and eating my phone was all in a day's work.

"But what about the Amazon?" Norma blurted out. She flushed as all heads swiveled in her direction... then they swiveled in ours.

Because I was so close to him, I heard the whispered "good Lord" he muttered under his breath. Then louder, he said, "As much as we appreciate all the well wishes and support, I think I need a moment to speak to Cam." When no one moved, he added pointedly, "Alone."

The crowd began to disperse, but not with any real speed. Bailey clapped her hands. "You heard the man. Let's go." She started making a shooing motion. "Move it, move it. Nothing to see here."

Rosy was the last to go, huffing as she walked off. And then we were alone—almost. We stared at Bailey as she stared right back at us. After an awkward five seconds of my life that I would never get back, her eyes widened. "Oh. *Oh!* Right."

I was hard-pressed not to laugh as she hustled off, urging Kona to come with her. "Well, the dog can stay," I called. "She knows how to keep a fucking secret."

Bailey threw up her middle finger, and I chuckled. When I

turned to Journey, my amusement faded. He looked so... so damned serious. I'd been under the impression that the hard part was over—Journey loved Cam, and Cam loved Journey, and that was all we needed to know—but I guess we had skipped over a few critical issues.

"Say it," I said with a sigh.

"I will. I'm just savoring this moment a little longer than that before I ruin it." He shook his head. "I've only had you for a freaking minute."

You've had my heart a lot longer than that. "Say it," I insisted.

"All right." He still looked a little hesitant as he forged ahead. "First off, I'd like to say that I was wrong to spring the whole rainforest thing on you. I didn't mean it as an ultimatum—either say yes and come with me, or we're done. I just... I got so excited about sharing that part of my life with you."

"I know."

He blew out a breath. "Good. I'm glad. Spending the summer here was an eye-opener for me. Turns out that travel isn't the only thing I like to do. I enjoyed teaching the kids at the center."

"Do you think that's something you want to keep doing?"

"Yes, I already talked to the director, and she was open to it." He smiled a little. "Livy is over the moon."

"That's fantastic."

He bobbed his head. "I also enjoyed working on your *Day in the Life of a Vet* videos. Don't take this the wrong way, but whoever was filming them before did a crappy job. I mean, the camera angles were all over the place, and sometimes the action even went off-screen."

"Thank you for the recognition," I said dryly. "I share this honor with my tripod, who would like you to know that we did our best."

"Oh, whoops." He smiled charmingly. "I guess what I'm saying is that I'll have no shortage of things to do around here. But I'm not willing to give up my job. Not entirely."

"Okay," I said slowly. "I'm not sure what that means."

"It means that I love my job. It's something I wanted to do my entire life, and I can't believe that I finally get to do it." When I opened my mouth to speak again, he hurried on. "I hope that's not a deal breaker."

"Journey—"

"I mean, I wouldn't be away all the time. My schedule isn't all that rigorous. And I could cut it down even more. Instead of seven trips a year, I could do three or four. Max."

"JJ—"

"Maybe just two times, even. And the trips are never for long," he rushed to say. "Well,

maybe I was in the Dominican for a while, but that was by design. I was catching up with a friend of mine, and I had no place pressing to be."

"That's—"

"Compromise," he said loudly. "It's the cornerstone of a healthy relationship, so just

think about that before you say no."

We looked at each other for a bit without speaking. He shuffled from one foot to the other. After a moment, he cleared his throat. "Cam?"

I raised an eyebrow. "Yes?"

"You're not saying anything."

"I wasn't aware I was allowed to speak."

"Oh, right. Your turn. I'll be perfectly quiet." When I opened my mouth to speak, he whispered, "But don't say no."

I barked out a laugh. "For God's sake, JJ!"

"Sorry." He made a zipping motion to his lips. "Last time, I promise."

"I'm not saying *no*. How could I say no to you?"

"You did before," he said suspiciously. "Several times. And not just about this, either."

"Well, having sex on the deck is always going to be a no," I said exasperatedly. "Anyone could've seen us."

"We don't *know* that."

"My point is that I'm all-in. You know, a little while ago, you told me that I reminded you of John, and I couldn't stop thinking about that."

"What does he have to do with anything?" His brow crinkled adorably. "Are you sure I said that?"

I chuckled. "Yes, you said that when he was looking for a partner, he was looking for an idea. Not a person. He thought he knew exactly what he wanted, but then he met Mindy and all those ideas went out the window."

He nodded slowly. "What's your point?"

"I'm done trying to make things go a certain way or fit a certain mold. I just want you. Everything else is negotiable." I wiped sweaty palms on my khakis. "I can't go with you this time around, but next trip, I'm there."

His eyes widened almost comically. "Really?"

I nodded. "Rosy is coming back to the clinic to help out. Officially, not just popping up when she's bored. Having someone on deck who can fill in for me will give me a little more wiggle room.

He still looked a little poleaxed. "Wow. That's... wow."

It was my turn to shift nervously. "That's a good wow, yes?"

"What? Yeah, *of course* it is." He let out a breath shakily. "I'm just so relieved. I had no idea of what I was going to say to you when I got here, but I knew I had to be honest. I'd pretty much convinced myself that you were going to say no."

I smiled. "I guess you don't know everything."

"I guess not." A hesitant smile crossed his lips. "I may be far away at times."

"I'll probably want you to be," I said cheekily. "I don't know if you know this, but you can be kind of annoying."

A laugh burst out of him. "Fuck you, Foss."

"Now, is that any way to talk to the love of your life?" I demanded.

"If I find him, I'll let you know." He grinned. "But for now, I'll take a kiss from you."

That was a fantastic idea. I closed the distance between us and cupped his jaw in my hands. The stubble abraded my fingertips lightly as I pulled him closer, close enough to see that familiar starburst pattern of gold in his amber eyes. And suddenly, I felt a little choked up. I couldn't believe we were going to be together—finally. It took us a while, but we'd managed to work out our shit.

I chuckled inwardly. That was going on the inside of our wedding bands, because eventually, someday, sometime, I *was* going to marry this man.

"Cam?"

I flushed as I realized I was just staring at him like a weirdo. Wasn't that partially his fault for being so damned beautiful? "Yeah?"

"Kiss me."

"You don't have to ask me twice."

His eyes crinkled with amusement. "Apparently, I do."

Okay, maybe he had a point. "Well, you certainly don't have to ask me three times."

"Apparently, I—"

I took his mouth in a soft kiss and that was the last thing we said for a while. Eventually we surfaced for air, and I rubbed my thumbs across his mouth before letting my hands drop away from his face. I checked my watch. It was getting late, and I had to help the rest of the staff pack up. Putting the adoption fair together took a while, but for some reason, taking it down took even longer.

"I have to get back to work," I said regretfully. I took two steps backward—big ones—because being near him was too damn tempting.

He didn't look all that pleased, either. "If you're going to be so responsible all the damned time, it's going to put a real crimp in our love life," he complained. "Come on. I'll pitch in."

"Why? So we can get back to my place faster?" I arched a brow to let him know I wasn't buying his sudden Good Samaritan act. "You're so obvious, Sutton."

"I'm a good goddamned citizen, Foss." He winked. "If we get home sooner, that's not my fault."

I furrowed my brow. *Home.* He'd called it home, and I didn't think it was an accident. Sure enough, his cheeks started getting a little pink. "What's wrong?" he asked.

He knew exactly what was wrong. "You called it home."

"So I did," he said carefully. "You know, I did a little packing when I was back in Seattle. Only... I didn't know where to ship everything."

I narrowed my eyes. "JJ."

He blinked innocently. "What?"

"You know what."

The thought of living with him was too freaking tempting. When he came back to Coral Cove on a more permanent basis, he'd probably get an apartment downtown or something, which meant he'd be far away. All right, downtown wasn't that far—it was Coral Cove, nothing was—but still. Farther than a fence was too damned far, but he probably wouldn't want to stay with his father.

I looked at him pensively. "It's too soon, isn't it?"

"Is it?"

"I don't know, I'm the one who asked you." I thought about it for a moment before I shook my head. I had to be practical. "Yes. It is. Way too soon."

"So, I shouldn't ask you what I was going to ask you."

"No."

"Okay. Then I won't ask if you're free next Saturday, which is when my stuff arrives."

"Good. I hate helping people move."

"And I won't ask you to make room in your garage for any... say, surplus furniture."

"Great." I eyed him suspiciously. "That would be awkward if you did, especially since we both said we're not doing the thing you're not asking me to do this soon."

"And I certainly won't ask you could clear out that utility closet you barely use at the back of the house. It would make a great space for a darkroom for someone."

"Would it?" I asked sardonically.

"I mean, that's if you knew a soon-to-be homeless photographer."

I growled. "You're freaking asking me without asking me."

"And if I am?"

"Then I'd have to say yes. Because it's stupid." I sighed, deciding to introduce myself to our imaginary group of fellow addicts. "Hi, everyone. My name is Cameron Foster, and I do stupid things."

"Hi, Cameron," he singsonged.

I laughed ruefully. "Wonderful."

"Cam," Bailey called. "I need your help loading the van."

"Coming." I sent her a little wave. "I gotta go."

He grabbed my arm before I could. "Wait."

"Yeah?"

"You remember at dinner, you told me that I was looking for something, and you didn't know what it was."

I nodded. I remembered a lot of things from that dinner that I wished I didn't.

"I thought about that a long time. That maybe you were right. I was looking for something, and I didn't even realize it. That's coddiwomple in a nutshell, isn't it?" He laughed a little self-consciously. "Traveling without a specific destination. Looking and searching for something that you can't quite put your finger on."

"And now?"

He kissed me softly on the nose and looked me in my eyes. The corner of his mouth lifted. "Found you."

EPILOGUE
JOURNEY

Three years later. . . .

Janice was such an ill-manned little monkey—literally. The capuchin was in a grabby phase, and she liked playing with my ears, my phone, my hair, my laptop... pretty much anything she could get her mitts on.

Cam had to stop volunteering us for fostering. Someone had bought the monkey illegally and dumped her on the clinic's doorstep. The sheriff didn't even think the individual was from this area, and I wasn't surprised. Cameron's *Day in the Life of a Vet* videos had taken off and given the clinic a lot of publicity.

The good news was that Charlotte, Cameron's ex, was in the wildlife business. She'd used her contacts to find Janice a spot in a sanctuary equipped to handle her needs. Cam was going to have to transport her up there himself—four hours, each way—but the good news was that Janice was getting her ass bounced from Hotel Foster-Sutton as soon as next week. She gave my ear a yank and I winced. Couldn't come soon enough.

I pulled her fingers away gently and resettled my AirPod in my ear. "I'm still here, Boz. What did you say?"

"I said, I thoroughly enjoyed your book. The *Lifelong Pursuit of Coddiwomple*? It was fantastic."

It was just a pet project, really—a collection of some of my favorite pictures from my travels and little stories to go along with them. I'd enjoyed writing the stories more than I'd thought I would. I'd thought it would just be fun to relive some of those trips through text and photos. I didn't expect that the process would make me introspective as fuck or that I'd start thinking about what I'd gotten out of each experience.

"I wasn't sure it was your type of book," I said, pulling my face away as Janice tried to stick her finger in my mouth. "You really liked it?"

He hummed. "Would I lie to you?"

"Yes," I said promptly.

He didn't disagree. "I enjoyed it so much that I already shopped it to a couple of publishers. One of them is looking for a coffee-table book, and I immediately thought of yours."

"Boz," I exclaimed. That little weasel. "That was just for you and me. I wasn't sure if I wanted to put that out there yet."

"That's why I did it for you," he said reasonably.

Little fingers tried to press a few keys on my keyboard, and I pulled Janice back. "Don't make me put you in one of those baby slings," I warned her.

"Now, if I can just pry you out of Nowheresville, USA for a few seconds, I have a job you might be interested in," Boz prattled on. "It's in Ireland, a month from now."

I was immediately intrigued. I hadn't been there in years. Maybe it was time for a repeat trip. I brightened. And I knew just what would make this trip superior to the last.

"Maybe Cam will want to go," I mused. "He loves Ireland. Or, at least, that's what I gathered from him playing 'Galaway Girl' so many times I was tempted to end my own life."

Boz made a sound of derision. "Sorry, I should've asked if you're allowed to go first."

I didn't bite. It wasn't the first time someone had accused Cam and me of being attached at the hip, and it wouldn't be the last. I didn't bother to explain our life to anyone else because it worked for *us*. That's all that mattered.

I'd been concerned the first year or so because I knew myself. Once I started traveling, it was hard to stop. I'd turned down at least four jobs until Boz and Cam sat me down to have a frank discussion. Boz's point had been that I had to come to terms with the fact that I needed to travel. That's just who I was. Cameron had followed that up with, *"Baby, we've talked about this. Trust that we can make it work this time."*

I did. But it wasn't easy.

I'd been worried that Cameron would get sick of me. He needed stability like he needed air—that's just who *he* was—but this time around was different. We were both determined to make it work, and that's why it would. So, I packed my trusty duffel and headed off to Alaska. It was the first trip of many since we'd gotten back together.

I hadn't been all that great at keeping to the two expeditions a year I'd promised. He never seemed to mind, and he usually made a point to join me once a year. Those were my favorite times. Well... I enjoyed it once we got going and he left his responsibilities behind. Before he left, he drove everyone bananas checking every box regarding the clinic. He always fretted that he wanted to make sure they had things well in hand. They always did.

How well we worked together really hit home during a four-day, three-night ride on the Maharajas Express. It was one of those times Cam had managed to get away, which made the journey from Delhi to Mumbai ten times better. I was amped and ready for Agra and the Taj Mahal—he was excited for Ranthambore, where we'd see Bengal tigers in the wild. He'd been sitting beside me, his head on the window as he slept through all the beautiful scenery that we'd traveled across the world to see.

I smiled fondly even as I moved his hair out of his eyes. He was jet-lagged as fuck and practically fell asleep anywhere and everywhere for the first few days. I couldn't get sleep because I was too nervous—I took his safety very seriously. When we traveled, I mothered him to death, and for the most part, he tolerated it.

I made plans in my head to surprise him with a dinner reservation the next night for our anniversary, and that's when I really thought about that date. We'd been together for three years. I didn't get caught up in dates, and I wasn't sentimental enough to mark every milestone in our relationship, but damn. Three fucking years, and we were making it work. I might always need to roam, but never for too long. Getting lost was kind of hard to do when sitting next to your one true North.

Boz was still going on, and I realized he was talking about that damnable show again. I rolled my eyes. "For God's sake, B. I don't know how many times I have to tell you that—"

"Not for you," he huffed. "For the hubby. And I hope to God he listens better than you do."

"He does," I said begrudgingly. "And we're not married."

"Please," he shot back, as if I was just too dense to be tolerated. "It's only a matter of time."

I wanted to deny it, but I'd only thought about it a hundred times already. It was something that I'd moved from the *maybe* category to the *just a matter of time* category.

"I think he would be amazing for the show," Boz yammered on. "He's got the looks, the personality—"

"I've got personality," I said, forgetting that I'd been saying for three years straight that I didn't want to do anything on television. And I didn't. But I *had* fucking personality.

"Please," Boz scoffed again. "It would be like that Rocky Mountain vet show or something. It would highlight some of his work with his stepmom. I mean, their story is just feel-good TV."

"Boz," I warned.

"Not to exploit him." He managed to sound wounded. "It would also benefit the animals. The better the clinic does, the more he can expand, the more animals he can help. Didn't you tell me that he already had to hire on another vet?"

"Yes," I admitted, "but he already has a pretty successful YouTube channel."

I heard a car pulling up in the driveway and pushed out of my chair. Janice clung to my neck like, well, a monkey. I headed over to the window and lifted the blinds. I smiled when I saw Cam getting out of his Jeep.

He bent over to reach something in the back seat—probably the groceries. I'd asked him to pick up a few things on the way home. He was still dressed in his work clothes and looked particularly edible. Those scrubs looked good on him, but I was pretty sure they'd look better on our floor. I idly wondered how long it would take me to get Janice down for a nap. Or, at least sleepy enough that she wouldn't screech her capuchin head off when I put her in her temporary habitat in the guest bedroom.

Cameron looked over his shoulder furtively, and my smile faded a bit. Just what the hell was he up to? It wasn't my birthday or even close to Christmas. Valentine's Day had come and gone. I frowned, hoping I hadn't missed a date.

"His channel is a hoot," Boz went on. "I watched that episode with the woman who had the two alligators in the pool about ten times."

"Calling it an episode is a bit generous, considering it only lasted a few minutes." I chuckled, remembering Cam's face as he blinked in disbelief at the pool. "I'm assuming you enjoyed watching Cam squeal like a little piggie and then hoof it to his Jeep."

"I enjoy watching Foster doing anything." Boz gave a little dreamy sigh, school-girl crush in full effect. "You can just tell he cares when he's working with those big, gentle hands—"

"Are you crushing on my husband?" I growled.

"I thought you said you weren't married."

I harrumphed. He was lucky I had a mystery to solve, specifically, why Cam was acting so *Mission Impossible* with our fucking groceries. "I still don't want you crushing on my nonhusband, Boz. I'll talk to him about the show."

And then, I saw the tail sticking up in the back seat and realized he'd brought more than bread home. I sighed exasperatedly, and a little fondly, too. "Thank God we've got the room," I murmured.

What we didn't have was time. He was so busy with work that I wound up taking care of the strays he brought home, and it was challenging to keep up with their feedings and whatnot. Okay, so maybe I volunteered. Maybe he'd also sent over a baby-faced vet tech a few times to feed some raccoons we'd fostered, and I'd sent him away. But the raccoons were so sweet and tiny, and only *I* knew how to do it right—or so I insisted.

I watched Cam ushering a baby goat out of the Jeep, a length of bandage around the animal's back leg. The goat looked just as conspiratorial as he waited patiently for Cam to close the door and come around.

"I gotta go, Boz. I'm hungry, and apparently, Cam chose to bring home livestock instead of groceries. There's also a kidnapping happening in my front yard, and I need to put a stop to it."

I hung up on his "wait, who's getting kidnapped?" Whoops. I probably should've said goat-napped, but I never could resist a double entendre. Cameron and the goat limped around the side of the house, Sneaky and Sneakier, and I couldn't help the smile that came to my mouth. That man. Yeah, I was going to give him the business, but I loved that man to pieces.

A few months after Goatgate…

Cameron

Journey was in a mood.

He was traveling with his father for the first time, which added an entirely new layer to things. Or, at least, that's what Journey had told me irritably the night before after hanging up with Jack for the sixth time. His father was a little nervous about flying, and that anxiousness was coming out in different ways. Most of those ways involved annoying Journey to death.

"Are you sure you can't go with me?" Journey asked for what had to be the tenth time. "I mean, Cam, it's Ireland. You love Ireland."

"I do love Ireland," I agreed. "I wish I could, but you know I can't leave the clinic right now. I've got surgeries all week, Rosy is at that conference in Tampa, and Marley is on vacation."

"Maybe I shouldn't go," he muttered, more to himself than anything else. "Who is going to feed the chinchillas?"

"I will," I assured him.

"Well, who's going to take Kona on our hikes? She needs the exercise, you know."

"I don't hike, Sutton, but I will make sure she's properly exercised. I'll even make her wear a headband and some spandex like we're in an old-school Jane Fonda video." I did a couple of stretching moves. "You'd betta *work*."

"That was not Jane Fonda's catchphrase, you weirdo." He sent me a superior look as he refolded a shirt to make it flatter. He carefully rolled it into a tube shape, making it about the size of a pair of rolled socks. No one could out pack Journey—no one.

"Are you sure?"

"She wanted you to feel the burn."

I squinted at him. "Like Bernie Sanders?"

"That's feel the *Bern*, Foss."

"Well, who said you'd betta work?"

"RuPaul, mostly, and every drag queen since the beginning of time."

I watched him as he finished packing his last-minute items in his trusty duffel. He slung his charger in the bag a little harder than necessary. I bit my lip to keep from smiling as I looked at his pouty face. A grown man. Pouting. It was adorable and ridiculous all at the same time.

Kona gave a soft whine as she brushed against me. I wasn't sure who was being a bigger baby at the moment, him or Kona. She could always tell when Journey was leaving, and she became super clingy and made sure to stay underfoot.

She wasn't sure which of us she liked better, even though I'd saved her ungrateful furry hide. I mean, let's put all this "dog" business aside and get real—I'd opened my home to a goddamned wolf. I wouldn't be surprised to find Red Riding Hood's coat in her kennel. I expected a little fucking gratitude. But alas, while my name might be on her Barkbox subscription, Journey had his own way to Kona's fickle little heart.

He always took her with him when he was off doing his photography thing. They would disappear for hours at a time, him in his battered jeans and faded shirt with his precious Cannon around his neck, and Kona in Doggles and rubber-soled shoes. I always had to try not to laugh when I saw her in them. He'd bought them to protect her paws from rough terrain, but they made her look like she was seconds away from breaking out into a tap-dance routine.

Off they would go, doing their Journey-Kona thing. They'd come back hours later, dusty and sweaty, and one particularly memorable time, completely muddy and wet. I didn't ask, and they certainly didn't tell. I had my suspicions, of course. My top theory was that *someone* had bounded into *someone*, and they'd both fallen into the river. I only wished I had video.

I came up behind him and wrapped my arms around his chest. He stiffened briefly until I kissed the side of his scruffy jaw, and then he melted against me. "I can't believe I got so addicted to having you with me," he complained.

"I know."

"It's not the same when you're not there."

I smiled against his skin. "I know, but your dad is coming with you."

"You say that like it's a good thing. We're probably going to wind up killing each other. Dead, right there in the airport." He shook his head as he finished zipping his duffel. "I'll admit that when I offered to take him with me, I never really expected him to accept."

"Are you sad he did?"

He turned around in my arms and linked his hands behind my neck, then stretched up to plant a kiss on my mouth. "No. He's finally starting to check things off in our dream journal."

"Don't you mean *his* dream journal?"

"I found it," he said stubbornly. "Possession is nine-tenths of the law. And he'll get it back when I'm dead."

"He's older."

"Exactly." He nodded. "A smart man would draw conclusions from that and start a new fucking journal."

I chuckled. "Real nice, JJ." Realizing he was looking at me, his cheeks a little pink, I tilted my head. "What? And it'd better not be something dirty that we don't have time to do."

"It's just that... I miss you already." He looked a little embarrassed. "How can you miss someone before you've even left?"

I gave a self-deprecating laugh. "God, we're disgusting. We're just going to get worse over time, you know."

"Good." He cupped my face and kissed me again. "I love kissing you. What if I forget how you taste?"

"That's impossible."

"You can forget the taste of something you haven't eaten in a long time, Foss. Like strawberries. I haven't had them in like, six weeks." He frowned as he smacked his lips together. "Oh God, I think I've forgotten what strawberries taste like."

I laughed. "You're so ridiculous. Now go. You're going to be late, and Boz will be pissed."

"Mm, maybe I'll just miss the plane altogether."

That was starting to look more likely, especially since he still had to go over to Jack's to pick him up. From the sounds of their conversation last night, Journey was going to have to repack his father's haphazardly packed bags. I knew I should make him get going, but I was enjoying his fingers moving along the scruff of my jaw too much.

"You think we should revisit what we were talking about before?" I asked, before I could think better of it.

"You mean the summer trip to Greece?"

I furrowed my brow. "No, but while we're on the topic, I thought we were going to Mexico. I had my heart set on it. I'm already taking Spanish lessons on Duolingo."

"I told you I know enough Spanish to get us by."

I shook my head with a little smile. He always claimed he knew enough of a language to get us by, but when someone sends you to the *banco* when you're looking for the *baño*, well, you don't need to learn that lesson twice. Luckily there had been a *baño* in the *banco*, and I'd avoided an *accidento*.

Hmm. That probably wasn't right. I needed to up my daily word goals.

"I'm not talking about the trip," I said. "I'm talking about the other thing."

"The other...." He stilled. "You said you weren't ready."

"Well, maybe I changed my mind."

Excitement flared in his eyes and he opened his mouth just as his phone rang. He checked the screen impatiently and sent it to voicemail. It started up again, and he did it again. "My dad," he sighed. "Well, you can't ask me now."

"I'm not," I said archly. "Who said I was going to do the asking anyway?"

"Oh. Well. Good." He dropped his hands and turned to grab his bag. "Glad we're on the same page and you're not asking me."

"Exactly." I nodded. "I'm just hoping that you'll want to stay with me forever."

"Baby, you know I do."

"And maybe live with me forever."

He eyed me suspiciously. "I already live with you. Why would that change?"

"Well, maybe we could get up in front of our family and ten or fifteen of our closest friends and tell them that. You know... that we love each other and want to be together forever. And if he's not busy, maybe Pastor Mike could swing by."

"Damn it, Cam, you're asking me," he huffed.

I sent him a cheeky grin. "I'm not. But if I was... what would you say?"

He gave me another long kiss and headed for the door. "God, I'm late. I'd say, I love you. I'd say, I gotta go because if I miss this plane, Boz is gonna gut me like a fish. I'd say, I already put our names down on a waitlist for the gardens, which I was hoping to secure before I asked you." He sent me a grin, one hand on the door. "I'd say, I melted down our old rings into new ones, and they're in a cigar box on the top shelf of my closet. *And* I'd say, you'd better have a nice suit ready by the time I get back. What would you say to all that?"

I laughed. "I'd say, it's a good thing no one is asking anyone anything."

"Right?"

Our laughter died and we stared at each other, the gravity of the moment catching up with us and surpassing the humor. When he spoke again, his voice was a little hoarse. "I love you."

I blinked back tears before I answered because I was *not* that sappy, and I was not that guy. Okay, maybe I was that guy a little bit. "Stop telling me things I already know and get your ass on that plane."

He gave me a little wave, and Kona's ears a quick scratch, and then he was out the door. This was always the hardest part, but the sooner he left, the sooner he could come back. I knew he knew the way home, which was a fucking miracle, considering his lack of sense of direction. The life we'd put together wasn't traditional, but it was ours, and I wouldn't change a thing.

I looked down to find Kona giving me a smug look. "Stop giving me the told-you-so face." She doubled down on it, instead. I chuckled as I gave her nose a quick boop. "Come on. I want to see those rings."

It wasn't hard to find them because they were exactly where he'd said they'd be. I shook my head as I opened the lid. I'd moved that cigar box out of my way no less than twenty times when looking for something else.

The rings were silver, simple, and unadorned. I spotted writing on the inside of the band and plucked it from its velvet bed. I guess it was only fair that he pick the inscription this time around. I had to fight back a swell of emotion as I rubbed my finger over the lettering.

The best journeys always take us home.

I couldn't have said it better myself.

ACKNOWLEDGMENTS

Thank you to my family for everything that you do. Thank you to Kiyle Brosius, who helped me whip this manuscript into shape. Hopefully, Ki will eventually be brought up on formal charges for trying to murder my fragments. Thank you to Leslie Copeland for an awesome beta read as usual. Any errors in the book are mine. And as always, thank you to the readers. I hope you enjoyed Journey and Cameron as much as I did.

ABOUT THE AUTHOR

S.E. Harmon has had a lifelong love affair with writing. It's been both wonderful and rocky (they've divorced several times), but they always manage to come back together. She's a native Floridian with a Bachelor of Arts and a Masters in Fine Arts, and now splits her days between voraciously reading romance novels and squirreling away someplace to write them. Her current beta reader is a nosy American Eskimo who begrudgingly accepts payment in the form of dog biscuits.

Website: https://seharmon.weebly.com/

Email: silkguitar2011@comcast.net

ALSO BY S.E. HARMON

Stay With Me

So Into You

The Blueprint

A Deeper Blue

P.S. I Spook You

Principles of Spookology

Spooky Business

The Spooky Life

Chrysalis

Cross

Love Is

Printed in Great Britain
by Amazon